JINGLE BELL
Wolf

TERRY
SPEAR

sourcebooks
casablanca

Published by Sourcebooks Casablanca, an imprint of Sourcebooks
P.O. Box 4410, Naperville, Illinois 60567-4410
(630) 961-3900
sourcebooks.com

Printed and bound in Canada.
MBP 10 9 8 7 6 5 4 3 2 1

To Malana Whited, her daughter, Hayle Morgan, and her daughters-in-law Ronda and Katelin Whited. Thanks for making the wolves a family affair—wolves stick together after all! You are the greatest!

CHAPTER 1

It had been ten years since that fatal accident in the snow in Montana that changed Gabrielle's life forever. She now stood at the edge of the outdoor part of the swimming pool at Timberline Ski Lodge, Silver Town, Colorado, the snow falling on her knit cap and ski jacket, mist rising from the heated water.

Although her last name meant "wolf cub" or "little wolf" in old French, Gabrielle Lowell hadn't been a cub for a very long time. After that night when her parents died, she'd returned to Pensacola to sell off their veterinary clinic and finish her degree. Once she had her license, she'd joined a veterinary clinic co-op in Daytona Beach, Florida. There wasn't any way she could have worked in her parents' practice with them gone.

Her jaguar friends, Odette and Zelda Bellamy, had convinced her to go on this winter adventure—she suspected as a way to prove to her that being in snow could be fun and not always deadly—and now they weren't even here yet. Coming here, Gabrielle realized, had upset her whole known world of beaches and sun and sea and reawakened her fear of snow and ice.

She loved the water—swimming, boating, waterskiing—but snow skiing? She figured she would end up killing herself in the process. Not to mention that all she could think about were the ski-vacation plans she'd had with her mom and dad before the fateful night that ended her dreams…and theirs.

Recollections of that terrible night made her hesitate to strip off her clothes and dive into the pool. It wasn't the same, she told herself. The night was cold and snowy, sure, but the pool was heated, and she wouldn't be trapped in a car, fighting for her life. As much as she hated to admit it, she still suffered from some level of post-traumatic stress disorder after dying in the crash, being revived, and finding she'd lost both her parents.

Gabrielle had arrived at the Silver Town Ski Resort after a late flight from Daytona Beach the day after Thanksgiving, having had client cases all day at the veterinarian clinic, and she felt the strongest urge to swim, to get the kinks out the best way she knew how. But the pool was closed, darn it. She was not normally adventurous, and she didn't usually break rules. But the water beckoned to her, the only thing in this snowy winter wonderland that didn't seem alien to her, if she didn't think of snow in conjunction with water and the lake that had swallowed her parents' rental car.

She figured she could swim a few laps in the pool before anyone would notice she was in there, and she would be as quiet as a mermaid, no splashing in the water. Just slip in, swim, and slip out, and nobody would be the wiser.

She would run later tonight as a wolf—though running through snow would be a whole new experience. All the snow made it so much more Christmas-like than living in Florida. The Christmas lights strung on the inside and outside of the lodge and restaurant and the decorations—Christmas trees and poinsettias and mistletoe—were so festive. Several fir trees were covered in lights reflecting off the outdoor part of the pool. Aqua, silver, and white balls and bows filled the trees. She felt like she was in a winter wonderland. The place was just beautiful.

Gabrielle swallowed hard. She knew she would feel better once she swam. Since she was wearing her bikini under the ski clothes, she hurried to strip out of her jacket. She was going to be at the ski resort for a little over a week, and she was determined to get over the phobia she had about snow and ice.

Landon Wolff had two pet peeves when it came to running the Timberline Ski Lodge at Silver Town: guests swimming before the pool was supposed to be open first thing in the morning, and guests who swam in the pool after it was closed.

If he'd known how many guests would ignore the posted rules, he would have suggested to his brother, Blake, and sisters, Roxie and Kayla, that they design the layout differently so they could lock the swimming pool area whenever the pool was closed to guests.

But they had wanted the area to be more open and picturesque. The Howling Wolff Bar and Grill overlooked the outdoor part of the pool on one end and had a great view of the mountains on the other. Plants and a glass wall provided a barrier to the swimming pool from the lobby, except for one entryway that had a sign posted with the pool's hours. Right now, the pool was closed. The lobby itself had a double-sided fireplace for anyone who wanted to sit and warm up while taking a break from snow activities. Large leather chairs and couches, warm honey-oak-paneled walls, and marble floors with tapestry throw rugs adorned the lobby. Not to mention a ten-foot Christmas tree that was decorated for the season.

The deep end of the swimming pool extended beyond a plexi-glass wall, so that guests could actually swim underneath the divider and into the pool outside, which was surrounded by a snow-covered patio. Landon loved swimming outside while it was snowing, the flakes falling on him and the heated pool water.

The pool was closed to guests during certain hours so that he and his family could have private use of it. They posted signs that said: PRIVATE PARTY ONLY. POOL CLOSED

So the day after Thanksgiving, when Roxie told Landon some-one was splashing in the pool before the night-shift staff came in—just after he had thrown on his board shorts to swim a few laps, his nightly routine—he was feeling like a growly wolf, ready to bounce the rule breaker out on his ass in the snow.

Roxie reminded him, "Remember, the swimmer is a paying guest." Then she frowned at him. "Maybe I should handle it."

Rosco, their avalanche-trained Saint Bernard and a loving family companion and mascot for the lodge, eagerly greeted Landon, his red-and-green bell collar jingling at the same pace as his tail, while his little barrel of doggy treats—decorated with a snowman and the words "Merry Christmas"—wobbled around his neck.

"Hey, Rosco." Landon petted him. "You stay put." Rosco was good about not swimming in the pool, most of the time. Landon just didn't want to have to get him back out of the pool, because then Rosco would shake all over and smell like wet dog next to the fireplace in the lodge. Landon said to Roxie, "I'm on my way to the pool anyway, and then I'll go home and have dinner with you and Kayla."

Landon headed for the pool with a beach towel in hand and wearing a red T-shirt with the name of their lodge and a wolf featured prominently on it, this one wearing a Santa hat. They didn't sell the T-shirts, sweaters, or sweatshirts in their gift shop, though several guests had asked if they could buy them. Instead, the owners and employees wore the special gear so everyone would know who was on staff if they needed help. Kayla was a marketing genius when it came to thinking up fun ideas to promote the lodge and the bar and grill.

In this case, wearing the T-shirt would help to show Landon had the authority to tell a rule breaker to get out of the pool. He knew he shouldn't get so steamed about it, but it was ingrained in him to live by the rules. His former girlfriend had been just the opposite. For her, rules were meant to be broken. Nothing really bad, just stuff like this. As wolves, they really didn't want to have to do any jail time. Not that royals—shifters who had wolf roots so far back that they could change at will—would be compelled to shift with the full moon like the others, but any wolf could get aggravated enough with being locked in a cage and dealing with a prison population and guards to go off the deep end and want to shift.

Christmas music played overhead: "I'm Dreaming of a White Christmas," which was totally appropriate as the ski lodge and ski resort had record snowfall this winter. The Wolff family had knocked themselves out decorating the whole lodge and bar and grill for Christmas, since the sisters were here too this year. Now that Blake had a mate, Nicole, she and her brother, Nate Grayson, had also helped. Even the siblings' parents had a blast helping to decorate the fireplace mantels, the check-in counter, and the gift shop—a new addition. It was truly a family affair between the Wolffs and the Graysons, who were now part of their extended family.

Landon finally made it to the pool and frowned at the woman swimming in it. From the moment Roxie had mentioned the guest swimming in the pool, Landon had thought it would be a man. For a second, he thought his ex was here, causing trouble for him. But the woman was wearing a white swim cap, something his ex would never have done, and a red-and-white-striped string bikini—like a candy cane—that showed off her curves in a revealing way. He just stood there like an idiot when he should have been hollering at her to leave, watching her swimming on the surface of the water and then diving under, headed to the opposite end of the pool.

Blake joined him, wearing a red sweater with their seasonal lodge logo of a wolf in a Christmas hat and pants and boots, dressed more for going out into the snow than swimming. "Roxie told me we had a rule breaker in the pool."

"Yeah. The swimmer just swam to the outside part of the pool."

Blake folded his arms, his eyes riveted to the pool. "Are you going after him?"

"Uh, yeah."

"Did you need me to stick around to make sure you don't have any trouble with him? I was going to head up to the bar and grill for a hot chocolate before I head home."

"No." Landon didn't want Blake to see the woman, or know that the swimmer was a woman, though his brother could see her if he went to the section of bar-and-grill seating that overlooked the outdoor area of the pool. He was sure Blake would, if nothing more than to ensure Landon didn't have any trouble with the swimmer.

Landon was seriously considering letting her continue to swim in their pool once he saw what she was wearing and how good it looked on her. She was all sleekness and curves. A candy-cane package. Human? Wolf? He didn't know. But he sure wanted to.

"I've got it, Blake." Landon put his phone and towel on a chaise lounge, then stripped off his shirt. He'd hoped that Blake would just leave, but his brother was still standing there watching for the swimmer to reappear.

"You don't think he's in trouble, do you?" Blake asked.

"Yeah, the swimmer's in trouble. The guest shouldn't be swimming after hours!" Landon wasn't as annoyed about it now that he'd seen the rule breaker, but he didn't want to let on to his younger quadruplet brother that a pretty woman was the reason.

Frowning, Blake shook his head. "I mean that maybe he is having issues swimming."

"I'll check it out."

"Okay. I'll check from the restaurant."

Great. Then Blake would see why Landon didn't immediately take the swimmer to task or correct Blake about the sex of the rule breaker. Landon kicked off his sandals and walked over to the deeper edge of the pool, worried when he didn't see the woman return to the inside pool. It was snowing like crazy out there tonight.

He dove into the warm water and swam to the divider with powerful strokes and dove under to reach the other side to make sure the woman was all right and remind her of the rules. When he came up into the chilly air, the snowflakes falling all over his hair, he found the woman had...vanished.

=====

Gabrielle had swum five laps the length of the pool before she figured she was tempting fate and a scolding and left. She felt good, having finally gotten over her fear of jumping into the pool in the snow. She knew her fear of snow and the water wouldn't go away overnight, but maybe this would be a beginning.

On the snow-covered patio surrounding the pool, she pulled off her white swimming cap, freeing her blond hair, and shoved the cap into her bag. Shivering, she yanked her green sweater over her head and her bikini top, and then struggled to pull her skin-tight black ski pants over her wet bikini bottoms. She slipped on her favorite Christmas howling wolves socks and shoved her feet into her snow boots. After pulling on her red-and-pink-striped ski hat, she shouldered her bag. Even though she knew she had dressed quickly, it felt like it had taken forever. She was just not used to this kind of cold.

At least she was well on her way up to the bar and grill on the crunchy, snowy walkway before anyone caught her entering the restaurant from the outdoor pool area.

She took a seat in a booth as soon as she entered the warm restaurant where guests were sitting and eating while Christmas music played overhead. She loved the way the glass dividers providing privacy for guests had illustrations of wolves etched in them. White Christmas lights were hanging everywhere, making the whole restaurant festive. A waitress came to take her order, and she realized several of the staff at the lodge were wolves.

The waitress, Minx, her name tag said, smiled at her. "We close in half an hour, just to let you know."

"Okay, thanks. I'll just take"—Gabrielle quickly looked at the menu—"the baked potato, salad, and a medium rare T-bone steak. And a cup of hot chocolate. On the salad, blue cheese dressing, if we have enough time for all that."

"We sure do. I'll bring it right out."

"Thanks."

Poinsettias and lighted red candles sat on each of the tables, which were covered in red tablecloths. It was the perfect place for a couple to have dinner, Gabrielle thought.

She noticed a man watching her, and then he smiled at her. Another soon joined him and garnered his attention.

"Did you find your swimmer?" the first man asked the newly arrived guy who looked so similar to him, they had to be brothers or cousins. They were both a little over six feet tall, the first one having light-brown hair and blue eyes, and the other light-brown hair and dark-brown eyes.

At the mention that the brown-eyed man had been looking for the errant swimmer, Gabrielle felt her heart hitch and she turned to look at the view of the outdoor part of the pool from the restaurant. Had the blue-eyed guy been watching her dress outside by the pool while he was in the restaurant?

Her whole body warmed with embarrassment.

"Nah. When I reached the pool outdoors, there was no sign of the swimmer," the other man said.

Well, the deed was done, and there wouldn't be any reason to talk to her about it unless she'd committed some major crime. She hadn't realized the restaurant patrons could have been watching her outside in the snow dressing poolside, or undressing before that. At least right now no one was eating in the section of the bar and grill with a view of the pool. Most were sitting where they could watch the nighttime skiers on the slopes before the lifts shut down for the evening.

The lodge owners probably had security cameras that would

have caught her actions. But again, why look at them if she hadn't really done anything bad?

So who were these men? Part of the security for the lodge? She suspected as much. And she guessed the guy who might have seen her dressing wasn't going to tell on her. She just hadn't expected one of them to be wearing soaking-wet board shorts that were clinging to his wet legs. His hair was also wet, and even his T-shirt that indicated the name of the resort was damp and clinging to his muscular chest.

The waitress brought her water, hot chocolate, a salad, and fresh-baked bread. Gabrielle's stomach rumbled, she was so hungry. She began to eat her salad and buttered her bread.

"Are you going to go swimming, Landon, or just drip water all over the restaurant?" the other man asked the one in the board shorts.

Gabrielle hid a smile.

Landon smiled at him a little evilly. "I'm swimming. See you in the morning, Blake." Then Landon, who must have actually swum after her in the pool since he was all wet—but thankfully missed catching her—left the restaurant, and the one named Blake grabbed a cup of hot chocolate, smiled at her, and left too.

Gabrielle sighed, relaxed, and enjoyed her delicious meal. After she finished her dinner, she was about to head up to her room when she got a text. Her jaguar friends were running late on a JAG mission they were working. They would see her tomorrow afternoon instead of tonight.

Great. They were the reason she was here at all!

Oh well, Gabrielle would run tonight as a wolf and then swim tomorrow, doing the things she loved anyway, and she wouldn't have to snow ski for a while. Normally, she wasn't afraid of any-thing...but falling down mountains in the cold, wet snow? It didn't appeal. She couldn't imagine how her friends had gotten into snow skiing, since they were jaguar shifters, but they loved the snow. Then again, with their catlike actions, she could imagine they would do well on the slopes.

She sighed, paid her dinner bill, and walked up the carpeted stairs to her room on the second floor to ditch her wet bathing suit and dress in other warm, dry clothes. She carried a bottle of water for after her run and a backpack to stuff her clothes into when she was ready to shift in the woods. The backpack was white and would blend in with the snow. But she would bury it too, just in case, not wanting anyone to find it and steal it or worry about a missing person. She could find the buried backpack with her enhanced sense of smell as a *lupus garou*.

Once she was ready to go, Gabrielle headed downstairs past the pool, though she glanced through the entryway to see Landon swimming with muscular strokes, his back, arms, and shoulders well sculpted, and she smiled, glad he hadn't caught her swimming.

Then she left the ski lodge and trudged through the snow past two beautiful two-story brick-and-stone homes, rustic but new, with white lights hanging from the eaves and around the trees out back. She headed for the tree line where she figured she could run safely through the woods on a snowy eve. She did briefly think about running into a frozen lake on her travels, but if she did, as a human or a wolf, she shouldn't be able to break through the ice. Not as cold as it was and for as long as it had been cold in Colorado. A big Saint Bernard barked inside the first of the homes, peering out a glass door. It looked like the one that had been sleeping by the fire earlier tonight when she'd first checked in and had to stop and pet him, minus the barrel around his neck.

Gabrielle moved a little faster through the snowdrifts, worried she might be trespassing in the houses' backyards, though there were no signs or fences, so she couldn't be sure.

When she finally reached the woods, far away from any residence, she hurried to yank off her clothes, stuff them in her backpack, and bury the bag quickly before shifting. The shift warmed her body all the way through at once, and she felt better as soon as she was covered in fur, standing on four legs, and ready to run as a wolf. Then she tore off into the woods, wanting to howl her delight but stifled the urge. She didn't want to alert any *lupus garous* in the area that she was running as a wolf in these parts if it wasn't allowed, or if hunters were illegally hunting to rid the area of the wolf "menace."

She was running along happily, the glorious, waning crescent moon peeking through the snow-bearing clouds, when she came into a clearing and saw four wolves—three females and one male—frolicking with each other in the powdery snow until the largest one caught sight of her and stood still. The others all turned to see what the male had seen. Two of the she-wolves were lighter-colored with brownish masks on their faces, their chests white. The second female was a little taller than the other. The third female was more reddish, her face a white mask, her chest light-red. The male had darker brown fur and more black guards on the saddle on his back.

But were they real wolves? Or *lupus garous*?

Maybe a whole pack of *lupus garous* lived here. Gabrielle had smelled wolves at the lodge. The waitress had been one and so had several of the staff members; was it a wolf-run lodge? Had to be and that's why so many of the decorations throughout the lodge featured wolves.

Her friends had found this out-of-the-way ski resort in Colorado and thought they might even get some running in as shifters in the backcountry. Like she was doing now. But the lodge hadn't been open to guests then, having recently been built when her friends came to Silver Town. Maybe the wolves at the lodge were all new to the area.

One of the she-wolves barked at her in greeting. Okay, Gabrielle thought, they were some of her kind and not a wild wolf pack that wouldn't want her in their territory. She exhaled the air she'd been holding in and breathed out a frosty mist.

The other two female wolves barked at her, and she barked back to let them know she was safe to be around. The male didn't respond, eyeing her, protective of the females in his harem, Gabrielle thought facetiously.

She wasn't sure what to do. Should she turn around and return to her backpack, shift, dress, and head back into the lodge? But then the three females approached her, greeting her in a wolf way, telling her they were safe. One turned her head, indicating she wanted Gabrielle to follow her and the others.

Okay, so this could be fun. She hadn't expected to come across any other *lupus garous* out here and she ran with them. The three female wolves began playing with her, and she hadn't expected that. The male was a little aloof, but he might have been worried about making her feel uneasy. The way he had been running close to one of the females, Gabrielle thought he was with her, as in courting or mated. The other wolves seemed just as familiar with him, so maybe related? She couldn't be sure.

She'd been playing with them for about an hour, and it was getting to be about eleven when she felt really tired. She hadn't gotten used to the time difference yet, and it was two hours later for her back home. She barked at them, telling them she was leaving.

They barked and followed her until she reached her backpack and woofed at them to let them know she was fine.

They woofed and she barked back and they hurried off to give her privacy, which she was glad for. She tugged her clothes out of her backpack with her wolf teeth, shifted, and hurried to dress. *Cold, cold, cold.* This was nothing like shifting after a run in Florida at night, even on the coldest winter days. Certainly, there wasn't any snow to stand in.

She finally finished dressing and trudged through the woods, past the two houses where the outdoor Christmas lights were still on. She could see the trail left behind by two wolves, the male and female she thought were mated. The other two females had left tracks to the house closest to the lodge.

So they weren't guests at the lodge, but owned the homes here in Silver Town.

Just then she saw the man called Landon heading toward the first house, and he glanced in her direction.

She mumbled "Hi" and hurried off as fast as she could through the deepening snow to the lodge. She glanced over her shoulder and found him still watching her.

He had to be a wolf like the others. Was one of the females his mate? He seemed wary. She hoped he wasn't putting two and two together and realizing she was the one who had been swimming in the pool, if he'd seen her face at all.

She kept going and finally made it inside the toasty-warm lodge, where she saw a new night staff working the front desk and a man polishing the floor. Gabrielle stood at the entrance to the pool and eyed it for a moment. Tomorrow, before it was open and before the restaurant opened, she would go for another swim when no one would be watching the pool.

She headed up to her room, eager to take a hot shower and climb into bed and sleep.

The funny thing was that she never broke the rules anywhere, so why now? She hadn't planned to do that until she realized the pool was closed because she'd arrived so late. But now, the business with Landon trying to locate her made her want to do it at least once more, to challenge him, to see if he would give up the search or if he would catch her—and then what? He had to be a wolf since so many of the staff were.

She smiled. He'd brought the devil out in her, and only the jaguar sisters had ever done that!

CHAPTER 2

WHEN HE REACHED HIS BACK DOOR, LANDON WAS STILL thinking about the pretty blond who had greeted him in an almost reluctant way in the snow behind his house. As soon as he went inside, he saw Roxie and Kayla straightening up the living room where they'd been putting together a wolf-pack puzzle. They had just finished making beef stew for a late dinner. He was curious about the woman who had been trespassing in their backyard, though since they hadn't put the fence up yet, anyone who wasn't from Silver Town wouldn't know that. "Did you happen to see the woman who just passed through our backyard, earlier while you were running as wolves?"

She had been coming from the same direction as his family, since that was the way they always went running when they were out in the snow as wolves. Plus that's where all the wolf tracks were coming from.

"She was probably the woman we met when we went for a run. We didn't see her shift. We were all playing as wolves when we saw her." Roxie served up bowls of stew.

"She was a wolf?"

"Yeah. She witnessed us playing and we all stopped what we were doing, surprised to see a new wolf watching us. We greeted her to let her know we weren't a danger to her, and she ran and played with us. She was a lot of fun. She's not from here, so she might be one of the guests at our lodge." Kayla smiled. "She was all alone, about our age, maybe an eligible she-wolf? You missed out on going with us when you could have played with her yourself."

"I was swimming." If he'd known his family had hooked up with a single she-wolf, he would have been there to check her out and forgotten about watching for someone else showing up at the pool. Though he had hoped to catch sight of the woman in the string bikini again. Still, someone just passing through Silver Town wouldn't have made for a permanent friendship—as in courting.

Kayla served the rolls and they sat down to eat.

Roxie smiled. "I know you. You were making sure no one else showed up to swim when the pool is closed, after what happened earlier."

Landon smiled at his sisters.

After dinner, he carried the dishes into the kitchen to clean up. "Dinner was delicious. Thanks for making it."

"You're welcome," Roxie said.

He finished cleaning up the dishes and told his sisters, "I'm off to bed. See you in the morning." But he couldn't quit thinking about the woman in the candy-striped string bikini. He wanted in the worst way to find her in the pool—not only by sight, but to actually catch her. He was a wolf at heart, but hell, when did he lose sight of his mission that fast?

After he'd showered and gone to bed, all he could think of was the woman diving under the water like a mermaid and then slipping under the glass divider and vanishing. As if she had escaped to the sea. He had desperately wanted to reach her while swimming—and he might have, if Blake hadn't interrupted him! But if she was human, that wouldn't be half as grand as if she were a wolf. And that's what he had to know. Was she or wasn't she?

The next morning, Landon was at the lodge early, taking care of guests who were looking for directions to town, gift shops in the area, eating places nearby. He gave them the brochures that Nicole's parents had made up for them at their stationery store.

While he spoke to the last guest about the Wolffs' gift shop and shipping policy for purchases, Roxie came over to speak with him, wearing a big smile, and arched her brows. "You know the pool's not open yet. But I heard a swimmer swimming across the length. Do you want me to tell the swimmer it's closed for two more hours?"

"I've got it." Landon hoped it was the woman he had seen last night in the pool. No way did he want anyone else to get involved. Despite his need to tell the woman she couldn't swim at this hour, he wanted to see her in the string bikini again. What could he say? He was a bachelor male wolf, and if she was a single she-wolf, he was going to have to rethink his notion that a guest couldn't swim when the pool was closed. But just for her. And someone, like him, would have to be there swimming with her to make it officially all right. He figured his family would rib him mercilessly about it if that happened.

He was wearing a sweater, pants, and boots, not ready for a swim, but if it happened to be the same woman, he was ready to ditch his clothes, wearing only his boxer briefs, and swim after her.

As soon as he reached the pool, he saw her heading for the glass divider to the outside part of the pool, wearing a red, green, and white bikini. She still looked like a sexy, sweet candy cane, but the swimsuit was not nearly as revealing as the string bikini. This time, her hair was floating around her, long and blond. Before he lost her again, since he couldn't swim after her, he called out to her, "Hey, what's your name?"

Not at all like what he should have said to the woman: *The pool's closed! You have to leave now!*

He suspected she might just ignore him and keep on swimming.

She turned, her smile radiant. He was a sucker for a pretty smile, yet the notion flitted through his mind that she was just like his ex, doing what she shouldn't because she thought she could get away with it with a pretty smile. And yet, he wondered, was she the woman he'd seen in the snow last night, walking past his and his sisters' house? It was hard to tell because the woman had been buried in clothes, a ski hat covering her head and her blond hair swept up in the chilly breeze, but a lighter color than this woman's wet blond hair.

"Gabrielle Lowell," she said, treading water.

"The—" He meant to say the pool was closed, but she interrupted him.

"Sorry. I'll be right out."

"You're a guest, right?" He wondered if she was staying at the Victorian Inn or Hastings Bed and Breakfast in town and wasn't even a guest here.

"Yes. My friends are late in arriving at the lodge, and nothing's open at this hour." She motioned to the outdoor area of the pool. "I have to go that way. That's where my clothes are."

He glanced around the pool and realized that's why he hadn't smelled her scent here before. She must have sneaked into the pool from the outside and left the same way so she didn't leave any clothes on one of the chaise lounges. Very clever. He would never have guessed it.

Now what? He hurried as fast as he could to the outside so he could reach her before she disappeared again. Though he could look her up on the computer and learn what room she was staying in, her car tags, where she was from. But he would much prefer talking to her first.

When he finally exited the lodge, having to take the long way around to reach a door, he found her sitting on a lounge chair, pulling on a pair of candy-cane socks and then snow boots with fluffy fur around the tops. Her parka was bright pink with a fur collar on the hood, and she was wearing black skintight ski pants. The same clothes he saw the woman in the snow wearing last night. She was a gray wolf like him. He smiled.

She gave him more of a precocious smile this time. Despite her saying she'd been sorry about swimming in the pool, he knew she wasn't really.

"So you are the lodge's security officer?" she asked, heading toward the restaurant as he hoofed it around the other side of the pool to join her.

"Part owner, along with my brother, his mate, and my two sisters. I'm Landon Wolff."

Her kissable mouth hung agape. "Wolff Timberline Lodge. And you're gray wolves."

He smiled and he was sure his look was on the predatory side. "Yeah, and so are you. You ran with my family last night. You passed by me when you were trespassing in our backyard."

Her enticing lips parted again. "Uh, if they live in the two homes next to the lodge, yes. Where were you? Wait, still swimming? Trying to catch me breaking the rules again?"

He chuckled darkly and led her to the restaurant, but the Saint Bernard came running after them to greet her.

"What's this, Rosco?" Landon asked, reaching over to pet the dog.

But Rosco quickly licked Gabrielle's hand and she gave him a hug. "You're such a good boy, aren't you?"

Landon smiled down at the two of them. They looked like they were the best of friends. "You've been holding out on us, Rosco."

The dog nuzzled his hand as if to say they were still friends.

"Come on, Gabrielle. Let's eat. He will want you to pet him for the rest of the day, if you encourage him."

"I'll pet you more later, Rosco." She frowned as she read the sign stating the bar and grill's hours of operation. "It says it's not open for another half hour."

"I'm one of the owners, remember?" He unlocked the door and let her in, then locked it back up so that no one would get the idea the bar and grill was now open for business. Breakfasts were being made for those who ordered room service, but he could have their breakfast made now.

"Wow. I call this royal treatment." She smiled at him. "What if I had a boyfriend?"

"He would be here with you now, and last night, I suspect." Landon couldn't imagine being her boyfriend and not being with her every minute of the day while on vacation.

She nodded. "You're right. What about you?"

"I don't have a boyfriend either."

She laughed and he brought her a menu, then they sat down in a booth. He got a call while she was looking over the menu and he said, "Yeah, Roxie?"

"So did you catch him?" Roxie asked.

He smiled at Gabrielle. "I caught the swimmer red-handed. I'm going to give the person hard labor—kitchen duty."

"The rule breaker, is it a she-wolf perchance?" Roxie asked.

There was no getting anything past his sisters.

Landon cleared his throat. "Yeah." He figured one of his family members would learn about Gabrielle soon enough. Not that he had any real plan to hide the truth from them long-term.

"Okay." Roxie hung up on him.

He'd expected more of a response from her than that.

"Hard labor? Kitchen duty?" Smiling, Gabrielle set the menu aside. She didn't look like she was worried about it in the least.

"Yeah, but we have to be open for a while or you won't have enough dishes to clean. Did you pick out what you wanted to eat?" Landon asked.

The waitress hurried to take their orders. "I didn't expect you here this early, Landon." She glanced at Gabrielle and smiled.

"Minx, meet Gabrielle. Gabrielle, this is Minx."

"Oh, a date." Minx offered them a carafe of coffee and smiled again, notepad in hand, ready to take their orders.

"Not a date," he corrected Minx.

"Sure." Minx sounded like she didn't believe him. "What would you like, then?"

Gabrielle motioned to the menu. "I'll have number three on the breakfast menu."

"One number three: sweet roasted tomatoes with eggs, sweet Christmas sausages, and hash browns. And for you, Landon?" Minx asked.

"I'll have a stack of pancakes and bacon."

A few people were beginning to gather at the doors to the restaurant, and Minx shook her head. "See what you did? Now they all will want to come in and eat early."

"Owner's prerogative."

"I knew you would say that," Minx said.

Suddenly, Roxie was at the door, unlocking it. Landon thought she was opening the bar and grill early, but she locked it back up and came straight to his table. "You know the trouble this gets us into when any of us eat early at the restaurant before we're open for business and everyone wonders why."

"As if any of us ever do this. Besides, we're wearing staff shirts or, in my case, a staff sweater," Landon said.

"True." Roxie smiled at Gabrielle and offered her hand. "You are the wolf who went running with us last night."

"I am." Gabrielle shook her hand.

Roxie folded her arms and looked sternly at Gabrielle with mock seriousness. "And you were swimming after hours last night *and* before hours in the pool this morning."

"I was. Now I have kitchen duty for my transgressions."

Roxie laughed. "I should have known Landon found a she-wolf in the pool—you must be unmated—and that's why he is 'buying' you breakfast instead of giving you a lecture."

"I figured she would take the lecture better on a full stomach," Landon said.

Roxie and Gabrielle smiled.

Blake peered in the window at them, shook his head, and left. Then Kayla came by to check them out. She looked through the glass at them just like Blake had, smiled, and walked off.

"That was our other brother, Blake, and that's Kayla, our

younger quadruplet sister. Blake's mate, Nicole, who ran with us last night, is working on a PI case with her brother, Nate, today in a town up north of here, or Nicole would be checking you out too," Roxie said.

Gabrielle smiled.

Minx served their meals.

"Where are you from?" Roxie asked Gabrielle.

Landon gave Roxie a look that said it was time for her to get back to work so *he* could ask Gabrielle all the questions.

"Daytona Beach, Florida."

"Wow. Have you skied before?" Roxie ignored Landon's annoyed look.

"Nope. This is my first time."

Roxie smiled at Landon. "He's an expert on the slopes. He can teach you all about it. When he's not working, of course. So what do you do in Daytona Beach?"

"Roxie…" Landon said, his annoyed tone of voice telling his younger sister to beat it, since she was disregarding his more subtle look of exasperation.

"All right, but you get all the details then and share them with us tonight. Oh, and ask her to run with us again tonight. Unless she sneaks into the pool area and you want to catch her at it and swim with her instead." Roxie smiled and hurried off as he opened his mouth to tell her to leave.

Gabrielle began eating her eggs. "You're paying for breakfast? Maybe I should because I broke the rules."

"We own the restaurant. The meal is on me."

Her mouth gaped, and then she smiled. "Wow. Was it the string bikini that did it?"

He chuckled. "It helped."

"I never wear it on trips, normally. I had to bring it because it was a joke gift my girlfriends, twin sisters, gave me last year before Christmas when we went to Cancun. They are coming here too.

None of us have any family so the three of us take trips together right after Thanksgiving. Only this time they got hung up at work and now they're late in arriving. I thought when no one would be in the pool, I could wear it and no one would ever see me in it."

He smiled. "Not everyone can wear a string bikini and look great in it."

"Thank you. As to the other question your sister asked—my occupation? I'm a vet."

"A veterinarian?"

"Yeah. I love working with animals, and nothing makes me feel better than when I can keep them healthy or take care of them when they're sick or injured."

"A veterinarian. That's great." He was really surprised, maybe because she was breaking the rules and she looked so hot in a bikini. Doc Mitchell was their veterinarian, old, white-haired, big and lumbering, and Gabrielle was a totally different version of a vet—all legs, blond, young, and beautiful. "Did you know we're wolf-run here?"

"Your lodge and restaurant? I suspected as much since all of your staff that I've met so far are wolves."

"Not just our place is run by wolves, but all of Silver Town."

Her green eyes widened. "Really?"

"Yeah, since its inception. The Silver family runs it, and all the businesses in town are wolf-run."

"Wow. That's amazing. So, the town is made up of just wolves?" she asked.

"Uh, yeah."

"My girlfriends are jaguars."

The restaurant doors were opened and several guests came in to grab seats and order their meals, a few of them looking at Landon, but upon seeing his staff sweater, they didn't say anything about him getting special treatment. Though a few of the people coming in for breakfast were wolves of Silver Town, getting a bite to eat before the ski slopes opened. Some were ski instructors or lift operators, so they knew who he was.

"They'll still be welcome, won't they?" Gabrielle asked.

"Jaguar shifters? Sure. We've had some stay at the lodge and ski a week or so ago. I think they were as surprised to learn about us as we were about them when we first found out they existed. But we all have a shifter secret and something in common, even if we're very much different when we're wearing our fur coats."

No one near them was human, so Landon could speak freely.

A couple of bachelor male wolves were sitting nearby, trying to listen in to the conversation, wondering just who Landon was eating with before the restaurant was even open. He and his family usually ate here for lunch, but grabbed breakfast and dinner at home. This morning, he'd missed breakfast to come in early, thinking he could catch her swimming, but Gabrielle hadn't been there that early and he'd ended up having to handle guest business after that. When Roxie told him that the swimmer was in the pool, he was glad it had been Gabrielle again and not someone new.

"You've never skied before," Landon said.

"No. I'm from Florida. There are no mountains or snow there, and when my friends and I have taken trips after Thanksgiving the past five years, we've hit beach resorts. But this is just beautiful. I have never seen such lovely decorations at Christmastime. The huge tree in the lobby—all the cute little hand-carved wolves, black bears, polar bears, Arctic foxes, and penguins. I took pictures of them to send to my friends. I'm getting some wolf decorations to take home with me."

"Many of our wolves did the hand-carved woodwork. The photography hanging about the rooms and lobby were done by Jake Silver, brother to our pack leader, Darien."

"How wonderful." Gabrielle buttered her toast and added marmalade on top. "A pack. I didn't think of that. So you and your family belong to a bigger pack?"

"Yeah. We have all kinds of events that our wolves can take part in. And the Silver Town Tavern caters to wolves only. Uh, I should say shifters. Your friends would be welcome at the tavern."

"Okay, we'll have to check it out. If they ever get here." She sounded disappointed.

He didn't blame her since the three friends were supposed to be doing this together and she didn't ski. Skiing alone wasn't safe or half as fun as skiing with friends.

"When are they coming in?" Landon asked.

"They were supposed to arrive here last night, then this morning, but they texted me to say they were delayed again until later this afternoon."

"Did you want me to take you skiing this morning?" Landon didn't intend to impose on her if she wanted to just wait for her friends, but if he could make her stay more enjoyable while she was here without them, he would.

"Don't you have to run the lodge or restaurant or something?" She finished off her toast and licked marmalade off her finger.

The sight of her licking her finger brought unbidden images to mind, such as how he would like to hold her close, kiss her, and tangle his tongue with hers. "I can be on call. We often take turns skiing. That's the whole point of having the lodge, so that we can take the time to enjoy the ski resort too. There's no sense in you sitting around the tavern waiting for your friends to show up. Do they ski?"

"They do. A lot. They finally convinced me to come with them this time. I left Florida early so I could have more time to get settled in here, but I had expected them to come in last night too."

Landon finished his bacon and took another drink of his coffee. "Well, I've been skiing since I was three. So if you want me to get you started, I certainly can."

"Three years old? Wow. I will be down on the ground more than I'm up, I'm afraid. I swim much better."

He laughed. "We all have to start somewhere. Have you got lift tickets?"

"No."

"Ski boots? Skis? Ski poles?"

She shook her head.

"Okay, first, I'll take you to the ski rental shop and get you set up." He smelled her tension. "You can do it. We can take this nice and easy. You can quit anytime you feel you've had enough."

"All right, but don't fault me too much if I spend most of the time on my bottom."

And what a beautiful bottom that was.

After she finished the last of her breakfast, he left a tip, then texted Roxie: Tell Blake and Kayla I'll be taking Gabrielle out for a few ski lessons.

Roxie texted: Are you serious?

Landon texted back: Just tell them.

He knew they would be laughing their heads off and he would hear more about it later.

Then he and Gabrielle left the restaurant. Kayla usually stayed in the office to work on marketing materials and anything else office-related with regard to the lodge and bar and grill. But she had to come out to meet the woman Landon was with. He introduced Gabrielle to Kayla, who shook her hand and smiled.

"Welcome to Silver Town. You'll have a blast here. Do you have a wolf pack back in Daytona Beach, Florida?" Kayla asked.

Gabrielle shook her head. "No. A few stray wolves coming through, mostly on vacation, but no real leadership or pack."

Kayla folded her arms and nodded. "We left Vermont for the same reason. We wanted to be with a pack. We love it here. The pack has been really good to us."

"They have," Landon said. "We're going to get some ski lessons in. Gabrielle's friends aren't arriving until this afternoon. We'll see you later."

"For another wolf run, right?" Kayla asked Gabrielle. "We loved having you play with us. And if Landon can skip swimming in the pool, he can come with us this time."

Gabrielle smiled. "Sure, I would love to. My friends too, if they arrive before we go for a run tonight? They're jaguars."

"Absolutely. That will be a new experience for us and we'll have fun," Kayla said.

"Okay, let's go and get you ready for your first ski lesson, Gabrielle." Then Landon hurried her off before Blake came along to talk to them too. Wolves were curious by nature, especially when it had to do with the family. When Blake began seeing Nicole, and she was taking care of a PI job at the lodge, the whole family got involved to help her out.

"So what do your friends do?" Landon asked Gabrielle.

"They're both with a JAG agency that deals with rogue jaguar shifters."

"Really." Landon had heard about them, and how they had a facility to actually incarcerate shifters—any kind now, but only shifters. No humans. It was privately funded by their own kind, so no one—especially no humans—were the wiser.

"Yeah. They were supposed to be through with the case they were on by now, so I'm not sure what the problem is. They didn't give me any of the details, just that they would be late in arriving."

Once Gabrielle was all set with skis, poles, boots, and a ski pass, Landon walked her back to the office where they had a storage area for the family's skis, poles, and boots.

"You're sure you don't mind at all?" she asked, looking uncomfortable about trying this out.

He could smell her anxiousness. "Yeah. I let everyone know where we're going to be in case they need me."

"All right." She sighed. "I could just hire someone to give me lessons."

"There's no need to waste your money when I can do this with you." He walked her past the Christmas tree in the lobby, sparkling with lights. They headed outside onto the deck of the bar and grill where early skiers were grabbing coffee, or hot chocolate, and pastries before they headed for the ski lifts. The deck had a coating of snow, though they cleared it every day so that it wouldn't end up being knee-high.

First, Landon took Gabrielle to the bunny slope where she rode the magic carpet up the 50-foot incline. He talked to her about giving right of way to other skiers. "People ahead of you have right of way. Which means you have to avoid them, not run into them. When you stop, you have to be out of the path of others, and you don't want to be someplace hidden from view as a skier comes up over a hill on the trail. Whenever your trail merges with another, you have to look uphill and not ski into a downhill skier's path. You have to always stay in control."

She laughed. "Oh, that will be a fun trial, I'm sure."

"You'll get the hang of it." He was sure of it. Though she might have to practice for several days to feel comfortable with it. "How long are you going to be here?"

"Eight days. Well, seven days left now. We leave on the night of day eight, so we'll ski in the morning, eat lunch, go to the airport, and fly out."

Seven days of teaching her how to ski? He could certainly go for it. But once her friends came, that would probably be the end of all the fun times he wanted to spend with Gabrielle.

———————

Gabrielle was so nervous about this business of skiing that she hoped Landon proved to be a good and patient ski instructor. She'd barely made it to the top of the bunny slope when she fell. She was just standing upright, doing nothing but just standing there. And then she wasn't.

"Okay, next lesson. How to get up. It's really important that you learn that lesson."

She laughed. "I can see that." She watched little kids get up easily since they didn't have half the distance to fall down or stand up. She was finally up and then she practiced forming a wedge, or a snowplow, with her skis to learn to control her speed and practiced turning. After that, she finally was ready to learn how to get on the ski lift and go down an easy green slope. She was beginning to feel like she might be all right with skiing, and she was having fun in Landon's company. It made her feel better about her girlfriends not getting here on time. Sure, she could have sat around the lodge watching all the skiers in their ski clothes laughing and smiling, with red cheeks and red noses, and looking like they were having the time of their life.

Gabrielle was much more of a doer, even if she did feel bad that she hadn't been able to do this with her dad like they'd planned a decade ago. She almost felt guilty about enjoying it. But she knew she needed to move on and put the past behind her.

She was hopeful that if she got good enough, when her friends arrived, they wouldn't have to teach her the very basics.

First, she was taking the ski lift to the top of the slope. At the top, she managed to get off the ski-lift chair just fine. Landon had told her to ski away from the lift so others could get off after her. She was standing in the way and felt panicked that she needed to ski away from the chairlift right away, but she was still trying to remember how to move her skis in the snow while trying to ski. Then she fell. *Ugh.* She envisioned everyone running over her as they tried to unload from the chairs and a pile of bodies fitted out in skis and poles all tangled up in that mountain of a mess. Landon skied around her to get out of everyone's path and waited for her to get up. At least she was getting good at that part. She thought she'd had the most practice at that—falling down and getting up.

Then she was at the top of the easy slope that looked a lot higher and scarier than she'd thought it could be—for being a green slope. But at least it was nice and wide and had a gentler slope than the intermediate and expert slopes had. Other skiers headed down the hill, looking like experts to her as they weaved back and forth, their skis close together, their turns like little hops. Not like she had to do it, by making a wide snowplow each time she pointed her skis downhill and picked up speed.

She couldn't imagine starting this at three years old. Though by now, if she came regularly to ski, she would be an expert.

"You can do it. And if you fall, lean against the slope to get back up. While you're skiing, keep your upper body and head leaning toward the valley and over the downhill ski. Keep your legs and knees and ankles equally bent. As you make your turns, your weight will be transferred to the downhill ski."

Oh, that would be easier said than done, Gabrielle thought. She began going down the slope, slowly, picking up speed, turning so she could slow her speed, turning again, and going down. This was fun. But scary. She sliced into the slope and felt her body lean downhill. She imagined falling all the way down the hill—rolling, gathering snow, and becoming a ball of snow with only her head, hands, and feet sticking out—and quickly fell against the snowbank so she could regain her balance. Then she figured out how to stand back up again, this time on the side of a hill.

Landon encouraged her every step of the way, which she appreciated. She assumed with running the lodge, he didn't often teach a new skier how to ski. And she imagined how boring that must be when he could just be enjoying the slope, winging his way down all the way to the bottom.

She slid down just a little with her skis against the slope, then took a deep breath and started her wedge and began the planned fall down the hill, back and forth, getting better, her wedge not as wide, and she wasn't falling down as much. She had this down.

She was nearly at the bottom of the hill when she took another spill. *Argh.*

Landon was right back at her side, smiling down at her. "You're getting really good at this."

She laughed. "Right."

"You are. This is your first time out. Lunch is on me in a couple of hours, but did you want to take a drink break?"

"When I'm getting so good at this? Let's go again." She was afraid she would forget everything she had learned if she took a break now.

"Okay." He sounded pleased.

That was one thing about her. She might feel like she couldn't do well at something, but she kept trying until she knew she could do it. Maybe not expertly, but at least until she felt more comfortable at it.

Gabrielle was not giving up, no matter how frustrated she might become.

"I don't usually instruct people on how to ski because I don't have a whole lot of patience, but when I was younger, and while I was helping to run a ski lodge with my family, I did earn some money as a ski instructor."

"With me, you seem to have plenty of patience."

"You have so much drive to do this, you make it easy on me. You're eager to get this right and laugh at yourself every time you fall. You're fun to be with."

She smiled. "You make a perfect ski instructor for a first-time skier—at least in my case. Thanks." She appreciated that he had made her feel good about something she thought she might never get the hang of.

Then they hit the slopes again. This time she didn't fall at all, either after getting off the ski lift or anytime on the hill, and not at the bottom either. She was ready to get in the lift line again. Several of the ski instructors smiled at her as she passed them by—they were all wolves. She couldn't imagine what it would be like living in a community that was made up of wolves who ran everything. Pretty cool, she figured. No need to hide what they were. As long as there weren't any humans around, they could talk openly about wolf issues.

She and Landon went up the chairlift and skied down the green slopes several more times. But this time when she was on the chairlift again with him, she was feeling cold, the wind blowing about them as they rode it up. "I think after we go down this time, I would like to get some hot chocolate." Despite wearing everything warm that she'd had at home, she still wasn't warm enough.

"We can do that and you can get warmed up."

Thankfully, she skied down even better than the last time, and they both skied to the outdoor part of the bar and grill where they could put their poles and skis on a rack before they sat down at one of the tables to have a drink.

"Indoors or out?" he asked.

"Oh, indoors. I'm cold." She rubbed her gloved hands together.

A bunch of skiers were sitting out at the tables, enjoying the sunny day, having hot drinks and talking about their ski day, their cheeks and noses red from the cold.

"Yeah, sure. We could have lunch early, if you would like," he said.

"And a swim?"

He laughed. "The pool's open now. Are you sure you want to swim when it's officially open?"

"Nah, what's the fun in that?"

CHAPTER 3

After Landon and Gabrielle took their seats in a booth in the restaurant, they ordered hot chocolates and then Landon called Roxie to ensure he wasn't needed. "Is everything going okay without me?"

"Yeah," Roxie said. "We don't need you, really."

Their mugs of hot chocolate arrived and Landon thanked the server.

"Okay, good, Roxie. You know to call me if you have any need of me."

"We will."

Then they ended the call.

"This is great hot chocolate," Gabrielle said, then took another sip, the whipped cream coating her lips. Landon wanted to lean over and lick the whipped cream off before she did.

"It's got extra chocolate to make it just right." He smiled at Gabrielle. "So when are your friends getting here?"

Gabrielle got a text message and read it. "Speaking of my friends, they said they're not going to be arriving until later tonight." She texted them back.

"It's a good thing we were able to go skiing, then. If there's one thing I hate, it's waiting on people who don't show up and then I've wasted all my time just sitting around and doing nothing fun," Landon said.

"I agree. I mean, honestly, I did think of just sitting on the sidelines for the day, but I'm so glad I won't be a total neophyte at skiing when they get here. By the time I have lessons with you after our hot chocolate break and then more after lunch, I'll be ready to go up on the slopes with my friends tomorrow. They're both experts. Not that I'll be able to ski at that level."

Landon gave an exaggerated sigh. "Looks like that will be the end of a blossoming relationship between the two of us, then."

She laughed. "It's supposed to work the other way around. The girl dumps her girlfriends for the hot guy."

"That definitely works for me." Not that he wanted her to ditch her girlfriends, but he would love to keep seeing her while she was here, if she could spare the time.

She smiled. "I'm sure they would be shocked."

"You don't date much?"

"No. I've been too busy with work, and there haven't been enough wolves around to go out with. I would see some wolves come through Daytona Beach on a vacation—some single, date one every once in a while, but nothing that would ever amount to anything."

"Ahh." That was good news. Enticing the she-wolf to join the pack would sure work for him. "So do you have any family back in Daytona Beach?"

"No." She looked down at her mug. "We were in a car accident while headed to a ski resort in Montana, first time ever for us to ski. It was ten years ago, but sometimes it still haunts me. In a blinding snowstorm, we met a moose on the road. Dad swerved to miss it and we ended up in a frozen lake. They didn't survive. I–I haven't ever been back to snow country since."

"I'm so sorry." He felt awful for bringing it up.

She took a deep breath and let it out. "I kept wishing I could have saved them. I did everything I could. It was a long time ago, but you know how it is when you lose someone you love. You always wonder what you could have done to prevent it. And I have to admit I really had a lot of qualms about coming to a ski resort at all." She gave him a sad smile. "What about your parents? Do they live here?"

"They're gone too. A hunter killed our mom, and our dad killed the man. He didn't have a choice. The hunter had seen her shift in death."

"Oh, that's so awful. He had to have felt terrible about losing your mother like that."

"Yeah, he died of a broken heart. He just wouldn't eat. You know how wolves can be. They mate for life. Sometimes they can move on. Sometimes they can't. He just couldn't. We were all grown, running the old lodge in Vermont on our own by then, my parents having retired. But we were all profoundly shaken by it. We tried and tried to bring him out of his depression, but nothing worked. It's another reason we moved here. It's safe to run as wolves, no hunters allowed on our properties."

"That's true."

Then Landon got a call from Blake and he figured there was trouble or his brother would have just texted him. "Yeah, Blake?"

"Hey, Rosco's not in the lodge. At least I've made a good search for him. You know him. He usually just chills by the fireplace, and if he needs to go outside to relieve himself, he comes to one of us. I went to our homes to see if he slipped back inside the houses through the wolf doors for some reason, but he's not there. He's been really good about not leaving the lodge without us."

"Okay, I'll look for him." Landon sighed. That would curtail his skiing for a while, and he hated to give up spending the rest of the day with Gabrielle. "I'll let you know if I find him or not." When he ended the call, he said to Gabrielle, "Blake called to say he couldn't find Rosco. He never leaves the lodge without us, but I need to search for him and make sure he's still here."

"I'll help you."

"But you wanted to ski. I don't want you to waste your vacation time on this. I could set you up with a ski instructor who can give you some more training while I look for Rosco and join you later for lunch. Or I could join you back on the slopes right after I locate him. I don't want you to miss out on skiing." Of course, he would only have asked someone in the pack who was mated to teach her to ski.

"No, no, that's all right. I would rather go skiing again with you, after we find Rosco."

"Are you sure?"

"Yeah. I would feel terrible if I were out there skiing and you couldn't find him, when I might have been able to help locate him. And if he has suffered an injury, I can take care of him."

"Okay, good."

They grabbed their skis and poles from the ski rack outside and put them in the storage room, then switched out their ski boots for their snow boots.

"We might as well go in separate directions to cover more area, right?" she asked.

"Yeah, if you can stay in this half of the lodge, I'll check out the other half," he said, and then they took off in different directions. But after half an hour of searching for the dog and finding no scent for him on the elevators, but a more distinctive scent for him near one of the doors, Landon suspected Rosco had gone outside. Landon saw Gabrielle coming out of the pool area, and when she noticed him, she shook her head.

They got together and he said, "I think he went out to the ski slope. He's never done that on his own before, but there's always a first time. I can walk through some of the snow in snow boots, but depending on how far he went into the unpacked snow, I might have to use snowshoes."

"Do you have a pair for me?"

He couldn't believe she wanted to come with him to continue to look for Rosco. "Yeah, I'll ask Kayla or Roxie if you can borrow a pair of theirs. Have you ever… Scratch that. You aren't from snow country, so you've probably never worn them."

"Nope, so you might need to give me lessons."

He smiled, and after he asked his sisters who could loan snowshoes to Gabrielle, Roxie quickly offered hers before Kayla could.

"I can't believe Rosco took off like that. If you don't find him, let us know and we can contact Darien to see if he can call up more of the pack members to help us find him," Roxie said, getting the snowshoes from the storage closet in their office.

"That's just what I was thinking," Landon said.

"I never imagined a wolf pack would go looking for a pack member's missing pet." Gabrielle thanked Roxie for the snowshoes.

"Yeah, there are all kinds of good things to be said about a wolf pack." Landon grabbed a prepacked backpack with a first aid kit and warming blanket out of the storage room, just in case Rosco was injured. He also grabbed three bottles of water and slipped them into the backpack.

Landon led Gabrielle outside, and they crunched through the snow in the direction they both smelled Rosco had gone. They called out for Rosco the whole while.

"Rosco, here, boy!" Landon said.

"Rosco!" Gabrielle called out.

They walked past the bunny ski slope, past the bottom of a green slope, then beyond a blue slope, all easy walking since the slopes were groomed. But when they came to the expert slope, the snow beyond it was soft, powdery, and deep.

"Time for snowshoes," Landon said, and helped Gabrielle on with hers, then put on his own.

Then they began calling for Rosco again.

"He definitely came this way." Landon pointed out the imprint of the dog plowing through the snow.

"Why this way?"

"Maybe he was chasing a rabbit or a squirrel. He's known to do that, though only when he's on leash."

———————

Gabrielle hoped they'd find Rosco soon. She was getting colder and colder, walking in the deep snow, and wearing snowshoes was a whole new experience too. Still, she was worried about the Saint Bernard. What if he had gotten lost? She didn't think Rosco would, but she'd known of cases where her clients' dogs had chased off after something and gotten horribly lost. She would think they would be able to trace their scent back to the owner's home, but nope.

She hoped the dog wasn't injured, but if he was, that's where she could really help. If she didn't freeze to death first. "Rosco!"

"Rosco!" Landon called out. He glanced back at Gabrielle, who was falling behind…again.

She couldn't help it. She felt the snowshoes were cumbersome and unwieldly, but at least they were probably keeping her from sinking too deeply into the snow. She still sank a couple of inches. She caught the tip of her snowshoe on a low-hanging tree branch and tripped. The snowshoe came unclipped from her boot, and her foot sank three or four feet into the snow. Man, she would never have believed the snow was that deep here.

Landon saw her leg buried in snow and came back to help her.

"Sorry," she said, apologizing for holding them up.

"You're fine. Rosco's the one in trouble for leading us on this wild-goose chase. Are you okay? I mean, cold-wise?"

"Yeah, I'm okay. I'm cold, but hopefully we can find him soon."

"If you get too cold, let me know. I don't want you getting frostbite." He picked up his phone and called someone. "Hey, Blake, we're on Rosco's trail beyond the last expert slope. We can smell his scent, but he hasn't stopped running through the deep snow. I might have to send Gabrielle back to the lodge. She's getting cold."

"I'm fine. Wait, I hear something. A scratching sound, maybe?" She got her snowshoe on and started to move again.

"Okay, Gabrielle thinks she hears something. We're going. Yeah, meet us out here. I'm afraid we're not going to be able to get him through the deep snow all the way back to the lodge when we find him, unless we've all packed the snow down enough for him. All right. We're on the move again. Just follow our tracks." He tucked his phone in his pocket and followed Gabrielle, listening carefully. "What did you hear?"

"I thought I heard digging. Rosco!" she called out, trying to get to the place she thought he might be. "Oh, Landon! There he is! He's digging at the snow beyond the stand of trees!"

"What did you find, Rosco?" Landon called out, trying to move as fast as he could to reach the location where Rosco was digging.

"You said he's an avalanche rescue dog, right?" Gabrielle asked, getting close to Rosco. "I hear someone buried in the snow—a heartbeat, a muffled cry for help." She began digging with her gloves as fast as she could right beside Rosco. And she could smell the human's scent: male.

Landon pulled out his cell phone as he joined Gabrielle. "Blake, we found Rosco. He's found someone buried in the snow. Okay, since you're already on your way, call ski patrol, will you? I've got to help Gabrielle and Rosco dig out the buried victim. Out here."

Landon quickly ended the call and began digging next to Gabrielle.

"I hear a faint heartbeat." Gabrielle continued to dig frantically. "I smell he is human."

"I do too. Man, am I glad you came with me. You and Rosco are a team," Landon said.

"You would have heard Rosco if you hadn't been talking on the phone." She felt something hard. A helmet, she thought. "Hold on, we're coming for you," she called to the man buried in the snow. "We almost have you."

"Emergency personnel are on their way," Landon said. "You're going to be just fine."

Then they uncovered the back of the person's black-and-white helmet and began to dig around his face so that he could breathe. He was breathing, and Gabrielle couldn't have been more relieved, but she still worried about any injuries the victim might have suffered. Working on an avalanche victim was definitely a first for her. "I'm glad we brought first aid gear."

"Yeah, me too. I thought we might be using it on Rosco. But you never know when you might need it, even for us if we'd gotten ourselves into trouble."

They continued to unbury the young man, Rosco pausing to lick the snow off the man's face, and Landon chuckled. That was a good sign. They finally removed enough snow that they could gently pull the man the rest of the way out. He groaned in pain, but they had to get him warmed up and hydrated.

Landon gave him some water. "What's your name?" Landon asked, while Gabrielle checked him over for injuries.

"Mick Johnson."

At least he was conscious and seemed lucid. The blond-haired guy groaned when Gabrielle touched his right arm. "It might be broken," Gabrielle said. "Do you have anything to use to stabilize it in the first aid kit, Landon?"

Landon was already pulling out the emergency blanket. "Yeah." He brought out the splint.

The splint was a moldable piece of aluminum enclosed in foam for comfort. After they splinted Mick's arm, they gently lifted him onto the emergency blanket and wrapped him in it.

"What happened?" Landon asked.

"I was snowboarding and then the snow buried me. I thought I was never going to make it out alive. I was trying to call out for help, but then gave up on it. I knew I needed to save my breath. Since I was not on a main slope, I was certain no one would be out here looking for me. Then I heard someone digging at the snow. I never would have figured it was a dog."

"Rosco is an avalanche rescue dog. So you were alone off-trail when it happened?" Landon asked.

Gabrielle realized they might need to look for someone else too.

"Yeah, my friend said he wouldn't go with me. It was too dangerous."

She was relieved they didn't have to search for someone else buried in the snow.

"Maybe he was right." Landon got on his phone again. "Hey, Blake, we've got a snowboarder, possible broken arm. Rosco was digging him out." Landon smiled and rubbed Gabrielle's back. "Gabrielle found Mick Johnson and Rosco first. They make a hell of a team." He laughed. "Okay. We need a pickup."

"You were there every step of the way." Gabrielle shook her head at Landon, then asked Mick, "Where are you staying?"

"The ski lodge."

"How old are you?" Gabrielle asked Mick.

"Twenty. My friend is so going to tell me I told you so."

Gabrielle started checking Rosco for injuries. She leaned down to check his paws to make sure he wasn't suffering from frostbite. "Do you have anything to put on his feet, Landon?"

"Yeah, I was just looking for his dog boots in the emergency pack. We added fleece lining to the boots to make them even warmer, but he normally isn't out this long in the snow." Landon couldn't seem to find them. "We can use some of the bandaging if we don't have them in there."

That was the good thing about wolves. They had more fur on their feet that protected their pads and toes and kept them from sliding on ice.

"Here they are," Landon said, sounding glad to have found them.

"Okay, thanks, and Rosco will be happier for them." And she would feel better if he was wearing them. She slipped them on his feet and secured them, and then she checked his nose, tail, and ears for frostbite. Bigger dogs and those that had heavier coats were at less risk than smaller, lightly furred breeds. It only took thirty minutes for a dog to develop frostbite in freezing weather.

"How's he doing?" Landon asked, concerned.

"He's good, but it's important to take preventive measures to make sure he stays that way."

After taking care of Rosco, Gabrielle rubbed her gloved hands together to warm up her chilled fingers.

"Are you cold?" Landon asked, crouching next to her and wrapping his arm around her shoulders.

"Yeah, maybe we can have lunch when we get back to the lodge and I can get warmed up before we ski again." She was at least glad the snowboarder seemed okay, his memory fine. She was hoping he didn't have any head injuries or any internal injuries that they couldn't detect, but he seemed okay.

"We'll do that."

"I'm sorry about this," Mick said, as if he suddenly realized he'd messed up their vacation plans.

"We'll get you out of here." Landon gave Rosco a treat from the treat barrel around his neck. "Good dog for rescuing an avalanche victim."

"Do you always do that?" Mick asked. "Give him a treat?"

"Yeah, it reinforces the idea that if there's an avalanche, he searches for any victim. If he finds one, he gets a treat. We just didn't know where Rosco had gotten off to. It's a good thing he came to help you and we went looking for him when he was missing from the lodge," Landon said.

"How would he have known about me?" Mick asked, just as surprised as Gabrielle was that the dog was that alert.

"If the door to the lodge was open and he heard the avalanche and you crying out, even from a distance, that could have clued him in," Landon said.

"Oh, yeah, I cried out for sure, all the way down the mountain as the snow followed me."

Landon smiled. "That was it, then."

"He's a remarkable dog." Gabrielle scratched Rosco's head.

Rosco lay down next to the victim to keep him warmer, but when she stopped petting him, he brushed at Gabrielle's hand with his muzzle to get her to pet him some more. She chuckled and continued to pet him. She was ready for Rosco to warm her up too.

Blake finally reached them, carrying another first aid kit. "How are you doing?" he asked Mick.

"Good, considering that I could be dead."

"True. You did good, Rosco. Here we thought you were a wayward dog." Blake rubbed the dog's head, slapped Landon on the back, and gave Gabrielle a hug. "Hey, you look cold."

"Yeah, I am." But hopefully this wouldn't take much longer.

"Landon, why don't you take Gabrielle back to the lodge and get her warmed up. I'll wait with the victim. The ski patrol will be here shortly." Blake offered them fresh bottles of water.

"No, we'll all stay together." Gabrielle wanted to be there if Mick's condition took a turn for the worse. She might work with animals, but she was still a doctor. She took a sip of the water.

Then they saw the members of the ski patrol coming for them and she was instantly relieved. She was so ready to get warmed up.

"Here they are," Landon said. "Right on time."

The guys of the ski patrol told them they had done a good job. They lifted Mick onto a stretcher and got him strapped on.

The ski patrol members smiled at Gabrielle. They were all wolves.

Then they headed back to the first aid hut so that the victim could be transported to the hospital in Green Valley. Poor Rosco was having a hard time getting back to the lodge through the deep snow though. Coming to rescue an avalanche victim? It appeared he could move mountains. But after all the work he'd done, he was worn out.

"Too bad he couldn't wear some snowshoes," Gabrielle said.

Rosco kept sitting down as if he wasn't going to make it. Landon brought out another bottled water and gave Rosco a drink. "Come on, Rosco, you can do this."

"Yeah, there's no way we can carry you," Blake said to Rosco, and then to Landon, "Did you want to get the ski patrol to come back for Rosco?"

"We might have to. That would be one for the record. A Saint Bernard needing a rescue instead of him always doing the rescuing." Landon petted Rosco's head. "Come on, buddy. Let's walk a little farther."

They continued to walk along the same path that most everyone had trampled, but with Rosco's weight and no snowshoes and the exercise he'd already had, he was having difficulty making it through the snow a second time.

Landon called the ski patrol. "Hey, if you guys can do it, we need Rosco carried back to the lodge. He can't make it." He smiled. "Thanks." Then Landon pocketed his phone. "Let's get out the other emergency blanket and get Rosco warmed up until the ski patrol can return with a stretcher for him."

Since Rosco weighed 160 pounds, similar to a man's weight, trying to make it through the snow while carrying him would be too much.

"Too bad we don't have a sled with us," Blake said. "Then we could just give him a ride on top of the snow."

"And me too!" Gabrielle really was ready for lunch and a warming up now.

CHAPTER 4

WHILE THEY WAITED FOR THE SKI PATROL TO ARRIVE, LANDON sat on the snow and reached his hand up to Gabrielle. "Come on, I'll warm you up."

She smiled. "All right. Thanks." Then she sat on his lap and he wrapped his arms around her. She did feel warmer like this, and it wasn't just from Landon's protection from the wind and cold, or his body heat either. She felt an attraction for him that she'd never felt for a wolf. Rather than a casual friendship between wolves like she'd experienced before, it was an intimacy between a man and a woman that she wanted to explore more deeply. Did he feel the same about her?

Never could she have imagined she would be sitting on a hot wolf's lap in the snow at the ski resort while waiting to have the ski patrol rescue the rescue dog—even if she had known wolves ran the whole place.

"Sorry, Blake, you're on your own," Landon said.

"Hell, the two, well, three of you had to do all that digging so you've had a lot more exercise than me and been out here longer than me. I'm good."

Gabrielle really wished they could continue walking toward the lodge. Moving got the blood circulating and warmed her up. She was envisioning sitting by the fire, roasting her fingers and toes, and not leaving there until she returned home to Florida. It wasn't as bad as when she'd been submerged in a frozen lake, but she really needed to get thawed out.

Though she had to admit that this was much more interesting than anything she'd ever encountered back home, and she was glad she could make a difference in the life of someone who wouldn't have survived if they hadn't gone looking for Rosco. Between the three of them, they had saved him.

"I bet you're proud of Rosco," she said, having never seen a dog locate and attempt to dig out an avalanche victim, not even in a movie.

"Yeah. You never know if the dog you train for that kind of work will be good at it. Many dogs wash out of the training. What's interesting is that dog rescues are comparable in success to human rescues using probes in locating victims. As wolf shifters, we can smell scents and hear so much better and can often find avalanche victims faster than either humans or dogs. Still, as Rosco proved to us, since he's trained for this kind of work, he remains alert when the rest of us are off doing other things," Landon said.

"When we realized he'd left the lodge, I really thought he'd chased after a squirrel," Blake said, sitting down next to Rosco and petting his head.

"Don't you feel guilty for thinking the worst of Rosco?" Gabrielle asked.

The brothers glanced at each other and smiled. Both said, "No."

She laughed, then grew serious. "I hope Mick is okay." She had thought to check on him when she finally reached the ski resort, but he should be on his way to a hospital by the time they arrived.

"He's in the best of hands," Landon assured her. "But he was lucky this time. Hopefully, he'll listen to his friend next time."

They didn't say anything for a while, and then Gabrielle worried she might be cutting off the circulation in Landon's legs. "Did you need me to give your lap a break?"

"Are you kidding? You're keeping me nice and warm."

She smiled and he tightened his hold on her as if he was afraid she might just leave him anyway.

"You asked about how the dating prospects were for me in Daytona Beach. What about you with dating?" Gabrielle couldn't believe she was talking to a male wolf about dating stuff near a ski resort miles and miles and miles from her home.

Blake was smiling, as if she meant anything by it. She just wanted to talk about something—other than rescues and snow and cold.

Landon said, "I gave up a girlfriend when I left Vermont and moved here. I haven't seriously dated anyone since then."

"What was your old girlfriend like?"

"She was a pretty brunette and had everyone wrapped around her little finger."

"You too?" Gabrielle was amused to hear it. She couldn't imagine anyone doing that to Landon. Then again, once he saw Gabrielle in her string bikini…

"For a little while. My sister Kayla thought she would change, given the chance, but none of the rest of the family did. Lyn was a rule breaker."

Blake shook his head. "That was for sure. She was bound to get herself in real trouble someday."

Gabrielle's lips parted. Then she smiled. "Like me."

"She was not anything like you. Okay, I have to admit the pool incident with you did remind me of her, but beyond that, nothing else," Landon said.

Blake laughed.

"So if I sneak into the pool tonight?" she asked.

"I'll be waiting to swim with you."

She laughed. "I'm glad you're one of the owners."

Then they heard people talking ahead and Rosco sat up and woofed.

"That looks like your rescue committee, Rosco." Gabrielle was glad they could start walking back to the resort now.

As soon as the men came into view, Rosco got off the blanket and headed for them under his own steam. The brothers laughed. He kept going until he reached the ski patrol, while Gabrielle, Landon, and Blake, who had grabbed up the blanket and secured it to the first aid backpack, headed out after him.

"Hey, Rosco," one of the men said. "If you can walk on your own, that's good news for us."

"But we'll be here if you need us," another of the men said.

"Thanks, guys," Landon said to them.

"Hey, Rosco's a hero," the first man said.

They all trudged through the snow but after another fifteen minutes, Rosco sat down.

That time, Landon and Blake made Rosco sit on the stretcher and they started up again. Landon stayed with Gabrielle, as if he was afraid that she might fall behind, and Blake helped the other men with the stretcher.

They finally reached the area where the snow was graded, and before Rosco wanted off the stretcher, several people took pictures of the rescue dog that had been rescued. Once they put him down on the snow-covered ground, he raced for the lodge.

Everyone laughed.

"It's lunchtime for him. You notice he perked right up when he saw the lodge," Landon said. "And it's lunchtime for us." He removed his snowshoes and helped Gabrielle with hers before they crossed the base of the ski slopes to reach the lodge.

"Thanks, guys," Landon and Blake told the ski patrol.

"No problem. Rosco's an important member of the team."

Then Blake had his snowshoes off, and the ski patrol headed back to the ski hut with the stretcher.

"I hope this experience didn't sour you for returning here in the future," Landon said.

"No. Though at one point I was thinking I might stay by the fire and never leave the warm lobby. Still, rescuing the man was worth every bit of the cold."

"Yeah, I totally agree with you there," Landon said.

Blake said, "I'm off to feed Rosco and take him for a walk afterward, but I suspect he'll do his business right away and the walk will be brief this time."

Landon and Gabrielle smiled. She imagined the Saint Bernard would be sleeping by the fire for the rest of the afternoon.

When they walked into the lobby, Rosco was lying by the fire, but as soon as he saw Blake, he raced to greet him, his tail wagging like crazy.

"Lunchtime, what did I say," Blake said.

"I feel the same way." Gabrielle was glad to see Rosco was just fine. She was ready for seafood.

They dropped off their snowshoes at the storage room. Once they were in the restaurant, they began stripping out of their ski jackets and gloves, hats, and scarves. When Minx brought them the menu, Gabrielle ordered shrimp linguini and Landon had veal scallopini. She'd worked up an appetite.

"How are you feeling?" Landon asked her.

"Oh, great, now that I'm inside and getting warmed up."

Minx quickly brought them hot tea and coffee and fresh-baked rolls hot out of the oven. "I heard the two of you rescued a snowboarder. Well, and Rosco, of course. Great job."

"Thanks," Landon said.

"Blake said to make sure I brought over hot drinks for the both of you pronto." Minx smiled. "Not that I wouldn't have, but he just wanted to make sure."

"We appreciate it." Gabrielle was already drinking her hot tea and getting even more warmed up.

"I'll bring your orders right out."

"Thanks, Minx," Landon said.

Gabrielle was just getting ready to butter her fresh potato roll when a man and a woman headed straight to their booth. She thought they might be guests who needed Landon for something. Or maybe they wanted to tell her and Landon how much they appreciated them for saving a snowboarder. News sure traveled fast in a pack.

Landon smiled at them.

Gabrielle smelled that the woman was a red wolf. The she-wolf wore a green sweater dress and black boots, her red hair hanging loose about her shoulders. She didn't look like she was here to ski. The man was a gray wolf, his dark eyes studying Gabrielle, his dark-brown hair mussed up by the chilly wind. He was dressed in a warm green sweater, as if they had dressed to match each other, definitely looking like a cute married couple.

"I'm Lelandi, and this is Darien Silver, my mate," the woman said, shaking Gabrielle's hand. "We're the pack leaders of Silver Town and wanted to officially welcome you." She smiled brightly at Gabrielle. "And we understand not only that you, Landon, and Rosco helped save one of the ski resort's avalanche victims, but also that you're a vet."

Gabrielle guessed the pack leaders wanted to know about all the shifters who came into the town in case they had any trouble with a rogue wolf. But still, how had they known she was a veterinarian? Had they checked her background completely? That was kind of unsettling. "Uh, yes."

"Do you have a sole proprietorship?" Lelandi asked.

"Four of us work at the vet clinic, and we have two others who come in once a week but also work at other clinics. It's a nice arrangement so we can cover for each other and take off if we need or want to." That question kind of ruled out that they had thoroughly investigated her background.

"Oh, how interesting. Doc Mitchell is our vet, but he wants to retire when we can find someone suitable for the pack who could take over his practice. Landon probably told you all our businesses are run by wolves. So if you ever think you might like a change of location and a friendly pack to join, we would be happy to have you," Lelandi said.

Darien agreed. "We have a lot to offer you that other areas can't for wolves."

Gabrielle was really surprised she was getting a job offer, of all the things that could happen to her on vacation in Silver Town.

"Thanks. I don't have any plans to move, but if I ever do, I'll sure give your offer serious consideration." Gabrielle had been born in Florida and had rarely left the state except to take a few beach-location trips with her jaguar friends. Certainly, after the situation with her parents, she hadn't ever considered moving to any place that had snow.

Though for Christmas it was fun. She could imagine how pretty the area would be in the fall. In Florida, they had no fall colors. Relief from the heat and humidity would be welcome too.

She hoped the pack leaders hadn't had the wrong impression that she was looking to move to Colorado, and that she was planning on or already courting Landon and they were ready to tell the whole pack the news. She had to admit she felt something deeper for Landon than she'd ever felt for a bachelor male wolf though. She really, truly liked him, but the thought of giving up her practice and moving to another state seemed too monumental.

Gabrielle loved her practice, her clients, the staff, and where she lived. Yet in beginning to get to know Landon, and seeing the other wolves in happy mated relationships, she realized she was missing out on a whole lot more in life by living a lone wolf's existence. If anyone could yank her out of the rut she was in, that wolf would certainly be one as hot and intriguing as Landon, who was so determined to be with her and show her a good time. Even so, there was more to the feelings she was experiencing than just having fun. Increasingly intense biological and physical needs were signaling her to change her notion of maintaining the status quo.

When they finished talking to Lelandi and Darien, the pack leaders welcomed Gabrielle to Silver Town again, and then they left the bar and grill. Gabrielle raised her brows at Landon, feeling a little blindsided.

He held his hands up in a defensive posture. "It wasn't my idea. I was as surprised as you to see them come to our table and talk to you."

"One of your sisters or your brother must have told them I'm a vet." Gabrielle drank some of her hot Earl Grey tea. "No one else here but you knew, unless you told the pack leaders."

Landon pondered that for a moment, then lifted his cup of coffee off the table. "I…don't know, then. Roxie asked you at breakfast what you do for a living, but I was eager to have her leave so she didn't hear your answer. I haven't told her or the rest of my family what you do back home. I do know the pack leaders have been looking for a qualified—as in also a wolf—vet for a while. Doc Mitchell wants to retire. Our regular doctor, Dr. Weber, is a red wolf and he's retiring, too, now that we have a family physician and pediatrician who can replace him. When Doc Mitchell learned Doc Weber had a replacement for *his* position, I think that made our vet want to retire all the more."

"Okay." Gabrielle still wondered if Landon had anything to do with it, which only meant he wanted to see more of her. That was a good thing, if she'd wanted to stay. Truly, she had felt honored that the pack leaders had come here to offer her the position if she'd wanted to move.

"Believe me, they don't welcome all new wolves who come through Silver Town."

"Really?" Now that was a shocker. She thought they truly did personally check out new wolves, just in case they might give them some trouble.

"Yeah, really." He smiled. "The only other time they checked out one of our new wolf guests was when Nicole arrived after the new year. She was from Denver, and we wanted her to stay. All of us did, but especially Blake. He would have done anything for her, even move to Denver, since she was a PI with an office there and her brother and parents lived there. They have wolves there, but no one she was interested in dating, and all of us were eager to do whatever we could to make her feel at home here so she wouldn't leave. She couldn't be happier living here with us. Her brother and parents are just as happy to be here. Her parents moved their stationery store to Silver Town, and Nate, her brother, ended up in the private investigator business with her."

"Was she a private investigator"—Gabrielle forked up more of her linguini—"on a job here or just on vacation here like me?"

"On a job. She was trying to catch someone who was staying as a guest at the lodge."

"And she figured she would have enough work to keep busy if she moved to Silver Town?"

"Yeah, Nicole and her brother still go to Denver when they have a case that clients want them to handle there. But here is where Nicole's heart is."

"Because of Blake." Gabrielle believed in happily ever after. But she had been certain her dream mate would be swimming in the Atlantic Ocean, leaving the water, then using a beach towel to wipe off the water beaded up on his skin when he saw her walking along the sand, and then he would sweep her right off her feet. She had never envisioned finding the wolf of her dreams at a ski resort. Though she had to admit she *had* met Landon when he was getting ready to swim and she was already swimming. Who said the dream would have to be perfectly accurate in real life?

Still, coming here to live was another thing. She finished her lunch and saw that Landon was already done. "That was delicious. Are you ready to ski?"

"You bet. Do you think you can manage the cold?"

"Sure, as long as we have a hot chocolate topped with whipped cream when I get too cold."

After lunch, they skied for some time. She had graduated to the intermediate slopes, narrower and longer and steeper than the easy slopes, and had done really well. When they finally stopped for a hot chocolate break to warm up, several men and women came by their table at the bar and grill, praising her for helping to save the snowboarder's life.

Gabrielle felt like a real heroine. Though she felt like that from time to time when she saved someone's pet's life, it was never to this extent. The family would be thrilled, but a whole wolf pack?

Landon was smiling at her.

At first, she kept saying if it hadn't been for Rosco, they would never have found the snowboarder in time. But everyone wanted her to know she was the reason they were coming by to thank her.

"Do you feel a little neglected? I mean, you were as much a hero as Rosco." Gabrielle rose from her seat and began to pull on her ski jacket.

Landon pulled on his ski jacket too. "Not at all. They are just so thrilled to—"

"See me. I know."

"Several were bachelor males, if you didn't realize it."

She laughed. "I should have known."

"But the thanks were sincerely given."

"They want me to join the pack." She put her hat on but carried her gloves.

"Do you blame them?"

She smiled. "No. I never envisioned a wolf pack would be this nice."

"They are. Not to say we never have problems, but for the most part, they're a great group to be with."

Before they could leave the lodge, a young man chased after them. "The dude at the check-in counter said you saved my friend's life. I want to thank you. I told Mick he was an idiot for going off slope. I guess he learned that lesson pretty well today." He ran his hands through his dark hair. "That's the end of snowboarding with him this trip. I just wanted to thank you again."

"And Rosco," Gabrielle said, pointing to the dog.

"Hell yeah. My friend and I ordered him a big box of doggy treats online. They should be coming in a few days."

Landon chuckled. "Thanks. We were glad we could help."

"I'm just glad Mick's okay." Then the young man shook their hands and took off for the parking lot.

Gabrielle was so glad she had gone with Landon to help him look for Rosco. She was relieved the snowboarder hadn't suffered any injuries. It would be one of the most memorable good experiences with a snow emergency she'd ever had.

The rest of the afternoon, Gabrielle and Landon went down the intermediate slopes. She did really great too. She wanted to ski on the slopes until they closed for the night so that she would be in good shape by tomorrow morning when she skied with her friends. But on the last run down, she fell twice. Her muscles had been used in ways they weren't used to, not to mention all the trudging through snow on snowshoes and digging out a buried snowboarder. She was tired. Happily so, though.

After she and Landon ditched their poles and skis and ski shoes for their snow boots in the supply room, they had dinner together at the bar and grill. Gabrielle wanted to order a pizza that came in the shape of a Christmas wreath, and he wanted the same. She took a picture of it when the server delivered it and texted that to her friends. And then she began eating it. "Your food is excellent here." She took another bite of her double-cheese pizza, topped with red bell pepper strips pieced together to resemble a red bow, green peppers, sausage slices, dried tomatoes, and basil leaves. Not only was it beautiful, but it sure tasted great.

Odette texted back: Save a slice for us.

Gabrielle smiled.

Odette texted again: Melany Williams, the woman we're trying to chase down, supposedly killed her husband and is on the run. I'm sure you saw it in the news. We tried to keep it quiet—given what we are.

Odette sent her a picture of Melany and Gabrielle frowned and texted: But?

Odette replied: Zelda and I think it might be a setup. Enjoy your meal!

Gabrielle studied the woman's photo. She was a pretty brunette with blue eyes and a lovely smile, and just from appearances, she didn't look like anyone who could kill anyone. But what did Gabrielle know?

"Is something wrong?" Landon asked.

"No, just my friends told me they were looking for a woman who might or might not have murdered her mate."

"Oh, not good."

"She might have been set up, they said."

"That's awful."

"It is. Sorry, I didn't mean to go on a tangent. The pizza is great," Gabrielle said.

"Only the best for our guests and for anyone else who wants to eat here, whether they live in town or are passing through. We take pride in making food that everyone raves about. You can leave five-star reviews anytime." Landon grabbed another slice. "So, did you want to go for a wolf run before we swim in the pool, or do you feel you've had enough exercise for the day?"

"Your family is going to fire you for neglecting your work."

"I'm doing my work—making sure that my guests are happy with the accommodations."

She chuckled. "Only one guest."

He smiled.

She loved how he was making her feel welcome when her friends weren't here. He probably could afford to take off a day while she was alone, but tomorrow, she would be spending the time with her friends. Though she wouldn't mind running with Landon as a wolf—and swimming—all week long when they were done skiing.

"Are you still up for a wolf run?" She was tired, but she knew if she ran, she would have a blast anyway.

"Yeah. And then we can break the rules and swim in the pool after hours?" Landon left a tip on the table.

"That's the only way to go, isn't it? Fewer people, no kids in the pool?"

He laughed. "You can strip out of your clothes and shift in the downstairs guest bedroom at our house to run as a wolf, if you would like, rather than in the woods. It's the first house after the lodge. The house after that is Blake's and Nicole's. Roxie mentioned you had shifted in the woods before."

"Yeah. I couldn't very well shift at the lodge and run out of there as a wolf. I did worry someone would see my backpack and sound an alarm that someone was lost or steal it. I guess when I passed your house I heard Rosco barking, warning that an intruder was in your yard."

"Yeah, that was Rosco."

"Okay, well, going to your place to shift works for me. Thanks a lot."

"You're certainly welcome."

After they pulled on their ski jackets, hats, gloves, and scarves, they left the restaurant and headed through the snow to the house. White Christmas lights trimmed both of the homes and a couple of trees out back, just like at the lodge. The lights reflected off the snow. So pretty.

When she walked into the house, Rosco greeted her as if she were family. Gabrielle laughed at the dog. "You look like you have recuperated just fine."

She glanced around at all the Christmas decorations—the beautiful Christmas tree filled with lights and ornaments all done up in blues and silver. Stockings hung from the mantel, and evergreens and red candles trimmed the top. But there was no fire going at the moment.

"Did you have someone professionally decorate the lodge and your home?" Gabrielle loved everything they had done.

"No, we did it all as a family. As soon as Blake and Nicole tied the knot, they began making plans to build their own home. We own the property up to the tree line, so we'll keep building homes along that way when a couple more of us are mated. The last one to mate will remain in this house."

"Wow, that's so nice to have a family like that."

"We are lucky. We all get along great. Not to say we don't have our squabbles from time to time, but we work out our differences easily enough. It's the same with the pack. To have a new business in Silver Town, you have to have the pack leaders' approval and every pack member gets a say in the matter. Sure, new owners have to be wolves, but the pack doesn't want to ruin the economy for the business owners who have been here for years. Or bring too many humans to the area, even just for sport."

"Oh, I totally understand."

"In your case, should you want to take over Doc Mitchell's clinic, it's already well established and you'll have all his clientele. In our case, I really believe they agreed for us to open the lodge not only because there was a need for it, but because we have two unmated sisters. There's a shortage of eligible she-wolves for mating in the pack."

Gabrielle would never have guessed it. "Was that also the reason Lelandi and Darien offered me a job? Just because I'm a woman?" She hoped she didn't sound as annoyed as she felt.

"You're a wolf and a vet, and you're young so you probably won't want to retire for a long time, at least to their way of thinking. I'm sure if you were a male vet, they would have been just as eager to meet you and make the offer for you to stay." He motioned to a room down the hall. "You can strip out of your clothes in the guest bedroom. I'll meet you downstairs in a minute."

That made her feel better. Once she had changed and shifted, she headed into the living room. Rosco was wagging his tail as he greeted her again, even though she was a wolf this time. He could smell her same scent. She nuzzled his face in greeting.

She listened for any sign Landon's sisters were here. She'd had fun playing with them and Blake and Nicole last night, and hoped they would all join in again in the wolf scuffle.

Then Landon came down the stairs as a big wolf, his mask a darker brown than Blake's, very striking black lines of fur above his eyes giving him the adorable look of having black eyebrows. His back was a mixture of black guard hairs and brown, blond, and gray, his chest mostly white. He smiled at her in a wolf way and nuzzled her face in greeting. She enjoyed the camaraderie as wolves, something that she didn't get to experience back home.

Rosco wagged his tail hard upon seeing Landon too. She wondered if they ever took him running with them when they were wolves. Then she and Landon headed outside through a wolf door.

She saw his family members gathered in the backyard of the other home, and they all woofed in greeting. Gabrielle relaxed. She was worried Landon had set this up to be a wolf-run date, trying to convince her to stay in the area. She did like that there seemed to be a number of eligible bachelors, if she ever had the notion of moving to Silver Town. That sure wasn't the case back home. But she just wanted to have fun with a group of wolves for now, no pressure. Not when she didn't live here and couldn't really consider courting a wolf.

They all ran off through the woods for about a mile and then they began playing. She was just as aggressive with the she-wolves as they were with her. She was glad they weren't giving her an inch just because she was not part of the family. Wolves had to show they had the mettle to take on other wolves. Landon and Blake just watched the four she-wolves playing as if they were putting on a show for them. Then Nicole tackled her mate, as if to tell him he had to participate or else, and the whole bunch of them began to play.

The wolves were all tackling one another until it seemed like the others faded away—all but Landon, who nuzzled Gabrielle's muzzle. She nipped at him in pure enjoyment and then tackled him. Play fighting was a great way to practice real wolf fighting—in case they had to battle a rogue *lupus garou* as a wolf—but it was a great way to play as wolves too. She'd never met any wolf who was into playing catch or fetch in his or her wolf form. That was more of a dog's game. Instead, the wolves chased each other, tackled the others, and ran together, racing each other. That's how they played.

They rose on their hind legs, snapping at each other, snarling, growling, biting. She had played with her jaguar friends, but they had to be more careful with her because of their stronger bite and their wicked cat claws.

Because of playing with them, she was used to their heavier weight and how agile they could be, and that had helped her to employ new tricks. She tackled Landon as if she were fighting a springier cat, and she was more aggressive too. Sure, he was a bigger male, but she was used to the rules of engagement being different with her jaguar friends.

Despite her aggressiveness, he was gentle with her. Then, he turned the tables on her as if he was just waiting for her to let down her guard, or maybe he thought she would respect him more if he was a little more aggressive. It didn't take him long to pin her to the snow, and she gave him a toothy grin. She didn't expect his brother and sisters and Blake's mate to tackle Landon all at once.

She was both amused and delighted that they had come to rescue her.

In short order, they pinned him down and were nipping at him in good fun while she watched with utter amusement. He finally woofed and they let him up. He licked their faces and then hers to say he'd had a great time. He woofed again to let them know he was headed in with Gabrielle. They were going swimming.

She couldn't wait, though she was having fun playing with the wolves in the snow. She had never thought she would be doing this with other wolves and loving it like she did. She thought she might be running with her jaguar friends, if they felt safe running as jaguars in the snow. And she thought she would be building a snowman with her friends—she'd never done that before—or throwing snowballs at each other.

That was if they ever got there.

CHAPTER 5

When they reached Blake and Nicole's house, the other wolves said good night with woofs and barks, and then Landon and his sisters and Gabrielle loped to the next house. Inside, Rosco greeted each of them with big tail wags and licks to their faces as if they were all part of a wolf pack.

Then they shifted in their rooms, dressed, and joined one another in the living room.

"Good night, Gabrielle. That was fun," Kayla said. "We're so glad you could play with us. I want you to show me later how you can spring and fight like you do. I've never seen a wolf do that before but that was really cool. We'll see you later, Landon."

"Yeah, that was amazing footwork you used out there." Roxie smiled.

"Courtesy of my jaguar friends," Gabrielle said.

"Ha! I thought maybe Florida wolves were different from the Colorado wolves." Landon was amused that that's how Gabrielle had outmaneuvered him a few times with her strange moves.

Gabrielle laughed.

Everyone said good night, then Landon grabbed a bag from his bedroom with a pair of board shorts and his beach towel featuring a wolf. With his bag in hand, he took Gabrielle out into the snow and walked her to the lodge.

"So what do you think of the ski lodge?" he asked, hoping she loved it as much as they did.

"It's beautiful. I love all the Christmas decorations and all the beautiful wolf details. It makes me feel like this is home. For a wolf, so to speak."

"That's what we love about having our own lodge. We can decorate it the way that makes it feel like home for all of us wolves."

"I agree. If I had a vet clinic of my own—" Gabrielle abruptly quit talking and smiled, as if she remembered she wasn't interested in taking over Doc Mitchell's clinic. "Where are you going to change clothes at the lodge?"

"In the room we have for our skis."

"All right, I'll run up to my room and change and meet you at the pool then."

"Meet me by the check-in counter so you won't give other people the idea you can swim after hours without one of us being there with you. I don't want to have to chase a mob of people out of there."

She chuckled. "What about you? Won't you give everyone the idea you're breaking the rules if they don't know you're one of the owners?"

Landon returned her smile. "We put up a sign that says 'Private Party,' and that way people know it's not open for guests."

"Okay, that sounds like it could work. How often do you get guests asking about reserving the pool afterward?"

"Often. That's why we also say it's for staff only."

"Okay, good. I'll be down in a few minutes." She headed for the stairs, and Landon was left thinking he'd gotten really lucky that she'd caught his attention the first night she was there, and that her friends hadn't arrived yet or she would have been busy with them the whole time. Though he reminded himself she was there for less than a week and then would be gone. He was glad Roxie didn't come swimming. She usually did when he did, except for the other night. But now she was allowing him some time alone with Gabrielle, which he really appreciated.

He dressed in a jiffy and headed to the pool, setting out the

Private Pool Party: Staff Only sign and leaving his towel on one of the chaise lounges before heading back to the check-in counter to wait for Gabrielle. He just wished there was something he could say or do to convince her to leave sunny Florida and live with the pack and continue dating him!

———————

Gabrielle entered her room and saw a red-and-gold-wrapped Christmas present sitting on her dresser. She frowned. "What is this?" She read the card, which said *From Secret Santa.*

Okay, her friends weren't supposed to do a Secret Santa with her.

She stripped out of all the winter clothes, tossing her parka, boots, gloves, socks, scarf, two sweaters, pants, and bra on the bed. She wasn't used to wearing so many clothes in the winter. Then she hurried to put on her bathing suit—the red-and-green-striped one. It was sexy enough. She didn't want to wear the string bikini while swimming with Landon and give him the idea it was a come-on.

She pulled on a cover-up, with no need to dress in her winter gear and do this out in the snow this time, for which she was glad. Her phone rang. *No!* She didn't want to leave Landon waiting on her for too long.

She grabbed her phone off the table and saw it was Zelda calling. "Hi, are the two of you getting in sooner than you expected? I was going swimming. I'll just meet you in the room in about an hour if you are coming in shortly."

"The pool is closed now, isn't it?" Zelda asked, sounding surprised.

Gabrielle slipped on her flip-flops. "Yeah, but I met one of the owners and he and I are taking a swim together, so it's okay."

"Oh."

"It's just a fun diversion until you get here." Gabrielle hoped her friends wouldn't think she would ditch them for a hot wolf, even though she would love to spend more time with him.

"Oh no, we're so glad you, uh, aren't just sitting in the lodge room waiting on us. We were feeling awful about it."

"No, don't worry. I've been having fun. Landon taught me some beginner ski lessons even."

"Really. But he's one of the owners of the ski lodge?" Odette butted in and Gabrielle realized Zelda had put the phone on speaker and her sister was right there listening in.

Not that Gabrielle was surprised. "Yeah. The town is run by wolves. It's just amazing. And they have a pub in town that is only for shifters. We'll have to go there one of the nights we're here. Who would ever have thought it, right? They even offered me a job as the vet here. Their vet wants to retire, and only shifters can run the businesses here. Of course I told them I had to return to Florida to my practice there."

"Oh no. With three other regular vets in the co-op and a couple of floaters, they have it covered. With all the wolves in Silver Town... I mean, just think of all the dating opportunities you would have. You should consider the move," Zelda said.

Odette quickly interrupted. "How nice. I'm so glad you're enjoying yourself."

"I'm not about to leave my practice." Gabrielle sighed. "Though I have to admit it has been fun. You can meet Landon and his family and say hi to them when you get here. I ran with the family tonight as wolves. Oh, and they want me to teach them about the training you've given me as jaguars."

The sisters laughed.

"They're eager to meet you."

"About that—" Odette said.

Gabrielle's heart sank. "Don't tell me you're canceling on me." As much fun as she was having here with Landon and his family, he couldn't entertain her for the whole time she was supposed to be here. Surely, he would have to go back to work. And being on her own skiing wouldn't be safe or fun.

"No, no, it's just that, well, we're so sorry for standing you up like this. We're still trying to get ahold of Melany Williams. We promise we're going to be there, after maybe a couple more days to wrap this up. If we can't capture her in two days, we told the boss we'll be on vacation, like we told him two months ago when we put in our leave form. Someone else can take the case if we don't catch her by then. In the meantime, she has led us on a merry chase for now."

"Two more days." Gabrielle wasn't sure what she was going to do by herself for that much time. So far, she'd done just fine because Landon took off the time to be with her. But she couldn't imagine him taking off any more time to keep her company.

"Yes. Just two more days. We had always talked about sharing the cost of the lodging split three ways, but now we're going to pay for your share," Zelda said.

"You don't have to do that."

"We want to. You didn't even want to go skiing until we finally talked you into it. And now you're there all by yourself," Odette said. "So yeah, like my sister said. The lodging is on us."

"Okay, well, thank you." Gabrielle really didn't feel it was their fault and they had to make up for it monetarily. She was having fun so far. "Do you still think Melany is innocent?"

"Yeah, but not that many people do, so she feels they're going to lock her up in the jaguar facilities and throw away the key and no one may ever find her mate alive or dead. But don't you worry about it. See if Landon can take you skiing again or take some paid ski lessons, and by the time we get there, you'll be on the black diamond slopes with us," Zelda said.

"Ha! I did manage the intermediate slopes yesterday, but the expert slopes? I don't think so. Not unless I lived here and skied all the time."

"Wow," Odette said. "We're so proud of you! But, hey, if you took the job there, you could! And when we come to visit, we'll all ski on the expert slopes together."

"Thanks, I have had a good and patient ski instructor." Gabrielle glanced at the Christmas present on the dresser. "Oh, before I forget, we weren't going to get anything for each other for Christmas. Spending the money on the trip instead was supposed to be it."

"That's what we agreed on," Zelda said.

"Yeah," Odette said. "For all the years we've known each other, that's the way we've done it, except for getting you that string bikini that one year on a dare."

Gabrielle smiled. Wouldn't they be surprised to learn she had reeled in a hot wolf while wearing it. "So one of you didn't give me a Secret Santa gift?"

There was a significant pause, then Zelda said, "No. Who did it say it was from?"

"It just said 'From Secret Santa.'"

"Was it left behind by the previous guest?" Odette asked.

"I don't think so. It wasn't here last night or today, but when I returned to change to go swimming, here it was, sitting on the dresser."

"What is it?" Zelda asked.

"I didn't open it. I wanted to make sure it was from the two of you. I didn't want to open something that wasn't mine."

"Well, it isn't from us, but maybe you have a secret admirer who is part owner of the ski lodge. So open it up and see what it is," Odette said.

"No one would have gotten me a Secret Santa gift."

"Are you sure?" Zelda asked.

"Yes. I guess I'll take it down to the front desk and see if the former occupant left it behind. Maybe it had fallen under the bed and the maid was cleaning and found it and put it on the dresser while I was out skiing."

"Can't you just take a peek under the wrapping?" Zelda asked.

"You know what they say about curiosity and the cat?" Gabrielle said.

"You're the one who piqued our curiosity," Odette said.

"Well, I thought it was from one of you, and I hadn't gotten either of you anything." Which made Gabrielle think about how she should get Landon something to thank him for teaching her how to ski and for all the free meals he'd shared with her. She should get something for his family, too, for welcoming her with wolf runs. "Oh, I've got to go. Landon's probably wondering if I forgot we were swimming next. I'll see you in two days then."

"You sure will. Have fun!" Zelda said.

They ended the call and Gabrielle grabbed her beach towel, Secret Santa gift, and key card, then left the room. She was going to call down to Landon to tell him she was coming, but she realized she didn't have his cell number. She called the front desk instead. "Hi, I'm meeting Landon Wolff at the check-in counter and was delayed. Can you tell him—"

"Here, you can talk to him," the clerk said.

"Oh, thanks."

"Hello?" Landon had the sexiest, deepest male voice.

"Hi, it's Gabrielle. I got delayed. My friends called, and I'm on the stairs now coming down."

"Okay, sure. Are they coming in tonight?"

"No. They're busy with a case. I told you that they work for the JAG. It's a case they handled, and the woman escaped her escort."

"Oh. But you're not leaving here, are you?" He sounded concerned.

"No." She smiled and waved at him as she entered the lobby and ended the call.

He eyed the Christmas package. *Great.* It looked like she had gotten him a gift. She switched direction and took the Christmas package to the check-in counter. "Hi, I think the previous occupant left this in my room." She gave the lady her room number.

The clerk checked the computer. "You've been in the room for two days."

Landon joined her. "What's wrong?"

"Someone left this in the room." Gabrielle shrugged. "I figured it was for a former guest and it fell under the bed or something. Anyway, it wasn't in my room until tonight, sitting on my dresser. My girlfriends said it wasn't from them."

He read the tag. "Secret Santa."

"Yeah, we don't do that."

He frowned. "Just set it behind the counter," he told the clerk, "and when you have time, contact the former guest and see if they left a Secret Santa gift behind."

"Sure thing."

Still looking concerned, Landon escorted Gabrielle to the pool. Maybe it was because Gabrielle's friends weren't going to be here, and he was afraid she would pack up and leave.

"I'll be here until my friends arrive. They said it would be two days from now." She kicked off her flip-flops and pulled off her cover-up and laid it on the chaise lounge, ready to enjoy swimming with her new wolf friend.

"Okay, that's good news." He was watching her, waiting for the show. "No string bikini this time?"

She laughed. "I only wear that when no one's watching."

"Well, it did the trick on me. Immediately, I forgot to tell you that the pool was closed." He kicked off his sandals and pulled off his shirt. Then he exchanged cell phone numbers with her so she wouldn't have to call the front desk to get ahold of him again. "We'll find out who the present belongs to and let you know."

"Okay, thanks." She dove into the pool and he joined her.

Then they were swimming laps back and forth. This was the life. Before she got here, she had learned the lodge had a pool, and that's why she'd brought a couple of bathing suits, but she hadn't thought she would be swimming with a male wolf. Two jaguar shifters, sure.

She reached the end of the pool near the lobby and turned and headed for the one that was outside in the snow. Landon swam beside her the whole time, not pulling ahead, but keeping the same pace, keeping her company, which she was thoroughly enjoying.

When they were outside, she paused and looked at the snow falling, the Christmas lights on the tree reflecting on the snow and the water, just beautiful. Landon came up beside her and put his hands palms up while he treaded water and caught the flakes. "So how does this compare to Christmas in Florida?"

She wrapped her arms around his neck. "This feels like a slice of heaven." And then she kissed him as they both treaded water.

"I couldn't have said it better." He wrapped his arms around her back, holding her close, and kissed her mouth gently.

His body was a perfect ten and she kissed him back, their tongues sliding over each other's in a long, meaningful caress, the heated water warm around them, their breaths frosty in the air, snowflakes covering their hair.

A winter wonderland for sure. Then she smiled at him, felt his growing interest in her pressing against her, their legs touching as they kept themselves afloat, his pheromones—and hers—coming to bear.

Now this was what she could have used earlier when they were trudging through the snow with Rosco, trying to return to the lodge.

"The question is," she said, nipping at his chin, "will you be available for more skiing tomorrow, or do I need to hire a private ski instructor?" She could do a group lesson, but since she had already had private ski lessons, she really liked the personal attention they afforded. If Landon could do this again with her tomorrow, she preferred that rather than trying to hire someone else to do it.

"Hmm, that sounds like a challenge." He kissed her mouth again, his hand sliding down her back, bringing her tight against his body. "I'm sure I can be off for the next two days and we can do more of what we did today, minus the snowboarder caught in the avalanche and the Rosco rescue, until your friends get here. When Nicole arrived here, we covered for Blake a lot—family helps out family—so it's no problem at all."

"Your family won't be getting the wrong idea, will they?" She kissed the water droplets off his neck and licked a snowflake from his cheek before it melted, the shadow of a beard darkening his chin, his dark-brown eyes smiling.

"Sure they will. But I'll assure them you're not staying beyond your vacation here. They want you to have breakfast with us tomorrow morning, so don't be surprised if they act hopeful that you'll change your mind about coming here for good though."

"Or that they told the pack leaders to invite me to take over the vet clinic here? I meant to ask your family who told them I was a vet, but I forgot." She would ask them tomorrow, and she hoped they would be honest with her.

"I, for one, had nothing to do with it, and I didn't mention it to any of them, so I don't know how Lelandi learned of it."

She believed Landon was being sincere. She licked his mouth and he kissed her again, this time holding her so she could relax and not have to tread water while he did all the work for them.

"That's not to say"—he kissed her nose—"that I wouldn't love it if you moved here. Though I would also love it if you continued seeing only me."

She laughed. "But there's a shortage of she-wolves. I would have my pick of bachelor males."

"You would. That's why I'm working hard at showing you I have what it takes to convince you I would be the only one you would want to date."

She kissed his cheek. "I wouldn't want to change partners at this point. Let's go back inside. Despite how hot you are, and as warm as the water is, my head is getting cold."

He slowly released her. "I'll give you a head start."

"No, I'll chase you this time." She didn't want to feel panicked as he raced after her. She figured he would catch up to her quickly with his powerful strokes. "And don't make it easy on me just so I can catch you."

He chuckled. "All right. I'll go first."

But she didn't want to lose either. And she dove right after him, not giving him more than a split second of a head start, going underneath the water and grabbing his foot before they'd even reached the glass divider. He turned and pulled her into his arms again.

He chuckled. "That was fast."

"You were going too slow. Try again. We're still out in the snow." She smiled at him.

"No head start this time."

As if she'd given him one the first time.

He dove under the water.

She dove right after him, not about to let him get away. He was kicking as fast as he could and made it under the glass divider. She came up under it and headed to the surface for a breath of air while he was still swimming for the end of the pool. She took off after him and finally grabbed his foot again.

He came up from under the water and laughed and pulled her into his arms again. "Damn, woman, you're fast, and I swear I didn't swim slowly so you would catch me."

"I'm from Florida, remember? I swim a lot."

He smiled. "I should have remembered that when you told me you were going to chase me."

"Don't tell me you couldn't have caught me if you had gone after me instead."

"Oh, hell yeah, I would have caught you. The incentive would be too great—not only because I want the prize, but because I have something to prove. Next time, I'm chasing you."

She smiled. She would panic for sure. "Do you want to swim in the morning before breakfast with your family? And then have breakfast and go skiing?"

"You bet."

"As long as you can square it with your family." She didn't want to take it for granted that he could take any more time off for her, despite Blake having taken off time for Nicole.

"It won't be a problem." Then Landon released her, and they climbed out of the pool.

They began drying themselves off. After he pulled on his shirt and his sandals and she pulled her cover-up over her head and slipped on her flip-flops, he wrapped his arms around her. "We've run together, saved a snowboarder together, played as wolves together, swam together, had meals together, skied together. It's high time I kissed you good night before you take off to your room."

As if they hadn't already kissed each other! Despite his declaration, he waited to see if she was all right with it.

"I can't tell you how much I've enjoyed doing everything I have with you and with your family." She wrapped her arms around his waist and tilted her chin up so he could lean down and press his mouth against hers. Warm, sweet, sexy, and memorable. She kissed him back and realized he was going to have a tough time walking through the lobby to the office and storage room with a full-blown erection in clinging, wet board shorts. She smiled up at him. "I can't wait to enjoy the day with you tomorrow." Then she released him.

"I'm looking forward to it also." Then he wrapped his wolf towel around his waist, helping to hide his arousal, and walked her to the stairs leading to her floor. "Good night, Gabrielle. Pleasant dreams."

"Believe me, they will be totally pleasant." If she had any say in her dreams at all. "Wow, what a memorable vacation already. Good night, Landon." Then she headed quickly up the stairs before she could invite him to stay in her room and cause even more speculation for the family and any other wolves who might have seen them glued together, kissing.

"It's all working according to plan," Odette told her sister, Zelda, at the hotel room they were staying at in Pensacola, Florida, even though she was aggravated they hadn't been able to catch up to Melany. She felt the jaguar would have gotten a fair trial and Melany had no reason to run. As soon as they could, they were checking into her story to see if they could find her mate—alive. Now the JAG had additional charges pending against her. Though if they could find her mate alive, they would drop all charges against her.

Zelda started stripping out of her clothes to take a shower. "Only if Gabrielle takes the bait. But I never expected her to hook up with one of the owners of that new ski lodge."

"I know. Me either. Lelandi said she would make sure Gabrielle met several bachelor males, all of whom are ski instructors and could show her how to ski since we wouldn't be there to teach her. Who would have thought the owner of the lodge would teach her how to ski?"

"She's going to be pissed off at us once she learns that we'd planned this all along," Zelda said.

"Not the part about that woman escaping her escort. That was all true."

"Just the part of how someone else could have gone in our place. We're not the only JAG special agents on the force, after all." Zelda pulled the pins out of her hair. "At least she didn't get suspicious about that part."

"She trusts us."

Zelda rolled her eyes. "Yeah, but when she learns the truth?"

"If she finds a hunky wolf mate that she can't live without, she will be thrilled we aided her in this way. She would never have done this on her own. Ever. She's a wolf, not like us big cats. She needs a mate for life and she needs a pack."

Zelda sighed and headed into the bathroom. "You're right about that. Lelandi's a trained psychologist. Hopefully, she can do some magic tricks to help Gabrielle see what a great place it would be and convince her to stay."

"Then when we want to take our annual ski vacation to Colorado..."

"We can stay with Gabrielle and her new mate." Zelda started the shower.

Odette turned on a movie to watch until Zelda was out of the shower. She'd had the idea of doing this once they had learned Silver Town was a wolf-run town and the ski lodge was just being built. They'd stayed at the Victorian Silver Town Inn and met Lelandi, who had welcomed them to their little slice of shifter paradise. And that's when Odette got the idea that their good friend, Gabrielle, could find someone to love there. At least Odette and her sister had hoped she would.

For the first time in the three years they had asked her to ski with them, Gabrielle had finally agreed to go, and this was the first time it really mattered—since they had found the perfect wolf paradise just for her. They knew how she had lost her parents on a ski trip, so they'd worried that might be an issue for Gabrielle. But they'd hoped the wolf pack would make a difference in convincing her to stay.

Odette thought about the situation with Gabrielle dating Landon. So much for their matchmaking efforts. Their best-laid plans were always being upset by someone or something else they hadn't counted on. But Odette smiled. So much the better.

Then she frowned. The main problem with this whole venture was that Gabrielle had lived in Florida all her life, and making changes that would be that great—new state, new clinic, new friends—could be a bit overwhelming.

Gabrielle had no mate prospects where she was now. And if she was still being stubborn-headed about taking over an established vet practice in a wolf-run town, Odette would have to ask Lelandi what else she could do to make it happen.

That's just what she would do. She lifted her phone and found Lelandi listed in her contacts and selected her number. "Hi, Lelandi, this is Odette. Things seem to be promising as far as Landon taking Gabrielle skiing and all, but she's not convinced that she should make any real changes in her lifestyle and move to Silver Town."

"I'm going to talk to Doc Mitchell. I have some ideas about what to try next. Thanks for keeping in touch."

"All right then. Work your magic." Odette ended the call. She and her sister would continue to do whatever they could to make it happen from this end.

CHAPTER 6

LANDON DRESSED IN HIS WARM CLOTHES AND HEADED HOME, crunching through the deep snow on this snowy night and thinking what a remarkable day it had been. He'd had such a great day and night with Gabrielle that he hadn't wanted it to end. She had really added some spark to his life.

Though he was concerned about the new-moon phase that would be upon them tomorrow. He and his family wouldn't be able to run and play with Gabrielle as wolves since they weren't royals and couldn't turn into wolves then. Maybe she wasn't a royal either. The royals had no issue with shifting at any time of the month because they had very few human-diluted genes. Instead, they had several generations of pure *lupus garou* blood. The only royals in the Wolffs' group were Blake's mate, Nicole, her brother, Nate, and their parents. It hadn't mattered to Nicole that Blake wasn't a royal; she loved him just the same.

Not all royals felt that way. It wasn't that they felt superior to those who had more recent human genes, but that being a royal carried somewhat less of a risk because the full moon couldn't compel them to shift. They wanted that same freedom for their offspring. Landon understood that reasoning.

He noticed lamplight and the Christmas tree lights still on in the living room at his and his sisters' home and wondered if his sisters were waiting up to interrogate him about Gabrielle. He'd thought they would be in bed by now. There was nothing for him to say. He thoroughly enjoyed her company and wished there could be more than that to it, but it wasn't happening. Not if she loved her workplace and home in Florida and wanted to stay there. She might not like the cold here, being used to the heat out there.

Then again, maybe his sisters had left the lights on so he wouldn't have to return home to a dark house. But as soon as he entered the house, he found both of them waiting in the living room.

"We suspect you need more time off to be with Gabrielle." Kayla was sitting on the couch, dressed in a pair of warm red-and-green-plaid pajamas, her feet in red slippers resting on the footstool.

Dressed in red footed pajamas, Roxie was sitting on the couch at the other end. "We're fine with it."

"Thanks. She's leaving when her vacation is done, but her friends aren't here yet, so I said I would take her skiing again tomorrow. Maybe for a couple of days if she would like that."

"And meals, and swimming, and wolf runs." Roxie frowned. "We won't be able to run with her as wolves the day after tomorrow, you know."

"Yeah, I was thinking about that. She may be like us anyway and can't run during the new moon."

"Or she may be a royal and disappointed that we aren't royals too," Roxie warned.

"True." There was nothing he could do about that, unless he got hold of some of the royals in the pack to run with her. He figured a whole bunch of them would take him up on the offer. Bachelors especially.

"When are her friends arriving?" Kayla asked.

"They won't be here for two more days. By the way"—he folded his arms and looked sternly at his sisters—"you wouldn't happen to know how Lelandi learned that Gabrielle is a veterinarian, would you?"

"Seriously?" Roxie asked. "I asked what she did in Daytona Beach when you were having breakfast at the bar and grill, but you didn't want me to continue grilling her, so I didn't have a clue. You were supposed to tell me that night, but I forgot to ask you. I didn't know she was a vet until now."

"Me either," Kayla said.

"Who else knew who could have told Lelandi?" he asked.

"Someone who overheard her tell you that's what she did? When did you learn about it?" Kayla asked.

"When we were having breakfast. She told me after Roxie had left."

"Minx then? She was the one serving you breakfast. There was no one else in the restaurant at the time," Roxie said.

"I'll ask her."

"Ask Lelandi," Kayla said. "She'll tell you."

"Why are you concerned?" Roxie asked. "Is Gabrielle upset about it?"

"I don't think she was really upset, just more surprised that the pack leaders would know. You know how you would feel if you visited a place and those in charge knew just what you did and where you were from."

"That would be unnerving," Kayla said.

"Exactly."

"That's a pack for you when we have a shortage of females. Though Kayla and I are available, we have been busy working on everything to do with the restaurant and lodge. Gabrielle should be thrilled the pack leaders want her to stay. They can be really picky about who can join the pack—and for good reason. They always check their backgrounds thoroughly. They checked ours," Kayla said. "That's great about her being a veterinarian, though if she hadn't had a job, she could certainly have worked with us at the lodge or restaurant. There's always something that needs to be done. But, hey, if she's at a human-run vet clinic, she's probably a royal."

"You're probably right." Then Landon frowned, trying to remember where Minx had been when Gabrielle told him what she did for a living. He hadn't thought she'd been anywhere near them at the time. He wondered why she would even be interested in telling Lelandi about it if she had.

"Oh, by the way, that was great how she helped you to find Rosco and the injured man," Roxie said. "I would say since she wanted to go with you, that was a good sign."

Kayla said, "Yeah, she didn't want to give you up."

He chuckled.

Roxie got up from the couch. "She wanted more of your personal touch." She headed for the stairs, then paused on the first stair when Kayla started to speak.

"You know, if she does take over Doc Mitchell's ranch and vet clinic, and if you and she mate, you'll be living out there, farther away from us," Kayla said.

"It's not that far, and it would give all of us another place to run. He's got a lot of acreage out there," Landon said.

Roxie laughed. "I told you, Kayla. Our brother is seriously making a go of this."

"I told you about them kissing in the pool." Kayla smiled.

"Is nothing sacred?"

"No," both his sisters said at the same time and laughed.

Landon was not at all surprised that his siblings were checking up on him and Gabrielle, and he wasn't bothered by it. If other bachelor wolves were wandering by and captured a glimpse of them, they would know he was serious about the she-wolf. And yeah, he definitely wanted to make a go of this.

Kayla left the couch and followed Roxie up the stairs. "I would love to hear what you learn about how Lelandi discovered Gabrielle is a vet."

Roxie called down, "No wonder Rosco loves her. She's good with animals."

Landon agreed with Roxie about Rosco. He still wondered who might have been the one to tell Lelandi that Gabrielle was a vet. Lelandi was known to be a matchmaker when a situation arose that she might be able to help along. He'd learned that when she ensured Nicole had enough mysteries to solve right here in

Silver Town so she wouldn't return to her home and practice in Denver.

He smiled. Well, hell, if Lelandi was attempting to do the same with Gabrielle, he was going to have to see what he could do to help make it happen.

He shouldn't be calling Lelandi right this minute. Not as late as it was, but he had to know the truth. Otherwise, he would be thinking about it all night. He picked up his phone and called Lelandi.

"This better be an emergency." Lelandi sounded sleepy.

Landon had hoped she was still awake.

"What's wrong?" Darien asked near her.

"It's Landon. What's wrong?" she asked Landon.

"Who told you Gabrielle was a veterinarian?"

There was a significant pause on the other end of the line, and Landon suspected that Lelandi didn't want to tell him the truth.

"That's why you're calling me at midnight? Why? Is Gabrielle upset that I asked her about taking Doc Mitchell's job if she ever wanted to join us?"

"I would say more surprised than anything. She thought I had put you up to it." Landon hadn't wanted Gabrielle to think that of him.

"Well, you can tell her with a clear conscience you didn't. Night!" Lelandi hung up on him.

He stared at the phone. He couldn't believe Lelandi did that! She was a psychologist and had to know that wouldn't work well with him. Not wanting to be thwarted, he called her back.

"Landon, it is *midnight*. If you want to get up with the kids at six, you're welcome to and we can talk all night long. But it will cost you. In professional doctor fees, I mean."

"If you're trying to convince Gabrielle to stay, I want in."

Again, a significant pause. "Okay, so you seem to be having fun with her, and she seems to like you, so do you have any suggestions that might work?"

"I don't know. Maybe take her on a tour of the businesses, have dinner at the Silver Town Tavern where it's just us wolves. Maybe—"

"Have a vet crisis and need her help?"

"That might be a little extreme."

"Right. Then again, I don't believe Gabrielle can practice veterinary medicine in Colorado without a license. Whatever we come up with, it can't be obvious, or our gooses are cooked. I'm talking to Doc Mitchell about ways to encourage her to move here and take over his practice. That doesn't mean she'll be convinced, but the more reasons she might have to stay, the better chance we have at changing her mind. You never know. Doc Mitchell has a beautiful place out in the country. He said he's willing to give it to her so he can retire."

"All right. I'll think about it." Landon was hopeful that they could convince Gabrielle to stay. Especially if she wanted to continue seeing him.

Then they ended the call and Landon stripped out of his clothes and climbed into bed. Now, he just had to think of something to do with animal care that would convince Gabrielle how much she would love it here and how much she was needed. Not just for her vet services though.

He frowned. Lelandi never revealed to him who had told her that Gabrielle was a vet.

—————

Lying on her back, her hands beneath her head, Gabrielle lay awake, trying to sleep, but her thoughts were going in a million different directions. She couldn't quit thinking about how fun it had been to play with Landon as a wolf in the snow—with his family, too, all of whom were friendly and welcoming. She hadn't played with a male wolf in wolf form in forever. When bachelor males had come through her area, she'd dated, had dinner out, gone to the movies, and walked along the beach, but only in her human form.

Swimming in the pool with Landon had been thoroughly enjoyable too. She'd certainly never done that with a wolf outdoors in the snow in a heated pool! Just way too fun. And free meals? She had never expected that. The food was the best ever. She didn't think she'd ever had such good meals consistently for breakfast, lunch, and dinner at one restaurant, which would have cost her a fortune. Not that they couldn't all afford the price of the meals, but Gabrielle and her friends tended to be frugal.

She sure hadn't expected to get free personal lessons from a hot bachelor wolf. She had planned to get group lessons while her friends had some fun skiing the expert slopes, though they had said they would start her out with lessons. If they had been teaching her, she could imagine the three of them laughing so hard at all her mistakes that she would never have learned how to ski and they would never have gotten in any skiing time. Landon had only smiled at her and waited patiently for her to get to her feet every time, making sure that she hadn't hurt herself.

Now her friends were going to foot the lodge bill too? She couldn't let them. But she was enjoying her time there, despite them not being there yet, and she certainly hadn't expected that. She realized she hadn't even had time to really feel disappointed that her friends weren't there. She felt a little guilty about that.

She thought about Lelandi and Darien coming to see her about replacing the current vet so he could retire. She still wondered who had told them she was a vet. Had they looked into her setup in Daytona Beach? That was another thing. Did they even know that's where she had a co-op with other vets?

Then she began to think about Odette and Zelda. She knew they were dedicated to their job as special agents, but they were supposed to be on leave. Several other special agents within the organization could have been tasked to do the job, she thought.

She couldn't imagine everyone being so busy that they couldn't have taken care of this so the sisters could go on their vacation.

Shifting her thoughts, Gabrielle hoped she would do even better at skiing in the morning. She was afraid that she would have forgotten all the moves and be at the beginning all over again. Sighing, she closed her eyes and rolled over on her side.

She thought about her co-op and how all the vets were human. How she didn't have a wolf pack to belong to. That's why when she'd met the jaguar sisters she'd become fast friends with them. Wolves loved to be with a pack. At least most did, based on the ones she'd met who were passing through Daytona Beach. And being around shifters afforded her the opportunity to talk about female shifter issues—like raising kids and having babies some-day, or dating shifter guys—which was really nice.

The idea of not only moving to a new state so vastly different from the one where she had always lived, but also leaving the only home she'd ever known and the first vet practice she'd ever worked at overwhelmed her. She wasn't sure she could handle all the changes. She was rather a stick-in-the-mud when it came to going places—other than Florida. She had never considered leaving her birthplace for good.

Then she thought of Landon again, his warm brown eyes, equally warm smile, easy manner, and hot bod. She touched her lips and imagined his mouth pressed against hers, his aroused body making her hotter. She knew if he had lived in Daytona Beach, she would be courting the wolf for certain.

No wonder she couldn't sleep!

CHAPTER 7

EARLY SUNDAY MORNING, GABRIELLE WOKE, STRETCHED, glanced at the time, realized it was much later than she'd planned to get up, and jumped out of bed. She had a swimming date with Landon—before the pool opened—and she hadn't wanted to be this late!

She tore off her night T-shirt and hurried to put on her bikini. She even debated wearing the string bikini. Was she crazy or what? But she left it in the drawer, not intending to bring it out again now that she was swimming with a hot wolf.

She finished getting ready, grabbed her room key and shoved it into her cover-up pocket, slipped on her flip-flops, and headed out the door. She had barely made it to the lobby when Blake met her and smiled. Rosco jumped up from his bed near the fireplace and hurried to greet her too.

"I swear Landon thought you were going to stand him up. He's been pacing across the lobby for an hour." Blake appeared amused.

"Oh, uh, we didn't set a time. I…overslept." She hadn't meant to upset Landon. She reached down and petted Rosco.

"Here he comes," Blake said.

But at the same time, a dark-haired woman caught Gabrielle's eye. Something about her seemed familiar. Her face. She was wearing jeans, snow boots, and a wool sweater and didn't look like she was going skiing, but she headed for the check-in counter. Then another wolf headed straight for Gabrielle, stealing her attention, and she couldn't believe who she was seeing. Brando Redfern.

She'd gone out with him a couple of times when he was in Daytona Beach on vacation. He was okay. Nothing to write home about. He was living with a wolf pack in Georgia, and he and two of his male wolf friends had come to Daytona Beach on a three-day weekend outing. He wasn't the least bit interested in moving to Daytona Beach, and he'd only walked with her on the beach and taken her out to dinner and then to a movie the next night. His friends showed up at the seafood restaurant to harass him good-naturedly, as if she and he were an item. Which they hadn't been. She guessed he was interested in saying hi because she was someone he had met before. She figured he wasn't here alone either and would have some friends along.

Landon was looking in a different direction, but when he saw Gabrielle talking to Blake and petting Rosco, he smiled openly. She loved how seeing her seemed to brighten his morning. She didn't remember a time when a wolf had acted that way when he saw her and really meant it. It couldn't help but make her feel special.

"I'll leave you two to it," Blake said. "He's all yours for the rest of the day and tomorrow. We'll see you for breakfast in a bit." Then smiling, he shook his head at Landon and headed for the check-in counter.

"So you're all mine for the next two days, your brother said." Gabrielle took hold of Landon's hand and headed for the pool while Rosco returned to his bed by the fire. She saw right away that Landon had already put out the private party sign.

"I'm glad about that. Tonight, if you would like, I'll take you to the Silver Town Tavern for dinner."

"Sure. Is their food as good as it is here?"

"It sure is."

She sighed. "But you would have to pay for it." As if the family wasn't already paying for the food at their own bar and grill. She could offer to pay, but she loved to tease him about it. A wolf without a sense of humor wouldn't be the one for her.

Landon chuckled. "Of course. That was the plan."

Brando had stopped to speak to a couple of guys—the men

Gabrielle had seen him with at Daytona Beach. He quickly spoke to them, then turned and hurried to intercept her and Landon on their way to the pool. She thought he would realize she was with someone and butt out. Instead, he pulled her into a hug, and she felt her face heat with embarrassment. She quickly pulled away from him and put distance between them, frowning at him for being so forward. He wasn't her boyfriend or anything else to her, for heaven's sake.

"What are you doing here?" Brando was all smiles, like they were the best of friends and had known each other forever.

"I'm here skiing, but I'm going swimming first." She turned to Landon, who looked like he was ready to trounce the wolf, his eyes narrowed, his expression grim.

Even though she wasn't Landon's mate, he still had the territorial wolf behavior down pat.

"This is Brando Redfern from Georgia. I met him once on the beach back home. Brando, this is Landon Wolff"—a real wolf, and one she had more of a time keeping her hands off, not this guy— "who is part owner of the lodge and restaurant."

"Swimming. That sounds like a winner. I'll go get my trunks and join you." Brando either didn't get the point or he was ignoring it.

"The pool is closed," Landon said. "It's only open to staff."

"You work here? As a vet?" Brando asked Gabrielle, as if he really thought they would have a vet clinic at the lodge. He was being facetious, and it certainly wasn't a way to win anyone over, as if he'd had any real interest in getting her attention and keeping it.

"She's an invited guest," Landon said, his voice terse.

"Oh, well, then you could invite me, since I'm a friend of hers." Brando's insinuation was that there was more to their relationship than she was letting on, and that irritated her.

"Sorry, it's a private party." She wanted him to just go away. Of all the times to run into someone she knew who had just been passing through Daytona Beach and had never spoken to her again. That's why she knew he wasn't someone she could be interested in. If so, he would have gotten ahold of her at some time or another and told her what a great time he'd had and how he wanted to see her again. "Enjoy your ski vacation."

"Yeah, I'll get together with you later then."

As if. She smiled lamely at him. "Let's go swimming, Landon." She walked with him into the pool area and stopped next to one of the chaise lounges, dropping her towel on the chair and kicking her flip-flops off.

Landon pulled off his shirt and removed his sandals. "So about this Brando…"

"I went out to dinner with him once when he was vacationing in Daytona Beach with his friends and then to a movie the next night. I never saw or heard from him again."

"I thought you looked a bit shocked when he hugged you."

She smiled. "You looked a bit growly."

He chuckled. "Sorry, instinctive wolf genes."

"No problem. He startled me with his actions. He isn't somebody that I know well."

"Not like me."

"Not at all like you. So, changing the subject, I sure feel the pull in my muscles. You work such different muscles when you're skiing. I didn't even know they existed."

"I agree. Every summer, we use different muscles to hike instead of snow ski, and then in the winter, we'll be back to skiing and we all feel it. A lot of skiers who just take a vacation at a ski resort once a year or so do too. So you're not alone."

"Good. I hate to think I'm the only one who is so out of shape." She jumped into the pool, and when she came up for air, he jumped in behind her and came up beside her. She was still wondering if her girlfriends would arrive tomorrow night like they said they would or keep calling or texting to tell her they were going to be even later.

She suspected that unless the woman gave herself up to Zelda and Odette, they were going to be at this for a while. Oh well, she should live for the moment, and for now Gabrielle was having a ball.

She and Landon swam to the outside part of the pool and then turned and headed back to the other side. When they swam back under the glass divider, she came up for air and saw a family of four removing their sandals and cover-ups, wearing swimsuits and getting ready to swim. Oh, great, more rule breakers. Only this time she was sure Landon would enforce the rules.

Landon came up some way beyond her and saw the family. "Excuse me. The pool isn't open yet."

"*You're* swimming." The man sounded aggravated with Landon. "And this doesn't look like a private party to me."

Gabrielle waited, treading water, hoping that Landon could resolve this without any trouble.

"I'm one of the owners."

The man looked disgruntled, his mouth turned down, his brow furrowed.

"The sign's posted for the owners and staff to swim. It's the only time we have to do it before we have to be on duty." Landon tried to sound apologetic, though he still showed he was in charge and the man and his family wouldn't sway him to allow them in the pool for an early-morning swim.

"Okay, sorry." But the man didn't sound sorry at all, more irritated he couldn't take his family swimming when he'd brought them all down to the pool dressed for it. "Come on, kids. We'll come later, after we finish skiing today."

"I told you it was closed." The woman sounded totally annoyed with the man, her tongue sharp, her face as much of a scowl as his.

The kids looked disappointed, but it was the man's fault for trying to buck the system and making the family think they could swim when it was posted that they couldn't. Gabrielle had been the exception—being a single she-wolf in a bikini helped.

As soon as the family left, Gabrielle turned and dove under the water again and swam to the outside end of the pool. She was glad Landon hadn't kicked *her* out of the pool the other day and was allowing her to continue to swim—with him, of course. And that was even more fun.

Landon swam with her, just doing laps like they'd done before, back and forth, back and forth.

She was glad. She loved swimming like this and did it at her own swimming pool back home a couple of times a day, once at night after work, and once in the morning before work to keep in shape when she couldn't run as a wolf. She'd never thought she would be able to swim at the lodge after hours like this—with permission, when there was no one else in the pool. This was so much fun.

But when she was done swimming laps, she chased after Landon, whether he was done swimming *his* laps or not. She grabbed his foot and he took a gulp of water, laughing. And coughing. She was laughing. He turned around so fast, she didn't have time to get away from him before he pulled her into his arms and kissed her.

What a way to start the morning. If she'd been here with just her friends, she wouldn't have had half this much fun! Well, fun in a different way. But this was sexy and romantic. Landon kept kissing her and she kept kissing him back. He was keeping them afloat with his legs as she wrapped her legs around his hips.

She sighed. "Hmm, I always love swimming, but this is nothing like what I would have imagined." Swimming in her own swimming pool back home with a hot wolfish hunk, sure. She'd envisioned it many times. But at a ski resort? Nope.

Landon smiled down at her and kissed her wet cheek. "I'm going to have to tell your friends to keep working, so I can keep seeing you."

She laughed. "At this rate, they may never arrive."

"I'll have to send them a Christmas card thanking them, if they don't."

"But can you afford to take that much time off from work?"

"Yeah, I can. I told you. Our guests are important."

"One guest."

He kissed her. "Yeah, you bet. Oh, and by the way, we called the guests that had been in your room before you arrived and they said the Secret Santa gift isn't theirs. So I guess since it was in your room two days after they left, it has to be yours."

She sighed. "Okay, I'll have to open it then. Maybe it's from someone who wants me to stay and be the local vet. But I'll check it out later. Let's go get some breakfast. Or we're bound to end up in my room doing stuff we shouldn't."

He let out his breath in an exaggerated sigh. "All right. If that's the way you want it."

"Yes. I'm starving, aren't you?"

"I am." They swam to the stairs and climbed out, then grabbed their towels and dried off. "I'm still waiting to see you in the other candy-cane bikini again."

She smiled. "All right. I'll wear it tonight." She really hadn't planned to, but after all he'd done for her, if that's what he really wanted, she would do it.

"Hot damn. I would howl if I could, but maybe tonight on the run."

She laughed and pulled on her cover-up. "I'll run up to my room and get changed and meet you downstairs in a few minutes." But she picked up the Secret Santa package from the front desk before she went upstairs. Her whole day was looking up as long as she didn't break a leg skiing.

CHAPTER 8

LANDON WENT INTO THE OFFICE, GREETED BLAKE, WHO WAS working on ordering more supplies for the lodge, and changed in their back room. When he came out, he said to Blake, "I'm taking Gabrielle to the tavern tonight for dinner. We'll have breakfast at our place in a few minutes, so you and Nicole are still eating with us, right?"

Blake turned off his computer. "Yeah, we are. Do you want any of us to meet you at the tavern tonight too? Will Gabrielle feel more comfortable with us there, since we've made friends with her already?"

"I'll see how she feels about it. I don't want to overwhelm her with making this look like a family affair, as though she's already joined our family."

"On the other hand, she might think that going out with you on a real date could be risky." Blake smiled and pulled out his phone. "If you don't want her to get away from here permanently, you'd better hurry and work on convincing her to think seriously about returning here for good."

"I'm working at it."

"You mean the kiss in the pool? That was a good start." Blake smiled at him. "Hey, one thing, though. Rosco's due for his vaccinations. You were going to do that after breakfast tomorrow morning. Can you still do that? One of us can instead, if you want to just see Gabrielle."

Landon frowned. "Uh, yeah, I'll still do it. Maybe that would be a good excuse for getting Gabrielle to come with me. She can see the clinic and stables for the large animals that Doc Mitchell takes care of."

"Unless she's only used to working with small animals. We didn't think of that."

"True." Then Landon spied her coming. "Okay, well, we're off to the house for breakfast."

"I'll come with you." Blake texted Nicole—to remind her about breakfast, Landon suspected.

Landon headed for Gabrielle. "Blake's coming with us. Nicole will join us."

"Okay, good. Where's Rosco?"

"He comes over to the lodge after breakfast," Landon said.

They all walked outside into the light snow to make their way to the house.

Gabrielle was wearing her hot-pink ski pants and jacket, the wrists and hood trimmed in the same color faux fur. He couldn't miss her in the snow, which he was glad for.

"I need to take Rosco in to get his vaccinations after breakfast tomorrow," Landon said to Gabrielle. "Do you want to come with me?"

"Sure, I'll go with you," Gabrielle said. "I might as well check out the vet clinic while I'm here, in case I ever decide I want to leave Florida and move here. That's not likely to happen, but if it does, at least I'll have seen the vet clinic beforehand. And I might as well meet with Doc Mitchell."

Landon was thrilled. From Blake's smile and raised eyebrows, Landon could tell Blake was too. "He's really nice, but older than some of the oldest trees in the forest. We need a vet, so he won't quit until we have a new one."

"Does he have a vet assistant?" she asked.

"A couple, and a billing clerk and an office clerk. They're all younger, so they can work for you for a long time. They're all royals, too, so you won't have to worry about them having to leave work for a week during the full moon because they can't control their shifting," Blake said.

"Oh, that's good. I hadn't even considered that a wolf-staffed clinic could have trouble with that. Everyone's human where I am, so no difficulty there. I guess Doc Mitchell is a royal then."

"He is," Blake said.

They finally reached the house and Landon unlocked the door. "We're here," he called out to his family.

"I'm here," Nicole said, greeting them. "I had stopped off at the house when Blake texted me, reminding me about breakfast, which was a good thing. I can get wrapped up in my PI work otherwise. A lot of it can be done online, which means I'm home when I can be. Sometimes I'm on the road with my brother, checking into a case."

Blake kissed her and she kissed him right back.

"I'm glad you could have breakfast with us. Where's Rosco?" Gabrielle asked Landon. "I know you said he comes to the lodge after breakfast, but he usually greets everyone who walks into the house, doesn't he?"

Landon figured Gabrielle's vet training told her something was the matter.

"We were busy making breakfast," Roxie said, Kayla agreeing with her. "He has to be around here somewhere."

"I'll check on him," Landon said, worried about him now because Gabrielle was right. He always greeted everyone who came into the house. He hoped Rosco was all right or he hadn't gotten out of the house again and gone searching for more avalanche victims.

Rosco was lying in his bed, looking up at Landon, but he didn't lift his head, and he was looking guilty. He appeared to be trying to hide something. "What have you got there, Rosco?" All Landon could see were some furry orange and white and black patches, like a rabbit. But the colors weren't right. Still, what else could it be? Rosco was known to chase rabbits and squirrels whenever he could. But when Landon tried to check out the animal, it moved and Rosco tried to keep Landon from touching the critter. "What is it, Rosco?"

"What is it?" Gabrielle asked, peering around Landon. "Oh, it's a calico kitten."

Landon's jaw dropped. "Where did you get a kitten?" As if Rosco could tell him.

"He got out of the house. We forgot to lock the wolf door," Roxie said, coming in to check on what Rosco had found. "He just came in covered in snow and went straight to his bed. We just knew that he had returned safely, and he was feeling guilty about sneaking out. We were too busy getting ready to fix breakfast to check on him further. We figured he was worn out after his wild run. We had no idea he had picked up a kitten from somewhere!"

"Let me see your baby, Rosco," Gabrielle said in a coaxing but firm manner.

He kept putting his head over the kitten, trying to discourage Gabrielle from taking it. Landon finally had to hold his collar so Gabrielle could pull the kitten out of his bed. Rosco was up on his feet in an instant, having a fit and wanted to take the kitten back.

"I'll give her back to you. Just wait, Rosco." Gabrielle checked the kitten over. "She's fine. I would say she's about eight to nine weeks old, which means she's perfectly weaned."

"That's good," Landon said, "since Rosco might be protecting her, but he certainly can't nurse her."

Nicole was standing nearby smiling, taking pictures of the kitten. "He loves cats. I'll have to investigate who might be missing a kitten."

"She'll need her vaccinations and such, if she hasn't already had them. But she looks perfectly healthy otherwise." Gabrielle was petting the kitten in her arms and then finally set her back in the bed where Rosco hurried to join her. As big as he was, he was still careful not to lie on top of her, and the kitten snuggled with Rosco as if he were her mother—a giant of a mother, nice and warm and cuddly.

"Well, if we don't find her family, we may have a new addition to ours," Landon said.

His sisters cheerfully agreed. Blake laughed. Nicole seemed happy about it too.

"We're having waffles—a choice of red velvet with a cream cheese glaze, or chocolate–peppermint. We also have plain waffles and just maple syrup if you don't want any of the fancy stuff," Roxie said, getting back to the business of breakfast.

"Red velvet waffles for me." Nicole took a seat at the table and then began texting someone. "You ladies make the best waffles I've ever had."

"Plain waffles for me." Blake told Gabrielle where to sit.

"Hmm, I think I'll have red velvet waffles. That sounds really good." Gabrielle sat down at the table while Landon got everyone coffee.

"Chocolate–peppermint for the rest of us," Kayla said.

"I don't know how the Silver Town Tavern meals can beat the food at your restaurant or here at your home. I love how you have all these Christmas dishes for the holiday season." Gabrielle smiled when she saw the waffles were made in the shape of Christmas trees. "These are so cute."

"It actually brings more of the townsfolk up here for special group parties, even if they're not skiing." Blake served everyone water.

Gabrielle sipped some of her water. "What with the decorations making your lodge and bar and grill a winter wonderland, and the meals, I can see it would be a real fun party place."

"It is. We enjoy it. Oh, and we have a big snowman and snow sculpture contest going on for the residents and businesses of Silver Town, so I can show you what some have done already before we go to dinner tonight. Also, the Christmas lights are up all over town. They have a lighting contest and a gingerbread house one." Landon helped bring the plates over with all the waffles on them.

"You're kidding. Really?" Gabrielle asked.

"Not kidding. Everyone likes to have fun at these celebrations. Since Blake and I were just here getting the lodge and restaurant open last Christmas, and our sisters were back in Vermont still trying to sell our old lodge, my brother and I didn't get involved in any of that. We put up lights, but that was it." Landon sat down next to Gabrielle and patted her thigh.

"But this year? Your lighting and decorations should be a winner."

Landon smiled and drank some of his coffee. "We hope so, but you'll have to see the others too. Everyone goes all out to decorate because it's a fun thing to do."

Kayla brought over a plate of sausages. Everyone else took their seats at the long wooden table after that.

"It's a lot of fun," Roxie said. "It's very different from when we were in Vermont without a pack. There's so much friendly competition that we're having a blast."

"I bet. I would love to see what everyone has done with their decorations." Gabrielle took a bite of her waffle. "This is delicious."

"Thanks," Roxie and Kayla said.

"They have a group who go Christmas caroling too," Blake said.

"We are having them come to the lodge on Friday night to sing for our guests. We'll provide free Christmas cupcakes, cheese, crackers, and punch," Landon said.

"Are you going to sing Christmas carols?" Gabrielle asked Landon.

"Not me."

"We're just providing the food," Roxie said, "but next year, we might sing."

"Not me," Landon said again.

Gabrielle laughed.

"So what are we going to name the kitten if she ends up being ours?" Kayla asked, getting back to the business with the kitten.

"Princess Buttercup," Roxie said.

"But if you name her and she belongs to a family, you're going to feel bad when you have to give her up," Landon warned.

Blake shook his head and poured maple syrup on his plain waffles. "They have already fallen in love with the kitten whether they name it or not."

"Princess Buttercup then," Kayla said, agreeing with Roxie.

Nicole and Gabrielle thought the name suited her.

"I can't believe Rosco adopted a kitten," Landon said.

Blake laughed. "And our sisters and my mate too."

"I've had clients come in with the unlikeliest of pet pals," Gabrielle said, "from a parrot that tells the dog to shut up when he's barking, a Labrador and a duckling that sleep together, and another Lab and a wild fox, to a wild boar piglet found starving in a field and a Jack Russell terrier that befriended it and brought it home."

"Aww, how cute," Roxie said. "Do you have any pictures?"

"Yeah, on our website." Gabrielle found the page on her phone and passed it around.

Everyone smiled and chuckled to see the unlikely friends playing or sleeping together. A Saint Bernard and a kitten did look cute together, Landon had to admit.

Once they were finished with their breakfast, they all looked at Rosco, sleeping with the kitten.

"I don't think he's going to come with us to the lodge today." Landon helped clear the dishes.

Blake helped with the rest of them. "I'll come and take him for a walk later. I might have to put Princess Buttercup in my pocket so Rosco will go with me."

Everyone laughed.

"I've already texted our pack leaders, and we'll get the word out via the alert roster to learn where the kitten belongs," Nicole said.

"We can bring her with us when we take Rosco in to have his

vaccinations," Gabrielle told Landon. "We can have Doc Mitchell check her out."

"Yeah, we'll do that."

Before they dressed in their coats, Gabrielle took some pictures of Rosco sleeping with the kitten. "I have to send this to my friends. They'll get a kick out of it."

Once the kitchen was clean, everyone dressed in their warm outer clothes and headed to the lodge together.

"You wouldn't happen to know how to make a gingerbread house, would you?" Roxie asked Gabrielle.

Everyone glanced at her to see if she had a foolproof way to make one so they would stand a chance at winning the gingerbread house competition.

"Every year I make one. It's a doghouse, though."

The guys laughed.

Roxie sighed. "I guess that leaves us still figuring out what to do." She smiled. "But you can build us a doghouse to go along with whatever we decide on if you're here long enough and have time."

"That would be fun."

When they entered the lodge, everyone went about their business while Gabrielle and Landon put on their ski boots. Then with skis and poles in hand, they headed outside to the lift for the easy and intermediate slopes. "Do you think you'll win any of the competitions?"

"I think we have a good chance at winning on the decorations this year. It didn't really matter to Blake and me last year, but our sisters are much more competitive. The Victorian Silver Town Inn usually wins with the snow sculptures—wolves," Landon said. "They're beautiful. Silver Town has begun to have two different categories for the competitions—the sculptures and the snowmen—because the snow wolves were winning all the competitions."

"Oh, wow, I would love to see them."

"It's right across the street from the Silver Town Tavern. We'll see them tonight."

"You haven't started any?"

"We planned to do it tomorrow. A couple of people take photos of the snowmen and snow sculptures, but the judges normally come by to see them first thing once they are made."

"So what will you be doing? Snowmen or snow sculptures?" she asked.

"None of us have a talent for creating snow sculptures, and our snowmen are just for fun, but I'm sure we'll do the snowman or a snow family."

"That sounds like fun. I've never made one."

"That will have to be remedied."

"What about the gingerbread house?"

"We've never done that before, so Roxie and Kayla are trying to come up with a design." Maybe that was a way to get Gabrielle involved in the family business in a fun way and make her feel like part of the family. "So about this gingerbread doghouse you created—"

"It was made of ingredients a dog could safely eat, and we gave it away the day before Christmas to one lucky winner last year. I made one this year too. We set it up on the front desk of the vet clinic. I even made a little dog for it."

"I'd love to see it."

She pulled it up on her phone and showed it to him.

"That really is great."

"People with pets coming into the clinic were taking pictures of it. I don't bake that often because it's only me, but every year I make one just for the clinic for some Christmas cheer." She sighed. "I thought about doing all this stuff—making snow angels, creating a snowman, and seeing the Christmas lights—with my friends, but I don't want to miss out on all this if they arrive too late to do any of it. Or don't show up at all."

"You can do it with us."

"But I'm not a member of the family."

Gabrielle and Landon finally reached the lift line.

"You can help us. No problem at all. You just aren't supposed to work on several different snowmen or gingerbread houses for the competition for different families. But you can work on one."

"And I imagine you're supposed to be a resident."

He smiled at her. "Believe me, everyone would be thrilled you participated."

"Especially if it makes me want to return here, become the local vet, and stay for good."

"Exactly. Besides, I thought you didn't mind breaking the rules."

"Ha! When it could hurt your chances at winning any of the competitions you're entering? No way. Oh, and I have to tell you, I have a secret, but you can't tell anyone else."

He was all ears and smiled down at her, but then they finally had to catch a chair, so they paused the conversation so she could concentrate on what she was doing. For him, it was second nature, as much as he'd ridden ski lifts up mountains since he was young. Gabrielle was having to watch that she didn't lose her ski poles or tangle up her skis, or even lose one. He'd seen everything with new skiers. Well, he'd been one at one time! And he'd experienced some of the same issues.

Once they were sitting next to each other on the chair and headed up the mountain, the wind in their faces and snowflakes whipping off the nearby trees, she continued, "I'm a mermaid."

He chuckled.

"Seriously. I have to swim two times a day most days, unless I'm sick or work just gets in the way. But I love to swim."

"So that's why you had to swim at our pool even if it was closed."

"You bet." She smiled at him, then pulled her dickey over her face to keep warm and nodded. "I had arrived too late to swim, but before the restaurant closed, I wanted to swim and then go eat."

"Do you have a pool where you live?"

"Yeah, my home has a pool."

"See, if you lived here, you could swim anytime you like, and there's no upkeep. We take care of it, and it's indoors so you can swim all year round. Unlike even your pool back home, I imagine."

"It's heated and I do swim in it year-round. Wait, you mean to tell me Doc Mitchell's home doesn't have a pool?"

Knowing she was teasing him, Landon smiled at her. "You probably wouldn't want the upkeep here because of the snow we have for months, but I bet you anything the pack leaders would put one in for you for free if you asked them."

She laughed. "So that means for them to get my valuable services, I can ask for more stuff?"

"Yeah, you're at a premium. Now the rest of us, no way, but you? Sure."

"Well, that's never happened to me before."

Landon hoped it would make a difference in her decision to return to Florida.

They came to the end of the ride and Gabrielle got off without a hitch. He was glad. If she moved here, he could just imagine taking breaks to ski with her, and if she could manage the long hours, he would swim with her anytime she came in before work or after the pool and her vet clinic were closed.

"How do you feel about snow skiing now since you've had a night to think about it?" Landon asked her.

"Oh, I love it. I thought I would take one trip down the green slope first thing to get my ski legs. I'll spend the rest of the day on the blues, unless I get tired and start to fall too much. Then it's back to the easy slopes for me. But I am loving it. I really hadn't thought I would."

"Okay, I'm glad for that, and it sounds like a good plan."

Then they moved to the green slope and she started down the

hill, doing great. He followed her all the way down, making sure she didn't fall. She was still a little unsure of herself, wobbling a bit, but she would get better, given practice.

She was doing super on the blue slopes after that and he couldn't have been prouder of her. He noticed she seemed to get tired about the same time they'd taken a break yesterday, and she was shivering some when they were riding up the chairlift again. "It's time for some hot chocolate, don't you think?" he asked. They had much more frigid temperatures today, and she definitely appeared to be feeling the colder weather.

She nodded, her face covered in the balaclava, her beautiful green eyes hidden by the mirrored ski glasses.

He had to remind himself he was from Vermont, so he was used to the cold. Her cold in Florida wasn't the same, and even when it was cold, it didn't last as long as theirs. She wouldn't be acclimated to it like he was. Plus she wasn't used to skiing and her muscles would weary the longer she was up on the slopes. His family all got some skiing in on a daily basis, usually with others in the pack at some time during the day.

When Landon and Gabrielle reached the outdoor patio of the bar and grill, they put up their poles and skis on one of the racks and headed inside. Gabrielle pulled off her balaclava and glasses and hat, her blond hair tumbling over her shoulders. He realized she did look like a mermaid—in hot-pink ski clothes.

"About tonight...I want this to totally be your decision," Landon said, after ordering their hot chocolates. "Do you want it to be just the two of us when we go to the tavern for dinner, or would you rather have the whole family there?"

She smiled, her expression radiant. "Okay, so—" She paused when the waitress brought their hot chocolate.

"Enjoy."

"We will. Thanks, Minx." Landon took hold of his hot chocolate and drank a sip. "It's hot."

"Thanks. If I go alone with you, everyone will think I'm dating you. If we go with the family, everyone will think I'm dating you." She smiled at Landon again and took a sip of her hot chocolate. "Hmm, this is so good."

"Okay, so your choice? What will it be?" He would be happy either way as long as she was with him.

"Either is fine with me, but since I'm not used to being around groups of wolves, and if your family would really like to go out to the tavern tonight, I'm all for it."

"Great. I'll let everyone know. They'll be thrilled. I think they believe you will like me better if they are around to help work things out between us."

Gabrielle laughed. "What are sisters and a brother and his mate for?"

Landon smiled, glad she wanted the family there because he knew they would want to be there—to act as a unified pack within the pack—saying "Paws off the she-wolf" because Landon was the one seeing her—for now, anyway.

He immediately got on his phone and texted Roxie first: Plan to have dinner at six at the Silver Town Tavern.

Roxie texted back: All of us?

Yes.

Roxie texted: Did you make reservations?

No.

Roxie texted: I'll do it. And I'll let the rest of the family know we have a dinner engagement tonight. They were all waiting for the word and they'll be thrilled.

Thanks!

He was glad that his family would do this for him. They would have fun. And Gabrielle would feel insulated somewhat from the rest of the pack, particularly if a number of bachelor males were there and they made her feel uncomfortable.

"You know, if you get too chilled, we'll come in. It wouldn't do for you to get sick. I know we heal faster than the general population, but there's no sense in pushing yourself if you're feeling too cold. If you need anything warmer to wear, some of the shops in town have winter ski clothes."

"Thanks. I might have to go shopping. Did you see me shivering?" She sipped some more of her hot chocolate.

"I felt you shivering when we were on the chairlift. You're doing great on the slopes, by the way."

"Thanks. You're a great instructor, and I'm really catching on a lot faster than I thought I would."

He drank some more of his chocolate and nodded toward a couple of ski instructors who waved at them as they came in to get something hot to drink on a break. "Well, you are the one who doesn't quit and that's the reason you're doing so well. It only gets better with practice."

"My friends will be amazed. I really am enjoying myself, when I didn't think I would. I envisioned spending a lot of time in the pool while they skied, and meeting them for hot chocolate breaks and meals, and maybe one or two trips down the slopes a day."

"You're doing a lot better than that. But truly, if you get tired of it, we can do some other things. I can run you into town and see if there's anything you want to buy so you'll be warmer."

"Let's run into town now. If I had a wool sweater, I'd feel much better. I should have gotten one off the internet before I left home, but I didn't think I would ever get any use out of one in Florida. I really hadn't thought I would return to a ski resort. I just wanted to do this the one time to prove to my friends this wasn't for me."

Landon smiled. "So you've changed your mind. That's good. All right, let's do that." He was glad she wanted to get some more winter clothes to go skiing further. She would feel better and so would he. Even more than that, it might mean she would return to Silver Town to ski again when she could get away from her job in Daytona Beach. And maybe they would have another chance to convince her to live here.

Once they finished their hot chocolate, he wondered if she would like to go with one of his sisters instead. He knew one of them would love to go shopping! Of course, he didn't want to give her up for even an hour or so, but he thought it would be a good move to ask. "Just an idea, but would you like to go with one of my sisters to shop?"

Gabrielle's kissable lips parted. Then she smiled brightly. "You don't like to shop."

He chuckled. "It's not that. Believe me, spending more time in your company, no matter what we're doing, is fun for me. I just thought you might like to go with Roxie or Kayla."

"Sure. I would love to."

It didn't hurt for his whole family to help win her over. Landon texted Kayla, the one he thought would want to go shopping with Gabrielle the most.

Kayla texted back: Yes! Roxie and I will both take her. We didn't think you would give her up to us for anything.

He smiled and texted: Only with reluctance. She needs more winter clothes so she's warm enough on the slopes. We are on our way to the office, and I'll let her know you both want to go.

Kayla texted: We'll get ready to go now.

At least his sisters were very good at switching gears. He turned to Gabrielle. "Both my sisters want to go shopping with you. They're thrilled."

"Oh good. We'll have fun."

"I'll take over from my sisters while you enjoy yourselves. Why don't you have lunch out at the tea shop in town, if the three of you would like."

"Sure, that would be great. I love tea shops."

Landon's sisters met them in the lobby. Kayla paused to give Landon a list of things she'd been working on, and then Roxie did the same with him. He gave them a look to get real. No way could he do all these jobs by himself in the amount of time they would be gone.

His sisters laughed. "We will be sure to have her back after lunch so you can go skiing with her again," Roxie said.

"Okay, good. Make sure she gets some warm clothes so she'll feel great on the slopes," he reminded them. Shopping for gifts to take home was one thing. He wanted to make sure she was nice and warm on the slopes too.

"We will," Kayla assured him, and then they took off with Gabrielle, looking excited to get away from the lodge for some shopping and lunch with their new she-wolf friend.

He hoped they would enjoy themselves but wouldn't keep her too long.

CHAPTER 9

GOING SHOPPING WITH THE LADIES WAS GOING TO BE enjoyable. Gabrielle couldn't wait to find some warmer clothes so she would have more fun on the slopes with Landon.

"We have to ask you if you're a royal," Roxie said to Gabrielle as Kayla drove them to the store that they said had the most winter clothing in Silver Town.

"I'm a royal. Are you?" Gabrielle asked.

They both sighed.

"No, we're not. Our great-grandfather was bitten by a royal wolf." Kayla sounded a tad regretful. "And then our grandfather and father both mated royals."

"Oh, well, since your great-grandmother, grandmother, and mother were all royals, you have more wolf lineage, at least on half your family's line. But it doesn't make any difference to me. I'm just so thrilled to have friends here who are wolves, period. This has just been a great experience for me."

"Yeah, but we can't run as wolves with you when the new moon is out," Roxie said, as if Gabrielle hadn't gotten the point.

"Right. But maybe we can do something else." Gabrielle loved running as a wolf. If her friends arrived soon, she could run with them. But she didn't want Roxie and Kayla to feel she would be upset with them because they couldn't shift and play with her. If she really wanted to go out, she could anyway, by herself, like she had planned to that first night she had arrived, before she saw the family of wolves playing. And she was having too much fun with the family to not spend more time with them if they wanted her to.

"Landon would ask other royals to run with you, if you really want to go. We know what it's like to want to stretch our legs as a wolf at night," Roxie said.

"Or we could do something else," Kayla suggested, "like Gabrielle said: have a pool party or play board games or something."

"Make a snowman? Landon told me you were entering one in the contest. He said I could help. I've never made one before, so I might just make a mess of it. But I could cheer you on."

The sisters smiled at each other. "Building snowmen is just what we'll do. The women and their mates who run the Silver Town Inn make wolf sculptures and have won the last two years," Kayla said. "So we'll stick to snowmen. But Roxie and I were thinking we could make a snowman for each of us and one of Rosco."

"You know, you could do your own thing, if you would rather. We don't want you to feel like you have to do something with us. You might be getting tired of being in Landon's company all the time too," Roxie said matter-of-factly.

But Gabrielle wasn't. She was glad to go with his sisters to shop and have lunch, but she couldn't wait to spend more time with Landon.

Kayla gave Roxie a look like that was *not* the right thing to say to Gabrielle and she would talk to her about this later.

Gabrielle smiled. "I like doing things with Landon. And with all of you. I want to make a snowman while I am here, but not by myself, so I would love to help you with yours." She wasn't going to lie about how she felt about being around Landon, and she suspected Roxie just wanted to know how far Gabrielle intended to take things with him.

Roxie's eyes widened all of a sudden and she did a facepalm. "Oh, I forgot Nicole is a royal, so the two of you could run together as wolves. She would love that since none of the rest of us can. She never runs when we can't."

"Oh, sure, I can do that. But building the snowman sounds like fun too. And it's on my bucket list for while I'm here."

"Okay, a snowman it is." Kayla gave her sister a look that said she had better not nix the plan.

Gabrielle didn't have any siblings, and she was always amused to see how they interacted with each other.

They finally reached the town and pulled into a parking spot in front of Silver Town Boutique, a women's clothing shop featuring winter clothes right now. It looked just perfect for outfitting Gabrielle for her snowy vacation. She would have to return here next year to put good use to anything she bought to wear skiing, though. She had thought she would come here only at her friends' insistence and never return—figuring they would realize how much she hated the snow. Now she was planning to return next year? She really hadn't believed that would happen. Of course she hadn't realized it was a wolf-run town either, but she liked the town and the people here.

Like the other shops, everything was decorated with Christmas lights, making Silver Town the most festive place Gabrielle had ever been at Christmastime. A Christmas tree covered in pink, silver, and white balls and bows stood in the middle of the big triple-paned windows of the boutique, and Christmas light icicles hung at the top edge of the window frame. When they walked inside, a little bell jingled. The shop was warm and cheery, the fragrance of hot holiday wassail and snowball cookies enticing them to take a drink and a bite to eat.

They greeted the shopkeeper, a pretty redhead with hazel eyes, a red wolf wearing a sweater dress and high-heeled boots, her hair swept up in a chignon. Gabrielle couldn't believe it when she saw her. "Maxine Fox?" She'd been one of Gabrielle's clients in Daytona Beach and had two adorable black-and-white tuxedo cats that would only see her and none of the other vets. Some of that, Gabrielle was sure, had to do with both Maxine and Gabrielle being wolves. But Maxine had sworn that her cats wouldn't tolerate any of the other vets on general principle. Gabrielle knew she'd moved, but not where to.

"Ohmigod, tell me you're our new vet in Silver Town. Puss and Boots adore you, and when they need their regular checkups and vaccinations, I'll bring them right in," Maxine said.

Gabrielle smiled. "No, I'm still back in Daytona Beach. I just learned about this place and am here on vacation. How are Puss and Boots?"

"They're loving it here. It's so great. Though I'm back to everyone checking me out because I'm a 'fox shifter,' you know, despite the word getting out to the pack that a new red she-wolf is here and owns a clothing store."

Gabrielle smiled.

"In the old days in England, my ancestor was a red wolf, of course, but they called him the Fox because he was so cunning. So the name stuck, and for generations, our wolf family went by the name of Fox," Maxine said. "I couldn't have been more thrilled to discover you were a vet and that I'd found a great doctor for my cats, but when I learned a whole community was filled with wolves, I had to move here."

"I don't blame you."

"I guess introductions don't need to be made since the two of you know each other already," Roxie said. "We're just delighted that Maxine opened her brand-new shop here. We've needed some stylish clothes to buy locally. She was so excited to have come here on a hiking trip with some human friends this fall and learned it was a wolf-run town. We are so glad she decided to make this her home."

"I am too. It's been wonderful. I've been crazy busy with just starting up, but it was fun to meet Roxie, Kayla, and their sister-in-law, Nicole, who all just moved into the area at the beginning of the year. So we're all newcomers. Everyone has been really welcoming." Maxine hurried to pour cups of wassail for them and then offered them the snowball cookies.

Despite the fact that they were about to eat lunch just down the street at the tea shop after Gabrielle found some winter clothes, they each drank the wassail and had some of the cookies.

"Well, I had hoped to get together with you before I left Daytona Beach, but this was just too good of an opportunity to pass up. I mean, where else can you find so many beautiful, single male wolves?" Maxine asked.

"Yeah, I know. I agree." Though only one sexy bachelor wolf really appealed to Gabrielle.

"I bet you're cold, coming in from Florida," Maxine said to Gabrielle. "I had a little time to acclimate. Are you here skiing?"

Gabrielle smiled. "Yeah. I'm not used to this cold and especially being outside in it for a fair amount of time. I've never skied before and I really didn't think I'd be returning for any more ski trips, but it's been a lot of fun." She realized Landon had made her feel better about being in the snow so that she was not constantly reliving the nightmare when she and her parents were submerged in the frozen lake a decade ago. Being with him had been so therapeutic.

"Oh, I need to try it too. I've been too busy, but a couple of guys—twin brothers—dropped by, to my surprise, and offered to teach me how to ski, free of charge. Once I've hired a couple of assistants to work in the shop, and when I finally have a breather on the day the shop is closed, I'll be able to take the ski instructors up on it. You have to move here. It's just the greatest place ever. But don't let me keep you. Take a look around, and if you need any help, I'm here for you."

"Thanks, Maxine." Gabrielle wiped off her hands on a Christmas napkin, disposed of it, and then began looking at the clothes on the racks.

Roxie was soon holding up a long-sleeved, black merino-wool sports shirt to show Gabrielle. "You have to have one of these, if you don't already. It wicks away moisture, dries really fast, and keeps you nice and warm. We all wear them under our clothes as a base layer. You can also wear it alone under your ski jacket if it gets warmer out."

"And merino-wool base pants too," Kayla said, bringing her a pair of black ones.

"You sold me on it." Gabrielle tried on two different styles.

"It goes perfectly with your ski clothes, and when it's even warmer for late-season skiing, you can peel out of your jacket. Wearing just a wool sweater and sports shirt, you would still be warm enough," Roxie said.

Gabrielle finished getting dressed and left the dressing room. "Okay, I'll get them. Even in the winter in Florida, I can wear these with just a light jacket."

Maxine came back to check on them.

"Have you convinced her to stay in Silver Town?" Maxine asked the sisters.

Gabrielle smiled.

"We're working on it. Lelandi and Darien offered for her to take over the vet practice from Doc Mitchell," Kayla said.

"Oh, that would be wonderful," Maxine said.

Gabrielle smiled. "Wasn't it hard for you to get used to it, Maxine? No beaches? All the snow and cold?"

Maxine sighed. "A beach shop was fun, but the problem was that in the winter, it was off-season, no sales. And of course, no wolves. But here? My shop doesn't have an off-season. I carry hiking clothes for the summer, bathing suits for year-round. You should see all the swimsuits I sell when guests stay at the lodge and realize they forgot to pack a bathing suit. Plus did I mention all the wolves?" Maxine smiled as if she were in wolf heaven. "How could you leave all this behind?"

Gabrielle was beginning to think Maxine was right. "I know. But it's still such a change." Mainly because she'd never lived any-where else in her life.

Roxie held up four pairs of heavy-duty socks. "To match the rest of your ensembles and keep your feet perfectly warm."

"And glove liners to keep your fingers nice and warm. You can even wear them by themselves if the sun comes out and you get too hot with the outer gloves." Kayla handed her the glove liners. "Once you pay for them, we can have lunch at Silva's Victorian Tea Shop. It's always outfitted with Victorian decorations, but she has a Christmas–winter theme going on right now."

"I love tea shops like that." Gabrielle hadn't been to one in eons, and whenever she had a chance to go with her friends, she did.

"She has grilled sandwiches or plain sandwiches, little cakes, scones, and cookies, and a wide assortment of tea flavors," Kayla said.

"That sounds delicious. It's my treat because I've been getting free meals at the lodge all along and you made us breakfast today."

"Thanks," Roxie said.

"We appreciate it," Kayla said.

Gabrielle was glad Maxine had found the perfect place to live and enjoyed the company of the wolves. Gabrielle was starting to feel the same way about being with Landon and his family. She paid for her clothes. "I'm feeling better about this already. I was so cold, but I didn't want to stop skiing. I really love it. I'm just not used to the cold."

"Yeah, it's like with anything, you have to dress right for the job. It would be like us going to Florida and, in the middle of summer, wearing merino wool," Kayla said.

"Oh, absolutely," Maxine said, "and for me, it was easier getting used to the cold, since you can just bundle up, than if you have to get used to the hot, humid Florida heat. There's only so much you can take off." She smiled.

"True." Gabrielle couldn't imagine anything worse than wearing wool in the summer in Florida. And forget about beautiful winter wolf coats. "Thanks so much." Gabrielle gave her a hug. "Give your cats some loving from me."

"I sure will. They will be thrilled when I tell them who I saw today."

Then Gabrielle, Roxie, and Kayla left the shop and dropped Gabrielle's packages off in the trunk of Kayla's car. From the boutique, they walked down the street to the tea shop on the snow-shoveled walks. Several of the shops had little red-and-white or green-and-white awnings. She noticed several wolf carvings at the various shops, too, that made her feel toasty and warm inside.

"I can't believe Maxine was one of your clients back in Daytona Beach," Roxie said. "We knew she was from Florida, but that was it. Talk about a small world."

"Yeah, she said she was moving to Colorado and needed her cats' shot and health records, but she never said exactly where in Colorado. And she certainly didn't say anything about the place being loaded with wolves. I used to drop in to her beach shop on occasion. I think if she and I hadn't been so busy, we might have run as wolves, but it never worked out."

"Well, if you join us here, I bet you can run with her. Is she a royal?" Kayla asked.

"She is. It's the only way she could have a shop on her own. No trouble with shifting any time of month," Gabrielle said.

Before they went inside the tea shop, Gabrielle had to pause to enjoy all the lights and the teapots and cups on display in the window. On the outside, garland and lights trimmed the big bow window and a small, lighted four-foot Christmas tree sat on a pedestal on either side. A seven-foot Christmas tree stood inside the window, decorated with blue, red, and gold balls and big red-and-gold-plaid bows. Christmas boxes beneath the tree were in the same color scheme with big bows. A shelf stood along one wall filled with every kind of tea imaginable.

It was so quaint and Victorian that Gabrielle loved it. She, Odette, and Zelda would go to a tea shop back home when the jaguars were in town and not chasing after bad guys. The shop was all very Victorian—no beach theme even though it was near the beach. The Silver Town tea shop was fun with all its decorations, including the little pastel-blue Victorian girl and boy figurines skiing or ice skating in the window, all a beautiful winter resort theme.

"Not only is the tea delicious, but the owner, Silva, makes the best peppermint hot chocolate," Kayla said.

"Let's go in, shall we?" Gabrielle said. "I'm getting hungry just thinking about it. Though I would love more of those snowball cookies Maxine had at her shop. They were so good."

"That's what's fun too about Silver Town. All the business owners try to have different items to offer to their customers so that we're not selling the same stuff or offering the same treats. It's an enticement to get people to drop in. That way, shoppers are encouraged to check out all our places," Kayla said. "It's a great marketing plan, and everyone is eager to abide by it because it works!"

"Oh, I agree." Gabrielle opened the door to the tea shop and heard a little jingle.

A woman wearing her dark hair swept up in a bun, a green velvet mini-dress trimmed in red fur with a black belt at the waist, high-heeled red boots with curled toes, and a green Santa hat trimmed in red fur hurried to greet them. "Welcome, ladies! I'm so glad to see you."

"Your shop is beautiful," Gabrielle said. "And I love your outfit."

"Thanks so much," the woman said.

"Silva, meet Gabrielle Lowell. Gabrielle, meet Silva. She is mated to Sam, the gray wolf who runs the Silver Town Tavern," Roxie said.

"Oh, we'll all be there tonight, won't we?" Gabrielle asked the sisters.

"Yeah, we sure will," Kayla said.

"I'll see you there, then. My shop closes before dinner and then I head over there to help Sam out." Silva directed them to a table for four and gave them menus. "You're the veterinarian Lelandi told us about."

Gabrielle smiled, not believing Lelandi would have told everyone in the pack about her.

"She is," Kayla said. "We are attempting to convince her she wants to be our vet."

"Is it working?" Silva asked.

Gabrielle chuckled.

"What can I do to help?" Silva asked.

Smiling, Gabrielle shook her head. "For now, we're just starving."

"We can certainly take care of that. I'll give you a few minutes to look over the menus."

They started to look over them, and Gabrielle said, "This looks good. Cranberry pecan chicken salad. And gingerbread linzer cookie with cinnamon apple butter. The Christmas tea looks good with Ceylon black tea, cinnamon, orange peel, and cloves."

"Hmm, I'm going to have a pumpkin bread and ham sandwich," Roxie said. "And the same with the cookie for me. I'll have the white tea."

Kayla pointed to the pumpkin bread and turkey. "That's the one for me. And the linzer cookie is my favorite dessert too. I'm going to have the eggnog tea."

Silva came back to take their orders and then brought their tea.

This was so much fun. Gabrielle had never expected to have a Christmas tea party during her stay. She would have to bring her friends here for more of the same. "Oh, Silva, do you know of anyone who had calico kittens and might be missing one?"

"No, but we got the alert from the pack leaders. Nicole sent a picture of Rosco protecting the kitten," Silva said.

"Yeah, he's not going to want to give her up." Gabrielle had seen it before. Fated fast friends.

"If I hear anything, I'll let you know. If you don't need anything else…" Silva said.

"We're good," Kayla said, and Silva went to wait on other customers.

"Rosco adores Jake Silver's cat, Mittens. I just hadn't expected him to get so territorial over a new kitten, as if he was protecting her because he knew she was so little and needed taking care of. Oh! That reminds me. We need to shop for cat supplies," Roxie said. "We don't have a litter box or anything."

"But what if she has a home and we have to give her up?" Kayla asked.

"Right, but in the meantime, she still needs a litter box."

"Okay, a litter box and litter and food, but no toys, collars, or sweaters for her, not until we learn if we can keep her," Kayla warned.

Gabrielle smiled.

Silva delivered their meals and then welcomed some new customers.

"We've never owned a cat before," Roxie said.

"I've had them. Dogs too. I adore all of them." Gabrielle didn't have any now, but over the years she'd had several dogs and cats. She began eating her sandwich. "This is delicious."

"Oh, mine is too," Kayla said.

Roxie loved hers also. "Then you can help us shop for the right things for Princess Buttercup, Gabrielle. Isn't it great having a vet along, Kayla?"

Kayla nodded.

Gabrielle smiled. They didn't need a vet to figure out what the kitten needed to have.

After they had their delightful lunch at the tea shop, they thanked Silva and then walked to the car and took a short drive to the grocery store to purchase the items for Princess Buttercup.

"We don't have a pet shop in Silver Town," Kayla explained, "so the grocery store carries a little of everything."

At the store, they found an enclosed litter box and cat litter, and despite what Kayla said about not buying the kitten any toys or anything, she picked out a pink rhinestone collar, and Roxie found a mouse-on-a-string toy, a scratch pad, and a string-on-a-wand toy. Each time, they asked Gabrielle if the items were safe for the kitten, amusing her, but she was glad they thought she could help.

Then with their packages in the trunk, they headed back to the ski lodge so Gabrielle could go to the slopes with Landon.

He smiled brightly at her when she reached the lobby with her packages. "Did you have a good time?" he asked as he glanced at his sisters with all the cat stuff.

"Princess Buttercup needs these things until we can find her home," Kayla said, defending their purchases. "I'll run these over to the house, Roxie."

"Okay," her sister said.

Gabrielle already missed Rosco. He would have hurried to greet her at the lodge, and she would have stopped and petted him. He was a big Saint Bernard and commanded attention when he wanted it, and Gabrielle couldn't deny him head pats and a hug. She thought it was cute that he had taken charge of the kitten and wanted to take care of her.

Roxie belatedly said to Landon, "We had a great time."

"The best," Gabrielle said. "The tea shop was a delight."

"And Gabrielle is a friend of Maxine Fox, the owner of the new boutique shop we were telling you about," Kayla told Landon. "Maxine is a former client of Gabrielle's, and she wants her to stay and be the vet for her two cats."

Landon smiled.

"Imagine my surprise to learn Maxine had ended up here, of all places," Gabrielle said.

"No better place to be for us wolves," Kayla said.

Roxie patted her shoulder. "Gabrielle will be nice and toasty warm on the slopes now, but if she gets cold anyway, do your best to keep her warm." Then she headed into the office.

"We'll see you later. Thanks for giving her up to us for lunch.

That was fun." Kayla was about to leave the lodge with all the cat packages, but Blake saw her and grabbed hold of the litter box to help her out.

"What is all this stuff?" Blake asked, frowning.

"For our new family member, for as long as she is with us," Kayla said.

Gabrielle sure hoped they could keep the kitten. "I'm going to take my clothes up to my room and get changed, and I'll meet you down here, Landon." She'd had the best time ever. She was really glad she'd gone shopping with Landon's sisters.

"Okay, I'll see you in a few minutes."

When she got to her room, she saw the Secret Santa present. What if it was for one of her friends? They would tell her to open it for them. She removed the Christmas wrapping and tore open the box. Inside was a cute stuffed jaguar.

Okay, so it had to be for her friends, she suspected. She texted them: The Secret Santa gift must be for you two. It's an adorable stuffed jaguar.

She took a picture and sent it to them.

Odette texted: No way.

Zelda texted: Uh-uh.

Gabrielle texted the two of them: Maybe one of you has a jaguar friend who's interested in you and you just didn't realize it. I've got to run. Talk to you later.

She set the jaguar on the table between the two beds where the sisters would be sleeping, but she realized that she didn't smell any sign that a jaguar had handled the box, card, or stuffed jaguar. She set the box, wrapping paper, and card on the table, too, so her friends could sort it out. They were JAG special agents after all. She was just a vet. What did she know?

———————

Landon went into the office to see Roxie, glad that she and Kayla had had a great time with Gabrielle and she'd had just as much fun. The cherry on top? Maxine had asked her to stay and be her vet. They couldn't have planned that better, even though they'd had nothing to do with it.

"We convinced her to buy several warm articles of clothing," Roxie said. "So we did our part. If she doesn't feel the cold, that will help. And we had a really nice time. We'll have a good time tonight at dinner too. We'll make sure she has fun. Oh, and she's a wolf with royal lineage. But she didn't seem to be bothered by the fact that we aren't. We told her Nicole could run with her. In fact, that would be one good thing about ending up with another she-wolf in the family who is a royal. Not that Nicole doesn't like to run with her brother and parents, too, but you know what I mean."

Landon understood, though he wondered how their nonroyal status would really affect Gabrielle's feelings about his family. Sure, it wouldn't matter if he didn't mate her, but if he did? "Nicole's parents don't get out that much to run, and her brother is often working."

"Right," Roxie said. "And Gabrielle said she liked seeing you, so that's good news."

He should have known his sisters would be trying to learn how Gabrielle felt about him—just in case there was a mating in the future. "I'm glad to hear it." *Really* glad. "I'd better go out into the lobby and wait for her." He didn't want to get caught talking to his sister about Gabrielle.

When he left the office, Gabrielle was coming down the stairs into the lobby looking like a sexy, huggable she-wolf that he truly wanted to court in an official way. She was all smiles, and that made him feel good.

"Are you warmer now?"

"Yeah. Thanks. I feel great. This is *so* much better. Even walking through the lobby with people coming and going from outside, bringing the cold air inside, I could get chilled."

"I'm glad the new clothes are keeping you warm. Let's go." He led her into their storage room, eager to spend the rest of the afternoon skiing with her.

Wearing their ski parkas, hats, and sunglasses, and with the rest of their ski gear in hand, they left the lodge, put on their skis, and headed for the ski lift. "What do you think of Silver Town now that you've had a chance to see the downtown area a bit?"

"It's a beautiful town. No beaches, though."

So they hadn't won her over yet. "But we have mountains, rivers, lakes, woods, and fall colors. You have to be here in the autumn. The spring, too. We do a lot of hiking when the snow is gone."

"That could be fun. It's so hot and humid in Florida, unless I'm walking along the beach, that I don't really want to do a lot of hiking."

"See there? Here, you can hike all year round. What about running as a wolf in your area?"

"It can be problematic. I will say that it's beautiful here. So many woods, so much land that you own that makes it feel safer to run as a wolf. Plus with the town being wolf-run, it's nice to have others to meet with and enjoy their company and share stuff about being shifters. I guess it would be really great to work with shifter families who bring in their pets to the animal clinic too."

"I agree. Doc Mitchell delivers wolf pups even, if you know what I mean."

Gabrielle's mouth gaped, right before they got on the ski lift. Maybe Landon shouldn't have mentioned that part of the vet's duties just yet.

CHAPTER 10

STILL PONDERING WHAT LANDON HAD TOLD HER ABOUT DELIVER-
ing wolf pups, Gabrielle got on the chairlift with him and began
the ride up the mountain. "You mean women shift and have their
babies as wolf pups?"

"Yeah."

"At the vet clinic?"

"Sometimes at the regular clinic. We have them isolated, and
most humans are shipped out of there after they're diagnosed with
whatever ails them, if they even come into the clinic, so we never
have any trouble with humans being there if that happens."

"Okay. Wow. I would never have considered being a vet and
delivering *lupus garou* pups."

"Yeah, a lot of the Silvers were delivered by Doc Mitchell. It's
just how things are done here because we can do it that way." Then
Landon switched topics. "Have you ever worked with horses,
cows? Big animals?"

"Yeah."

"Okay, good. We weren't sure if you'd only worked at a small-
animal clinic. Doc Mitchell works with both."

"I've done both." Gabrielle smiled. He was acting as though
she'd taken the job already. Her thoughts switched to Rosco and
the kitten. Where in the world had he found her? She just couldn't
stop thinking about it. "Can Rosco get into the lodge on his own?
Or would he?"

"Yeah, he can. The doors open and close enough, and with the
treat barrel around his neck, everyone knows he belongs at the
lodge. So even if the door wasn't open, someone would let him in.
Why do you ask?"

"I can't imagine him finding the kitten in the snow. So that makes me think he returned to the lodge and found her there somewhere, then brought her home to take care of her."

"We don't allow guests to have pets in their rooms. We did at one point at the lodge we owned in Vermont, but we had too much of a mess with it, and sometimes guests complained a prior guest had a pet that had left fleas behind. Some guests were allergic to dogs and cats. Sometimes a dog would bark in the room while the owners were out skiing. And we had trouble with some guests with pets not cleaning up after their dogs, so we had to change the status on allowing pets in the rooms to no pets at the lodge. When we came here, we decided not to allow pets at this lodge from the beginning."

"Does anyone mind that Rosco is in the lodge?"

"He's an avalanche rescue dog, besides being our beloved pet. Sure, we've had some guests ask why they can't bring a pet when they see Rosco there, but when we explain what he does and how he has saved lives, they drop the subject. I'm sure they understand that if they ever needed a rescue, he might be the one to save their lives."

"Good. The lodge wouldn't be the same without his friendly face greeting everyone."

They were coming to the top of the run and the end of their ski-lift ride and Gabrielle prepared to get off, needing all her concentration for this. Every time she did it, she worried she would fall and be in everyone's paths, causing a major pileup of skis, poles, and bodies. But she'd only had one fall in all the times she'd come up on the chairlift, though she'd had a couple of near spills last night when she was getting tired.

They had gone down the intermediate slopes a couple of times when suddenly Brando and his friends—she had never known their names—came up behind them on the slope as if they wanted to ski with them. She'd had no idea they had even skied before seeing Brando in the lodge. And she didn't like it when anyone crowded her on the slope. She was trying to concentrate hard on her form and not take a spill because they were making her nervous. They had to realize she was a newbie. What was Brando's problem, anyway? He only acted interested in her when *he* was on *vacation*? And only if he somehow ran into her?

That would make for a great relationship. *Not.*

When they reached the bottom of the slope, Brando skied up close to her and she didn't like it. His whole wolf posture said he was interested in her and he wasn't giving up. Why? Because she was with another wolf this time, and Brando had to prove to her that she should be more interested in him because she'd been out with him before? He had no idea if she and Landon had been an item for years.

"Hey, I'd like to get together with you. Dinner tonight? We could go for a wolf run. It's up to you," Brando said, as if he thought he really had a chance to see her further.

"I'm afraid my dance card is totally full. With my friends coming in, and Landon being so nice to teach me to ski and take me out for meals, swimming, and wolf runs and more, I just don't have any time for anything else." She smiled sweetly at Brando and hoped she didn't fall down in the middle of the brush-off. That would not have the right effect for what she was going for. Cool and collected.

Brando glanced at Landon and then gave him a conceited smile. "Gabrielle makes for a fun date."

Landon shook his head. "She's the kind of woman you don't ever let go of once you meet her. And you do everything in your power to show her a good time."

Gabrielle smiled brightly at Landon. He was being her hero. She'd never had two wolves act interested in her before. She hoped that wouldn't happen with other wolves here. But she realized none had really approached her, as if they had an unwritten rule that once a she-wolf was seeing a male wolf, the others waited to see if they'd have a chance later, if things didn't work out between the wolves.

Brando smiled. "Hey, so I'll see you around, Gabrielle. You've got my phone number, if you change your mind."

She wouldn't. But he skied off before she could say so, and his buddies hurried off after him.

"One good thing about a wolf pack that runs its own town is that we can tell wolves that don't behave to leave," Landon said.

Gabrielle smiled. "Brando is just being Brando. I swear he has shown more interest in me this time because I'm with a wolf than he did the first time I met him."

"Too much competition for him this time. He didn't have any when he saw you in Daytona Beach. Are you ready to go up on the slope again?"

"Yeah. I'm having a great time. And the clothes your sisters helped me pick out are just perfect for this weather. I'm feeling much better."

"I'm glad Maxine had just what you needed for skiing and braving the snowy cold."

All afternoon they skied, and Gabrielle was really enjoying herself, except for seeing Brando and his friends hitting the intermediate slopes right behind them several times during the late afternoon, annoying her.

"Are you sure you don't want me to say anything to them?" Landon asked her again before they made their way to the chairlift.

"No, they'll get tired of following us eventually." She didn't want to make an issue of it. Not because there were three of them against Landon and her and she worried Landon would get hurt. She knew the whole pack would be behind her and Landon, and the ski patrol would kick the men out of the resort completely. That was the thing about Brando and his friends being wolves. They had to realize that a pack would dictate their behavior. She just wasn't into confrontation. "I will probably make a complete fool of myself and fall down and ruin the moment, but can you kiss me?"

"Hell yeah, kissing you anytime makes my day." Landon skied beside her so that his skis were on the outside of her left ski, and he wrapped his arm around her and kissed her. She hoped that they were out of the way of anyone skiing. She should have thought of that beforehand. But he warmed her right up, and she realized Landon was the reason she was enjoying skiing so much. And… kissing. He was the perfect kissing partner whether they were in the pool or standing in the snow.

Brando and his friends skied past them. She wondered how often they skied and if they were new like her and that's why they were sticking to the blue slopes, but she suspected they weren't. Especially when she heard one of Brando's friends say, "Hey, we're hitting a diamond slope. You stay on the blues until closing if that floats your boat."

His friends didn't wait for him to say anything. They just skied off in the direction of the chairlift that would take them to the hardest diamond runs. Finally, Brando relented and went with his friends, glancing back at Gabrielle.

She said to Landon, "Come on. We have a couple more runs to go before they close."

"Blue or green?" he asked, skiing with her to the chairlift.

"Blue for this one." She was thrilled to be able to ski down with Landon without Brando and his friends tailing them.

But by the time they took the chairlift up for the last ride, she opted for the green slope. "I'm getting tired."

"No problem. It's better to take it easy on the way down and keep your confidence."

"That's what I figure." Plus she didn't want to injure herself.

She couldn't wait to go to the tavern tonight, and how would that work out if she sprained an ankle or broke a leg? She concentrated on her form all the way down the mountain, her legs really getting weary. When they reached the bottom—no spills, yay!—she and Landon headed for the lodge. They hadn't taken that many breaks from the cold this time, and she was delighted that her clothes were keeping her warm enough.

"What does everyone wear to the tavern?" She didn't want to be overdressed or underdressed.

"Anything from casual to dressy. No suits for the guys, normally, but anything is fine, really. We have Victorian Days in the fall and we dress up for that, though."

"Oh, that sounds like fun. Okay, so I'll meet you down in the lobby?" Gabrielle asked.

Landon hesitated to say as they put their skis and ski boots and poles in the storage room.

"Landon?" She thought he seemed to be a million miles away, and she hoped he wasn't still irritated about Brando and his friends stalking them on the slopes.

Landon was frowning. "Do you think someone has a cat and kittens in one of the rooms?"

Oh, that was what had stolen his attention. "Uh, yeah, possibly. When I was a kid, we had a trip planned and that's when our toy poodle suddenly had her puppies. My parents wouldn't leave her at their vet clinic's kennel. They were both vets and wanted to look after her and the puppies.

"My parents never made reservations for hotels in advance when we traveled, never knowing how long they would drive, and when we finally reached a town, they were having a big car convention and nearly everything was booked. The one place that wasn't didn't say one way or another if they allowed pets, at least I don't think so. But I was a kid. What did I know? Anyway, they sneaked her and the pups in, put them in the bathroom, and then my dad learned we had no bath towels. So he called to the front desk, and when a guy brought them to the door, he did it so quickly that we didn't have time to prepare. In a panic, we all scrambled to keep Taffy quiet, while Dad went to answer the door.

"She had jumped out of the bathtub carrying two pups with her that were still nursing and she woofed, but not loudly, thankfully. I don't know if her actions were her natural instinct to guard the room and her human family or to let an intruder know she was protecting her puppies."

Landon smiled.

"Anyway, I put the pups back on the blanket we had in the bathtub for Taffy, and Mom grabbed Taffy and hurried her back into the bathroom, while my dad was trying to keep the door only partially open so he could grab the towels and not let the clerk see the wild happenings in the room. We don't know if the clerk saw or heard anything. He probably did and was amused."

Landon laughed.

"It made me think that maybe someone sneaked a cat and her kittens into one of the rooms here, and one got loose somehow. And Roscoe heard her meowing. The guest didn't want to say anything about the missing kitten because he wasn't supposed to have them in the ski lodge in the first place."

"Well, it's easy enough for us to learn the truth since our wolf sense of smell is so good," Landon said. "We'll have to check for the scent of the cats in the lodge after dinner."

"Right. Okay, I'm heading up to my room and I'll be down as soon as I'm changed."

━━━━━━━━━

That night when Gabrielle came down to the lobby before Landon took her to the tavern, she was wearing a red sweater, a red-and-black-plaid vest, black snow boots and black leggings, a red scarf wrapped around her neck, and a black knit hat on her head, her blond hair loose about her shoulders. She had a black fleece jacket hanging over her arm and black gloves in her hand. She looked like the perfect present for Christmas—just for him.

He smiled, glad she was with him, and then took her out to the car he'd parked in the lodge's lot, rather than walk through the snow to the house. Once they were in the car, he drove her around to see all the Christmas lights on the homes and the shops in town.

"Oh, they are all beautiful. I bet you still will win the lighting competition though. Your place just lights up the dark mountains at night when the ski slopes are shut down. It's spectacular." Then she saw the snow wolf sculptures in front of the Silver Town Inn and began taking pictures with her phone. "Those are just beautiful. They must have made them while we were on the slopes. I don't remember seeing them at lunchtime. They've got to win."

"I'm sure they will. Others won't give up the competition, even if they're sure they're going to lose."

"That's the spirit."

After he showed her the snowmen others had made for the competition, he drove Gabrielle to the tavern, where everything was decorated in lights and evergreen garlands. Inside, they met up with Blake, Nicole, and his sisters who had already gotten a table. He was glad Roxie had made a reservation when they normally didn't when they went as a family. Silva had ensured a table was set aside just for Gabrielle and Landon's family, with a little card sitting in the center: *Wolff*.

Landon helped Gabrielle out of her jacket, then pulled his own off.

"See?" Roxie said. "Silva is doing her part to keep you here, Gabrielle."

Gabrielle smiled and she and Landon sat down next to each other. Everyone ordered a roast beef sandwich, and an appetizer of balsamic mushrooms. The ladies all wanted brandy Alexanders, the guys, beers.

Landon noticed right away that Doc Mitchell was sitting

with Doc Weber at one of the tables. When the veterinarian saw Gabrielle with the Wolff family, he waved at them and came over to say hello. Landon was glad he did, but hoped he wouldn't scare Gabrielle off.

"Hi. I'm Doc Mitchell. Everyone calls me that. And you must be the young lady that everyone says needs to take over my clinic." He smiled at her. "My clinic and ranch will be at a bargain basement price, but only for you. The market value for the land, ranch, and clinic is quite high."

She smiled back. "Gabrielle Lowell." She shook his hand. "But I work in a vet practice in Daytona Beach."

"A co-op, Lelandi says. They've got enough people to handle the patient load. They're not wolves, are they?" Doc asked.

"No, they aren't."

"Well, we...um, well, I desperately need someone to take over the clinic. Hell, at this rate I could be here for another forty years serving as the pack's vet, if I live that long and we don't get someone else in to replace me." Doc Mitchell sighed.

That had all to do with their longevity. That was one thing about having their own wolf-run town. They didn't have to worry about hiding their identity when they didn't age as fast as humans. Which could be a problem for Gabrielle at some time in the future at her current job.

Landon hoped Doc Mitchell wasn't coming on too strong though. Landon felt they needed to ease Gabrielle into the idea of moving here and taking over the clinic by showing her the fun they had as wolves and how many friends she would have.

"I have an excellent staff. They're eager to meet you," Doc Mitchell said.

Gabrielle sighed and smiled. "We're bringing Rosco in for his vaccinations tomorrow. I mean, Landon is, and I'm coming along to see your place and your clinic."

Landon smiled, grateful that she was going to at least check it out. He hoped when they arrived there the doc wouldn't try to pressure her into moving here. He was afraid it would have the opposite effect on her and put her off.

Doc Mitchell was a grizzled, white-haired gray wolf. He loved animals and didn't have any use for humans who didn't take care of their pets properly, but since they rarely had a human pet owner come through Silver Town and need to make an emergency stop at the vet clinic, that normally wasn't an issue. He didn't smile a whole lot, even though he was pleased with life in general. But he did smile at Gabrielle, as if she was the angel who would save him.

"I bet you have some stories to tell," the doc said.

Gabrielle smiled. "I do."

"I had to help out at a vet clinic in Green Valley once when their doctor got sick. Human, you know. And"—Doc chuckled— "well, I have some stories to tell too."

She laughed. "I bet you do."

Now Landon wanted to hear them! He was sure the rest of his family did too.

"Well, I'll see you tomorrow then."

"We have to bring in a kitten, too—a calico about eight weeks old. Have you seen any calico cats at the clinic that gave birth a couple of months ago?" Gabrielle asked.

"No, can't say that I have. I saw the message from the pack leaders, though." Doc rubbed his bearded chin. "But I'll certainly check her out for you."

"Thanks."

Landon was pleased Gabrielle had asked Doc the question about Princess Buttercup. He hadn't thought of it.

As soon as Doc shook Gabrielle's hand, he said to Landon and the others, "Make sure you convince her she needs to stay here."

Silva brought over their drinks and balsamic mushrooms. "We all have to convince her of that, Doc. Even you."

"I'll do my damnedest. I'll see you tomorrow, Gabrielle, Landon."

"See you then," Landon said.

When Doc Mitchell returned to the table to sit with Doc Weber, Silva said, "You should have seen me fighting with patrons about keeping this table reserved for you. Now, if you hear anyone mention it's because the new vet is here, I only had to say that to keep the others from fighting over the table."

Gabrielle shook her head. "When people learn I'm returning to Daytona Beach on Friday, they're going to be really disappointed." She took a sip of her brandy Alexander. "Oh, this is good."

"Thanks. I'm glad you like it. It's one of our most popular drinks," Silva said.

"I can see why," Gabrielle said.

Landon knew that Silva was making up a story about the reserved table. Sure, the tables were filled with wolves tonight, like they often were, but if Silva said a table was reserved, it was reserved. Her mate, Sam—a wolf who looked like a big bear, with his black beard and amber eyes and tall stature—wouldn't have allowed anyone to give Silva trouble. And the only ones who would have considered giving her trouble would have been rogue wolves passing through. Everyone in here tonight—except for Gabrielle—was local.

"I'll get your sandwiches. They should be ready by now." In a few minutes, Silva returned with their sandwiches and chips. "Enjoy."

"Thanks," everyone at their table said.

"Sorry about that, Gabrielle," Landon said. "You're just on vacation, and we want you to enjoy your time with us. We don't want you to feel that you're being pressured to stay and then you would feel rotten about being here."

"That is the sweetest thing anyone has ever said to me. I'm having a great time with you. I can understand how Doc Mitchell feels and the problem with replacing him with a wolf veterinarian." Gabrielle drank some more of her cocktail. "I sure do like this drink."

"They are good. The sandwich is great too," Roxie said.

"And the homemade vinegar potato chips." Nicole took another bite of one of hers.

"The mushroom appetizers too." Gabrielle took her first bite of the roast beef sandwich. "Oh, this is delightful."

"Their food is always great," Blake said. "At the lodge, we offer different fare, but when we want to be with only wolves, this is the place to be."

"This is wonderful." Gabrielle bit into one of her vinegar potato chips. "Hmm, this is so good." Then she sipped some more of her drink.

Christmas music was playing overhead and conversation and laughter filled the air.

"Maybe it's fate that you came to ski with us at this time," Nicole said.

"Fate?" Gabrielle asked.

"Yes. A few years ago, Doc Mitchell might not have wanted to give up his clinic."

"Have the pack leaders tried to find another vet?" Gabrielle asked.

"You know how it is with our kind. The only wolf veterinarians they might learn about would be with a pack, and getting them to leave their pack would be counterproductive," Blake said.

"Hmm, so it's fate then." Gabrielle smiled.

The way she smiled at Landon told him she didn't believe it. Not that he did either. They just got lucky that Gabrielle had arrived and they learned she was a vet. Especially if they could convince her to return here and give them a try.

"So, what vet stories do you have to tell us?" Kayla asked. "You can't leave us hanging like that."

Gabrielle laughed. "Okay, well, we had a case where one cat patient wouldn't tolerate any dogs when she came in to see the vet. We had to move all the dogs out of her sight so she would calm down."

Roxie laughed. "Here I thought *we* spoiled Rosco."

"That cat definitely ruled the roost." Gabrielle took a sip of her water. "You know, pet owners can get really upset if their pet suddenly is injured or sick in the middle of the night. I had to go in during the middle of the night to meet with one client like that who called to say he thought his pit bull had broken his leg. When the client arrived, he was stark naked."

Everyone laughed.

"Being what we are, I was just amused. Poor guy. I gave him some scrub pants and took the dog into surgery. Melvin, the dog, *had* broken his leg. I can only imagine what happens in the emergency room in a hospital for humans if they have a child who is needing emergency care in the middle of the night."

"That is too funny," Kayla said.

"It was. You probably have heard the old tale where someone's at a party and they want legal advice from a lawyer or medical advice from a doctor. Well, being a vet, I've had to field medical questions from our human clients too. I've had a number of clients remove their shirts to show me rashes or other ailments they have while I'm supposed to be seeing to the pets."

The group laughed.

"What do you say?" Kayla asked.

"Well, in one case, the client's dog had a heart murmur and the client said his was even worse. He pulled up his shirt and wanted me to listen to his heartbeat."

"Did you?" Kayla asked.

"I was reluctant at first, but he was insistent so I listened to his heart. He was right. His heart murmur was much worse than his dog's. But the human client was having heart surgery a few days later, and he called me afterward to tell me he was perfectly fine. I have to say I love my clients."

Landon was glad they'd met Gabrielle. She was so much fun.

"One client said her cat was going to the bathroom in her house even though she let her outside a couple of times a day. I asked her what kind of litter box and litter she used. Sometimes cats can be finicky. The client didn't have either. That was the problem. After she bought them, she called me and was thrilled to tell me it worked!" Gabrielle took another sip of her brandy Alexander. "I imagine you've had some funny cases of your own at the lodge."

"Oh, yeah, we've had several funny stories too," Blake said. "One time we had someone call the night manager and ask for a Jacuzzi in a room. The manager had to tell the person we didn't have Jacuzzis in the rooms. The guest was irritated and actually called to speak with one of us about the rude manager who refused to give her a Jacuzzi in her room."

Gabrielle laughed. "That's what I want."

"We've had the same thing with pillows," Kayla said. "One irate man said we didn't give him fluffy pillows like he had asked for. The clerk said the guest hadn't requested any fluffy pillows when he checked in or at any other time, but that he would make sure the maid staff knew to leave him some fluffy pillows the next time. Then there was the time we had someone complain bitterly because someone was making a lot of noise in the room next door, but they didn't tell us until they were checking out."

"Oh, I know how that is. I had that happen to me once where someone had their TV blaring half the night. It was loud enough to annoy humans, but for wolves? Even worse. I suspected he fell asleep through it, though I sure couldn't imagine how he could," Gabrielle said. "I finally had to call the front desk. They went to his room, woke the guy, and he turned off the TV. Blessed silence. I just wished I'd called them sooner. We were staying several days, and he pulled the same thing every night. I smelled alcohol on him when he was leaving his room one night when I was arriving at mine, and I suspected he was drinking himself to sleep every night."

"We've had a similar complaints—loud TV or a party going

on," Landon said, "but if a guest tells us about it, we'll take care of it right then and there. One time we had a pot-smoking party going on. It's legal in Colorado now, but we're still a nonsmoking lodge because wolves don't smoke and it's so pungent to us. We kicked the partygoers out and had to air out the room for three days before anyone could stand staying in it."

"Ugh," Gabrielle said.

"When we were in Vermont, we had an incensed woman who came to the lodge two months after she'd stayed there and said she'd left some items behind. She didn't remember who booked the room, what the room number was, and best of all, she didn't remember what she'd left behind," Blake said.

Everyone laughed. Landon was the one who'd had to calm the woman down.

"Yeah, and another time, this was at the lodge in Vermont when we allowed pets, a woman brought in about ten cats, unbeknownst to us, and left them in the room with a hundred-dollar bill and a note that said 'Take care of my cats, and I'll return in a week.' She never did return to take care of the cats, and we ended up having to find homes for them," Roxie said.

"Oh, that's awful," Gabrielle said.

"Yeah, we thought the same thing. Now we have another cat mystery case we're trying to unravel at this lodge," Landon said.

"Princess Buttercup," Roxie said. "I asked all the cleaning staff to smell for signs of a litter box or cats in any of the rooms when they start their cleaning tomorrow morning."

"Good." Landon had told the rest of the family what Gabrielle had suspected, and they figured she was right. "But I imagine guests who would sneak in the cat and kittens, if that's the case, would not ask for housekeeping. They'll have a Do Not Disturb sign posted on their door."

"True." Roxie ate another chip. "We could just check all rooms that have a Do Not Disturb sign on the door afterward if we don't find the cats. We could knock on the door, and if someone opens it, we'll be able to smell if cats are in the room."

"Well, hopefully, we'll find the cat before long and settle this," Landon said.

"You won't kick the family and the cat and kittens out in the snow, will you, if you find them staying in a room?" Gabrielle picked up another chip.

"No." Landon took a sip of his beer. "They can have the cat and kittens boarded at the vet's clinic. The owners can't keep the pets in a room. We have rules. But the guests are welcome to stay."

"Oh, good."

Roxie laughed. "We're animal lovers. We would make sure the cat and kittens were well taken care of."

"Rosco could take care of them," Kayla said. "But he has to be on call for avalanche searches. He normally loves to sleep next to the fire during the day at the lodge, loving to be near us and around people. I guess we could bring the kitten to the office and have them curl up in there so she'll be with us during the day at least and Rosco can check on her anytime he wants to, if he leaves her in the office."

"We can do that," Landon said. "I miss having him around the lodge. I just want to make sure the kitten doesn't get lost."

"I agree." Blake finished off his sandwich. "I can see us now, running all over the place looking for the kitten if it wandered off."

They all chuckled.

"A couple of people said they've heard of friends who thought someone had kittens in the pack, but none of the stories panned out," Nicole said. "I'm continuing to learn what I can."

"Good. I hope we can keep Princess Buttercup," Roxie said.

"So are the two of you going swimming again tonight?" Blake asked Landon and Gabrielle.

"Yeah," Landon said, then glanced at Gabrielle. "Right?"

"Yeah, we sure are." Gabrielle finished her sandwich. "This has been great. Thanks for dinner. I've had a ball."

"We have too," Kayla said. "You're so much fun to be with."

Gabrielle drank some of her water. "You are too."

She and Landon were about to leave when Brando and his friends unexpectedly showed up at the tavern. There were no tables for them at this point so they had to order their meals and drinks at the bar and stand in one corner, out of the path of everyone using the bathroom. It was the only spare spot to stand in. No one made a move to leave the tavern, and the way the wolves in the place were eyeing Brando and his cohorts, Gabrielle had the distinct impression they knew they'd been hassling Landon and her. Otherwise, he was sure someone would have offered them a table to sit at.

Which was confirmed when Silva came to the Wolff table and refilled their water glasses. "They're on the pack's shit-list."

Gabrielle frowned. "How—?"

"Several of the skiers on the slopes today that belong to our pack and some of the ski patrol are in here. They passed along the word that these guys have been giving the two of you grief. Lelandi and Darien were made aware of the situation, but Lelandi said as long as nothing gets out of hand, you can deal with it as you see fit. Of course, since she's the pack's psychologist and co-pack leader, everyone is going along with it. Though I can tell you right now, several of our pack members are ready to start crowding them and see how they like it."

Gabrielle smiled. "Wow, I never realized just how tight-knit pack members can be."

"You better believe it. We want good members, and wolves like them who try to start trouble with our own wolves certainly aren't going to be coddled." Silva smiled brightly. "If you want to have them tossed out on their ears, Sam will take care of it."

Gabrielle shook her head. "I think Landon and I are about ready to go swimming."

"Yeah, that's exactly what we're bound to do next." Landon got

Gabrielle's jacket and helped her into it, then grabbed his own and pulled it on. "Night, all. I'll see you later," Landon said to the rest of the family.

They looked like they weren't leaving just yet. He didn't blame them. They didn't have a swim date next. But they might be stubbornly holding onto the table too because of Brando and his friends needing one. But then Nicole and Blake walked out with them, and Landon thought they might have needed some special alone time together at their home.

"We're calling it a night," Blake said, his arm wrapped around Nicole's shoulders. "Though our sisters are staying for a while longer to hold onto our table so Brando and his friends don't get it. See you in the morning."

Landon laughed. "See you tomorrow."

After that, Landon and Gabrielle headed back in his car to the lodge. "Are you still going to wear the string bikini for me?"

Gabrielle smiled.

CHAPTER 11

WHEN THEY REACHED THE LODGE, GABRIELLE TOOK THE stairs up to her room and Landon changed in the storage room. He came out of the office and saw Gabrielle running to join him, still wearing her warm clothes. She was waving frantically at him, appearing out of breath. She must have gone up to her room and run back down the hall and then the stairs. She was definitely worried about something.

"What is it?" He was wearing his board shorts, sandals, and a shirt, and he hoped they didn't have some kind of trouble out of doors that was an emergency and needed to be taken care of right away, though she had been inside the whole time, so maybe not. Unless she'd seen something out her guest-room window that was cause for alarm.

"I heard kittens meowing in a room I passed on the way to mine. I just turned around and came back down here, figuring you could get a key to the room and check them out, if the guest isn't in the room."

"Okay, which room?" he asked, heading to the check-in counter.

"Two-oh-two."

Landon got the skeleton key. "I'll take care of this while you go to your room so you can get changed."

She glanced down at his bare legs.

He smiled and shrugged. "Always on call in this business, no matter what I'm in the middle of doing."

"Unless you're in the shower at home, right?" she asked as they headed up the carpeted stairs.

"Then one of my siblings could take care of it. At least I'm not soaking wet from having been in the pool already."

"True."

They reached the second floor and headed in the direction of Gabrielle's room. She was supposed to walk on past, but she whispered, "I'm a vet, and they might need looking after."

He nodded and figured she was just as curious as he was about the kittens and had to see them. He knocked on the door. "Management!"

No one answered.

Landon knocked again. He didn't hear anyone in the room talking, a TV going, shower running, or anything else that indicated someone was in the room. "Management!"

Still no answer. He unlocked the door and heard kittens meowing in the bathroom where the door was shut.

He called out "Management" one last time, just in case someone was in the bathroom and hadn't heard him.

Gabrielle held the door to the room open. No one was in the room, unless they were in the bathroom hiding. Landon knocked on the bathroom door. No one responded. He turned the door handle, expecting it to be locked, but the door opened with ease.

A calico momma cat with four kittens the same age as Princess Buttercup ran out of the bathroom, making their escape.

Gabrielle quickly closed the door to the room so the kittens and their mother wouldn't flee down the hall.

Landon got on his phone and contacted Blake. "We found the cat and kittens."

"At the pool?" Blake asked, since that was where Landon and Gabrielle were supposed to be.

"In a room close to Gabrielle's. She heard the kittens crying."

"Oh, okay. Good. What's the room number?" They could access the lodge computer with their own at their homes, thankfully, so Blake wouldn't have to run in to check on it.

Landon hoped he hadn't interrupted anything going on between his brother and Nicole, but he figured their sisters were still at the tavern and wouldn't be able to access the computer as quickly. "The room number is 202."

"Okay, I found the guest's name. Mr. Adam Jeffries checked out half an hour ago."

Landon shook his head. "Well, he left a calico cat and four kittens behind. Can you call him on his cell phone and ask if he left the cat and kittens behind on purpose? We don't want to find homes for them if he just made a mistake."

"I'll do that, Landon. What are we going to do with them in the meantime?" Blake asked.

"We'll have to have Roxie and Kayla take them home to Rosco. Hopefully, the momma cat will be all right with Rosco watching over all of them at home." Though not all cats were okay with dogs. The kitten didn't seem to know any better, but the momma cat might take exception.

They ended the call but Blake called Landon back a few minutes later while Gabrielle was checking the momma cat and kittens out, talking away to them as if they were her own babies. "Yeah, Blake."

"Mr. Jeffries won't answer his phone. I'm afraid since we all have the name Wolff on our caller ID, if he left the cats on purpose, he might not answer our calls. All except for—"

"Gabrielle." Landon glanced at her.

She looked up at Landon.

"Can you text me his number, and I'll see if Gabrielle can try calling him? Since she's a vet, she could learn if they've had their vaccinations if he doesn't intend to keep them," Landon said to Blake.

"I'll do it." Gabrielle was cuddling one of the kittens. She set it down with the other kittens, all of them rubbing up against both Landon's and her legs.

"Okay, she's going to give it a try," Landon said.

"I texted Roxie and Kayla and they're heading to the lodge,

disappointed they had to free up their table but excited to pick up the cats. They will meet you at the room. Did he have a carrier for them? Or do we need to get one from someone?" Blake asked.

"He has a cat carrier, litter, a litter box, cat food, and some toys."

"All right, sounds good. Roxie and Kayla will be up in a few minutes."

"Thanks, Blake. At least we know now where Princess Buttercup came from. Though not how she became separated from the others. We'll talk later." Landon ended the call with his brother and sent a text with the number of the guest to Gabrielle. At least Princess Buttercup had to be from this batch. He couldn't imagine more of them running loose in the lodge.

Gabrielle got out her phone and sat on the floor to let the kittens climb on her lap. "They're not wild at least." She was glad for that. They were adorable, and hopefully they could find homes with the wolf community. She called the number and an older man answered.

"Hello?" He sounded like he was in his vehicle and on Bluetooth from the noise in the background—tires slushing through snow, wind whipping about the vehicle, engine rumbling, and the heater blowing on high.

"Hi, I'm Gabrielle Lowell, a veterinarian in Silver Town"—not a lie since she was a vet and in Silver Town currently—"and I'm checking on the situation with the momma cat and kittens you left in your room at the ski lodge when you checked out. Room 202? Did you leave them behind on purpose or accidentally forget them?"

She noticed the room had been cleaned out. No clothes in the closet. All the dresser drawers were open and empty, all but one that was still closed. The bed was unmade, and two damp bath towels were lying on the floor of the bathroom. It looked like he'd left the cats there on purpose, unless he'd forgotten to check the bathroom for anything he might have left behind. But she doubted anyone would forget a passel of cats in the room when he wasn't supposed to have them there in the first place.

Since Mr. Jeffries didn't answer her, she continued, "I need to know if the cat and her kittens had their vaccinations and wellness checks. How old is the momma cat? How old are the kittens? Mr. Jeffries? We'll find good homes for them. We believe you lost one of your calico kittens earlier, and we have a good home for her already. But we need to know if you're returning for them so we don't find homes for them and have to give them back."

He was human. She suspected if he'd been a wolf, the pack leaders would have taken him to task.

"All"—he choked up—"of their records are in a drawer in the chest of drawers. I'm sorry. My wife and I just adopted a little boy. We didn't know it when we adopted him, but he's deathly allergic to cats. We've been on a trip in an enclosed car for a couple of days, and his condition has been worsening. We had to take him to the emergency room in Green Valley. We couldn't take the cats with us. Find good homes for them. Please. Ambrosia is the momma cat and she's two years old. The kittens are eight weeks old and weaned. I had all their shots taken care of. I…I'm sorry. We didn't have any choice. If it wasn't for our son, we would never have given them up."

"We'll take good care of them and find them good homes. I hope your son recovers quickly. How did the one kitten get away from you?" she asked.

"I opened the door to the hall to bring in a bag, and they all took off running. The escaped kitten ran down the stairs while I was catching the other kittens and Ambrosia. After I had put them back in the cat carrier, I went looking for the lost kitten but couldn't find her. We'd stopped late last night at the lodge, hoping to give our son some fresh air to breathe, but he's just really sick. This morning, we made the difficult choice to leave them as we took him to the emergency room."

"You should have told us," Gabrielle said to Mr. Jeffries, her voice stern.

Landon was sitting on the floor next to Gabrielle and playing with one of the kittens with a cat toy he had found in the cat carrier. All the other kittens began chasing after it. Gabrielle thought Landon was cute. The momma cat went over to the window, jumped onto the windowsill, and sat there to watch passersby. Great. Now if anyone saw the cat in the window, they would think it was okay to have pets here.

Roxie opened the door to the room and she and Kayla came inside. Their eyes widened and they both beamed at the sight of the kittens and their momma as Roxie quickly shut the door to keep any of them from escaping.

"Ohmigod, they're so adorable," Kayla said. "Can we keep all of them?"

"I left a couple hundred dollars with the shot records to pay for extra cleaning of the room and any fees you might incur for caring for them initially. I also left their food, cat litter, and the cat carrier so you could transport them safely," Mr. Jeffries said to Gabrielle. "What else can I do to rectify what I did?"

"Just don't do it again. And like I said, I hope your son gets better quickly. We'll take good care of the cat and her kittens," Gabrielle said.

With the network the pack had and because of how much everyone in the Wolff family loved them, Gabrielle knew the kittens and momma cat would find homes for Christmas.

Then Gabrielle and Mr. Jeffries ended the call and she explained to Landon and his sisters what had happened. She went to the one drawer that was still shut in the dresser and found the money and shot records Mr. Jeffries said he'd left behind.

"He left $200 for incidentals and their shot and health records." Gabrielle looked over the shot records, and it was as Mr. Jeffries said. The cats were all set.

At the window Kayla was petting the momma cat which was purring up a storm. "At least that means we get to keep Princess Buttercup. What about the rest of them?"

"We can send word to the pack about the rest needing adoption. A couple of pictures should do the trick. In the meantime, we'll take them to our house until they find homes," Landon said. "Several will love to have them, and we have enough to take care of as it is now. Not that we don't love pets, but I mean with managing the lodge and restaurant."

"True," Roxie said, cuddling one of the kittens, looking as though she didn't mean it.

She and Kayla gathered up the cat and kittens and put them in the carrier. Roxie took the cat carrier, Kayla grabbed the litter box, and Landon gathered up the money, vet records, cat food, and bagged cat litter.

"I'll meet you down in the lobby once you're dressed for the pool?" Landon asked Gabrielle.

"Yes. I'll be down shortly." She took off for her room while the others left with all the cats and their things. She was so glad they had resolved the business with Princess Buttercup and the Wolffs could keep her, and that the cats had all been taken care of, vet-wise.

CHAPTER 12

IN HER ROOM, GABRIELLE STRIPPED OUT OF HER WARM clothes and put on her string bikini and her cover-up, grabbed her beach towel and key card, and headed out the door. She was glad she'd heard the kittens meowing or it would have been tomorrow when they finally had maid service clean the vacated—or mostly vacated—room and learned of them.

She saw the same dark-haired woman she'd seen when Brando first sidetracked her, but the woman was in a rush to leave the lodge this time. Gabrielle still couldn't recall where she'd seen her before.

Gabrielle saw Landon stalking across the floor to meet up with her. "My sisters are elated you found the kittens and their mother. I think they would have felt bad if they couldn't have kept Princess Buttercup. Kayla texted me and said the momma cat and the kittens adore Rosco. He could have been a momma dog, it seems." He led Gabrielle to the pool.

She laughed. "I'm so glad we have that mystery resolved and that they can stay at the house with Rosco for now."

"Yeah, Blake and Nicole would have taken in the cats otherwise, but everything worked out just fine."

They put their things on a chaise lounge, and before he could get much of a look at her string bikini, Gabrielle dove into the pool.

"Hot damn," Landon said and jumped in after her. He soon caught up to her, even though she was planning to do laps first.

No matter how much she told herself not to panic, she couldn't swim fast enough away from him, and when he caught her leg and pulled her into his arms, she squealed in delight and laughed.

He kissed her. "You know we don't want you to leave at the end of your vacation. I don't want you to leave."

She wrapped her arms around him. "I have to tell you I'm really not good with change."

"You've met all of us so it's not like you won't already have friends here. Not to mention you already have a client here waiting for you to take over the practice. And a vet who also wants you to take over the practice."

She smiled. "I have to admit the idea of leaving the wolf pack to return to a place that doesn't have wolves doesn't appeal very much now, despite being the only home I've ever known. The notion of running and playing with wolves when I have time to do it sounds much better. And I think it's great you have so many pack functions to enjoy."

"Not to mention me, right?"

She laughed. "And your family. What…" She looked up at him. "What if I can't manage the clinic by myself? I've never had my own clinic." She did worry about that. She knew what she was doing but she was afraid she would get overwhelmed.

"You have a whole pack to help you out, and trained assistants. Believe me, you'll be fine."

With vet matters? She wasn't sure about that. "I've never lived anywhere else. It's hard to think of moving to somewhere out of state. What if I didn't like it after a while? I would have left my practice behind and someone would have taken over from me, so where would I be?"

"Here with us, a pack. Wolves. If it's something you're really interested in, you can do it. It won't take you long before you'll feel right at home. Believe me, it's not the same as living among humans. We had never lived anywhere else but Vermont before we moved here this past year. It didn't take us long to enjoy being with this wolf pack and part of a wolf-run town. If you need more time to think about it, you could return here next year to ski with your friends and see if you missed us enough that you want to stay for good then—if Doc Mitchell can hold out that long."

She smiled and kissed Landon on the cheek. "But Vermont is similar to Colorado in that you had snow and cold. And you still have your family with you." She paused. "I have to admit it's really nice having a pack to stick up for you if wolves, or humans, hassle you. I hadn't expected that. Humans would mind their own business for the most part, I figure. They wouldn't want to get involved and would let you deal with the trouble on your own. It's nice to think you have someone, or a lot of someones, to call on if you need help."

"Several of us are deputized, including me. So we even have the law behind us."

"That's good to know." She ran her hands over his perfectly muscled shoulders. "So what do you think? Do you like this bathing suit better than the other?"

"I love anything you wear." He kissed her on the nose. "But this one is really hot—because you make it really hot."

"Thank you."

He kissed her mouth and she hugged him close. This was what she was going to miss the most. Landon, his protectiveness, his helpfulness, his playfulness. And this—his hotness.

His arousal pressed against his board shorts and against her, and she welcomed his sexy touch. His mouth was hot on hers, seeking connection, the promise of more, and she parted her lips to give him openmouthed kisses. Then she inserted her tongue into his mouth and started stroking his. She wanted more. Wanted unconsummated but passionate foreplay in her bed tonight.

"Hmm, I guess we ought to get on with swimming before someone complains about our public display of affection, even though it seems quiet everywhere."

He sighed. "Yeah, I agree. Let's get our laps done. After that, we can plan our day out for tomorrow."

They swam back and forth, and like before, he kept pace with her. She enjoyed the companionship. She was used to always swimming alone, but this was really nice. After they finished their laps, they played in the water, diving under, capturing each other. This was just as fun as playing as wolves. They came up for air and hugged each other.

"You are so addictive," she said to him.

"So are you." He treaded water, his arms wrapped around her. "I was thinking that we could swim first thing in the morning, have breakfast at the bar and grill, then take Rosco in for his vaccinations. After that we would ski, have lunch, and build our snowmen in the afternoon instead of skiing. Then we could ski that night."

"Oh, that would be fun. I keep thinking how pretty the ski runs are at night with the lanterns lighting the way, the illumination reflecting off the snow."

"They are. You have to experience this while you're here."

"I do. Thanks." Of course her friends might have taken her up at night, but going with Landon was a different kind of fun—much more romantic. "Let's go up to my room and we can talk about it some more."

She had no intention of talking about anything more, but she wanted to continue kissing him and more in the privacy of her suite.

He looked a little surprised, then he smiled rather wolfishly, getting the gist of it. "Yeah, sure. You don't mind if I grab my clothes from the storage room first, do you?"

"No, we'll drop by there first."

After they got out of the pool, she dried off and pulled on her cover-up, and he dried himself off, pulled on his shirt, and wrapped his towel around his waist. They put on their shoes and headed for the lobby and the storage room.

She hoped she wasn't being presumptuous that he would want the same thing as she did. But she wanted to know what it would be like to be with him. She'd never taken it that far with a wolf before, and as long as they didn't consummate the relationship, they would be good. But she really wanted to be with Landon. He was like no other wolf she'd ever met. She felt comfortable around him, and when they were apart, she looked forward to being with him again. She fantasized about him in bed with her, something she'd never done with any wolf she'd met passing through Daytona Beach.

"You can get dressed in my room since my friends aren't here yet."

"Thanks, I appreciate it."

Of course she didn't want him to get dressed right away. She just had to get him to a nice private place to reveal her own plan. Forget thinking about tomorrow's planned activities.

After he grabbed his bag, they walked upstairs to the hallway and then headed to her room.

She glanced at 202, thinking about the cats they'd found.

"I'm glad we found the cats," he said, taking her hand and going to her room as if they were courting already.

"Yeah, me too."

When she reached the room, she used her security key card and opened the door. Then she pulled him into the room with her. She slipped her cover-up off and tossed it on a chair to the dining table while he closed the door. She kicked off her flip-flops and he removed his sandals.

He motioned to the bedroom. "Do you want me to change in there?"

"Um, we have to straighten some things out between us first." She headed into the bathroom to remove her string bikini.

He joined her in there and set his beach towel on the bathroom counter. "Do you need help?"

She smiled. "Sure. You can untie the strings since they can be difficult to untie when they're wet." Just a little bit. She really didn't have to untie all the strings either, but if he was game, then maybe he would be for all the rest too.

"This is just like untying the ribbons on a Christmas package." He untied the back of her bikini top, then ran his hands up her bare midriff to her breasts under her top and massaged.

She smiled. His warm hands on her chilly breasts felt marvelous. He pressed his body against her back, his mouth caressing the side of her neck with whisper-soft kisses.

Ohmigod, yes, this was just what she had wanted and he was doing everything right.

He moved his hands around to her back and untied the neck of her bikini and let it drop to the floor. Then his hands were on her breasts again, his mouth hot and sexy as he kissed her shoulders and back and then the side of her neck again. She felt so incredibly needy, and she'd never thought she would feel that way about a male wolf. He had all the right moves to get her pheromones raring to go. Not to mention she could smell his testosterone spiking, a total turn-on. His body moved deliciously against her backside, his arousal eager for her stroke.

This would be even better, she thought. That way there would be no sign that she and he had sex in her bed. Instead, they could wash the chlorine off their skin, have unconsummated sex in the shower, wash away the evidence, and dress. Now that was a plan. And that was the problem with their sensitive sense of smell. It was challenging to keep anything hidden when everyone around them also had such a keen sense of smell.

She slipped her hands down to her bikini bottoms and was going to just pull them off, skipping the ties. It was easier than having to tie the swimsuit bottoms back on if she wanted to wear them in the pool again. But Landon was eager to finish what he had started, and he moved his hands down to untie first the right side of her bikini bottoms. She kept them from slipping down her legs by closing her thighs around the crotch. Then he untied the other and she let the bikini bottoms fall to the floor.

"Should we shower first before we dress?" she asked.

"Yeah. That's a good idea." He was letting her set the pace, and she was glad he didn't just take charge and act like she was desperate to have him, even if she was.

She stripped off his damp T-shirt and tossed it on the floor, then pulled him against her to kiss him. "First, I don't... I haven't ever done this with another wolf."

"Taken a wolf into a bathroom after swimming to shower with him?" The devil sparkled in Landon's dark-brown eyes; his mouth curved upward.

"Anytime, bedroom, bathroom, anywhere."

"Me either."

She chuckled. Then she kissed him again and he cupped her buttocks with his hot hands, making her realize her tush was cold. But the front of her pressed against his body? Sizzling.

Their tongues slid over each other's in a mating dance, even if they weren't about to mate. This was more of a test to see just how compatible they could be in the affection department. And he was winning points all over the place.

He nuzzled her lips with his, his heart beating hard like hers was. They sucked on each other's lips and rubbed their scent over each other's bodies. It was really an innate wolf need, and it stirred things up even hotter between them.

He felt divine and she wanted to take this to her bed, but she didn't want the maid service to know she had been with Landon like this.

She slid her hands down his backside, cupping his wet board shorts clinging to his muscled gluteus maximus. And then she pressed him harder against her, wanting to feel the extent of his steel-rod erection. Beautiful. She slid her hands down the waistband of his board shorts and ran her hands over his bare buttocks. His felt as cold as hers. Now it was time to hit the shower.

She pulled off his board shorts, watched his arousal spring free with fascination, and gave him a hug and kiss, wanting to feel his bare skin against hers.

He ran his hands through her damp hair, kissing her right back. "You are irresistible."

"So are you." Which was a problem because she had to return to Daytona Beach *without* him.

She pulled away from him long enough to turn on the shower and got it just hot enough, and then she climbed into the bathtub and reached out her hand to him. She hoped the pulsating shower worked for him. It seemed to suit the romantic mood. "Join me, if you don't mind using coconut snowball shampoo and bodywash. I know you have shampoo samples for the lodge guests, but I always save them for my friends."

He smiled and took her hand and joined her in the bathtub. "Coconut snowball shampoo works for me. It sounds like a mixture of you being from Florida and me from the snow country."

She laughed. "It does."

Though Gabrielle realized if he smelled like coconut instead of chlorine when he went home tonight, his sisters would know something more was going on between Landon and her. Then again, anything he used would clue them in that he'd showered before he returned home.

It couldn't be helped. She wanted him. And she knew he wanted her.

She settled her arms around his neck, and he slid his hands down her sides until he reached her hips and pulled her snug against his body, the warm water sluicing down their skin. She thought of soaping up his glorious, muscled body first, but then they would have to clean up again, so she went right to kissing his mouth and rubbing her body against his hard erection and chest.

His mouth was hot on hers, languorous at first but then building up the passion, and she matched his actions move for move, totally in sync. He was a dream lover in the flesh.

His hands moved to her breasts and he massaged them before kissing her throat and licking the water off it. His tongue licking her skin tickled, and she smiled and kissed his forehead. His hands were warm and strong but gentle on her breasts. Then he moved one of his hands down between her legs and began to rub her clit. She moaned with delight.

She was already slick with need and he was making her even hotter and wetter. He tilted his head and kissed her mouth again, his tongue roaming over hers. She had to cling to his shoulders while his thumb was doing such sweet caresses to her nub. He leaned down and kissed her breasts.

Every one of his moves pushed her sexual buttons just right, and she felt as though she were a shooting star, high above in the heavens, reaching a place of no return. Her body craved his, wanted the sexual fulfillment of him penetrating her feminine sheath with his rigid erection.

The climax hit, and she shattered, falling from that high place of pure enjoyment. He muffled her cry with a well-placed kiss, and she kissed him back and then smiled up at him. She hadn't considered that he would make her cry out in pleasure when they were in the bathroom in her room at the lodge. The walls weren't all that thick!

Now it was his turn, and she hoped she could do as great a job on him as he had done on her. She slid her hands down his chest and reached out to touch his erection, but as soon as she took a firm hold and began to stroke him, he cupped her face and kissed her.

What a beautiful way to end the day.

Landon had no idea he would end up in Gabrielle's bathtub in her room, both of them pleasuring each other. He was kissing her mouth, trying to enjoy the sweet taste of her, but her stroking his cock was garnering most of his attention. She was soft in all the right places, her breasts and bottom, her mouth—so kissable.

He had envisioned being with her like this, pleasuring her… well, not quite like this—he was a wolf after all—but nothing he could imagine would have readied him to feel the heady experience of just how wonderful being with her could be. And unwrapping her like a Christmas present had made it all the more titillating for him.

Their tongues laved over each other's and he felt the end coming, but he wished it was just the beginning. He was too aware of the time quickly approaching when she would leave for home.

The shower water was still hot as it poured down over them, but she was making him even hotter as she continued to stroke him. And then he came with a groan of pleasure, and he kissed her again, feeling intoxicating delight that he wished he could experience with her forever.

The soap regimen began as she poured bodywash on her hands and started soaping him down and he did the same for her. He was in heaven. Silky skin made even silkier with every soapy stroke. Then she quit running it over his skin and leaned against him and began rubbing her body against his, beautiful breasts, mons, thighs. Man, she was a wild wolf. Using both his hands, he rubbed her silky shoulders and leaned down to kiss her. He didn't want this to be the first and last time they would enjoy each other's company like this. He didn't even want to leave her tonight. He wanted to see her for every minute of the day and night until she left. And he already knew he would miss her terribly when she was gone.

After kissing and cleaning each other up, every inch feeling like they were getting ready to have sex again, he began soaping up her hair. He felt like he was on an island paradise with the mermaid wolf of the sea as he leaned down and let her soap his hair also. Her fingers massaged his scalp in a loving way, and he felt like he could collapse in her bed and pull her into his arms and sleep the night away with her.

Then they rinsed off and grabbed towels and began drying each other off.

She smiled up at him. "Well, I hadn't expected to do this, just saying, but I'm glad we did."

"Yeah, I feel the same way."

She hung her towel up on the rack. "I'm worried the maid service would know you slept with me if you stayed—"

"It doesn't bother me."

"Hmm, what if they talked to the whole pack about it?"

"They won't tell. I promise." They would be fired if anyone in his employ did.

She sighed. "Well, I don't want you to go home tonight, but your sisters will know that you stayed with me and—"

Landon smiled. "They'll know I'm doing my job in trying to convince you that you belong here with us."

"With you."

He smiled even more. "Yeah, well, that much is true. I'll just text them and tell them I got hung up at the lodge and I'll see them tomorrow."

"Oh, I can hear all the conjecture now."

"My sisters would know something was up when they smelled your coconut fragrance on me."

"Yeah, I figured that too. Well, tell the family that you're too tired to take that walk through the snow tonight."

He laughed and texted Kayla: Staying at the lodge tonight. See you all in the morning.

Kayla texted back: We were about to send out a search party!

He smiled and texted: I'm good.

Hell, better than good. Walking-on-the-moon good.

Kayla texted: We'll bring a change of clothes for you first thing in the morning. Mum's the word, right?

Yes! Night!

Kayla texted: Night, you clever wolf, you.

Landon smiled since it had been all Gabrielle's idea for him to join her in her room. He set his phone on the bedside table.

"When my friends get here"—Gabrielle had finished blow-drying her hair and climbed under the covers naked—"we can't do this."

"We could make other arrangements." He climbed under the covers with her. "You could stay at my sisters' and my house. We have a guest room downstairs."

Gabrielle curled up against Landon. "Are the walls more solid?"

He chuckled and ran his hand through her silky, soft hair. "Nicole and Blake used it until their house was built. We couldn't hear them from the upstairs bedrooms. So yeah, it's more soundproof."

"My girlfriends will be shocked."

"Hey, they were the ones who haven't joined you yet."

She smiled and kissed Landon's chest and took a deep breath. "I sure was lucky for that."

Landon sure was too.

CHAPTER 13

IN THE MIDDLE OF THE NIGHT, GABRIELLE HAD WOKEN WITH A start when she felt a hot, sexy male body that she'd been curled up against. For an instant, she hadn't remembered that Landon was in bed with her. Then she recalled the shower and steamy shower play with him, and then more in bed. *Hmm.* Forget worrying about the maid service knowing what they had been up to. Landon certainly had stamina, and she didn't want to get up yet.

Cradled in his arms, she wanted to sleep in all the rest of the morning. She kissed his scruffy cheek. "Hey, do you want to skip swimming? We could get room service before we go to the animal clinic." She really didn't feel like going anywhere first thing this morning—not after such a wild night—and she was thoroughly enjoying Landon's company.

He smiled at her. "Yeah, let's do that." He kissed her. "Are you sure you want to skip swimming?"

She stretched out in bed and ran her hand over his head. "Yeah. Some things in life are more important than swimming, even."

"For a mermaid, that's saying a lot."

She chuckled. "Okay, so what's on the menu?"

"Besides you?"

She laughed. "We do have a vet's appointment and"—he opened his mouth to speak and she quickly silenced him—"you can't keep the doctor waiting."

He sighed dramatically. "How about a loaded potato-tot waffle—the bacon and waffle are the best."

"Hmm, okay, sounds good to me. I'm going to take a shower and get dressed." She left the bed and he ordered breakfast.

"Yeah, Minx, room service for Gabrielle. Two orders of the

potato-tot waffles and coffee. Uh, yeah, she's extra hungry," Landon said over the phone.

"Earl Grey tea for me." Smiling, Gabrielle started the water for her shower and climbed in. She kept telling herself she couldn't move away from Daytona Beach, but after a night with the wolf in her bed? She had to seriously start rethinking things.

======

While Gabrielle was in the shower, there was a knock on the door and Landon opened it to find Roxie with his change of clothes. She smiled brightly at him and handed the bag over. "You had a good night, I hope. We looked to see if the two of you were swimming this morning before the pool opened, but you must have skipped that part. Oh"—Roxie took a deep breath—"I love your new shampoo."

He smiled.

They heard the cart coming with breakfast. "Hmm, breakfast in bed. You're doing good. I better go before Gabrielle catches me talking about the two of you."

"Thanks, Roxie." Running his hand over his stubble, Landon hoped Roxie had put a shaving kit in his bag.

Then Roxie wished them both well and headed down the hall and the breakfast was served. When the waiter left, Landon said, "Breakfast is here."

Gabrielle came out of the bathroom wearing a towel. "I forgot to grab my clothes."

He smiled. "No problem there. I'll take a quick shower and join you for breakfast." He carried his bag into the bathroom and took a superfast shower, dried off, shaved, dressed, and joined her.

"Ohmigosh, this is so good." Gabrielle was sitting on the chair, wearing jeans, blue socks, and a bright-blue sweater featuring a Santa waterskiing in a swimming suit and Santa hat.

It suited her, but he was thinking she would look better in a shirt with a Colorado wolf wearing a Santa hat. He sat down at the table. "Yeah, this is my favorite breakfast dish."

"Who delivered your bag?"

"Roxie."

"And?" Gabrielle dunked a tea bag in a mug of hot water.

"She noticed the coconut shampoo right away." Landon took a bite of his waffle.

"I'm sure your family is getting a kick out of it."

"Yeah, they were watching for us to come down to swim in the pool."

Gabrielle laughed. "We'll just have to keep them guessing."

After they ate their breakfast, Landon picked up Rosco, the momma cat, and the kittens and loaded them into the car, then drove them and Gabrielle to the Silver Town Animal Clinic out in the countryside. He was hoping the clinic and Doc Mitchell's home would impress Gabrielle enough that she would want to move here and give Silver Town a chance. And him.

When they arrived at the clinic, little Christmas lights hung from the eaves and lit all the windows. The ranch house was glittering and a couple of trees were twinkling with lights too. Doc Mitchell hadn't decorated for Christmas last year when Landon brought Rosco for an annual checkup. Landon wondered if Doc had asked someone to hang up the lights before Gabrielle saw his place. It was much more festive that way and Landon was glad for it. If Gabrielle came back here to be their vet, the family would help decorate everything for her for the holidays.

Landon carried the full cat carrier inside, while Gabrielle brought Rosco in on a leash. A tree filled with dog, cat, and bird decorations, lights, and bows caught his eye. Gabrielle smiled at it, then Landon made introductions. "This is Doc Mitchell's receptionist, Tammy MacGregor. She's been here for a few months."

"Hi," Gabrielle said, shaking her hand.

"Please tell me you're taking over for Doc Mitchell," Tammy said, a pretty auburn-haired woman. Her green eyes were taking Gabrielle in as if she was assessing whether she would be her boss soon or not. "Doc Mitchell is so wanting to retire. And we would love to work for you."

Gabrielle smiled.

"Doc's currently giving a Jack Russell terrier a health exam and vaccinations. Hold on one moment, please." The phone rang and Tammy answered it. "Silver Town Animal Clinic, Tammy speaking, how may I help you?"

One of Doc Mitchell's technicians came out of the back and smiled broadly at Gabrielle. "I'm Callahan O'Rourke." He had nearly black hair a little on the shaggy side and brilliant blue eyes. He shook her hand. "And I'm single."

Gabrielle and Landon smiled, but Landon was standing close enough to her to tell anyone in the office she was with him.

"I'll tell Doc you're here." Callahan hurried into the exam room. Doc Mitchell finished the terrier's exam and came out to greet them, his client leaving with the dog. She smiled at Gabrielle and Landon and paid the receptionist at the counter for the vet services.

Doc Mitchell welcomed Gabrielle and Landon. "Come on in! I'll take care of Rosco, and Kayla called and told me about the cat and the rest of the kittens, so I'll check them over too. Then I have a clear schedule for an hour so I could show you around."

Landon was glad that Gabrielle could see the whole place without interruption. It really was beautiful out here.

"Rosco looks great," Doc Mitchell said, checking him over. "Teeth are good, good weight, he's fine." He gave the dog his shots.

Landon petted Rosco on the head. "Thanks, Doc."

"The cat's records say her name is Ambrosia. Let's take a look at her and her kittens," Doc said, looking over the shot and health records. "I can't believe anyone would abandon them like that."

He checked Ambrosia over, then Princess Buttercup and each of the other kittens. "They all look good. I saw the text from Lelandi saying they need homes. I'll take Ambrosia in. I lost my own calico a couple of years ago, so she'll be a nice little companion."

Gabrielle smiled. "Thank you."

"No problem at all. She's my Christmas present to me. Let me show you the rest of the clinic and the house. We can leave Rosco and his feline friends here." Callahan took Rosco and the cat and kittens behind the counter so they could visit with the staff for a while. "We all love Rosco."

"He's a lovable dog," Gabrielle said.

Landon was studying Gabrielle to see how she seemed to like the vet facilities. She was smiling and looked impressed. He was hoping that it would be enough. They walked out to the stables that could house ten horses. There were no horses there now, but sometimes Doc Mitchell provided vet care and boarding, mostly in the summer.

Then they went to the rehabilitation facility and Gabrielle's mouth fell open when she saw the wild animals Doc Mitchell was taking care of. A moose calf and a fawn were housed in the same place, lying down together on a bed of fresh straw. "Since both are herd animals and had been found abandoned, I put them together. They're best of friends."

The moose and fawn both got to their feet and greeted them.

"Aww, I can see that." Gabrielle petted each of the animals. "Landon never told me you take care of abandoned and injured wildlife too."

Landon had been afraid Gabrielle wouldn't want to take care of wildlife when she would also be responsible for delivering *lupus garou* offspring if the other doctors didn't, but Doc Mitchell winked at him, indicating he thought she was just fine with it. Landon was glad to see it.

Then Gabrielle finally turned her attention to two barn owls in an enclosure, and she talked to them. "What beautiful barn owls you are. Are they family?"

"Yeah, one of our people found them by themselves in the woods, not yet old enough to fly. The mother might have died. We don't know for sure. So one of our wolves brought them to me, and they've been growing to a healthy size ever since."

"They are adorable. And the bald eagle?" she asked.

"A hunter illegally shot her and broke her wing. She's well on the mend. As soon as we can release her back to the wild, we will."

"Oh, that's so good."

Landon smiled, so glad she was fine with the wild animals. Gabrielle would be perfect as their vet. She talked to the eagle after that, offering her words of encouragement, and then Doc escorted Landon and Gabrielle to the house.

Everything from the clinic to the stables and the rehab facility was beautifully maintained. Doc employed several wolves to make it happen. And when they went to the house, Gabrielle smiled.

"This is gorgeous," she said. "Charming. I love the woods surrounding the home and vet clinic, especially the woodsy, fresh out-of-doors fragrance. The big decks all around the ranch-style house would be great for parties. The view of the mountains is extraordinary. In Daytona Beach, I'm surrounded by houses and only have a view of the other homes in the development."

"For a wolf, this has to be better. A small lake is situated a short distance from the house on the property and is great for fishing and swimming in the summer." Doc let them into the house.

She marveled at the size of the kitchen, with granite countertops, warm oak cabinets, and marbled floor tile. The open living room had a large stone fireplace, Christmas stockings hanging from the mantel, and big windows showcasing the views of the mountains.

"This is just awe-inspiring," she said.

"You should see it in the fall when the leaves change colors. It's just beautiful," Landon said. "The quaking aspen are bright yellow against the backdrop of the Colorado blue spruce, the Douglas fir, and the bristlecone pines. Bigtooth maples are bold orange to red. You will enjoy the autumn fireworks display."

"In the spring, when the trees are covered in fresh green leaves," Doc said, "and in the summer, when the wildflowers like blue columbine, larkspur, phlox, and bluebells are in bloom, you would love it here."

"I would have to take up photography."

"It's worth it. And Jake Silver, who is our resident photographer, would give you lessons and tips on how to take beautiful pictures. We get a lot of deer, birds, an occasional cougar or bear—though with the wolves around, they usually stay clear." Doc took her through the house. "I've recently updated all the bathrooms and the kitchen in the hope of convincing a wolf vet to take over." He showed her the four bedrooms and three baths, the three-car garage, and the large patio with a firepit for parties.

When they came back inside, Doc Mitchell made them hot chocolate topped with whipped cream and started the gas fire in the fireplace. "I converted it from a wood-burning fireplace to gas because it's faster and cleaner."

"This is so nice," Gabrielle said.

They all sat down in the living room on the brown leather couches, and Gabrielle looked out the windows at the majestic view.

"So what do you think?" Doc asked.

"It's really beautiful. How much does the clinic, house, stables, and land cost?" She sounded like she was really considering the move.

Could they be that lucky?

Doc smiled. Landon practically held his breath, hoping Doc said the right thing that would convince her to stay. Hell, Landon was ready to help pay the cost of buying the place so she would say yes!

"For you, bargain basement. *Free*. Sarandon Silver, one of Darien's cousins, has moved to another city in Colorado to be with his mate and her family. He said if I find a wolf vet to take over the clinic, his home in Silver Town is mine. So if you want to take over the property and be our new vet, the place is yours, free of charge. I have no family to leave anything to at some future date, and if it means you'll join us here, I'm willing to give the whole kit and kaboodle to you."

Doc had made the offer and Landon wanted to pump his fist in victory, but what if giving her the place for free wasn't enough to convince Gabrielle to want to stay?

"Oh." Gabrielle looked astonished, her brow furrowed. "Are you sure that's what you want to do? Won't you need the money from the sale of the house and clinic if you're not earning an income any longer?"

Landon thought the world of Gabrielle for being concerned for Doc Mitchell.

Doc shook his head. "I have plenty in savings and investments to tide me over. I won't want for anything, and if I did, Lelandi would make sure I got it. The land was given to me years ago by Darien's family. They helped pay for the cost of the home, clinic, and stables while I got started. You've got a great staff to work with, and I'm always available to help you out if you need an old vet to come to your aid." Doc looked hopeful that she couldn't give up a deal like that.

———

Gabrielle couldn't believe it. She hadn't ever thought she would consider leaving Daytona Beach, but to be with a hot wolf she was coming to realize she couldn't live without?

She'd kept thinking someday the right wolf would come along in Florida and settle down with her there and they would live happily ever after. That didn't seem to be in the cards. But to move to Colorado and a totally different way of life? To have a clinic all her own that didn't cost her a cent? To be with a wolf pack? To continue to see Landon? Right now, she was feeling that she needed to enjoy all the days she had left with him before her time ran out—and she was feeling panicked about leaving him.

She wanted to continue to take pleasure in seeing his family and to meet more of the members of the wolf pack. She knew when she returned to Florida she would just be working her regular routine—swimming in the pool, taking walks along the beach by herself—and missing everything and everyone here and all the interesting things she could do with other wolves.

She had been trying to figure out if she could afford all this, once she sold her own home. She couldn't believe Doc Mitchell would give it all to her for free.

"Can we see the lake?" she asked Doc. She had to bite back the concern that the last time she saw a frozen lake she was in it, fighting for her and her parents' lives. Maybe seeing it in a different way, in a less menacing way, would help her to overcome her earlier trauma.

She did like the idea she would have someplace to swim when the weather cooperated. But also she could swim as a wolf in the lake with no worry about leaving fur behind to clog up the swimming pool filters.

"She loves to swim," Landon said.

"Yeah, you'll love this. Even as old as I am, I love to swim in it from time to time. I have a dock, a swimming platform, and a boathouse with a couple of canoes for when friends want to paddle with me. It's great in the spring, summer, and fall. And if you're into ice-skating, you can skate on it too."

She clenched her teeth. Going on ice wasn't something she was really excited about doing.

"I can teach you. My whole family knows how to ice-skate, so we could have a skating party," Landon said, "if you ever want to give it a try. It's safe this time of year. I wouldn't let you go on it if it wasn't safe."

"Don't ask me," Doc said. "I gave my ice skates up years ago. Oh, and the property includes 125 acres of forested land, and a river runs through it. Great fishing if you're into that."

"Oh, wow, 125 acres? That's…that's wonderful." She would have to be crazy not to jump at the chance to accept his offer. Ice-skating? She took a deep breath. Another challenge to help her get over her fear of a frozen lake. "I've never really gone fishing, but if I find someone who can teach me the ropes, I'd be willing to learn."

"You've got a fishing partner," Landon said, jumping in to be whatever she needed him to be.

She figured Landon would offer, even if he wasn't into it. She could imagine having Landon and his whole extended family out here to fish and have a barbecue. And others in the pack, too, once she got to know more of the wolves. She could even have her staff at the vet clinic over.

Ice-skating? She would have to give it a try. Oh, and sledding. Just so many winter sports she'd never tried. Now that she had some warmer clothes, and she could always invest in more, she would be warm enough to do them. But mostly because she'd have friends to do it with.

They all pulled on their parkas and hats and scarves, and Doc Mitchell walked them the short distance through the woods to the lake. It was a lot larger than Gabrielle thought it would be and she loved it. Like the house, the lake had striking, snow-covered mountain views. Majestic Colorado blue spruces reflected on the frozen water.

"We pull in the swimming platform and dock before the lake freezes."

"That's great." Gabrielle stood there looking at the lake, envisioning swimming in it—both as a wolf and as a human. Though she couldn't help but recall the accident, her parents' car headed for the lake and breaking through.

She quashed the memory and thought how this could be—so much fun. Boating, racing Landon and his family, having even more boats out here. This could definitely take the place of the beach that she had to share with lots of tourists. Here, she could enjoy the natural surroundings with lots of wolves instead. And this was much more attuned to their wolf nature.

This was the wildest, craziest, most life-altering decision she'd ever made, and she'd never thought she would make such a decision without really considering all the ramifications for some days at least, though she'd been thinking about it ever since Lelandi had proposed it.

But seeing the beauty of this place, Gabrielle sighed. It was just amazing. She couldn't imagine returning to Daytona Beach—where she might run into a single male wolf only once in a blue moon—when she would have a whole pack of wolves to play with here. And she'd never thought the clinic and the house would be this beautiful. She loved the beach back home, but this was amazing, too, and the idea she could run as a wolf much more safely anytime she wanted really appealed. Being with her kind would make all the difference in the world. She hoped she wouldn't regret it, but how could she turn down such a remarkable offer?

"When would you like me to start?"

"As soon as you can take it over, I would be grateful. I can stay here for as long as you like and work with you until you feel comfortable running the clinic on your own. And I would still be available anytime you need me," Doc Mitchell said.

"I will need to give two weeks' notice to my current co-op. And I need to get a Colorado state license to practice as a vet here." She didn't want to put her co-op in a bind, though she figured they wouldn't miss her since there were so many working there already.

Being here was a different story. Doc Mitchell didn't have anyone else to help him out.

Doc shook her hand. "Two weeks it is, and I'll continue to work with you as long as you need me. As far as the state license goes, we'll see if there's any way to expedite it. I'm on the board."

"Oh, wonderful. I can't wait." She smiled brightly, realizing that she had been feeling much more reluctant about returning home than she had been about staying here. It would be a big move, but she really felt that this was what she was meant to do. Not to just take care of pets in Daytona Beach, but to attend to a wolf pack, their pets, and the wild animals that also needed her help.

"Do you need any of the furniture I have?" Doc asked.

"No, thanks. I'll start from scratch and make this my new home."

"I'll start moving stuff to the other house then, and get this one cleaned up for when you are ready to move here. If you have the time, I'll take you around to meet all the staff I have here today." Doc Mitchell motioned to the clinic.

"Yeah, sure." She hoped they wouldn't feel bad that their boss was leaving, and she hoped they would all be a good fit.

But everyone there today had been practically holding their breath, she thought, and now that Doc told them Gabrielle would be coming to stay there for good in a couple of weeks, they were thrilled.

"Did Doc tell you that we have potluck Fridays?" Tammy asked at the receptionist desk.

"No, but that works for me."

Doc smiled. "Remember, she might want to do things differently from me."

"Whatever you're doing, if everyone loves it, we're going to keep doing it." There was nothing worse than someone changing a good thing. She thought Doc appeared much less tired in the few minutes since she had said she would take over the clinic. No one needed her that much back home.

Doc glanced at the clinic clock and sighed. "I've got another appointment in a couple of minutes."

But when the woman came in with her pug, Gabrielle stayed to watch Doc do the exam and vaccinations, and the lady was grateful to learn Doc Mitchell had his replacement. Gabrielle couldn't officially say she was working there as a vet until she received her Colorado state license.

"We're so glad you'll be joining us," the woman said.

"Thank you. I look forward to it."

"Are you ready to get some skiing in?" Landon asked Gabrielle, as if he was worried Doc would keep her there the rest of the day to help out and get acclimated to the way his clinic operated.

"Yeah, I am. And thanks, Doc," Gabrielle said.

"I should be thanking you." Then he turned to Landon and said, "Take good care of Rosco, the kittens, and our new vet in the meantime."

"You know it." Then they said their goodbyes and Landon put Rosco and the cat carrier in the car. "I can't tell you how glad I am that you're joining us for good. But I'm curious. When we were at the clinic, what made you decide to take it over?"

"When I saw the baby moose and the fawn, the baby owls, and the injured eagle. My clinic wouldn't take care of injured wild animals like that, for one thing. For another, we wouldn't even have them out there. Of course, you and your family and the pack-run town were really big considerations. But seeing the rehab center made me feel like it was all the more important that I take this job."

On the drive back to the lodge, Landon said, "And then getting the place for free helped."

"Before I knew Doc Mitchell was giving the whole business to me for free, I was ready to say yes. I was just hoping I could afford it, once I sold my own place and used some of the savings I have. I still can't believe he isn't selling it to me. I hope he doesn't regret the decision, but I can always pay him something for it in compensation if he needs the money later. Besides, returning here to stay for good has become a necessity for me. There has never been a wolf in my life like you, someone who could turn my whole world inside out and make me want to ditch Florida for the unknown."

"You won't regret it. I promise you."

She smiled at him. "You are the best. I need to tell my co-op I'm leaving, and I need to get the paperwork together concerning my qualifications to meet those required by the Colorado board for licensing."

"Okay, do whatever you need to do, and I'll help you with whatever I can. Living here in Silver Town was the best decision my family ever made. Any reservations we might have had were gone once we settled here."

Gabrielle got a call on her cell phone and smiled. "Lelandi."

"It doesn't take long for good news—or bad—to spread in a pack." Landon smiled at her.

"That's something I will have to get used to." She answered her phone.

"Hi, Gabrielle? This is Lelandi. Doc Mitchell told us the good news. He might not have told you, but we help move our valued new members here, at no cost to you. Everyone will help."

"Oh, thanks. I have a lot of furniture I'll be leaving with the house, or selling there. It suits a Florida home, not a woodsy Colorado mountain home. But thanks. The idea of moving is a nightmare though."

"We'll help you every step of the way."

"Thank you. I really appreciate that." Gabrielle was surprised. When she and Lelandi ended the call, Gabrielle called the co-op and gave them her notice, though she would also send written notice as soon as she could email it.

"You can't," their office manager said, sounding flustered and upset.

Of course Gabrielle could. She only had to give two weeks' notice, per the co-op's agreement, but she was surprised to hear their office manager's concern. "What's wrong?"

"One of the vet's licenses has been suspended as of today. It's Dr. Clarkston. He was charged with drug abuse. But it wasn't just that. He had eight prior DUI convictions and several other incidents that prompted this. Another vet was in a car accident and broke his leg. He won't be able to return to work for about six weeks. Can you believe it? And then you want to go? That leaves us with only one full-time vet. Can you please wait until we hire two vets to replace you and the other doctor? Otherwise we'll be really short on help."

"Let's see how it goes. If you can't find a couple of vets before I'm scheduled to leave, I'll stay there until you do." She still needed to sell her house and get a vet's license in Colorado, so she didn't mind helping her co-op and her clients a little longer.

Landon was frowning at her as he pulled into the lodge's parking lot.

"Okay, thank you. It's just been such an awful upheaval right now. We've got the part-time vets trying to take care of all the clients the other two vets and you were responsible for," the manager said.

"The vet here has no one to cover for him."

"Oh, okay. Is the vet clinic in Colorado where you are skiing? If so, you'll have to get your state license for there, won't you?"

"Yes, I will."

"Okay, well, I already put out the word we were looking to add one more vet on the staff at the clinic, so I'll send out the notice we're looking for two now. Thanks so much, Dr. Lowell. We'll see you first thing next week then."

"Right." *Ugh.* Gabrielle finished the call and turned to Landon. "Okay, so we've lost two other vets at the clinic, one permanently." She explained what had happened as she got out of the car. "I might have to stay a little longer than planned. They may need to hire another vet technician to help out until the injured vet returns to work."

"That's not good." Landon held onto the carrier of kittens and walked Gabrielle and Rosco into the lodge. "What can I do to help you get everything done?"

She smiled. "Don't worry, I'm coming here. I do need to get my vet's license in Colorado. I have all the credentials: I graduated from an approved school of veterinary medicine and I've passed the computerized national examination. I just need to send all the information to them—complete the application, indicate where I've been practicing and give them my license number, and send them the fee. I'll do that today. I have all my documents saved on the cloud."

"Okay, good. If there's anything you need me to do, don't hesitate to ask."

"Lelandi said that some of the wolf pack members will help me move."

Landon laughed. "I haven't heard them offer to move *anyone* else here. When we came here, we were on our own. They really want you here. But I'll be there to help as soon as you need me to."

Gabrielle unhooked the leash from Rosco's collar in the lodge, and he greeted Roxie and Kayla, who were both coming out to greet Gabrielle.

They both gave Rosco a hug first because he was in the way. Then gave Gabrielle hugs, and she knew the whole pack had already heard that she was going to be their new vet. She felt welcomed like she'd never felt before in her life. She knew she was doing the right thing.

She explained to the sisters about work, and then repeated the news to Blake who hurried to meet up with them in the lobby and give her a hug.

"What can we do to help?" Blake asked, the sisters looking on eagerly to learn what they could do too.

Kayla took the carrier of kittens from Landon.

"Nothing for now. I just want to have fun on my vacation. Before long, I'll have to leave here and be back at work in Daytona Beach." Gabrielle took Landon's hand. "We're going skiing before lunchtime, if you can spare him for a little while longer."

"He's all yours," Kayla said, smiling. "I'm heading to the house with the kittens. I'm thrilled Doc Mitchell already posted on Facebook about adopting Ambrosia."

Gabrielle was glad that he had taken the momma cat in.

Everyone agreed.

"Yeah, and we can't be any gladder you're returning to us, Gabrielle," Roxie said.

"Thanks. I'm looking forward to it." Then Gabrielle and Landon took off for the ski slopes. She was glad she would be part of a wolf pack. And some year in the distant future, she wouldn't be hoping to find a wolf to replace her at the clinic. She would be working with another wolf to train him or her to be her partner at the clinic eventually.

"Since I've been here, I haven't seen Doc any happier than he is now. I suspect he'll be celebrating at the tavern tonight," Landon said. "Speaking of celebrating, we'll be doing that at our house too."

"That will be fun." When she became a vet, there hadn't been anyone to congratulate her. Of course the three vets and the staff had welcomed her to the co-op, but there hadn't been any big celebration. This was so different from the way it was back in Florida.

Everyone who was a *lupus garou* who had gotten word about her becoming their new vet had to stop them and congratulate her as she and Landon headed for the chairlift through the snow. She felt like a celebrity. No one paid any attention to her back home. It was almost embarrassing to have so many people excited about her moving there and becoming part of the pack, but she knew they were really happy to have her and it wasn't all put on.

She and Landon finally made it to the chairlift line.

"That's only a few members of the pack. I'm sure you'll find everyone welcoming," Landon said, smiling at her.

"It's great to feel that way."

"It is. We had a mixed reception. Some were concerned that our business would take away business from the rest of the town, and then Blake snagged Nicole's attention when she dropped into the lodge, which meant no bachelor males in the pack had a chance with her. With you, it's different. You fill a need that helps everyone out."

Gabrielle and Landon had been so busy talking, and she'd been so busy thinking about what she had to do next, that she wasn't paying attention to the chair when they got ready to ride it up. It slammed into them from behind and she bounced off. Landon jumped off and joined her, and they moved out of the way of the chairs.

Everyone continued to move off on the chairs until Gabrielle and Landon reached the beginning of the line and the next couple motioned for them to go ahead of them. Man, that was embarrassing. From feeling on top of the world to nearly falling on her face. She laughed at herself when they got on the chair this time, and she held on tight.

He smiled at her. "It happens all the time."

"Yeah, but it's the first time for me. That was scary."

CHAPTER 14

AFTER SKIING THE REST OF THE MORNING AND HAVING LUNCH, Landon gave Gabrielle a hug and kiss in the lobby. "I never tell anybody my dreams, but I just have to tell you mine, considering how I met you. I dreamed a beautiful she-wolf would swim into my life. Since I run a ski lodge, I figured it was just nonsense, like most dreams are."

"Was this before or after you saw me swimming in the pool when I wasn't supposed to be?" She arched a brow.

"Before. About a week before, actually. The she-wolf was diving off the swimming platform at Doc Mitchell's lake. Like I said, I didn't put much stock in it. Not even after I saw you swimming in the pool and learned you were a wolf and a vet. It just came back to me all at once when we saw the swimming platform at Doc's lake. And immediately I thought of you swimming there."

"What was I wearing? In your dream?"

He smiled.

"Not the string bikini."

"Nope. It was summer and you weren't wearing anything at all. But your hair was definitely blond."

"A naked woman. Were you swimming with me?"

"I was just about to."

She laughed. "In the raw or...?"

"In the raw. Of course." He was already thinking about making his dream come true next summer.

She smiled and kissed him. "I'm going to run up to my room and get some paperwork for the licensing done, and I need to officially send off a letter that I'm giving notice. Do you have a computer I can use to type it up? I can email my resignation to the vet clinic. As to the Colorado board, I need to mail my paperwork to them, so if we can print it all out, I can send it in."

"We sure do and then we'll drive the car over to the house since I left it parked at the lodge. And we'll make snowmen."

"Sounds like a winning plan to me. I'll let you know as soon as I'm headed down."

"All right. I'll help my brother and sisters out in the meantime."

"I'm sure they will appreciate that." Then she headed for the stairs to her floor.

Landon walked into the office and his sisters both smiled at him.

"So," Roxie said, "Brother, it looks like your dreams might come true."

"I'm hoping that some other wolf doesn't convince her he's the one for her instead once she moves here."

"No way. Just keep doing what you've been doing. It's been working so far," Kayla said. "Snowman building next, right?"

"Yes." He told his sisters what Gabrielle was doing.

"Oh, I hadn't even thought of the issue of Gabrielle having to get a state license. Doc Mitchell is thrilled about her taking over," Roxie said. "He sent a message to everyone in the pack."

"I heard about the text message but didn't have time to check it. I think Gabrielle will be really happy once she's able to move and get settled in," Landon said.

"You know Doc Mitchell will be celebrating tonight," Kayla said.

"I think a lot of people will be," Landon said.

Blake joined the siblings in the office. "You just have to make sure she doesn't see all the other bachelor males."

Landon laughed. "What do I need to do to earn my keep here?"

"Everything's covered for now," Blake said. "Let's head out."

"Go ahead," Landon gestured. "I'll wait for Gabrielle."

Gabrielle felt lighthearted about this whole situation. Maybe in a few days, she would be more anxious, but right now, she was excited. She finished the application for the state license and then she texted Landon: I'm on my way down.

Landon replied: See you in a minute. My sisters and brother already headed over to the house with Rosco.

Gabrielle hurried down the stairs and across the lobby. When she reached the office, Landon set her up on the computer and she typed up her letter. She printed it off and then sent the email to her vet office, giving them official notice. After that was done, she printed off all her documents for the Colorado state board and one of the Wolffs' staff said he would take it to the post office for her and mail it right away.

Then Landon and Gabrielle drove over to the house, saw Nicole with his sisters and brother all working on a snowman, and parked in the garage.

"This is going to be so much fun," Gabrielle said.

"It is. We haven't built a snowman as a family in forever. And Nicole said she hasn't either."

Ready for some serious snowman work, Gabrielle and Landon joined the others and she asked the family, "So what are we making, then?"

Using a snow shovel, Roxie was filling a bucket with snow. "We're making a giant snowman. We were going to make a snowman family, but there are getting to be too many of us and so many of the pack family members do that already. So we decided on a giant snowman."

"That sounds like fun," Gabrielle said.

The others had started the base of the snowman and Gabrielle and Landon jumped in to help.

After building the smooth base, they took a hot chocolate and Christmas sugar cookie break.

"This has been so enjoyable." Gabrielle eyed the growing snowman. "I imagined a small snowman, nothing like this."

"We haven't ever made one this big before, either," Roxie said. "This has been great."

They brought out a couple of ladders and began making the middle section of the snowman. But sometime during the work, they ended up in a snowball fight. Landon pelted Blake, who had to get him back. Nicole threw a snowball at Roxie, and Gabrielle threw one at Landon. Everyone ran to the deeper snow where they could gather their balls of snow.

Snowballs were flying fast after that, and Gabrielle laughed so hard her stomach hurt. Kayla threw them at everyone as fast as she could gather a snowball. Nicole made a pile of them first. Gabrielle got hit more than anyone since she was still laughing so much.

After a few more snowball tosses, they were back to building more of the middle section of the snowman.

"Will others try to copy you?" Gabrielle asked as they loaded another few buckets of snow on a wooden sled where the snow was still deep and pulled it to the cleared-out section where they were building the snowman.

"No. That's one thing about a wolf pack: we're family. No one tries to create the same kind of wolf snow sculptures like the Victorian Inn's ones, and no one will copy us," Landon said.

"That's good. After all the work we've put into this, it would be awful to hear someone else did the same thing," Gabrielle said.

All afternoon they worked on it until they had the base and middle part of the body done. The sun was beginning to set and colored the snow pink and yellow. It was beautiful. Gabrielle had never considered how pretty a sunset reflecting off the snow could be.

"Let's have supper," Landon said. "Then Gabrielle and I are going night skiing."

"We can finish the snowman tomorrow afternoon," Roxie said.

"Yes, I agree," Blake said. "It's supposed to be cloudy and snow all day, no sun, and the weather will continue to be freezing so that will help to preserve our snowman."

Everyone headed inside, banging snow off their gloves and boots at the door.

"So we're having steaks and mashed potatoes and broccoli," Roxie said, "to celebrate Gabrielle's becoming our vet. No spirits for you two, though, if you're going skiing."

They chuckled.

Rosco greeted them all, and even the kittens ran out to see them, getting as many pets and hugs as Rosco. Then everyone began getting ready to make dinner, set the table, and Nicole even set out candles and lit them. She was glad Ambrosia was now at home with Doc Mitchell.

Instead of the rest of the family having wine, Nicole and Gabrielle made wassail and the whole family toasted to their new pack member and future veterinarian.

"We are so thrilled you're joining us," Roxie said. "Once a month, Nicole and Kayla and I take a shopping trip to Denver. We would love to have you come with us."

"If I can arrange it, I sure will." Gabrielle was thrilled that not only had she found a pack to be with, but she had also found some real girlfriends. And girlfriends were always important.

After dinner, Landon and Gabrielle returned to the lodge. They grabbed their skis and headed out, the night sky filled with stars but no moon. Gabrielle was having a wonderful time, not caring if she could run as a wolf with her friends or not, the brisk wind blowing around them as she rode the chairlift with Landon. The clothes she had bought at the Silver Town Boutique felt nice and warm—much warmer than what she had been wearing—and Landon's body pressed against hers helped too. She loved seeing the lights all along the slopes, lighting the skiers' way.

One man took a bad spill on the slope below the chairlift and Gabrielle cringed, thinking that could have been her. Luckily, he got up fine. She and Landon reached the top, and she managed to get off the chair without mishap. They skied down the slope in the dark of night, and when they reached the bottom, she was eager to get on the chairlift again.

"You are doing great," Landon said.

"Oh, to think I will be able to do this lots—after work, of course—and someday even make it to the expert slopes. This is so much fun skiing at night. But"—she paused dramatically—"we still have to swim at night."

"Guaranteed."

They went down the intermediate slope again and again. But when they were on their fourth run down, they saw someone had taken a spill down below them and hadn't gotten up yet. A lone skier.

"Are you hurt?" Landon called out to the skier before he reached him.

"Yeah, and I'm fighting the shift."

Gabrielle made her way down slowly so she wouldn't race past the injured skier or run into him and Landon, who was already checking him out. She heard that the skier was a wolf and was fighting the change because of the injury. He had to be a royal if he could shift while the new moon was out.

Landon called the ski patrol. "We need a sled for an injured skier, one of ours. He appears to have—"

"Broken his left femur," Gabrielle said, crouching down to check on the skier.

The man was trying to pull off his gloves. She held his hand. "Can you hold on? Just for a few minutes? We'll get you down to the first aid hut as soon as we can."

He smiled up at her while Landon was setting the injured skier's skis up in an X to warn others to stay clear. A couple of people slowed down to offer help.

"We've got it. A sled is on its way," Landon said, and as they skied on past, she smelled they were human.

Did Landon know the injured man? He was probably one of the pack members. Then again maybe not, just like she wasn't. Then she smiled a little. That would soon change.

She held the man's hand and smiled down at him. "The sled is coming. Do you hear it?"

"Yes," the injured skier gritted out.

"Do you have a ski partner, someone with you at the resort we can notify?" Landon asked.

"My friend, but he was ahead of me. So he has to be down at the bottom by now."

"All right. Give me his number, and I'll let you talk to him." Landon had his phone out.

The man gave Landon the number and he called it for him. "Hi, I'm Landon Wolff, and it appears your friend broke his leg up on the slope. We have a sled coming for him, but he wants to talk to you." Landon handed his phone to the injured skier.

The skier said, "I'm trying to hold on." He glanced at Landon. "Yeah, the man and woman with me are wolves."

"You can do it," Gabrielle assured him.

The skier nodded at Gabrielle and said to his friend, "Yeah, dude, I'm trying not to shift." He handed the phone back to Landon. "He wants to keep you on the line, and you can keep him posted as to my progress."

Then two members of the ski patrol tore up the hill on their snowmobiles. They soon lifted the injured man onto the sled while Landon loaded the man's skis.

Landon was still talking on the phone to the skier's friend. "He's on his way down now."

Then the ski patrol sped off with the injured man. Gabrielle and Landon headed down the slope. She didn't ski to the ski lift, but to the first aid hut instead. No one but the ski patrol members were there, both wolves, and the injured skier and his friend who met up with him there. Everyone was a wolf.

Even though they had called for an ambulance, Gabrielle planned to check him out.

Instead of lying still, the injured skier was trying desperately to remove his clothes. No wolf liked to be wearing human clothes when they shifted.

Everyone was helping the injured man to strip out of his clothes but Gabrielle, who was trying to keep the skier from injuring himself further. As soon as he was naked, he shifted, howled in pain, and passed out.

She stabilized his leg. Even though she wasn't licensed as a vet here, no one would fault her for taking care of an injured wolf. Besides, no one would dare tell anyone she'd practiced veterinary medicine on a wolf in a ski hut.

Once she was done, they took him to the vet clinic so Doc Mitchell could set his leg.

"Was he a pack member?" she asked Landon as they left the first aid hut.

"No. He must be a guest. Thanks for taking care of him. Being a wolf, he should be good in half the time it takes humans to heal." He frowned at Gabrielle. "Do you want to ski some more?"

"Absolutely. Let's go." They hurried off to the chairlift. She just hoped she wouldn't ever do that—fall and have to shift because she was injured.

Landon appeared glad she wasn't afraid to ski further. "He'll be okay."

"I agree. I just didn't think he would shift like that at the ski resort." Having never dealt with an injured *lupus garou*, she really hadn't expected to see anything like that. "Have you had trouble with anyone like that who has been injured before?"

"Every once in a while. We have to put up the privacy screen when that happens and hope if anyone else—an injured human—is in the hut at the time, our injured wolf doesn't howl in pain."

Gabrielle laughed. "At least no one else was in the hut this time."

Suddenly, out of the corner of her eye, she saw Brando and his friends starting to follow them again. *Great.* She'd thought he'd given up on her. But then two members of the ski patrol skied up to talk to Brando and his friends.

"Let us give you some advice. Gabrielle's part of our pack. Landon is too. I don't know how they work things where you're from, but pack members stick up for each other, and if you didn't realize it, the town is entirely run by the pack."

"Gabrielle and I have a history," Brando said as if that said it all.

"Yeah, well, apparently *you* are history," one of the ski patrol members said. "So keep your distance from them or leave Silver Town."

After that, Gabrielle couldn't hear what was being said, but she loved the pack already.

Landon smiled down at her. "Do you see what I mean? You'll have all the protection you can get anytime you need it."

"Yeah, that's really nice."

She and Landon rode the chairlift up the mountain and headed down the intermediate slopes several more times. Brando and his friends steered clear of them the rest of the night too. Thankfully.

When the ski lifts closed for the night, they headed inside the lodge and she said, "Swimming, right?"

"Yeah, I'll meet you—"

"Your swimsuit is in my room."

The night manager waved to Landon that she had an issue with a customer. "I'll be up in a few minutes, after I take care of the problem."

"Okay, see you in a few minutes then," she said.

That night, Zelda said to her sister, "Odette, listen, we're not going to find the woman. We've lost her for good this time. We need to call the boss and have some other agents take care of it, or we'll miss out on our whole vacation with Gabrielle."

"Do you think Gabrielle's had enough time with Landon and the others to convince her to move to Silver Town and take care of their vet clinic?" Odette asked, wishing they could have at least found the woman and arrested her so they had finished their mission, and the fact they hadn't met up with Gabrielle at the beginning of their vacation would seem more legitimate. Besides, she hated not finishing a mission.

"That's another reason for us going to Silver Town. If Landon and the others haven't done enough to convince Gabrielle she needs to be with a wolf pack, we'll have to help."

Odette smiled at her sister. "As long as we don't make a muddle of it. I mean, if we go there and Landon's busy taking Gabrielle out all the time, and then here we are taking her away from him, that would be at cross-purposes to what we're trying to accomplish."

"Right. Though he probably has work to do. We will have to make sure they can still spend plenty of time together. Like, we can visit the diamond slopes, and since Gabrielle's a new skier, she won't be able to join us. You remember what she told us. She would sip hot toddies in the ski lodge so we could get in some expert-slope runs."

In her heart, Odette knew they had to join Gabrielle, but she really hoped their she-wolf friend wouldn't feel obligated to be with them all the time. Odette also wanted to meet the Wolff family that had taken Gabrielle in and see that they had her best interests at heart.

"I'll call her," Zelda said. "She'll be expecting us to join her tomorrow."

"All right."

Zelda got on the phone, and when Gabrielle answered, Zelda put it on speakerphone. "Hey, good news. We're flying in by late afternoon tomorrow. We will probably get to the resort about three or four."

"Okay, great, and we can have dinner together and night ski, if you want to," Gabrielle said.

"Wow, you're getting adventurous," Zelda said.

"I'm impressed," Odette said. "What are you planning to do now?" She hoped Gabrielle wouldn't be calling it a night at nine already.

"Landon and I just finished skiing and we're going to swim next."

"Oh, we don't want to hold you up." Zelda winked at Odette.

"Wait, I have to tell you something. I hope you are okay with it. I'm going to move to Silver Town to take over the vet practice here as soon as I can leave Daytona Beach. It might take a little while to get my state license before I can practice here, but… Well, what do you think?"

Zelda and Odette's mouths gaped. "Ohmigod, yes!" Zelda said.

"Oh, yes!" Odette said. "We'd so hoped you would feel that way."

"What?" Gabrielle asked.

"Well, you know. When we came out here before, we learned it was a wolf-run pack," Zelda said.

"You knew all along and you didn't tell me? You…you set me up? You've been trying so hard to get me to come skiing with you this year. Now it all fits." Gabrielle laughed.

Odette smiled at Zelda. She was so glad Gabrielle wasn't angry with them.

"Yeah, the other places were just regular ski resorts. But when we came here, we knew we had to get you here at all costs just so you would see it for yourself and maybe want to make this your home."

"You…you didn't make up this business about the person you were supposed to take into custody, did you?" Gabrielle asked.

"No," Zelda said. "It was as we explained, but when we learned you were having a good time there, we sure didn't want to give up our business and mess things up for you."

"But how did you know Silver Town needed a vet?"

The sisters exchanged looks. "I'm sorry," Odette said. "We looked into it when we were here the last time to see if they might have an opening at the vet clinic. We heard rumors their vet, Dr. Mitchell, wanted to retire."

"Wait, you did not talk to Lelandi, the pack leader, about this, did you?"

Zelda chuckled. "I told you, Odette, it would come out before long. Gabrielle would make a good JAG agent."

"So that's why she offered me the job. You told her I was a vet," Gabrielle said.

"Yeah," Zelda said.

"And Landon?" Gabrielle sounded concerned.

"Oh, he was a mistake," Zelda said.

Odette punched her sister lightly on the arm. "What she means to say is that Lelandi was supposed to ensure you had some nice bachelor ski instructors all lined up to teach you how to ski and to show you around town until we could get there. And maybe you would fall head over heels for one of them. Then everything would have worked out beautifully. But you took care of that on your own when you hooked up with Landon."

Gabrielle laughed. "That's why you were so surprised when I said the owner of the lodge was giving me ski lessons."

"Yeah, no one thought of that." Zelda held her hands over her heart. "It was fate."

"With a big push from you two," Gabrielle said.

"Well, it worked, didn't it? If we hadn't convinced you to come this year to the ski resort, you might not have ever learned about the wolf-run town, found a hot guy to hook up with, and decided to take the job offer." Odette just couldn't believe it had all worked out.

"I'm sure you would have finally come right out and told me about the town, if I hadn't checked it out anyway."

"Yeah, but you might have been even more reluctant to meet a whole pack of wolves if we'd told you that part. We've never seen you around other wolves much," Odette said.

"That's true. What about the two of you?" Gabrielle sounded worried that they would miss her.

"Are you kidding?" Odette asked. "You know we're constantly out of town on missions, so we don't get to see you all the time anyway. But now? Every vacation we get, we're coming out there to see you, okay? Free room and board, right?"

Gabrielle chuckled. "Yeah, sure. And you can come in the summer too. Doc Mitchell has a lake you can go swimming in, no problem with humans seeing you. The property's all surrounded by woods—125 acres of it."

"Oh, wow, now you're talking about a jaguar paradise." Zelda smiled.

"Well, it's two hours later here than there and we still need to pack. We'll see you tomorrow," Odette said. "Lelandi's having someone pick us up at the airport—I love your pack already—and they'll drop us off at the lodge."

"All right. I can't wait to see you!"

Odette just had to make sure that she and her sister didn't stand in the way of a wolf romance when they arrived in Silver Town after all the work they had put into this. Convincing Gabrielle to go to Silver Town to ski had been a job and a half as it was, though they understood why.

CHAPTER 15

"YOU WOULD NOT BELIEVE WHAT MY GIRLFRIENDS DID," Gabrielle told Landon as he joined her in her room to change into his board shorts. "They just called me while you were resolving the issue with the guest."

"Are they finally getting in or did they cancel on you again?" Landon looked almost hopeful that they weren't coming.

She smiled. "They're coming in around three or four tomorrow afternoon. You and I will have the whole day together, and I want to help you and your family finish building the snowman. I'll have dinner with my girlfriends when they come in and catch up with them. Maybe we'll night ski."

Landon looked a little bummed as he stripped out of his clothes, baring his hard, sexy body to her, and then slipped on his board shorts, T-shirt, and sandals. She would so miss seeing him like that when she left for home.

"Hey, we will have a blast, and believe me, my friends will want to be on the expert slopes for most of the time, if you're free to ski with me on the intermediates."

He smiled. "You bet."

They left the room and walked downstairs and across the lobby to the swimming pool area.

"But I couldn't believe what they had pulled. They set this whole thing up."

"What do you mean that they set this all up?"

"When they came here last year to ski, they learned Silver Town was wolf-run. And they decided it was the perfect place for me to visit—to be with other wolves."

"To find a pack to join?"

"Yeah." She pulled off her cover-up and laid it on the chaise lounge. "Talk about being surprised. They're good at keeping secrets."

"I don't remember any jaguars staying at the lodge last year." Landon removed his shirt and set it next to her cover-up.

"I think they stayed at the Silver Town Inn, but they wanted to be on the slopes this year and stay at your lodge. Anyway, they talked to Lelandi and had been trying to get me out here to ski ever since."

Landon laughed. "So that's how Lelandi knew you were a veterinarian. She is a bit of a matchmaker."

Gabrielle heeled off her flip-flops. "Yeah, but she didn't get it right this time."

"Lelandi?" Landon removed his sandals.

"Right. She was supposed to set me up with a bachelor ski instructor."

Landon's eyes sparkled with good humor as he pulled Gabrielle into his arms. "It's a good thing fate would have it that I caught you swimming in the pool after hours—not one of my sisters or my brother."

"Would they have kicked me out?"

"You bet."

She laughed. Then she kissed him and hurried to the pool and jumped in. Laps first. She was very much a goal-oriented person. Then playing in the water came next.

When they finished swimming laps and playing, Gabrielle left the water first and dried herself off while Landon joined her, grabbed his towel, and began running it over his body.

"You can stay with me if you want tonight," she said.

He smiled broadly at her. "Hell yeah. I was trying to come up with a reason you needed me to spend the night."

She smiled at him and slipped on her cover-up and flip-flops. "I'm just glad *I* don't have to beg you to stay."

He laughed. "No way."

The next day, Gabrielle and Landon swam, skied, and had lunch, and then they joined the rest of the family to build the top of the snowman and decorate him.

The last section of the snowman took them longer than they anticipated because they had to take the snow up two different ladders. When they were finally done, they were able to decorate the snowman. The largest carrot Roxie could find in the grocery store worked for the nose. Landon and Blake found fallen tree branches in the woods for the arms. Nicole and Gabrielle sorted through Nicole's button supply, Roxie and Kayla going through theirs until they had the largest black buttons they could find for the snowman's clothes. Kayla gave up her red-and-green-striped elf ski hat with a long tassel and matching red and green scarf to dress the snowman.

Nicole brought out some blush she'd picked up just for the snowman, and they gave him rosy cheeks. Red buttons made the smile.

They stood back and looked at their snowman that was about ten feet tall, trying to figure out what else they could add.

"A string banner of Merry Christmas in red, green, and white!" Roxie said. "I'll go get it."

"This is great," Gabrielle said. "Next year, I think he should be holding a wolf puppy."

"A giant snowman holding a wolf pup it is. Though we're going to have to practice making one." Landon wrapped his arm around Gabrielle's shoulders.

With the banner in hand, Roxie ran out into the snow. The whole area around the snowman was wiped clean, and Blake and Landon got on the ladders to string up the banner. "How about Sparkle for the snowman's name?"

"Yeah, I like that. Do you have birdseed?" Gabrielle asked.

"Yeah, we feed the birds year-round," Roxie said.

Gabrielle smiled. "Maybe we can prop something on the snowman's hat and the birds could come and feed."

"I've got just the right dish for it. It's plastic but has poinsettias on it, so it's the perfect color scheme," Kayla said, and headed inside.

Once she came back outside, Landon put the dish feeder filled with birdseed on top of the snowman's hat and climbed down the ladder. "I hope we don't have to keep refilling the feeder."

"No, it's just for the display," Roxie said.

They called for Jake Silver to come take pictures for the snowman and snow sculpture contest.

When he arrived, Jake smiled. "I heard about the giant snowman. Don't be surprised if people hear about it and come to take selfies."

Gabrielle figured that was a good indication the Wolff family could win.

"Anyone is welcome to do so," Blake said.

"You know, we should add some battery-operated Christmas lights to Sparkle to light him up at night," Roxie said. "Then that really suits his name."

"I'll go get some. We had extra lights left over, and I wasn't sure what to do with them," Nicole said and returned to her house.

"I'll come back later to take pictures of the lighted, um, Sparkle, tonight," Jake said. "I suspect you might just have the winner this year."

Everyone smiled to hear it. It had been a lot of work.

After Jake left, Nicole returned with the Christmas lights and they all helped to hang them up all over the snowman.

Gabrielle couldn't wait to see it all lit up at night. "It's probably time for my friends to arrive. And I need to get warmed up," she said.

"Thanks for all your help with this," Nicole said. "This is the best snowman ever."

"Yeah, it is," Roxie said. "I can't wait to capture some photos of birds eating off the birdfeeder when we're not all gathered around scaring them off."

The others went inside the houses, but Landon walked Gabrielle back to the lodge.

"More hot chocolate to warm you up before your friends arrive?" Landon asked Gabrielle.

"Yes, thanks. Hot chocolate is perfect for a place like this. I rarely drink it back home. Iced tea is just about all I drink."

"I don't blame you. In a hot climate, I would be drinking a lot of cold drinks. Do you want to sit by the fireplace with Rosco?" He wasn't sure if she wanted him to let her wait for her friends alone while she gathered her thoughts or if she would like his company.

"Yeah, let's do that." As if she knew what he was thinking, she reached over and took his hand and squeezed. "Thanks for waiting with me. I keep thinking they will text again to say they're not coming."

"They're coming. They're on the plane and should be here soon. Lelandi said she's picking them up at three and their plane is on time." Landon had checked with Lelandi because he was hoping Gabrielle's friends wouldn't disappoint her again, but if they had, he was going to cheer her up.

When the jaguar sisters finally arrived at the lodge, they were just as happy to see Gabrielle as they were to meet Landon. Both were dark-haired and blue-eyed, but Odette was the taller of the twin sisters, and the older. Zelda, the younger, had sun-lightened streaks in her dark hair. They hugged Gabrielle, giving her warm smiles. Then they both gave Landon hugs as if he was just as important to them as Gabrielle was.

It cheered him that Gabrielle's friends treated him with friendship. "We're glad you finally made it and that I had time to be alone with Gabrielle for the last three and a half days."

"Well, now that we're here, you are not going to get rid of her so easily," Odette said, patting him on the shoulder.

He smiled. "That is good to hear."

"We're going on the expert slopes tonight after dinner, and we hope you'll take her down the intermediate slopes," Zelda said. "We hope you'll join us for dinner too."

He opened his mouth to speak, thinking the ladies would like to have dinner together alone, but Gabrielle smiled. "I agree. We'll go up to the room and Odette and Zelda can unpack and then we'll come down and have dinner."

"All right. I'll see you in a little bit." He was delighted.

———————

Up in their suite, Gabrielle sat on one of the beds and watched the sisters unpack. "Thanks for being so nice to Landon. Here I thought you both were falling for the wolf."

"Ohmigod, if he was a jaguar, I sure would be," Odette said, unpacking her panties and bras into a drawer. "You wouldn't stand a chance. I would steal him right out from under you." Then she paused and sighed. "I love the lodge too. It's so beautifully decorated for Christmas."

"Oh, me too," Zelda said. "As for Landon, he is gorgeous and so sweet. If he had been a jaguar, you would have had to fight me for him, Odette." Then she finished hanging her clothes in the closet. "How can you even stand to return to Daytona Beach without him, Gabrielle?"

"I will be so busy working and getting ready to move, I won't have time to think."

"Ha!" Odette said. "You will be thinking of him when you are away from here as much as I'm sure he will be thinking of you. So you might as well get him out of your system in the next few days until you can return here."

Gabrielle laughed. Odette's words were so true. Though she was certain she wouldn't get him out of her system before she left.

"Odette's right. You know if we had met a hunky...well, jaguar, we would want you to do the same for us."

"But we were supposed to do all this stuff together," Gabrielle reminded them.

They smiled at her.

"We were supposed to help you find a wolf and encourage you to join the pack and take over the vet clinic." Odette shrugged. "Now it's up to you to hang on to that sexy wolf. The part owner of this beautiful lodge? You are sooo lucky."

"I told you it was fate that Lelandi didn't pair her up with a hot ski instructor instead," Zelda said. "Oh, and tell us you're not staying with us at the lodge now, but you're staying with that hunky wolf. You know, it could be dangerous to room with us, just in case our perp tries to track us down."

"You never mentioned that before." Gabrielle didn't believe it for an instant.

"You never told us just how hot Landon is," Zelda said.

Yet, that's just what Gabrielle had wanted to do—move in with Landon at his house and stay in the guest room, if it was truly more soundproof. But she hadn't wanted her friends to feel she was slighting them.

"Yeah, what Zelda says. We're trained in hand-to-hand combat, if the woman shows up here. We sure don't want you to be in the midst of danger," Odette said.

Gabrielle smiled. She knew they were just teasing her.

"Right. We're serious about this." Zelda looked perfectly— serious. "What if it takes you a couple of months or more before you can return here? You would be kicking yourself for not spending every precious moment with Landon for as long as you could before you have to leave."

"Landon did say I could stay in the guest room at the home that he shares with his sisters."

"There, see? Pack your bags. When we are finished with dinner, or skiing, you'll need to haul your bags right over there," Zelda said. "Though if he's busy with lodge business, we'll help you."

"Well, after we ski, we'll want to swim." Gabrielle did want to stay with Landon for the rest of the time she was here. Once she was finished packing her bags, but leaving her swimsuit out, she glanced at the stuffed jaguar. "I didn't smell any jaguar scent on your gift."

The sisters took a minute to look the box, paper, card, and jaguar over.

"Hmm, so we have a new mystery." Odette was frowning as she tried to smell anything from any of the items. "I smell wolves have touched it. And you, of course, Gabrielle."

"Same here," Zelda said, checking all the items over.

"Are you sure there wouldn't be anyone you know who might send you a Secret Santa gift and who knew you were coming to the resort?" Gabrielle asked.

"You, our boss, and a half-dozen other people with the JAG agency who knew we were going on vacation," Zelda said.

"And no known boyfriends?" Gabrielle couldn't believe a random jaguar who didn't leave a scent on the package would have sent it. She knew the sisters had dated a lot of jaguars, but neither of them was interested enough to settle down with any of them. What if one of them had a secret admirer who was afraid to just come out and say so?

"Nope," the twins said at the same time.

"Then it must be a secret admirer," Gabrielle said.

"Yeah, but if so, it's a secret as to which of us he's admiring too," Odette said. "That doesn't work for me."

"Me neither," Zelda said.

"Okay, well, it sounds like a mystery for the two of you to

unravel." The radio/alarm clock on the table caught Gabrielle's attention. "Are you ready for dinner?"

"Yeah, I'm starving." Odette grabbed her purse.

"Me too." Zelda lifted her room key off the chest of drawers. "We're eating at the restaurant here, right?"

"Yeah. The food is great." Gabrielle led them out of the room and down the stairs and saw Landon talking to somebody in the lobby. Then she realized it was Brando. *Ugh.* She hoped he wasn't causing trouble.

"Hey, isn't that the guy you went out to dinner with in Daytona Beach? He was from Alabama or Georgia or somewhere close to there," Zelda said.

"Yeah, he's from Georgia. I never heard from him after that and then he saw me here. I figure he wanted to have a couple of dates, nothing real between us, but just as a diversion."

"He's not alone, right?" Odette asked.

"No, he's got a couple of his buddies with him. They came with Brando that time I saw him in Daytona Beach too." Gabrielle waved at Landon, and he smiled at her and said something more to Brando, then headed toward them.

She wondered what was up with the talk between Landon and Brando.

Landon glanced at her bags, smiled, and gave her a hug.

"My friends are kicking me out of the room," Gabrielle said. "I left our swimsuits in the room so we could change, and then we can change back after that." She shrugged. "Maybe my friends thought we might get carried away. I have no idea where they would come up with that idea."

"They're JAG agents. Very intuitive. I'll take your bags to the office, and we'll carry them to the house after we swim." He took her bags off to the office.

"Man, he's droolworthy," Zelda said.

"Oh, yeah. He has got all the right moves," Odette said.

Gabrielle was amused. She'd never heard her friends talk about a wolf like that. If they were trying to convince her Landon was the one for her, she didn't need much convincing.

Landon hurried back. "Are you ladies ready for dinner? It's on the family."

"Wow, thanks," Zelda said. "Here we planned to pay for dinner for you since you've been so good about taking care of Gabrielle while she waited for us to join her."

"It was totally my pleasure."

"Well, thanks so much," Odette said.

Then they all went inside and got a booth. Gabrielle and Landon sat together on one side, and the sisters on the other.

"I love all your wolf decorations," Zelda said. "This is such a fun place. We had made reservations at the Silver Town Inn last year before you had built the lodge, so we never got to see it."

"Yeah, this is a great addition to everything the resort offers. Gabrielle told us that the Silver Town Tavern is for shifters only. We would love to try it out too."

"It's a great place to have dinner," Landon said.

"Hmm, okay, then tomorrow night, if you don't have any other plans, we'll take you to dinner there," Zelda said, "if you can drive us."

Landon chuckled. "Thanks, sure, we can go there."

Gabrielle was glad the ladies had asked him to go with them tomorrow night too. "So what was the deal with Brando, Landon?"

"He wanted you to know he really likes you and he had planned to get together with you again in Daytona Beach."

"And you told him I'm going to be returning here to live and work permanently?"

"I did mention it. And that you're seeing me, and it's not a one-time affair. He said he'd been busy but he had planned to get back together with you."

"Yeah, like that would ever have happened. He hasn't thought of me since he left, until he saw me here."

"Hopefully he'll quit pestering you from now on."

"Let's order the pizza," Odette said. "Ever since you sent us the picture of the one you were having that they made in the form of a Christmas wreath, I've wanted to try it."

"Yeah, that's what I want too," Zelda said.

Landon waited for Gabrielle to decide on something.

"I think the blue-cheese-topped burger is the one for me. And the vinegar fries."

"Okay, I'll have the mushroom burger," Landon said.

Zelda and Odette agreed on the toppings they wanted on the pizza they would share.

"After skiing tomorrow night, we thought we would take a run in the snow," Zelda said.

"We'll be going swimming after skiing." Gabrielle didn't want to give up what had become her fun routine with Landon.

"Oh, sure, we could run after that, unless you are too tired," Odette said.

"No, we can do that."

"Since it's safe here, we wanted to make the most of our runs. We did last year when we came. We did startle a couple of wolves accidentally, but I'm sure they had a good laugh over it later," Zelda said.

"We sure did," Odette said.

Landon laughed. "We missed hearing about it. I'm sure the wolves who had been scared by a couple of jaguars running through the woods here would have mentioned it to the rest of the pack."

"We would be honored if you all came with us," Odette said.

Gabrielle cringed. She hadn't told her friends that Landon and his family couldn't shift to run the rest of the time she was here. The moon wasn't strong enough.

"We're not royals, if you know anything about that," Landon said. "But Blake's mate, Nicole, can run with you if she would like."

"I'll ask her," Gabrielle said. "But she might want to spend the time with Blake instead."

"We were thinking it would be fun to run on Doc Mitchell's acreage. You haven't really seen the property as a wolf, right?" Odette asked Gabrielle.

"No, I haven't and yeah, that would be fun. I need to ask Doc Mitchell if it's okay. It has a river, too, and I want to see it."

"The pack leaders own tons of acres of land and that's where we ran last time. So if Doc Mitchell is reluctant to have us run on his land, we can run on the pack leaders' property," Zelda said.

Their meals came and Gabrielle said, "I'll call him, just to be sure." She got her phone out, and while her friends were taking pictures of their Christmas pizza pie to share with their friends, she called him. "Hi, Doc Mitchell, this is Gabrielle."

"You haven't changed your mind about taking over the clinic already, have you?" Poor Doc Mitchell sounded worried.

"Oh, absolutely not. I'm returning as soon as I can. My friends arrived and they want to run with me tomorrow night on your property. Is that okay? They're jaguars."

"Yeah, come by the house and I'll give you a survey of the land and you can run around the acreage to your heart's content."

"Oh, thanks, that would be wonderful. Thanks so much, Doc."

"The place is yours. Enjoy it while you're here."

"We will." Gabrielle thought he was such a nice man. She hoped he would work with her for a while once she began to see patients here. She called Nicole next. "Hi, Nicole. This is Gabrielle. I'm going swimming with Landon after skiing tomorrow night, but I wondered if you would like to come with my jaguar friends and me and run on Doc Mitchell's property."

"I would love to. That would be too much fun. I've never seen jaguar shifters in their fur coats. Maybe they can teach me some of those fun moves you did with us the other day when we were playing as a family," Nicole said.

"They would be happy too. We'll have fun. We're eating dinner now. I'll tell the sisters you'll be running with us and will let you know when we're ready to go tomorrow night. I guess we'll actually need you to drive us."

"I'll be happy to. I'll see you later. I can't wait," Nicole said.

Then Gabrielle and Nicole ended the call. "It's a go at Doc Mitchell's place, and Nicole will be with us."

"Yes," Odette said.

Landon smiled. "I wish I could run with all of you."

"Next time we'll have to plan it better. We'll come to visit when the new moon phase isn't here and run with you too," Zelda said.

"I would love that."

Gabrielle didn't want Landon to feel left out, but she would be going to bed with him after running anyway so he would see her the rest of the night.

"Tomorrow morning, the two of you are welcome to join us when we go swimming," Landon said, then took a bite of his mushroom-loaded burger.

"We'll see. We do have to get our beauty sleep," Odette said.

"Yes, unlike Gabrielle. I swear she can live on only a few hours of sleep and keep working away at it," Zelda said. "Boy, is this pizza great."

"It is." Odette smiled at Gabrielle.

Gabrielle knew the sisters would love to swim because they were jaguars and they loved the water. But they would have to wait until spring thaw to swim in Doc Mitchell's lake as big cats. She also figured she would swim with the sisters sometime while they were here—during regular pool hours, if they felt more comfortable about doing that. They were special agents with the JAG after all. And they did abide by the rules.

After they ate, the sisters insisted Landon take Gabrielle up on the intermediate slopes while they hit the expert slopes. Which kind of surprised Gabrielle because she figured they would need to get their ski legs first. They hadn't skied since last winter.

They all geared up and then her friends rode the chairlift following Gabrielle and Landon. She figured they would ski off to the right trail where it led to one of the expert slopes, but she and Landon were already headed down the intermediate slope and she was concentrating on her form by the time the jaguar sisters left the chairlift.

At the bottom of the intermediate slope, Gabrielle turned to head for the chairlift again, Landon right beside her, when she saw her friends sailing down the intermediate slope. She smiled.

Odette shrugged. "We figured we would take one trip down the intermediate just to make sure we remembered how to do this."

Gabrielle sure had wondered about that, but she figured the real reason they came skiing tonight was so she and Landon could still ski together. Skiing with him during the day was so much fun. But at night, with the sun setting and the lights coming on, it was romantic and spectacular. The shadows of the skiers followed them down the slopes.

She and Landon went up again, and when they reached the bottom of the slope, they headed for the chairlift, wanting to make the most of the skiing tonight. This time she saw her friends coming off a black diamond slope. She smiled and waved at them with her ski pole and nearly fell. Landon grabbed her shoulder to steady her.

No waving with ski poles in the future.

Then she and Landon were on the chairlift again. "It really is okay with your sisters that I stay in your guest room, isn't it?"

"Yeah, you bet. I'm surprised they hadn't suggested it already."

Gabrielle laughed. "Well, I wanted to do it, but I was afraid my friends would feel I was forsaking them for you, but they really wanted this too."

"I will forever be in your friends' debt. We'll have to have them over to the house for dinner the night before you leave, to thank them properly."

"That would be nice."

After several more trips down the mountain and at closing time for the ski lifts, they saw the sisters skiing toward them from the bottom of another expert slope. They were all smiles.

"Wow, to think we can do this several times a year with a free room here when we come in the future," Odette said.

"Yes, I so agree. We'll be able to cook at your place and save on meals, and take you out to the tavern since we can't buy you meals at the lodge," Zelda said as they all skied toward the lodge.

"Oh, tomorrow I've got to take you into town to see the tea shop. Maybe in between skiing in the morning and the afternoon? It's only open afternoons. And I can show you the giant snowman we built named Sparkle." Gabrielle remembered the snowman was lighted now, and she couldn't wait to see it after they swam and went to the house.

Then she thought about how they had no transportation into town.

Landon quickly said, "I'll drop you off in town tomorrow. I need to run some errands anyway."

"You could eat lunch with us," Zelda said, and Gabrielle knew she meant it.

He shook his head. "It's okay. Once I finish errands, I'll grab a hamburger, and when you're done, I'll take you back to the lodge."

Gabrielle thought the world of him for wanting them to have their own time together too as she, Landon, and her friends skied to the lodge together.

CHAPTER 16

LANDON KNEW THE SISTERS DIDN'T WANT TO SEPARATE Gabrielle and him, but she needed some time with her friends, and he was perfectly happy to give them their space. "Do you all live near each other in Daytona Beach?"

"We live about a half mile from each other," Zelda said. "We were all at the beach one night really late. We were as surprised to see a wolf as she was to see a couple of jaguars. Odette and I were playing in the surf, and she was standing on the beach watching us. Of course, as soon as we noticed her, our first thought was that she was a big dog that looked like a wolf. We were certain no wolves lived in Daytona Beach, and we didn't know about wolf shifters at the time."

"Exactly," Gabrielle said as they reached the lodge deck and removed their skis. "I knew right away they were jaguars, of course. This happened about eight years ago. I didn't even know jaguar shifters existed back then. At first, I thought they had escaped from a zoo. Or maybe there was a big-cat rescue organization somewhere near Daytona Beach that I hadn't heard of. I was really worried they were real cats and not shifters. They could easily have killed me if so."

"We weren't sure what to do," Zelda said. "We just watched Gabrielle, not wanting to give her a heart attack if we left the water. She didn't bark, like a dog would, or make any sound at all and she wasn't leaving. We were afraid she thought if she turned away from us and ran off, we would attack her. If we had been all jaguar, we probably would have. We carefully left the water, trying not to look like big cats prowling on the hunt, but that's just the way we move. Then I figured if I shifted, the dog would just realize we were human and go on about its business. Imagine my surprise when the dog, or in reality a wolf, shifted too."

"We were totally in awe of Gabrielle," Odette said.

"Yeah, like I was of the sisters. I invited them to my house for drinks after that. We shifted back into our respective furry forms, loped off to our vehicles, shifted, dressed, and they followed me home. We must have talked until three in the morning." Gabrielle smiled. "We even went for a swim in my pool. We've been friends ever since."

"We sure have been," Odette said. "You couldn't find a better friend than Gabrielle."

"I just didn't know you were in the matchmaking game," Gabrielle said to her friends.

"Well, we knew you needed to be with a pack," Zelda said.

"Before it gets too much later, we'll get some hot toddies and nachos so the two of you can go up to the room and get changed into your swimsuits," Odette said.

"Okay, thanks." Gabrielle led Landon to the office's storeroom where they left off their skis, poles, and ski boots while the sisters went to the rental place and dropped off theirs.

It didn't take Gabrielle and Landon long to reach her room, and then the two of them were quickly stripping out of their clothes in her room and exchanging them for their swimsuits. They didn't want to take too long in case the sisters wanted to return to their room while Landon and Gabrielle were swimming.

Then they went downstairs and Landon put out the pool party sign. They waved at the sisters who were drinking their hot toddies and snacking on red and green nachos fireside, both smiling at them and raising their mugs to them.

They smiled and waved back at the sisters.

Landon wanted to swim their laps and return to the room and change so he and Gabrielle could free up the room. He was certain the sisters would like to relax in their room soon, after their flight and because they were still on Eastern Standard Time, two hours later, but they seemed to be enjoying themselves for now.

In the swimming pool area, Gabrielle seemed to have the same notion and was out of her cover-up and flip-flops before he even had time to pull off his shirt. She moved to the deeper end of the pool and dove into the water.

He yanked off his shirt and removed his sandals, then jumped into the water after her.

Gabrielle was too enticing to just want to swim laps with, so Landon swam after her as she did a breaststroke across the length of the pool. He dove under the divider to the outside part of the pool and caught her foot, then pulled her into his arms and kissed her.

"I'm going to miss this with you." He kissed her cheek. Their warm breaths and the warm water collided with the cold air and created a magical mist.

"Hmm, me too with you. I never believed I would be swimming with a hot wolf in a pool surrounded by snow and trees covered in Christmas lights." Gabrielle wrapped her arms around his waist. "I'm so glad I'll be with you at night until I leave. You are sure you're all right with taking us into town tomorrow so I can show Odette and Zelda the tea shop?"

"Yes. You need time to be with your friends too. Otherwise, I would happily monopolize all your time." He kissed her nose. "Ready for our laps, then we'll head up, change, and go to the house?"

"Yeah, I figured we wouldn't spend as much time frolicking as we usually do so we can free up the suite for them."

"Exactly."

They swam more laps, but frolicking just seemed to be part of the routine and though he was trying to just swim, she fell behind on her lap and grabbed his feet. That had him laughing, though while they were in the pool after hours, they tried to suppress any loud laughing or conversation so they wouldn't bother anyone who might be putting kids to sleep or was trying to get some sleep themselves.

They kissed and hugged and chased each other, then called it quits so her friends could return to their room.

They left the water and he pulled on his shirt and sandals while she was getting on her cover-up and flip-flops. The sisters were still enjoying their snacks when Gabrielle and Landon reached the lobby.

"We'll be right back and you can go up to your suite," Gabrielle told them.

"Take your time. We're fine," Zelda said.

But they would be as quick as they could. Besides, he was sure Gabrielle would want to see the lights on the snowman like he wanted to, and then he was eager to go to bed with her. He was glad the guest bedroom had its own bathroom en suite so they would have more privacy.

Once they had dressed, they pulled on their warm outer gear and put their wet bathing suits in the pocket of the bag that Gabrielle had left in the room for him.

They stopped on their way through the lobby so she could give her friends hugs before she and Landon left the lodge.

"Night, you two. We'll see you in the morning," Zelda said.

"Breakfast at the bar and grill," Gabrielle said.

Odette smiled. "Okay, night all."

Then Landon and Gabrielle headed out into the cold to drop off all their stuff at the house. Once they reached the house, they could see the snowman all lit up. "Oh, I wish my friends could see it like this."

A family was taking pictures of themselves while they stood at the base of the snowman. They waved at Landon and Gabrielle who smiled and waved back.

"We can bring the sisters over here to see the snowman

tomorrow night after going to the tavern," he said as Gabrielle took a picture of the snowman and sent it to her friends.

"What will we do about taking showers?" she asked as they went inside the warm house. His sisters had already gone to bed, giving them privacy.

"We have a bathroom attached to the guest room. Totally private."

"What are we waiting for then?"

He smiled and carried their bags into the room and closed the door while she began stripping out of her clothes in a hurry.

He was soon joining her in the shower, thinking how his showers had become wild and exciting instead of just a time to wash up. It sure wouldn't be the same without her.

Then they were in bed together, and he thought this couldn't get any more perfect. Unless they were mated.

———

The next morning, Gabrielle and Landon woke late, and though she absolutely loved being with him in bed, all cuddled up to him and nice and cozy and warm, she groaned. "Being with you is not conducive to getting up early. If we ever did mate"—he raised his brows looking hopeful, and she smiled—"we would really have to work things out better than this."

He smiled and kissed her mouth. "We will, if it comes to that. I think I heard my sisters leave earlier."

"And you didn't wake me?"

"It was way too early and I fell back to sleep. Wild night, you know."

"Hmm, well, I smell the eggs, ham, and hash browns they made. Coffee, Irish tea." Gabrielle grabbed her phone off the bedside table and texted Odette: Did you already have breakfast?

Gabrielle was afraid they already had.

Odette responded: Yep, and the food is great at the bar and

grill. We're off to ski. Meet you for a break of hot chocolate topped with loads of whipped cream at ten.

Gabrielle groaned again and texted: Okay. Sorry about that. I meant to have breakfast with you.

Odette responded: No way. This is all working out just as we planned. Off to get on the chairlift. See you later.

Landon had already dressed. "What did they say?"

"They'll meet us for hot chocolate at ten."

"Okay. What do you want for breakfast?"

Gabrielle was still lying in the bed, not wanting to get up. "What your sisters had. It smells delightful."

He leaned down and kissed her forehead. "Do you want breakfast in bed?"

"No. Go work on it. I'll make myself presentable and I'll come in to help you. I have to admit it's tempting, but we'll never get going if I don't get my lazy butt out of bed."

Landon smiled. "Sure. See you in a bit." He left to make breakfast, and she got up and dressed.

What a way to wake up, though, with a hot wolf willing to make her breakfast in bed! Not to mention all that came before that.

Gabrielle soon joined him to help make breakfast, but he was about done and beginning to serve the food. All the kittens were coming to greet her, including Princess Buttercup, and she stopped to pet them.

She washed up and then made Landon some coffee and started some tea for herself. "Wow, you are sure handy."

She brought her tea and his mug of coffee to the table.

"I am only too happy to make us breakfast."

"Your sisters must have been super quiet this morning. I think I heard a little bit of noise, but so barely audible that I drifted off to sleep again. I had no idea you had been awake too."

"Yeah, my sisters are the best. I figured we both needed the extra sleep." He took a sip of his coffee. "Perfect."

"Great. I watched you add all that milk and sugar to it when we had breakfast here before, so I winged it."

"You winged it just right. Hey, I've been meaning to ask you, did you ever figure out the Secret Santa gift? Who it was for and who it was from?" he asked.

"Oh, yeah, it had to be for one of the jaguar sisters. It was a stuffed jaguar, but they claim that they don't have a clue who might have given it to them, and there wasn't any scent on it indicating a jaguar interested in either of them gave it to them."

"Nicole or her brother could always look into it," Landon said.

"The sisters are good at what they do too. But we can mention Nicole to them, if they think they might need someone else to help them check into it."

"Okay. About swimming—"

"The pool is open already to guests." Gabrielle smiled at him. "We can swim tonight after going with the sisters to the tavern for dinner. I'm ready to ski right now."

"You got it."

Before long, they were out on the slopes having a great time skiing. When it was finally ten, they met up with the sisters to have hot chocolate. Gabrielle's friends were beaming.

"We were talking about how great this is going to be with you moving here. We're making plans for several trips already," Odette said.

Gabrielle laughed. "You would be welcome to visit anytime."

"Hey, we thought we would take turns skiing with Landon down the expert slopes while one of us skis with you," Odette told Gabrielle.

"Oh, I would love that. Great thinking!" Gabrielle hoped she wouldn't screw up too much while she was skiing with her friends. She was used to messing up with Landon, and he was so good and helpful about it with her. It was funny how she'd thought it would be more embarrassing to fall in front of strangers than if she was falling all over the place in front of her friends. But she was comfortable with Landon now.

They finished their hot chocolates, and Gabrielle and Odette went on the chairlift first while Landon and Zelda followed behind them. Odette was the firstborn of the twins, and she was usually in charge, but the twins got along famously. They would disagree with each other sometimes, but it never lasted long, and then they were back to being a united front.

Gabrielle said to Odette on the ride up, "Landon asked me about the stuffed jaguar. Do you have some idea of who might have sent it to you?"

"A really far-out notion," Odette said. "Still, we didn't want to discount it, and it's another reason we wanted you to stay with Landon and his sisters."

"You were teasing when you mentioned the she-cat you were chasing down might show up here, weren't you?" Gabrielle asked.

"Only half-heartedly. All the evidence suggests the woman killed her mate. They had a fight the night before at a restaurant and she said he'd started it, egging her on. And then he turned it around as if he was trying to calm her down and be the good guy in the whole situation. So what the patrons saw was her blowing up and him trying to settle her down."

"And then he was found dead after that?" Gabrielle had bad outcomes with her clients sometimes because of pets dying, but she couldn't imagine trying to track down a jaguar who had murdered his or her mate.

"Okay, well, that's the thing. He convinced her to go boating with him in the Gulf of Mexico to make up for the fight they'd had. Again, that was witnessed. She seemed moody and not at all happy. He was cheerful, greeting everyone at the marina—"

"Making a show of it," Gabrielle said. "As if he wanted everyone to remember them for the final scene to play out."

"Exactly."

They reached the top of the ski lift, and Gabrielle wanted to hear the rest of the story. She guessed Odette and her sister hadn't wanted to mention the situation in front of Landon because he was a civilian. So was Gabrielle, but they knew she wouldn't tell anyone about it.

They moved out of the way of the chairlift and skied off to an intermediate slope.

"You know Landon is deputized to arrest people in Silver Town," Gabrielle said.

"Oh, okay, then I guess we should clue him in later. Are you ready to ski?"

"No, Odette."

Odette smiled at her and they moved way over out of everyone's way so other skiers could ski down the slope. "They went out on the boat, had dinner and cocktails, and she felt overcome with sleep—"

Gabrielle frowned. "Knockout drug!"

"Zelda and I considered it. Then she wakes sometime in the night, lights are out, she's got blood all over her, there's blood in the boat—"

"And he's lying dead on the floor of the boat in a pool of blood." Gabrielle could just visualize it.

"Nope. No body. It appears she killed him and dumped his body overboard. Of course she says she believes pirates boarded the boat while she was passed out, and she didn't have anything to do with it. She calls for the Coast Guard and they come out, take her into custody, take the boat into shore, the sheriff's department tests the blood, and it comes back that it's her husband's."

"But?"

"When we find no body, that's always…suspect." Odette texted her sister, then pocketed her phone. "She's released on bond, she runs. We track her down, turn her over to the agents that will incarcerate her in the JAG confinement facility, and you know the rest. Are you ready to ski down now?"

"Yeah, here goes nothing." Gabrielle skied down the slope as Odette followed her. She did really well, and she was so glad that she didn't mess up. When she got down to the bottom, Odette quickly joined her and got a text.

Odette pulled out her phone and responded to it. "I told Zelda I was telling you about our perp. She said if I wanted to go down with you a few more times, I can, and then we'll swap partners. She's having a ball skiing the experts with Landon. He's even given her some tips."

"Oh, great. He's super patient and a really good instructor." Gabrielle started to ski toward the chairlift again. "So about your runaway jaguar?"

"She doesn't remember killing her mate. The thing I thought was odd was that both drinking glasses had been rinsed out."

"So he washed up the glasses and then she killed him."

"Right. But if it was as she said, he got rid of the evidence that he gave her a drug to knock her out."

"But what about all the blood?"

"He could have taken some from himself earlier and then smeared it all over the boat in strategic places. Even donated some for the 'project,' saved it until he needed it, and voilà, no dead body, but it sure looks bad for her."

"Okay. Did a doctor check for a drug in her system?"

"It was too late, way past the twenty-fours that would show the drug was in her blood by the time she came to and notified the Coast Guard to get her back into the marina."

Gabrielle didn't ask anything more about the situation because she was too busy concentrating on getting on the chairlift. When they were both seated, they rode it up.

"So how does he benefit from pretending to kill himself off when he could just divorce her? At least jaguars can do that, unlike wolves."

"He was in debt up to his eyebrows—gambling debts, was

losing the house, and some loan sharks were after him. Zelda and I figured if he pretended to kill himself, he could get rid of both his debts and his wife, who he fought with more and more over his gambling issues."

"That makes sense, then."

They reached the top of the slope, got up to off-load from the chairlift, and skied down a couple more times. Then Odette switched with Zelda to ski with Gabrielle several times.

"So Odette told you about our perp." Zelda and Gabrielle rode up the last time on the chairlift before it was time for lunch in town.

"Yeah. I feel sorry for the woman." Gabrielle couldn't imagine having a mate who would set her up to take a murder charge just so he could get out of the financial bind he was in from gambling. "Do you think the stuffed jaguar might have been from her? If so, why would she send one to you?" Gabrielle got off the chairlift, and Zelda joined her as they skied to the intermediate slope.

They stopped off to the side of the top of the slope like Gabrielle and Odette had done to stay out of other skiers' way earlier.

"Because she likes us. She genuinely made a connection with us. While we waited for the other JAG agents to take her into custody, we mentioned we were supposed to meet you at the lodge in Silver Town after Thanksgiving. So she knew we were here. And she talked about her future plans, once she's cleared of the crime. We never suspected she would escape her escort and flee again. She believes we're on her side."

"Are you?"

Zelda let out her breath in the frigid air. "Yeah. We believe her. Which was why we were trying to catch up to her so bad and missed out on part of our vacation to be with you. Of course once we learned you were having fun with a wolf, we felt better about not joining you right away. Making sure you wanted to join the wolf pack was also our priority."

Gabrielle smiled at her friend. "Landon sure made a difference when I hadn't had anyone to be with all this time. But I'm glad you're here. I sure hope you can learn the truth soon about the jaguar."

"She did mention double jeopardy. If she's found guilty of murdering her husband by the jaguar court, and she learns he's alive and she's finally set free…"

"If he ends up dead for real this time—by her hand—they couldn't try her again for the same crime. Payback's a bitch." Gabrielle mentally prepared herself to ski down the slope.

"Don't you know it."

Gabrielle skied off down the hill, Zelda following behind her. Both her friends had said nothing but praise about how well she was doing and how grateful they were that Landon had taken her to this level already.

But now it was time to regroup and have lunch with the ladies at the tea shop, and Landon was ready to have his hamburger.

"The ladies gave me a run for my money." Landon gave Gabrielle a hug and a kiss. "This afternoon, I'm ready to go back to skiing with you down the intermediate slopes."

She laughed.

"Don't you believe it. He looked like a professional skier zipping down the slopes," Odette said. "We're going to sleep well tonight."

"Yeah, for sure," Zelda said.

CHAPTER 17

AFTER LANDON DROPPED THE LADIES OFF AT SILVA'S TEA SHOP, Gabrielle made introductions. Silva was delighted to meet the twins. "I rarely get jaguars in here. I'm so excited to see you. Any friends of Gabrielle's are friends of mine."

"Since Gabrielle will be moving here, we'll be coming to see her and I'm sure we'll drop by the tea shop whenever we do. We love tea shops. And your place is just adorable," Odette said.

"It sure is," Zelda agreed.

"And the food and beverages are wonderful," Gabrielle said.

"Thanks, ladies, and we're so glad you are returning for good, Gabrielle." Silva gave the ladies each a menu.

"We are too." Zelda opened the menu. "Now she just has to pick up a mate and she'll be all set."

Silva smiled. "Well, if she hasn't decided on one yet, there will be a lot just champing at the bit to date her."

"That's what we like to hear." Odette was still perusing her menu. "I would love to have the corned beef on rye. And peppermint tea."

"A grilled ham-and-cheese sandwich, please." Gabrielle considered the teas. "White Christmas tea for me."

"Oh, white tea with vanilla, almond, and cardamom sounds good to me. I'll have one of those. And a brisket sandwich with onions and blue cheese. Yum. All of it sounds good." Zelda gave Silva her menu.

"We'll pick out pies afterward if we're still hungry." Gabrielle had worked up an appetite.

"Sounds good, ladies." Silva went back to the kitchen to give the orders to their grill cook.

"We'll have to show you our giant snowman all lit up with Christmas lights when we return from the tavern for dinner tonight."

"Oh, we had hoped to make a snowman with you, but we're glad you got to make one with their family. We're so short on time, we'll have to do it some other time with you when we visit you in the winter," Zelda said.

"That sounds good."

"Besides, we want to spend tonight's time running as jaguars with you," Odette said.

"Yeah, that will be fun with Nicole too." Gabrielle sipped from some of the water one of the waitresses had served.

A few minutes later, Silva came back with all their meals.

"Boy, these look delicious," Gabrielle said.

"They sure do." Odette took a picture of her and Gabrielle's meals.

Zelda took a picture of her own.

Gabrielle knew the sisters loved to share the meal photos they took on various assignments with others in the JAG agency. "You might entice a whole bunch of jaguars to visit here."

"Yeah, wouldn't the wolves be surprised." Zelda took a bite of her sandwich.

Odette sipped her tea. "This is so good."

"Mine too. I tried something different last time. Everything they have here is good." Gabrielle took another bite of her sandwich.

"So what do you think about Landon? Is he your dream mate?" Odette asked.

Gabrielle smiled. "He is. I figure I'll continue to see him when I return."

"And only him." Zelda sounded like she would be in his corner if Gabrielle decided to check out the competition.

But Gabrielle didn't have any need to. He was the kind of guy who was more real than anyone she had ever imagined being with.

He was great fun, and her time spent with him was thoroughly enjoyable and the nights—heavenly. She knew she wanted to continue being with him like that when she returned here.

"You're going to miss him, aren't you?" Odette said.

"Yeah. I am." Terribly, she knew. She hadn't even left and she was already feeling a quiet desperation to wrap things up in Florida as fast as she could and hightail it back here to be with him.

"Then like we said, we're giving you every opportunity to see him as much as you can before we all leave," Odette said.

"You two are the best friends ever. I didn't want you to feel I was ditching you to be with a guy," Gabrielle said, then finished up her sandwich.

"No way. This is why we coerced you into coming here." Zelda drank some more of her tea.

"You did, and boy am I grateful."

"We know you would do the same for us if you had the chance," Odette said.

"I sure would. You two are so picky when it comes to male jaguars." Gabrielle finished her tea.

They laughed. "We haven't gotten lucky like you." Odette poured herself some more tea. "This is so nice. I just love Silva's tea shop."

"It's lovely. We always enjoy visiting tea shops wherever we go. When I came to this one with Landon's sisters, I knew I had to bring you here. And you'll love the Silver Town Tavern too."

"I'm sure we will," Odette said.

"We need to get you back to the lodge and skiing with Landon though, before it's too much later," Zelda said.

Gabrielle paid for their meals, despite their objections. "You earned it. Thanks for coercing me to come here."

"What are friends for?" Zelda asked.

"I couldn't have asked for better friends, that's for sure."

"We feel the same way about you," Odette said.

They all said goodbye to Silva. "We'll take a rain check on the pie," Gabrielle said, "and when we return, we'll be sure to come for another girls' luncheon."

Silva smiled. "I'm so glad to have met you all and I look forward to seeing you again."

Gabrielle called to tell Landon they were ready to go. "Are you ready to ski?"

"I sure am. I'll head over there now."

The ladies all walked outside to free up their table and wait on Landon.

"Did you have a good hamburger?" Gabrielle asked him on the car's Bluetooth as he drove from the direction of the Silver Town Tavern just down the street.

"Yeah, Sam made me an extra big one. He said that was because he knew the jaguar sisters were running me ragged on the expert slopes. I still can't believe how fast the word gets around in a pack like this one."

"It's a close-knit pack, that's why." And Gabrielle was glad to join them.

———

Landon pulled into a parking space and parked at the tea shop, and the ladies all climbed into his car. He was ready to enjoy more time with Gabrielle, no matter what was on the agenda next. "Did you ladies have a nice meal?"

"The best," Zelda said as Odette got a text on her phone. "Well, not better than your bar and grill, but it was just as good."

"Silva's food *is* good. We're glad she realized her dream and opened it up and mated Sam, the wolf that owns the Silver Town Tavern—with Silva now," Landon said.

"So they own two of the eateries in Silver Town?" Zelda asked.

Landon drove them back to the lodge. "Yeah, they do."

"Okay, while I was skiing with Landon, I told him about our case, since Gabrielle told us he was a deputy sheriff."

"Yeah, if you need my help with this in any way, I'm here for you," Landon said.

"Well, we might just need you. I just received an update from the jaguar we were trying to chase down." Odette read the text off her phone. "'I know you're good at your job.'"

"So good we didn't catch up to her." Zelda sounded annoyed.

"I know. Right?" Odette read some more of the woman's message. "'Instead of trying to hunt me down, why don't you go after the real bad guy and get me off the hook?'"

"Her husband, I bet," Gabrielle said.

"Yep." Odette continued, "She wants us to clear her name and she wants to help us do it."

"She shouldn't have fled the JAG agents," Landon said.

"She needs to be in custody for her own protection. Otherwise, I'm all for looking further into the situation," Zelda said. "Even if the boss says we have another assignment, we can certainly investigate it, too, but she's not trained to do this kind of investigative work. If her husband learns she's trying to get him arrested for setting her up for murder, no telling what he might do to her."

"I'll tell her we'll help her, but no on her assisting us. It would be too dangerous." Odette texted her.

"And if she's guilty of the crime—just saying—you don't want her involved in anything that might look like collusion on your part," Landon said.

"Agreed," the sisters said.

"Can't they trace her phone?" Gabrielle asked.

"She said she's got a burner phone," Odette said.

"Did you ask her about the stuffed jaguar?" Gabrielle asked.

"Yeah. She said it was from her. She suspected our boss had made us come after her, and she wanted to give us a small token of appreciation for what she'd put us through when we were supposed to be on vacation. She appreciates us for believing her about her mate." Odette got another text. "Okay, she's glad we're going to help her. And she has a clue he's alive."

"What? Why didn't she tell us before?" Zelda asked.

"She just had a friend send a video to her that appears to be her mate getting money out of an ATM. So apparently she's solicited a friend to help."

"Oh, wow," Zelda said. "Let me see it. Yeah, that sure resembles him. But her friend could be as much at risk if she has no law-enforcement training."

Gabrielle looked at the photo of the guy. "So he's a blond. Color of eyes?" Gabrielle asked.

"Blue. He's a good-looking guy. It's too bad he's such a heel," Zelda said.

"You're right about Melany's friend though, and the danger she could be in. I'll tell her again she has to let us handle it. She says her husband didn't have an account at the bank that she knew of. Which means he must have socked some money away and planned this whole thing sometime earlier. He had to get more money before he disappeared for good," Odette said.

"You would think he would have gotten it beforehand." Landon parked back at the lodge and they showed him the photo.

"Something must have happened and he didn't have a chance to grab the money," Odette said. "When he went to clear out his account, the bank wasn't open, so he went to the ATM."

"Man, okay, we need to get on this," Zelda said. "He had to have used a different name when he went to the bank."

"Exactly," Odette said.

Landon asked, "Why don't we have Nicole and her brother check into it while you enjoy the rest of your vacation? Nicole has actually worked several cases where a person pretends to be dead for whatever reason and they take on a new identity. I'm sure she would be glad to help if her caseload isn't too bad."

"Yeah, we can do that," Odette said. "Since she's worked other cases like this, she might have some good ideas about what we need to look for. We've never had a case to work that's similar to this one."

They got out of the car and Landon called Nicole as they headed into the lodge. "Hey, Nicole, we need your services. Nate also, or if you are too busy, he could help out."

"Yeah, sure, I can. What did you need looking into?" Nicole was always there for the pack first.

He explained the situation with her while the sisters and Gabrielle waited to see what would happen next. "I'll give the phone over to Odette and Zelda, and they can give you more details."

After they spoke for a few minutes, Odette said to Nicole over the phone, "Thanks so much for helping us out. I'll send you the video, bank location, all of that." She sounded cheered.

Landon was glad Nicole could help the sisters with their case.

Then Odette ended the call and gave Landon a hug. "Thank you! Now we can meet with Nicole. Afterward, we'll have dinner and then later, a jaguar–wolf run with Nicole and Gabrielle."

"Yes!" Zelda said.

"That's great news," Gabrielle said.

"Nicole is good. If anyone can track down Melany's mate, she can." Landon took Gabrielle's hand. "Are you ready to ski?"

"I sure am."

Nicole waved at the sisters and joined them. "My brother wants in on helping to solve this case too."

They smiled.

Zelda said, "I'm so thankful. If we can absolve the woman of the crime and charge her husband, that will be the best Christmas present ever."

"I agree," Odette said.

"We're off to ski." Gabrielle snagged Landon's hand and headed for the office. "Let's go. Unless you would rather ski with the expert skiers."

"No way. I'm with you the rest of the afternoon."

"I'm so glad you said that. I don't know what I would do about it if you preferred skiing with them."

"Ditch me for someone who was a better sport."

"No way." In the storage room, they put on their ski boots and then she wrapped her arms around Landon. "You are the best sport of all. You were willing to give me up to allow me some time to ski with my friends, and you were a good sport in skiing with them too."

"Well, I had fun with the ladies. They certainly know how to ski. I think, being jaguars, they have some natural skills that make them really good at skiing, even though they don't go to the resorts that often." Landon kissed Gabrielle, and then they grabbed up their skis and poles.

"I agree with you there," Gabrielle said.

They headed out of the office, through the lodge, and outdoors to ski. It was snowing lightly, which made skiing all the more fun.

While they were in line for the chairlift, Gabrielle sighed. "I hope Nicole and her brother help the sisters solve the case."

"I do too. What an awful situation for Melany. I hope they can find her husband and clear her quickly." Though he still wondered if she had killed her husband and it was all a ploy on Melany's part.

Then they were getting on the chairlift and Gabrielle got quiet. Landon knew it was because she wanted to concentrate on getting on the chairlift without mishap. Once they were seated, she said, "How did the Secret Santa gift get into the room?"

"What?" This reminded him of when Gabrielle had been pondering how Rosco had found the kitten.

"The stuffed jaguar wasn't shipped to the hotel. It was wrapped up and then left in the room. How would it have gotten there?"

Landon was thinking she was just like Nicole in the way she

solved puzzles. "I'll have to check with the staff that was on duty when you found the package in your room. Since we hadn't thought it was anything sinister, I hadn't checked into it. But if you think Melany is here, we need to make sure the sisters know about it."

"That's what I was thinking."

They got to the top of the ride and left the chairlift and skied to the slope. Landon paused to pull out his phone and text Roxie: We need to know who delivered the Secret Santa package to Gabrielle's and the sisters' room. How did they know it belonged in their room? What did the person look like who left it?

Roxie texted back: So we have another mystery afoot.

Landon replied: Agreed.

Roxie texted: I'll get right on it.

Then Landon put his phone in his jacket pocket and zipped it. "Roxie will question everyone about it."

"Oh, good."

Then Gabrielle skied toward the expert slope. He was so surprised.

"One time down an expert slope," she said. "Then when I've moved here and can ski more regularly, I'll get better at it, but I wanted to just try it this one time before I get too tired this afternoon."

"Right. You're still acclimating to our higher altitude too. I'll be with you all the way." He was glad the altitude difference hadn't made her sick.

She pointed down the slope. "There's Odette! And Zelda is probably at the bottom."

Then Gabrielle took a tentative slide and started down the slope. She was doing well, slowly but surely turning on the steeper slope, the moguls more defined, resting on top of them, and then going to the next one, taking her time.

He was skiing down far enough to get close to her but pausing on a mogul above her, waiting for her to navigate the next section so he'd be there for her if she got into trouble.

She kept going until she was finally at the bottom of the slope, and he skied in to join her.

"Woo-hoo! I did it. Just this once, though. I'll have to get better at this. That's tiring."

"You did great."

She had made it down without any spills, and her form would get better with practice. For now, she did swell with taking on an expert slope and making it down fine.

She smiled up at him, her nose and cheeks rosy. "Well, it was fun. More fun if I could have just zipped down it like other skiers were doing."

"We all have to start somewhere," he said.

"That's true."

He maneuvered next to her to hug her, wrapped his arms around her, and kissed her mouth. "You are so much fun to be with, and I'm proud of you for trying new things even if you don't feel you're ready for them yet."

"Hmm, you are such a great instructor. You say all the right things."

"You're a great student, willing to try anything just once."

"But we're skiing the rest of the time on the intermediate slopes," she said.

He chuckled. "That works for me."

"And maybe a green one at the end of the day."

He smiled. "Whatever works for you."

They skied the rest of the day on the intermediate slopes, even for the last run down. "Swimming in the pool after the tavern tonight," she said.

"Absolutely."

"Ohmigod," she said suddenly, "I know where I had seen the dark-haired woman in the lodge. That's Melany. She had her hair up in the photo so I couldn't place her. But she's Melany Williams, the jaguar Odette and Zelda are looking for." She immediately got on her phone. "Odette, I think Melany is staying at the lodge!"

"Yes! She is," Odette said.

Gabrielle and Landon headed into the lodge where they met up with Odette and Zelda talking to Nicole.

"She's here, Melany Williams, our perp," Odette said excitedly to Gabrielle and Landon. "You were right. We gave her photo to the clerk, and she remembers her registering and asking if we had come in yet. It turns out Melany was afraid to actually get in touch with us once we got here, just in case we were only humoring her that we believed she wasn't lying to us about the status of her mate."

"You have her in custody?" Landon asked.

"Yes. Your sheriff took her into custody until our people can pick her up," Zelda said.

"Do you want to come with us to the tavern for dinner, Nicole?" Gabrielle asked.

"I'm going to have dinner with Blake and then run with you all later," Nicole said.

They said they would see Nicole in a bit, and Landon drove the other ladies to the Silver Town Tavern for dinner.

CHAPTER 18

At the tavern, Silva had reserved a table for the group of women and Landon. Sam came over to bring them water and took their drink orders: brandy Alexanders for the ladies, since Gabrielle had raved about them, and a beer for Landon.

Sam raised a brow at Landon. "You sure have a lovely group of ladies to dine with tonight."

Landon smiled and reached over and squeezed Gabrielle's hand, telling Sam and everyone else in the tavern that Gabrielle was with him.

She leaned over and kissed his cheek and he kissed her back.

"I love this place," Odette said. "I wish we had a tavern like this back home—for shifters only."

"It makes it nice for us to be ourselves and not worry if any humans are about. Roast beef sandwiches for everyone?" Sam asked.

"Yeah, sounds good to me," Zelda said, and everyone agreed.

"We'll bring them right out." Sam left to handle the food while Silva checked on other tables.

"We do have a jaguar hot spot—a dance club, the Clawed and Dangerous Kitty Cat Club—in Orlando, but it's open to everyone. Of course, humans don't realize the owners and staff are all jaguar shifters, nor that a lot of its patrons are too," Zelda said. "But it's really fun."

"I've never heard of it. I guess we don't have any in Colorado," Landon said.

Gabrielle sat back in her seat. "They took me once to see it. There were no wolves there, just jaguars and a few humans. It was a real eye-opener."

"The jaguars were fascinated with her," Odette said.

"But she wouldn't dance with any of them, which fascinated them all the more," Zelda said.

Landon laughed. Gabrielle was precious. "What if I had been there and asked you to dance?"

"You would have stood a chance."

He knew he would have convinced her to dance with him, if for no other reason than he was the only male wolf among jaguars and humans.

Silva delivered their drinks. "Food will be right up."

Odette began telling Landon and Gabrielle more of the details about Melany's situation. "She actually met Jim at the same jaguar club. He was so sweet and fun to be with, she said. She didn't know he had a gambling problem. He was free with his money, buying strangers drinks. No one was a stranger to him. She couldn't believe he would set her up to take a murder rap so he could convince the Mob, or whoever he owes money to, that he is dead. Untouchable."

"It takes all kinds," Landon said.

Silva served their food. "Enjoy."

"We certainly will," Landon said. Once Silva left, he asked Odette and Zelda, "Did they have life insurance policies for each other?"

"No. Nicole already asked us that. She said that was one reason people faked a death or were truly murdered, for the money. It would have given Melany more of a motive to end his life. Someone would…" Zelda was staring at her water glass.

"What are you thinking?" Odette asked.

"What if someone did get life insurance money for his death? Not Melany. She didn't think he had any on himself, and she certainly wasn't the beneficiary if he did have a policy, but what if he had a girlfriend on the side and they fixed it so she would get the money and then they would live together off the proceeds?"

"Do you have any idea who he might have been seeing?" Landon asked.

"Melany had mentioned a best friend, Belinda Montgomery. Melany said she always thought the two of them seemed more like lovers than just that Belinda was friendly toward him because he was Melany's mate. Shared looks, catching them together in the kitchen and the living room in more intimate poses than Melany thought seemed right. But then he would be so loving toward her, and Melany would think she was just making something out of nothing. Of course, Belinda was her best friend, so Melany figured she would be in her court when she told Belinda she hadn't killed him. She said Belinda was so upset, sure he was really dead, but Melany knew she hadn't killed him," Zelda said.

"Belinda didn't believe Melany?" Gabrielle asked.

"Nope. Melany said Belinda reminded her of all the times she and her mate had fought, as if saying she had to have done it. That it didn't look good. The whole thing was so upsetting, and Melany didn't even have her best friend to back her. Then we were assigned to her case and we found where Melany was hiding and believed in her," Odette said.

"We tried calling Belinda and she didn't answer. We dropped by her house, and she wasn't home. Maybe she was out, who knows, but we wouldn't be surprised if she just—vanished, like Melany's mate did," Zelda said.

"The thing with a gambling addiction is he'll blow through any money they have and be in the same predicament he was in with Melany. But of course if Belinda helped stage this, she deserves everything she gets," Odette said. "Someone had to pick Jim up from the boat, if he didn't fall overboard. He had to have an accomplice."

"There are no family members or other friends that might have helped him out?" Gabrielle asked.

Odette drank some of her water. "A brother, but as far as we know, Jim is estranged from him, and from his parents. He kept asking for more money from them because loan sharks were going to kill him. They would loan him the money and he would spend it gambling. They finally just cut him off about two months ago."

"Unless he had other relatives—aunts, uncles, cousins, grand-parents. His parents said they weren't sure about what happened on the boat. They hoped Melany was okay. She said they never reached out to her. We sent them the video of him at the ATM. Who would be better able to identify him than his own parents or his brother? But they didn't respond," Zelda said.

Landon took a swig of his beer. "They're probably too ashamed to admit he has lied to everyone once again."

After they finished their delightful meals, they drove to the house to switch out vehicles so Nicole could drive the ladies to Doc Mitchell's ranch house to run as shifters.

"Oh, wow, this is the giant snowman you all built?" Zelda said. "It's fantastic. Gabrielle, you don't start small, do you?"

Gabrielle laughed.

CHAPTER 19

WHEN GABRIELLE, NICOLE, AND THE JAGUAR SISTERS ARRIVED at Doc Mitchell's house, he gave them a warm welcome. "You can use any of the rooms to change clothes and shift. The back door has a wolf door, perfect for jaguars too."

"Thanks, Doc," Gabrielle said.

"Thank *you*. Oh, here's a map of the property." He showed her the map while the other ladies went into one of the guest rooms and stripped off their clothes. "I can't tell you how much I appreciate you for taking over the clinic for me."

"I'm glad to. I can't wait to move here and get started." After she looked at the boundary lines to the property, she went to the guest room to remove her clothes. The ladies had already shifted, so she said, "Doc Mitchell has the map if you ladies want to look at it and make sure we don't stray too far."

Nicole barked in agreement and the ladies all left the room. Gabrielle hurried to strip out of her clothes, shifted, and joined them. She was so excited to be running with Nicole and the jaguars.

They all dashed out through the wolf door and ran through the woods, past the lake, all the way to a river bordering the property, startling white-tailed deer that bounded back into the forest.

It would be so much fun doing this again in the spring or summer when they could swim in the lake, too, but Gabrielle was having a blast running through the snow for now.

The jaguars suddenly pounced on each other in play, and Nicole and Gabrielle watched in fascination. Now Nicole could see where Gabrielle had gotten some of her wilder moves that weren't quite wolfish.

Then Zelda broke off to play with the other two shifters and went after Gabrielle. The jaguar sisters weren't going to let her get out of playtime with them.

Gabrielle played with Zelda, but wasn't sure Nicole would be game. Nicole had been watching the jaguars' maneuvers, and she came in to attack Zelda in fun as if she were protecting her wolf sister.

They all got into a grand game of it, mouthing each other's muzzles rather than biting, the jaguars' claws sheathed, until they'd had enough and were heaving with exertion. Then they ran off again to explore more of the property. If Gabrielle hadn't already decided she wanted to move here for good, this would have decided it. The land was beautiful, and she could imagine the fun she could have out here whenever she was free.

When they returned to the lodge, Nicole left to walk to her own house. The jaguar sisters headed into the lodge, and Gabrielle went back to Landon's house, eager to join him.

He quickly opened the door for her as if he'd been standing there half the night waiting for her return. It was late and his sisters had gone to bed.

But Rosco was there eagerly waiting for her too and had to be greeted first before Landon got his turn. Once she'd petted Rosco, and then greeted the kittens that were late in coming for some attention, Landon pulled Gabrielle into his arms and kissed her. "You're cold."

"You're so hot."

He was. She was cloaked in the cold out-of-doors. He was nice and toasty warm. He must have been sitting in front of the fireplace.

"While you were out running, we ended up finding homes for all the kittens. Princess Buttercup, too, if we had wanted to rehome her," Landon said.

"No. You couldn't."

He smiled. "No, she's ours. But the rest will be picked up

tomorrow. Do you want to go swimming?" He waited to hear what she would like to do.

She pulled off her gloves and her ski hat. "It's late. I would rather just hop in bed with you."

He unzipped her ski jacket and helped her out of it. "That's just what I was hoping to hear."

"I'm glad you're so agreeable."

"When it comes to you, it's easy. Let me turn things off here and we can retire to the guest room."

"I'll help."

He hung her ski jacket on the coat-tree and went to turn off the gas fireplace, while she switched off the Christmas tree lights.

She headed for the bedroom and he caught up with her. "Did you have fun?" He shut the bedroom door.

"Yeah." She pulled off her snow boots. "The jaguars are fun to watch while they play and run in the snow, and Nicole enjoyed playing with them too."

"Next time they visit, we'll have to all go out with them."

"I agree. You know, I was thinking about the first time I saw you. You had come into the bar and grill and were talking to your brother, though I didn't know you were brothers at the time. You were wearing a wet bathing suit and had been dripping water all over. You were quite intriguing."

He smiled at her and pulled her into his arms. "Oh, yeah?"

"Yeah. Your brother asked you if you were going to swim or keep dripping water all over the place after you couldn't find me in the swimming pool." She ran her hands up his sweater-covered chest.

He chuckled.

"I think Blake saw me dressing after I got out of the pool outside. He was so sweet. He didn't tell on me."

Smiling, Landon shook his head. "Coal in his stocking for Christmas, then."

She laughed.

With a whisper of a kiss, Landon caressed her mouth with his, his hands running over her shoulders.

She enjoyed how he always made their lovemaking special. "Hmm, I had fun, but coming back here to be with you… This is extra special." She licked his lips and kissed him. She was going to have to leave him way too soon. She wished she could pack him up in her suitcase and take him with her.

His kiss was exploratory, sampling her, taking his fill of her, and she was luxuriating in the feel of him, her tongue sliding over his, the way his hands were sliding down her backside and pressing her tight against his body. And what a body.

His arousal was ready for her to stroke him to climax. She really wanted to go all the way, but she knew she needed to get her affairs in order back home, move here, and get settled before she even thought about committing permanently to a relationship with him.

His hands massaged her buttocks, heating her core, and already she was feeling moist and needy for him. And hot. The new clothes she had bought to keep her warm in the cold out-of-doors had to be ditched whenever Landon made her blood sizzle with his kisses and his tender touch.

He moved his body between her legs, the action meant to increase the contact between his erection and her mons, stirring his pheromones, telling her he wanted her in the worst way. Just as much as she wanted him.

She had to remove her sweater or turn on the air conditioner! She reached down to lift it up, and when she had made a little progress and he realized she was trying to pull it off, he slid it up her arms and over her head and tossed it onto the chair. But she was still wearing the merino wool base shirt underneath that.

Instead of removing that one, he molded his hands to her breasts, the top formfitting and making her feel sexy under his ministrations. Her nipples were aroused and sensitive to his touch as her nether region ached for his penetration. It was probably a good thing she was leaving Silver Town for a while or she would just cave and mate him.

He was just too sexy for her own good. She kissed his mouth as he stroked her nipples with his thumbs in an erotic way. But she rubbed against his erection in a way that was just as stimulating. He groaned. She captured his tongue and sucked, then kissed his lips.

She swept her hands down to his sweater and began to pull it up. He quickly yanked it off, but it landed on the floor. He was too hungry for her to mind where the clothes went now. Or maybe he only worried about taking care with her things.

She was still too hot and getting hotter, though the room was comfortable. It was just the wolf who was making her burn up. Grabbing the bottom edge of her merino wool shirt, she lifted it and he quickly dispensed with it. The shirt landed on the chair. She smiled at him. He was cute.

His hands were on her bra-covered breasts. She'd brought a red lace one for Christmas, just to get in the spirit, never expecting to be showing it off to a bachelor male wolf this season!

But he seemed to approve as he ran his hands tenderly over her lace-covered breasts. He reverently kissed one, then the other. She slid her hands up his chest, eager to run her thumbs over his extended nipples. His erection strained against his pants, and he moaned a little under his breath. Then he cupped her head for a well-placed and thorough kiss, the passion running rampant between them.

Their hearts were beating wildly, their pheromones teasing each other's, the call of the wild upon them. She slid her hands behind his back, pulled him against her body, and rubbed hers against his, sharing her scent, her desire, her need to be with him in the throes of passion.

Tell him you want to mate him, a little voice in her head said. *Tell him you don't want to lose him.*

But then he was unfastening her bra, suckling one nipple then the other, teasing them with his tongue, and she lost all train of thought. Ohmigod, he did wonders to her body.

She reached for her ski pants, but he slid his hands down her waist to remove them instead. She liked how he enjoyed undressing her. Then he pulled her pants off, but this time they hit the carpeted floor with his things. With her fingers on his buckle, she began to unfasten his belt while he was sliding his fingers down her merino wool base pants and panties, cupping her bare buttocks.

Once she unfastened his belt, she unzipped his zipper and ran a fingernail down the opening, stroking his erection in his boxer briefs. He quickly stepped out of his pants and kicked them aside, then pulled down her base pants clinging to her legs. After he removed them, he set her on the bed and removed her socks and yanked off his own. Before he could pull off his boxer briefs and show off his glorious arousal, she was back on her feet doing the honors, kissing him all the way down. He was definitely past ready for her.

He slid her red panties off and climbed into bed with her, but this time he moved her to lie with her back against his chest, and pulled her leg over his so he could stroke her that way. She was in heaven when he began to kiss the side of her neck, her ear, her shoulder, his breath warm against her skin, making the fine hairs at the nape stand to attention. He reached over her waist and down to stroke her clit. To be with him like this always, to enjoy the intimacy, the special touches, whisper-soft kisses, heated craving between them—that's what she was missing from her life.

But she reminded herself that she had already impulsively made the leap to quit her job, sell her home, and move here. She needed to be more circumspect about taking a mate that would be for the rest of her life, which for them was long indeed.

He was stroking her with just the right amount of pressure, the right speed, and she was certain her scent and reactions to him were cluing him in as to just what she needed to send her over the edge. She felt as though she were melting against him, melding, becoming one, even though they weren't joined. Which made her want to turn and join him in the worst way.

She was a sensible veterinarian, not prone to whimsical notions, always thinking things out before she made any major decisions. Her jaguar friends were much more spontaneous than she, yet at this moment, and practically every time she was in Landon's company, she wanted to be more like her friends, let go, and just take the plunge. Turn and tell Landon she wanted to mate him. Give herself fully to him. But the peak was nearly at her fingertips and she was immersed in the pleasure of his strokes pushing her to the end. She cried out and sank happily against the mattress, not moving right away, lost in the afterglow of the climax.

Then she slowly rolled over and lay with his back against her chest as she began to kiss his neck and shoulders, her hand sweeping down his muscular arm. She teased his nipple and slid her hand down his stomach before she felt his erection, wrapped her fingers around the hard length of him, and began to stroke. Like with him being attuned to the nuances of her scent and reaction to his touch, she felt the same thing with him. His shuddery breath, the way his arousal jumped in her grip, the way his body was tensing, all guided her to pleasure him in the best manner possible.

———————

Landon groaned as Gabrielle's hand on his cock sent sensual electrical pulses straight to the brain. He felt like he would end up with sensory overload, her touch was so exquisite. Her musky scent and his, their pheromones all added to the mix, created a carnal pleasure that he'd only felt when he was with her. He had never expected her to turn the tables on him and have his back to her while he was locked in her erotic exploits. With all the foreplay, he was ready to come, but he fought coming too soon, wanting the sensation to last. He imagined being deep inside her, thrusting, penetrating her inner chamber, her inner muscles clamped around his cock.

He shouldn't have envisioned being with her like that, no matter how much he longed to make love to her all the way. But the images plying his brain of her beneath him, him inside her, kissing her, body to body—man, that was all she wrote. He groaned out loud, shuddering, spent, at the pinnacle of the world.

She wrapped her arms around his body and kissed his back. "I guess we need to get some…clean sheets, unless you want to sleep on the wet spot."

He groaned. "Tomorrow, I will have to do laundry." He turned and smiled at her. "With you, a little extra laundry is worth it though."

Once they'd showered and changed the sheets, they snuggled together in bed.

———————

Dating Landon had been surreal, meeting in a winter paradise, no jobs to deter them, no chores to do, just all fun and games. Which was great, but would the magic last once he was back to helping out at the lodge and Gabrielle was busy with pet care—both returning to their regular routines?

Yet she knew from the way she craved being with him, there was more to them than just strictly friendship.

"What do you want to do tomorrow?" Gabrielle asked Landon after making love with him, wanting to spend the time as much as she could with him but still have fun with her friends before she had to fly out with them soon.

"Whatever you would love to do." Landon kissed her head.

"If we can get up in time for swimming, we could do that." But the way she'd been feeling mornings after waking in Landon's arms, she hadn't wanted to go anywhere.

CHAPTER 20

THE MORNING FINALLY CAME WHEN GABRIELLE HAD TO leave, and Landon wanted to spend the rest of the time in bed with her until she had to fly out tonight. He was totally hooked on her. She was still sleeping, one arm draped over his chest, her cheek snuggled against his shoulder. She was his. She had to be. He wanted to give her time to decide that she wanted the same as he. All he knew was he adored her—every waking moment and in his dreams. The only nightmare he had was if she didn't return to him.

His sisters had breakfast before they left the house, but he was just enjoying these few precious moments to lie with Gabrielle before the busy day ahead of them. He wouldn't have any more time to do this with her until she moved here permanently.

She finally opened her eyes, kissed his chest, and looked up at him. "I think we missed swimming."

"We can still swim."

"No way. The pool is open by now."

"Breakfast, then?"

She stretched next to him like a happy she-wolf, her hand caressing his chest. "Let's have breakfast. My friends said they'd eat on their own. That it was more important that we enjoy our time together before I leave."

"What would you like to eat?"

"Waffles."

"Okay." But he didn't make a move to get out of bed, and she didn't make a move to get off him either.

And then they fell asleep again.

When they woke, it was time for lunch. So much for going

skiing. Or having breakfast. Or going swimming. Being with Gabrielle was all that mattered.

"Oh, Landon, I can't believe we've spent all morning in bed together."

"We needed it."

"We did, but we need to go to the lodge and have lunch with your family and my friends before we drive to the airport."

"I don't want you to go."

She smiled at him. "I never thought I would be saying this, but I don't want to either. Still, I'll be back before you know it. Hopefully."

Then they got their lazy selves out of bed, dressed, and he went to make them some coffee and hot tea while she packed her bag. Gabrielle left the clothes she'd bought to go skiing on top of the dresser. She wouldn't need them in Florida, and she couldn't wait to wear them here when she returned.

She went into the kitchen to drink her tea, but he pulled her into his arms and kissed her. "I'll put your bags in my car, and we'll drive over to the lodge so we can load Odette and Zelda's luggage in my vehicle."

"Okay, that sounds good. You're not disappointed we didn't have time to ski, are you?"

"No way! I couldn't have spent the day with you in any better way." He finished his coffee and then loaded her bags in the car.

Then Gabrielle joined him. "I got a text from the sisters. They said we don't have to join them for lunch if we want to spend more time with each other. We'll be together waiting for the plane and all the time of the flight. But I told them we would have lunch with them. Besides, your family is meeting us at the bar and grill to say goodbye."

Landon agreed. "Though I would keep you to myself always if I could, everyone wants to wish you a safe journey back to Daytona Beach."

"I promise I'll see you soon."

They headed over to the lodge, and the first thing they had to do was greet Rosco before they went to the bar and grill. "I will so miss you, Rosco," Gabrielle said, giving him a hug. He greeted her with big tail wags and licks. And she said goodbye to Princess Buttercup. The other kittens had already gone to their homes this morning.

Smiling, Landon petted Rosco on the head. "You are so going to miss Gabrielle when she's gone." Like Landon would. He petted Princess Buttercup too.

Then Landon and Gabrielle joined her friends and the rest of the family for lunch at the bar and grill.

"I can't believe it's only been a little over a week that you've been with us," Roxie said at the long table for groups that they had reserved for the send-off. "But boy, will we miss you."

Nicole agreed. "We're so glad you came and are returning as soon as you are able to."

Blake agreed to that and they all ordered their lunches— everything from crispy salmon to beef tips. Wolves and jaguars both loved their meat. Not a vegetarian among them.

Kayla was smiling and saluted the jaguar sisters with her glass of water. "And we can't wait to see you both again too. Nicole was telling us how she played with you when you went for a run. We want to do that, too, so you'll have to time a visit with us when there's not a new moon."

"Definitely," Odette said.

"Yeah, that's in the works," Zelda agreed.

They talked about Gabrielle settling into the vet's house and how Doc Mitchell was already moving his belongings to his new home so that he could paint her house and get it ready for her.

"Wow, he is the sweetest," Gabrielle said.

"He thinks the same of you," Roxie said. "He couldn't be more excited about you returning to take over the clinic."

After they finished a lovely lunch with the family, Landon helped the sisters load their luggage into his car. Then he drove the jaguar sisters and Gabrielle to the airport in Green Valley.

Once he'd parked, he helped them take their luggage into the airport and then the sisters waited nearby with their bags while he said his goodbyes to Gabrielle.

"Can you return here and spend Christmas with me and my family?" Landon asked her. He couldn't imagine anything worse than being alone at Christmastime, especially since he and his whole family would love her to be here with them. The jaguar sisters had already said they had a mission and would be out of town. He wondered if they really did or if it was a way for him to be together with Gabrielle.

"I'm not sure. I might need to be on call."

He really didn't want her to be all alone in Daytona Beach without him. Which meant if she couldn't return to Silver Town by then, he was going to spend it with her in Florida, no matter whether they were going to be mated or not.

"Then I'll come out there to be with you."

She smiled, gave him a hug and kiss, and smiled again. "You are sure trying to win brownie points."

"I'm going to miss you. You haven't even left and I'm already missing you, knowing what it will be like this afternoon—no skiing with you, or swimming, running as a wolf when I can, or sharing meals and conversation, or playing." And making love to her and snuggling with her the whole night through.

"Your family will be glad to get you back to work."

He laughed. "I'm sure they will. I know you'll be super busy at work during clinic hours. Having lost two of your vets, you'll be even more swamped, but I'll keep in touch as much as I can. When I email you or call or text you, just let me know if you're busy and I'll try not be too much of a nuisance."

She kissed him again and gave him another heartfelt hug. "If I'm in surgery or seeing a client, I'll just text you back later. Otherwise, I won't ever be too busy."

He was sure glad Gabrielle felt that way.

"But she has to make her flight," Odette said, waiting for Landon to give Gabrielle up.

Zelda was smiling at them, looking as though she didn't care as long as she got to see the love scene going on.

"All right. I'll let you go. Text me when you get there safely," he said to Gabrielle.

"I will." Gabrielle kissed him again, then went through the security checkpoint with the jaguar sisters. She waved at him one last time, and then she and her friends were out of sight.

As soon as Landon saw Gabrielle and her friends off at the airport, he felt like his whole world went with her. He couldn't believe he would ever feel that connected, that attached to someone. Much like he was with his sisters and brother, and Nicole now, but he felt something even deeper for Gabrielle. And he knew he wanted her for his mate, now and forever.

Yet he felt compelled to give her time to get used to the whole idea of moving to Silver Town, to settle in—though he would help her get set up. Then he would date her—not for every minute of the day and night the way he'd done when she was all by herself on vacation, but in a courtship way while they both had jobs to do.

Once he returned to the lodge, he tried to concentrate on guests' issues, but he kept thinking about Gabrielle, glancing at the clock in the lobby, knowing she had hardly started home on her flight but already wanting to get her text saying she was safely back home.

Roxie came over and patted Landon on the back. "Why don't you check on Kayla and see how she's coming along with the plans for the refreshments for the Christmas carolers when they come tonight."

He knew Kayla didn't need his help, and he was sure she

would feel he was in the way. But Roxie was right. He couldn't concentrate on what the guests' issues were so Roxie stepped right in to take care of them. Man, was this what it felt like to be lovesick?

He texted Gabrielle: Miss you already.

Landon knew she wouldn't get his message for about three hours, but he had to tell her how he felt. He went into the office and found Princess Buttercup curled up in her favorite chair. She loved the family, but she was just as happy to sleep when they weren't playing with her.

Kayla was working away at the plans for the refreshments. "Do you need me to help you with anything?" he asked her.

Kayla's eyes widened to see him standing there. "I thought you were… Uh, no, thanks, Landon. Would you take Rosco for a walk though? He seems to be missing someone, and he's been in here looking for her five times already."

Hell, Landon knew just how Rosco felt. Just then, he felt a nose bumping his hand. He looked down to see Rosco trying to get his attention and Landon chuckled.

"See? What did I tell you? That makes six times." Kayla smiled at the two of them.

"I'll take him for a walk." Maybe Landon would stop thinking about Gabrielle for a while then. But as soon as he bundled up and took Rosco outside, waved at Blake who was talking to some of their pack mates out front, and headed for the path through the woods, all he could think of was how he wished Gabrielle was with him and Rosco, taking a walk in the snowy woods. He had to get back on track, keep busy, and quit thinking about her every second she was gone. She would be back here before he knew it, and then he would have all the time in the world to see her after they both finished their workdays.

"You miss her too, don't you, buddy?" Landon asked Rosco, as if the dog knew what he was saying.

Rosco looked up at him, his tongue panting, his eyes bright and his tail wagging frantically.

"Yeah, me too."

———————

On the flight to Florida, Gabrielle was thinking about how she had so much to do when she returned home and feeling overwhelmed. Odette was sitting next to the window, Gabrielle in between, and Zelda in the aisle seat.

"You have a whole new life ahead of you," Odette said, glancing from the window to Gabrielle.

"There's just so much to do." She had already begun making lists so that she would stop worrying about all the up-in-the-air stuff.

Zelda patted her knee. "You know we'll help you out when we can. You told us the wolf pack of Silver Town would help you move, too, so don't worry about it so much. Your Colorado state veterinarian license will come through just fine. You'll get a couple more vets to work for the clinic before you know it. I mean, who wouldn't want to be living in beautiful Daytona Beach? You're only leaving because you have a much better offer, being the wolf that you are. Just sell your place before it's hurricane season."

Gabrielle chuckled. Her friends always knew how she was feeling.

"We're thinking of moving to the Houston or Dallas area with the JAG agency so we can be closer to where you are," Zelda said.

"Yep, so we can visit more often," Odette said. "You'll have a guest room just for us, right?"

"And the lake surrounded by woods and with a mountain view, yes." When Gabrielle thought about being settled in there, she felt good. It was just the getting moved there and the settling in that had her stomach tied up in knots.

And then there was Landon. Gabrielle closed her eyes and all she could envision was him looking down at her in the swimming pool, smiling, his dark eyes gazing upon her with interest and intrigue. She sighed and thought of his hugs, his hot body wrapped around hers, telling her he wanted to continue seeing her when she returned. She hoped while she was away no she-wolf would attempt to seduce him. She would have a thing or two to say about that when she returned, if so.

When she and her friends finally arrived at the airport in Daytona Beach, she turned on her phone and found she had ten text messages from Landon. Every one of them said he missed her and he couldn't wait to see her again.

She smiled and texted him back: I'm here and I miss you too and can't wait to see you either.

———

For the twelve days after Landon and Gabrielle had parted company, he had tried to give her some space and not text or call her constantly. During the family dinner at Landon's and his sisters' house, he poked at his chicken wings, everyone's favorite food, yet he wasn't hungry. He missed Gabrielle's cheerful smiles and warm hugs, going to bed with her at night and playing with her during the day.

"Listen," Blake said to Landon, "you're feeling just like I did when Nicole was still thinking of returning to Denver and her PI practice there. Except Gabrielle lives even further away and she's got to take care of her furry patients before she can move here. She's got a ton of things to do with getting ready to move, and you aren't able to focus much at the lodge with her gone right now. So we all took a vote and agreed to call her on your behalf to see if you could help her out."

Landon's jaw dropped. He couldn't believe his family was

looking out for him like that, or that they'd noticed how distracted he'd been. Or that they would call her and see if it was all right for him to help her without talking to him about it.

"We know you didn't want to get in her way while she's working, and you wanted to be here for us after taking off that one week, but you're not able to concentrate on anything that needs to be done around here," Roxie said. "She is thrilled you want to go out and assist her. She's been feeling overwhelmed, but after you spent so much time with her during her vacation, she didn't want to ask you to take off any more time to be with her. Or to upset us that you would not be helping us out. We quickly assured her that's not the case. That you're hopelessly stuck on her and aren't any help at all."

Landon chuckled. He loved his family.

"We bought you a one-way ticket to Daytona Beach," Kayla said. "All of us pitched in for it. You're leaving tomorrow morning, and she'll pick you up at the airport during her lunch break. She said to be sure to bring your swimsuit. Her pool is heated."

Landon smiled. "You are the best family ever."

Nicole scooped up a forkful of green bean casserole. "I couldn't wait to get settled in here with Blake. I spoke with Gabrielle too. She's swamped with work, but she's thrilled you're coming to be with her. She said it won't be all about work, and I didn't ask for clarification."

"Besides," Blake warned, "you had better make sure you're mated before you return with her so you don't have to fight off the other wolves who are trying to garner her attention. I saw Doc Mitchell today at the lodge. He came by to see how things were going with Gabrielle and hadn't realized she had gone home already. I think he's worried she might change her mind once she is back in Daytona Beach. He said three of our bachelor males who have trained avalanche rescue dogs have canceled their dogs' annual physicals so they can reschedule for when Gabrielle is running the clinic."

Everyone laughed.

"I will make every effort to convince her I'm the only wolf for her."

Now, Landon had an appetite again and he began to eat some of his wings. "Are there any more?"

As soon as dinner was done, Landon began packing for his trip to Daytona Beach. He paused to call Gabrielle though. "Hey."

"Hey, you. I hear you've been missing me."

"Hell yeah. I think I've been making a total nuisance of myself at the lodge, but I don't want to upset your work or process, if you think I'll be more trouble than it's worth. I'm packing and I'll be there if you're good with it."

"Well, I told your family to warn you I've got packing boxes all over the place."

"That's what I want to hear. I'm really good at packing."

"You've got a job, then. When I get home at night, I'm too tired to pack much and I'll never be ready to leave when I need to."

"I'll get it done." He would do it all for her so she wouldn't have to lift a finger when she got home from a day at the clinic. He was ready to give her back rubs and any other special attention she would need.

"Oh, thank you. I've been wishing you could join me, but I was afraid your family would miss your help too much."

"Ha, they're so eager to get rid of me, they even bought the plane ticket to send me on my way."

Gabrielle laughed. "*I* was planning to send you the airfare. I'm so glad you're coming."

"I was going to join you for Christmas no matter what, if you couldn't get out of there by then to spend it with me and my family."

"Oh, good, because I wasn't sure if I could get out of here in time for Christmas. If we get a new vet or two in, they can take the Christmas on-call issues. They'll be the newest ones on staff. But if we don't, the rest of us will have to take turns and I won't be able to join you in Silver Town."

"I'll be there, then." He wasn't going to leave her until she was ready to go for good. He couldn't wait to see her tomorrow.

CHAPTER 21

THE NEXT MORNING, ROXIE GAVE LANDON A LIFT TO THE airport. He was as excited as when he was a kid getting a favorite toy at Christmastime. He had every intention of doing everything he could to help Gabrielle and not stress her out any more than he knew she had to already feel about the move.

"You two have fun. I know you both have work to do, but this is also a time to get to know each other better in her own domain."

"I agree. Tell everyone thanks again."

"I will. You deserve it, Landon, as hard as you work. At least until Gabrielle came into your life. You are absolutely no good without her." Roxie smiled and gave him a hug and kiss. "And I mean that in a good way."

He hugged and kissed her back. "I'm seriously going to have to get some Christmas presents for all of you."

She laughed. "I've seen the packages under the tree for us already. Take care, Brother, and have a good time."

"Hopefully, we'll see you soon."

Then Landon checked his bags, went through security, and boarded the plane. The flight to Florida seemed to take forever, probably because he was so anxious to see Gabrielle again. He was envisioning swimming in her pool and catching her, like the mermaid she was. Then before he knew it, he was at the Daytona Beach International Airport and Gabrielle was waiting for him at the luggage carousel, collecting him and his suitcases. She was all smiles, hugs, and kisses and he knew—if he'd even had any doubts—that he had done the right thing in coming here.

She motioned to the suitcases. "Did you pack enough stuff?"

"Yeah, just in case it takes us longer to get you moved. But if you get tired of me being around, you can send me packing."

"Ha! You will have way too much work to do. Now that you're here, I'm not letting you go, just in case you get homesick."

He wrapped his arms around her back and kissed her again. "God, I've missed you. You fill a special place in me that I never knew existed."

"Oh, I feel the same way about you. I've been really busy with work with the shortage of vets, believe me, and still trying to get rid of stuff before I move and put the house up for sale, but whenever I was free—swimming in the pool in the evening for a respite, trying to sleep at night—all I could think of was you and seeing you again. I was serious about sending you airfare, but I had to make sure that your family wouldn't miss you."

He laughed. "They were so ready to be rid of me."

She smiled. "They love you."

"They sure do." He kissed her cheek, then grabbed two of his bags, leaving his laptop for her to carry.

"I picked up some Reuben sandwiches and bottled waters for lunch. I wouldn't have had enough time to make us lunch or for us to drop by somewhere to eat in. I'm afraid I've got to get back to work after I drop you off at the house."

"That's no problem at all. Did you want me to drive and you can eat on the way?" he asked.

"No, that's okay. I know my way around and we'll get there quicker. How was your flight?"

"Long, but shorter than when we return home, since we'll be driving. If you want me to stay until you are able to return."

"Oh, yeah, you're helping me drive to Colorado. We can stop someplace on the drive to Silver Town and enjoy ourselves. No sense in rushing to get there," Gabrielle said.

He took his fill of her, her blond hair done up in a bun, her green eyes bright with excitement, her shiny, pink lips curved in a perpetual smile. She was wearing black slacks, pumps, and a long-sleeved black shirt, professional. He suspected she wore a lab coat over them at work.

It was hot and humid here, seventy-one degrees this afternoon. When they reached her car, he admired the silvery-blue Camaro convertible. A cool car for a sexy mermaid of a wolf. He loaded his bags into the trunk.

Before he got into her car, he pulled off his sweater and rolled up his long-sleeved shirt.

"Are you hot?" she asked.

He gave her a wolfish smile.

She laughed. "I sure missed you. Well, I received good news while you were on your flight coming here. The Colorado state board has all my vet documentation. So now it's just a matter of them taking the time to approve my Colorado license." She got into the car, started it, then got out and set the partition in the trunk, and folded the top down as Landon watched in fascination.

"That's great news, and that's one fantastic car." He climbed into the passenger seat.

She sat in the driver's seat and smiled at him, then drove to her house. "I figured you would like the car. In other great news, we have two veterinarians coming in for interviews this week. We're hoping they like the facility and the rest of the vets in the co-op like them so that we can hire them."

"They'll still be short because of the vet with the broken leg though." He hoped that didn't delay things further.

"Right, but they said it wouldn't be a problem for me to leave."

"Okay, good." He was glad to hear it because he didn't want to have to hold out here too long, though he knew his family could do without him for as long as it took. "It seems surreal not to see any snow here."

She laughed. "That's something I'm going to have to get used to at a ski resort. But I'm excited about seeing the fall colors, and it's fun dressing up for the fall. Here, it's hot, hotter, hottest, and cool."

He laughed. "You'll definitely get all the seasons there."

"Did you make your gingerbread house?"

They had skipped making it while Gabrielle was there so she could spend more time alone with Landon at the end of her trip. Next year, it would be a family affair. He hoped.

"Yeah, but it didn't win. Silva at her tea shop won. She made one of a teapot, featuring windows and a door."

"How cute. I'm glad she won."

"The MacTire sisters of the Silver Town Inn won on the snow sculptures again. We did win on the lighting of our lodge."

"That's great! And Sparkle, the giant snowman?"

"That was a big hit. Everyone loved it because no one had thought to create a giant snowman. Everyone has been creating snowman families because we're so family-oriented, so ours took first place. Tons of people, both guests in town and pack members, took pictures of it to share."

"I'm so glad I got to help you make it."

"Me too. But remember, next year—"

"Oh, next year the vet clinic will be in direct competition with you."

He laughed.

"I'm serious."

He laughed again. He couldn't help himself. He had missed her lighthearted sense of humor.

When they arrived at Gabrielle's place, he loved the white stucco one-story house with the red tile roof. He noticed she didn't have any Christmas decorations out, no lights on the trees or house.

"You didn't decorate for Christmas."

"I have boxes of decorations, but I wasn't planning on having anyone here for Christmas and I was gone right after Thanksgiving, visiting Silver Town, so it didn't seem like enough time between when I returned home and when Christmas arrived to bother."

"Gotcha." And she was working and she didn't have anyone to help her with it anyway.

She carried his laptop and the sacks of food into the house and he brought in his suitcases.

Several packed and sealed boxes were stacked against one wall in the living room. Otherwise, everything looked neat and tidy and like she wasn't going anywhere. He hoped to remedy that in short order.

"I've got to eat and run. If you start packing, just try and only pack things I might not need for a few weeks."

"Like your pictures hanging on the walls?"

"Yeah, though I'm thinking of selling any of the ones that have beach themes. You can take them down and set them against a wall. I have spackle sitting on the kitchen counter. You could putty up all the nail holes."

"I'll certainly do that."

"I should have asked," she said, opening her sacked sandwich. "You are a handyman of sorts, aren't you?"

"I sure am."

"Good. Could you clean the pool, if you don't mind? The sweeper is running, but I noticed some leaves fell into the bottom and it's not getting them. So go for a swim, unpack, make yourself comfortable. I have a list of things on the counter that I'm trying to do. If you see anything on there that you could do, feel free to. Or if you think of anything else that might need to be taken care of before I put the house on the market, feel free to handle it."

"I'm your man."

"Hmm, and a wolf at that. I feel so relieved that you're here. I know we can knock a lot of this stuff out, but don't worry. I don't intend to make you work the whole time. I want to take you to the beach and out to eat, swimming in the pool, stuff like that. I want to enjoy being with you."

"I can't wait. Don't worry about a thing. I'm here to help, not to make more work for you."

"We'll have fun too. I need some downtime." She ate her sandwich and drank some of her water. "I hate to eat and run when you just got here, but I really need to get back to the clinic before my next client arrives."

Landon rose from his chair and drew her into his arms and kissed her. "More of this later."

She smiled. "I will hold you to your promise. God, I'm glad you're here." She gave him a big hug and a brief kiss, then headed for the door. "The place is yours."

Then Gabrielle left the house, and Landon texted Roxie to let her know he'd arrived just fine and Gabrielle had gone back to work.

Roxie texted: Make sure you show her a good time. Don't just do a bunch of work to get ready to move.

Landon replied: We're going to have fun.

Roxie texted: Good. Talk to you later.

Landon took the rest of his sandwich and water outside to the patio that overlooked the swimming pool, sat down at the table, and smiled. He would never have come to Daytona Beach if Gabrielle hadn't been here. All this was going to be work, but they would make it fun. He did see the appeal of her home, though, and how different it was here from her new home in Colorado. He hoped she wouldn't miss it too terribly. He, his family, and the wolves in the pack would have to make sure that didn't happen.

He spent the rest of the day taking down pictures throughout the house and setting them in a spare sewing room. Then he began putting all of the nail holes. He didn't want to paint until they had more of the stuff cleared out of the house. He looked at the list she had on her table. She wanted to have a garage sale this weekend. He smiled. He'd never done that before. It should be fun.

He made up signs for the garage sale and set them in the corner of the living room. Then he went through all the Florida pictures and placed them against the wall with the garage sale sign. He figured if she wanted to keep any, she could sort them out and set them aside.

Then he found his board shorts in one of his suitcases and stripped out of his clothes and put them on. He thought that her request to have him clean the pool really meant she wanted him to have some fun and not work all the time while she was at the clinic, but he didn't mind helping out wherever she needed him to. That was a good part of why he was here.

He walked outside. It was still seventy-one degrees Fahrenheit, which felt hot to him after being in the freezing weather in Silver Town. He dove into the heated pool and swam across the length. It was a nice-sized pool, the water perfectly warm. A pretty landscaped yard provided privacy from the neighbors, though all the places here were one-story and they had six-foot wooden fences. He suspected a lot of the homes had swimming pools. If he had lived here, he certainly would have invested in one.

He left the pool, grabbed a net from a storage building, jumped back into the pool, and began cleaning. When he was done with that, he swam some more laps, but he wanted to swim with Gabrielle later too.

He went inside, grabbed his clothes, went to the guest bathroom, and took a shower. He was thinking of making dinner for them when he heard the garage door open, and he hurried to dry off and pulled on his clothes. "You're home." He was so glad to see her.

"Yeah. We're only open until six thirty weekdays, and on Saturday until one thirty, closed on Sunday."

"Okay, good. I was going to make us some dinner."

She smiled and hugged him. "Are you sure?"

"Yeah. I can cook something on the grill. It's perfect weather for it."

"Sure, that would be great." She glanced at his suitcases still sitting in the living room. "Oh, I'm sorry, I should have told you before I ran back to the clinic that you could stay in my room. I'm trying to keep all the rooms as neat as possible for when it comes time to put the house up for sale so I wanted to use only the one bedroom. Did that sound convincing enough *without* sounding like I am claiming you for my mate?"

He laughed. "Yeah, I agree with your logic." He hadn't wanted to assume she would want him in her bed at night here, though he'd sure hoped that's where he would be staying.

"Thanks for the garage sale signs. They're great. And so is the spackling. I'll price the paintings tonight, and we can store them in the sewing room until the sale this weekend. I don't work this Saturday, but I'll be working the next Saturday, which is why I planned the garage sale for this weekend."

"Okay. If you want me to start it on Friday, I can do it by myself."

"Oh, that would be a great idea. We could keep bringing more stuff out on Saturday and Sunday." She pulled out a package of chicken thighs. "Here, you can grill these and I'll make us mashed potatoes and chicken gravy and broccoli."

"That sounds good."

"I have boxes of stuff in the sewing room I planned to get rid of. And furniture too. I listed them in the garage sale ad."

"Okay, great."

After they had their dinner, Gabrielle cleared the table. "Let's go to the beach. I might not have very much longer to visit it, and being able to go with you will make it even more special to me."

"I would love that."

They dressed in jeans, and she wore a sweatshirt while he was wearing a T-shirt. She was going to wear a light jacket. She made him take one, too, just in case, but he insisted he wouldn't need it.

She let him drive the short distance to the beach—he loved her car!—and they parked and saw the hotels featuring tons of Christmas lights. Then they got out, rolled up their pants legs, and began walking along the boardwalk until they reached the stairs to the sandy beach. The sun had already set, but with their wolf vision they could see perfectly well. A cool, steady sea breeze swept over them.

"This is great," Landon said, walking on the sandy beach with her. "Not that I want to convince you to stay here, but I can see why you enjoy it."

"I'm going to love taking hikes with you in the woods and running as a wolf, and we'll still have a lot of fun. It won't be the same, but we can always take trips to other places that have beaches."

We? He took her hand and looked down at her. She was eyeing the sand under their feet, then glanced up at him. And smiled.

"I look forward to being with you in the new place. I realize it won't be the same as here, but being with a pack more than makes up for it," he said.

"Being with you makes up for most of it," she said.

"Most of it?" He laughed.

"Well, we will have to see, won't we?"

Then she pulled at his hand and ran into the shallow water, back out of it, and down the beach. He chased after her, loving this, coming here, being with her in her world.

———

When they were ready to go home, Gabrielle pulled a couple of beach towels out of the trunk of her car and handed Landon one. "I have them in my car for trips to the beach." She brushed the sand off her legs and shook out the towel. He did the same, then they climbed into the car. She let him drive home. She swore he was torn between loving her and the car. She suspected whenever they had a chance to drive in warm weather in Colorado, he would want to be the one driving the car.

Once they reached home, they headed inside the house. "Let's go for a swim." It was her usual routine and now his too. But what would happen after that wouldn't be routine at all. She wasn't sure she could hold out that long though.

They stripped out of their wet jeans and shirts and underwear and put on their swimsuits. She grabbed a couple of fresh towels for them and then they went outside to the pool. She dropped the towels on the chaise lounge, then dove into the pool before he did. He quickly dove in after her and caught up to her. He pulled her into his arms. This time he wasn't letting her swim laps first.

He encircled her waist with his arms and kissed her smiling lips. She wrapped her arms around his neck and kissed him back, his stiffening erection already pressing against her body.

"I have caught you and you are mine," she said, even though he was the one keeping them afloat and keeping her pressed against his hard body.

"You are mine as well, sweet wolf. All mine." He kissed her thoroughly.

She would miss this with him, their private pool with no prying eyes watching them, like they could have at the lodge. But they would have the lake in summer too.

And the woods to run in as wolves.

"I am so glad I'm here." He finally let go of her so they could swim their laps.

But she wanted him to be her mate and she was much too impatient to delay the inevitable. She couldn't wait to make love to him all the way. As long as he was agreeable!

"I've dated off and on over the years, but I never met a wolf like you who means everything to me. I can't wait for this. In between clients, that was all I'd been thinking of." She took his hand and walked through the shallow end of the pool to the stairs. "Laps later. You are the only wolf for me."

"Hell, you mean you're going to agree to mate me?"

She loved it when he looked like he was ready to eat her all up. She smiled, kissed his chest, then grabbed a towel and wrapped it around herself. He might be hot in the Florida winter weather, but she was cold. "Yeah, I can't resist you any longer. If I have to persuade you further, I will. But if you love me the way I love you…"

He grabbed his towel and dried himself off in a hurry. "Oh, hell yeah, I do. Why do you think I came out here after you'd only been gone for a short while? It seemed like forever. I was hopelessly lost without you. Hopelessly in love with you. Nothing was the same after you left. I would have done anything to convince you that you were the only one for me."

She smiled up at him and kissed his warm mouth. "Then let's make this official."

"I'm beyond ready for that!" He dropped his towel on a chair, grabbed her up, and carried her into the house and then into the bedroom. "Shower first?"

"Yeah." They ended up in her walk-in shower and she turned on the hot water.

He pulled off her bikini top and then kissed her breasts.

She ran her hand over his rock-hard erection, his wet swimsuit molding to him. "Hmm," she said as he started to kiss her, their tongues making contact, sliding, tasting, teasing.

"How could I have ever gotten so lucky," he murmured against her wet hair.

"You were determined to catch me breaking your pool rules."

He kissed her lips again, his hands sliding down her wet back until he reached her buttocks and slipped his hands under her bikini bottom waistband. His hands were hot on her cold bottom, and she loved how heated she felt whenever he was holding her close, kissing her, hugging her.

She pulled at his board shorts, and once he slipped them down his legs, he kicked them free and pulled off her bikini bottoms. Then he was wrapping her legs around him and holding her against the tile wall, kissing her again.

"You're sure you want to mate now? No doubts?" he asked.

It would be forever as wolf mates, so she knew why he wanted to make sure she was absolutely ready for this. "Yes, I want to mate you now. And it's all your fault."

He chuckled, then set her feet on the shower floor. "I knew I couldn't live without you once you came into my life."

She ran her hands over his muscular buttocks and marveled at his ripped, muscled strength—all of him, from his abs to his pecs and biceps, all the muscle groups and more. His sizzling brown-eyed gaze took his fill of her, as if he thought she was the most beautiful she-wolf in the world. To her, he was the most beautiful he-wolf known to wolfkind and he was about to be all hers.

He kissed her mouth, pressing gently, then deepening the kiss until their tongues were tasting and teasing each other's. He moved his warm mouth from her lips to her neck and began kissing her with sweeping, nuzzling kisses, making her tingle with need. The sexual attraction had been there from the moment she'd met him. She'd never felt this way toward any male she'd ever been with. Landon was the one for her—forever and ever.

Their hearts were pounding hard as she nuzzled his chest with her mouth. She reached his taut nipples with her lips, brushed them over each nipple, and licked each in turn. He growled softly. She nibbled on his nipple and he groaned. "You take my breath away," he said hoarsely.

She smiled, loving that she could practically bring him to his knees. But he nearly did the same to her when he massaged her breasts, licked her nipples, and slipped his hands under her buttocks. He pulled her tight against his rock-hard body. God, he felt good.

She kissed his chest. "I sure missed you."

He ran his fingers through her wet hair. "I sure missed you too. I couldn't wait to be with you again." Then he kissed her mouth again. "I adore you, cherish you." With his fingers, he spread her feminine lips to find her nub and began to stroke her.

The hot water was sluicing over her back, as she continued to cling to him or she would have melted right into the tile floor. She was kissing his mouth, their tongues licking and tasting. She sucked on his tongue and he groaned. She wanted to howl.

He was stroking her feminine nub, working her. He had such a marvelous way of bringing her to the top. He was so good. "Ohmigod." She was nearly there, so close. "Oh, yeah."

She was about to come. As if he realized just how close he was to bringing her to climax, he lifted her up, and she wrapped her legs around him. This time, he pressed his stiff arousal into her and thrust. This was just what she wanted. Him as her mate for all time. His erection embedded deep inside her, filling her, making her feel glorious and loved.

He held her tight, her legs wrapped around his hips, her arms around his neck, and she kissed him as he pulled his cock nearly out and thrust deep inside her. She moaned as the crescendo built and then she shattered, feeling a million pleasures all at once in the center of her core, spreading out, making her feel one with him.

He ground into her and then began to thrust again, her legs still wrapped securely around his hips, her anchor, her mate.

He began to kiss her mouth again, hot and firm, pressuring with passion. She felt loved, satiated, happier than she'd ever been, with a man and wolf who had made her dreams come true.

———————

Landon had hoped it would come to this, making love fully with Gabrielle, consummating their relationship, becoming mated wolves. He hadn't thought they would do it the first night he was back with her, but he was glad he didn't have to beg her to mate him before long.

She was his dream wolf, and he couldn't have been more thrilled she hadn't wanted to wait any longer either. He knew in his heart she had been the only one for him the moment he had caught her breaking their rules while wearing the string bikini at the lodge swimming pool and learned she was a wolf. And everything from then on had worked toward culminating in this—a mating between two wolves in love.

He was thrusting hard, not wanting to come too quickly, but he had no intention of stopping there for the night. Later tonight, he was ravishing his beautiful mate all over again. But no matter how hard he tried to keep from coming, her sweet and sexy shewolf scent, her moans of pleasure, their pheromones enticing each other, her soft body wrapped around his—all propelled him toward the summit. With one last powerful surge, he came with an explosive climax and howled his delight.

She chuckled, but then she made him hold her still. "Hold on, I'm almost…" She couldn't get the words out, as he realized just what she needed. He worked his hand between them and began to coax another climax out of her while he was still embedded in her. She was so perfect for him.

"Oh, ah, yes," she cried out, and collapsed in his arms.

He set her down on the floor and began to soap her up with her watermelon bodywash, and she washed his hair with her peach shampoo. He laughed. He would be happy to always smell like her fragrant shampoos and bodywashes—and her.

They finally finished rinsing off and left the shower stall so they could dry off and retire to bed. He knew she had a long day ahead of her and she needed to get her sleep. But if she wanted more loving in the middle of the night, he would do whatever he could to make her happy. He knew he would be ready for more at a moment's notice.

About two in the morning, she began kissing his chest and running her hand over his erection and he growled low with intrigue. It was time to love his she-wolf all over again.

CHAPTER 22

The next day, Gabrielle had the worst time leaving the bed, Landon, and the house, but finally she managed to dress for work, and he made hash browns and sausage for them before she was out the door.

Despite all Landon's help with packing, she was feeling inundated and hated that so much stuff was in boxes, though he was keeping the place as neat and orderly as possible. She was just ready to move, like, yesterday. "Thanks for all the help with doing the garage sale." She hoped she sold a ton of stuff before the weekend even got here.

She was looking forward to seeing who was coming today for the vet interview. When Phillip Reddington arrived, interested in working at the co-op, she realized who he was. A former vet student, though he'd transferred the first year she was in school with him, which was why she hadn't remembered his name.

"When I saw that you were one of the people who is part of the co-op," Phillip said to Gabrielle, "I was ready to sign on the dotted line to join you." He smiled broadly at her and then gave her a hug. "I'm so glad to see you."

She was surprised he remembered her. He was always a charmer, more of a playboy than anything even just the year she'd known him. He'd been dating a college student at the time. Of course, Gabrielle hadn't been interested in him in the least. He was strictly human.

"Thanks. It's good seeing you too. But I'm one of the vets that is quitting."

"No."

She smiled. "Yes, I'm needed at a clinic in Colorado. As soon as we can hire a couple of vets to fill our vacancies, I'll be leaving." She'd never thought she would be so happy to leave.

Phillip's mouth gaped. "Wow, here I thought we would be working together."

"Please don't change your mind about joining the clinic. We have a great staff and the part-time vets and the full-time one are wonderful to work with. I would never have left here if I hadn't met someone who lives in Colorado."

Phillip smiled. "The good ones are always taken. Can you show me around the clinic?"

"I sure can." She was thrilled that he was interested in working there.

"I've always wanted to live in this area, but I'm disappointed that you won't be staying."

"You will have a great time. And if you're looking for a home, I have one I'm putting up for sale that has a heated pool even and is close to the beach." She figured she would throw that out, just in case he was interested.

"I'll certainly take a look at it if you want to show it to me."

Yes! "Do you want to drop by and see the house and have dinner with us tonight?"

"Sure. I would like that. Thanks."

"Oh great." She showed Phillip all the exam rooms, the surgery rooms, and the kennels, and then they met with the other vets, two who came in a couple of times a week and the full-time vet who was staying.

Phillip was a likable guy, so she hoped everyone would welcome him with open arms. In the meantime, between clients, she texted Landon: We are having a guest join us for dinner. I met him at vet school, and he's interested in being part of the staff at the clinic.

Landon texted back: That's great.

Gabrielle texted: Wait until I tell you all of it. Can you straighten the place up? He's going to look at it with maybe hopes of buying the house. Fingers crossed.

She hadn't meant for poor Landon to have to get her home ready for viewing by a potential buyer, but if it made a difference in a sale, she was sure he would want to help out.

Landon texted: Hot damn! It will be spotless. I'll close up the garage sale around one to fix us lunch. What do you want me to make us for dinner?

She knew he was the wolf for her and texted: Barbecued ribs?

Landon texted: It will be my pleasure.

She texted: We'll see you at 6:45 for dinner, but I'll come home for lunch at 1.

Landon texted: See you then.

Her heart soared with hope that Phillip would buy her house. Since Doc Mitchell had given her a free home and clinic, she could afford to reduce the price on her home if Phillip could take it off her hands. Not for free, of course. He wasn't a wolf, and she could easily sell it to someone else for the price. The list price for the four-bedroom, two-and-a-half-bath home was $392,000, but she'd paid considerably less for it when she bought it. And with inheritances and her own savings, it was paid off. So she could furnish her new home just the way... Ohmigosh, it really hadn't sunk in that she and Landon were mated and would be living in the doc's house...together. So she and Landon would set up housekeeping just the way the two of them liked it—which meant when they returned to Colorado, they were going to have to make some trips to the furniture stores. They could use the money from the proceeds of the sale of the house to buy whatever they needed. If they didn't go through a Realtor, that would also be an expense she wouldn't have.

Phillip had lunch with a couple of the vets while Gabrielle went home to see Landon and have a bite to eat. The place looked immaculate. He had moved the paintings to the sewing room, the garage sale signs too. He had cleaned the bathrooms and kitchen and had made them grilled cheese sandwiches for lunch.

"So, what do you think?" he asked.

She wrapped her arms around Landon's neck and pressed her body against his. "I'd think you're a keeper, even if I hadn't already mated you."

He smiled. "I'm in it for the long run and I'm not giving you up for anything either, but I meant about the house. Do you need me to do anything more with it?"

They sat down to eat their grilled cheese sandwiches.

"No, just relax. We'll have dinner with Phillip, and if he wants the house, he'll buy it. If he doesn't? No sweat. I'll list it with a real estate agent and put it on the market when I'm ready," she said. "How did the garage sale go?"

"You sold a couple hundred dollars' worth of items. You had buyers for thrift stores come right after you left when I was just putting stuff out. They hung around to see what all you were selling."

She smiled. "Good."

"Is Phillip taking the job?"

"I sure hope so. We just need another taker and then I can leave. We have another vet coming in tomorrow who is checking out the clinic. When I can leave, if I still don't have my Colorado state license, I might have to hang around the ski lodge and be a ski bum." She arched a brow.

"I'll keep you company."

She laughed. "I'm sure your family would love that. *Not.*"

"They will be so happy it worked out between us that they will agree to anything where you're concerned."

She sighed. "Good. That's partly why I mated you, you know. I gained your family too."

"Speaking of which, it was too late last night to call them to give them the good news, and then you had to leave for work right after breakfast. So, if you think we have a moment...?"

"Absolutely. They'll stop worrying about us then."

They finished their sandwiches.

"The sandwich was really good. Now I know you can make us meals if I'm too tired to do it after work," she said.

"You bet." He pulled out his phone and called Roxie. "Hey, Sis, we have some news. We're mated." He put it on speakerphone.

"Yes!" Roxie yelled. "Wait, hold on. Blake! Kayla! Come here!"

"Yeah, what's wrong?" Blake asked, his breathing heavy. She suspected he'd run from some distance, worried something was wrong.

"They mated! Landon and Gabrielle!" Roxie said.

"Woo-hoo," Kayla said. "We need to celebrate when you come back."

"Yeah, we're so glad," Blake said. "Nicole's on a job so we'll tell her when we end the call. Do you want to tell the pack leaders, or do you want us to?"

"Gabrielle has to go back to work. She was just on a lunch break. I'll call them as soon as she goes in."

"What about the job situation?" Blake asked.

"One vet appears to be interested. They have another coming in to check things out tomorrow," Landon said.

"Okay, well, that sounds hopeful that you'll be joining us soon," Roxie said.

"This is all such great news," Kayla added.

"I've got to run, but my first ski experience turned out to be the best ski experience I could have ever had," Gabrielle said.

Everyone laughed.

Then Gabrielle gave Landon a hug and kiss and hurried back into work while Landon continued to talk to his family. She was feeling really hopeful that she could be moving with Landon soon. She spent the rest of the day working at the office, and that night, Phillip arrived to have dinner with Gabrielle and Landon.

She showed Phillip the house, and he looked through the

Florida paintings. The way he was smiling at the size of the kitchen, the views of the swimming pool, and the layout of the open living room and dining room, she could tell he was impressed with the house. Then they sat down to have ribs and they were out of this world.

"These are great, Landon," she said.

"Yeah, the best," Phillip agreed.

Afterward, they sat poolside, having Christmas margaritas. Christmas lights sparkled in the pool, and she was so glad Landon had found the box of lights in her garage and hung them up on the trees and on her back patio. They made the pool and setting even more spectacular.

"This is sure a nice place. How much is the property going to be listed for?" Phillip asked.

She could envision him having a bevy of girls over to join him in the pool. "It's valued at $392,000, but I was thinking if you would buy it, no Realtor—so no agent's fee—and since you're a friend and taking the job at the clinic so I can have a chance to leave, I would offer it for $370,000. It's on a half-acre lot too."

Phillip's eyes widened.

She wasn't sure if he wasn't expecting it to cost that much, or if he was surprised that she would drop the price that low just for him. She would have to pay about $20,000 for a real estate agent's fee otherwise, if she couldn't sell it on her own. "But I would only offer that price to you. Once it goes on the market, my price is firm. It's worth every penny."

"And the furniture?"

Her lips parted. Now she was surprised. "The major pieces of furniture can go with the house." She wouldn't get that much for used furniture, she figured, and if it helped sell the house, she would give it to him.

"The Florida paintings?"

She smiled. "Those too."

"Okay, let me think on it." They finished their margaritas, and he looked longingly at the pool.

She would have invited him to swim, but she figured he didn't have a bathing suit with him and she really didn't want to see him swimming in her pool in his underwear.

Phillip took pictures of the house and the swimming pool, thanking them again for the wonderful meal.

When Phillip left, Landon smiled and grabbed a couple of the margarita glasses and took them into the house while Gabrielle grabbed hers and followed him inside. "Do you want to go for a swim?"

"I sure do." Landon set the glasses in the kitchen. "So what do you think? Will Phillip take the job? Will he buy your house?"

They went to her bedroom and started to strip out of their clothes. "I think he'll take the job. He might not decide to take the house."

"That would be unfortunate." Landon tugged on his board shorts, and she quickly pulled on her bathing suit.

"Thanks for the nice touch with the Christmas lights. With them shining into the pool, it gives such a festive touch."

"Anything to help sell it to a potential buyer."

Then they headed to the pool. This time, they would swim their laps first, before they made love. She loved swimming and playing with him in a pool, whether it was his or hers. Then she and he were toweling off for the next part of their mated adventure.

The next day when Gabrielle went to work, Landon hoped the new vet would work out for them and he hoped Phillip would decide he wanted to work at the vet office too. He hadn't actually confirmed it in writing.

When Gabrielle came home for lunch, she was all smiles and he assumed Phillip was a go on taking over the job.

"Well, the other vet has a family and they're ready to move here because of the nearby beaches. Phillip dropped by to tell us he is taking the job. He was showing pictures of my home to the other vet."

"Does Phillip want to buy your home?" Landon asked.

"The other vet wants my house." Gabrielle smiled and gave Landon another hug. "It's going to sell to one of them, I bet, but it'll sell even if neither buys it. But you know, I was thinking, when we actually move into Doc Mitchell's house, we'll have to furnish it. How are you at furniture shopping?"

"Roxie and Kayla always do it."

She laughed. "Well, it's up to you. If you don't want to shop with me for furniture that you would love, too, I'll take your sisters with me."

"Nicole too. She and my sisters also helped her furnish her and Blake's home."

"Okay, well, that works for me," she said. "But maybe we could decide on the bedroom set?"

He smiled. "Of course. The bed especially. We want it to be just right for all our activities."

She laughed. "Yes." She got a call and saw it was from Phillip. She hoped he hadn't decided to back out of the co-op. He had his state license and had been working in Orlando, so he was perfect for the job.

"I'm taking the house. The other vet wants it, too, and I didn't even tell him how much it was. He was sold on the swimming pool, the other features of the house, and the close proximity to the clinic. I was afraid you would sell it to him first if I didn't make an offer."

Gabrielle laughed. "Yeah, in Florida, a swimming pool is wonderful to have, and no commute means you can come home for lunches. I'm glad you decided to get it. I can have the contract drawn up this afternoon."

"I'll give you your down payment this afternoon."

"That will be great." She was so excited about it. "Thanks so much. You will love it here."

"I know I will. Okay, I'll see you about three. And if you're ready for me to start working, considering how short-staffed you are right now, I'll begin on Monday. Since I don't have any family, I'll work the Christmas holidays."

"Super. Thanks so much. I'll see you back here in a little while then." Gabrielle had a client coming in so she quickly called Landon. "Hey, I hadn't thought I would need to draw up a by-owner contract to sell the house this quickly. Could you look up what it needs and write one up for me? Phillip's coming over at three to give me a down payment and to sign a contract."

"Great! I'll get it done. I saw your printer in your office, and I'll get a taxi to get me over to the clinic."

"Okay, you're a dream and my superhero."

He laughed. "See you soon."

As soon as Gabrielle was done checking over the client's cat, Gabrielle got a call from the jaguar sisters. She'd been hoping they would tell her that they'd caught Melany's husband.

"Hey, Odette, what's happening?" Gabrielle asked.

"We haven't discovered anything more on Melany's husband, but we're back in Florida on leads on another case and we wanted to see if you could take any time off to go to Orlando to the Clawed and Dangerous Kitty Cat Club for Christmas Eve. We want to celebrate that you're mated—and that we are the reason it happened."

Gabrielle laughed. She was glad that when she'd had a moment between clients, she'd texted the sisters to let them know that she and Landon had mated. They had been ecstatic. "I know you two. You want to see me finally dance at the club."

"With the wolf of your dreams."

"Christmas Eve it is!"

"Good. We'll pick you up and drive you down there at four, get some dinner there, drinks, and dance. Oh, and we did pick up Melany's best friend, Belinda Montgomery, for questioning. We told her we learned about the life insurance proceeds she got for Jim's supposed death, that he's alive and well, and if she doesn't want him to pull the same thing with her—as in frame her for a murder because of his gambling addiction—she'd better come clean."

"Ohmigod, did she talk?"

"Not at first. Hard case, you know. We told her she would go to prison for receiving money for a dead man when she aided and abetted him in the ruse. We learned she rented a boat on the day Melany supposedly killed her husband. Belinda had to have picked Jim up to simulate he had been killed and thrown overboard. We had witnesses who confirmed Belinda had driven the boat in the direction that Melany and Jim's boat was anchored. We had to get her to confess to what had happened and confirm Jim was alive— since we didn't know for sure at that point—and that he orches- trated the whole thing."

"And she talked?"

"Yes. Very chatty when she thought she was going to prison for a very long time. The jaguars could make it happen too. Anyway, she said she hadn't been in contact with Jim… Both of them afraid they would get caught. She's a receptionist at the dental clinic where Melany used to work as a hygienist. Belinda didn't want to suddenly leave, in case anyone suspected her of wrongdoing. How would it look if she received a big insurance payout for Jim's death and then she vanished? She was planning to leave the state after a couple of months, hoping Melany would be tried and convicted and then she and Jim would be in the clear."

"Some friend. And the bank where he had an account that Melany hadn't known about?" Gabrielle asked.

"He cleaned out the bank account."

"Great. So he has still got money."

"Yeah, but the way he pisses it away on gambling, he won't have the money for long. Several jaguar agents and my sister and I have been watching all the gambling places for him to show up. So hopefully we'll catch him before long. Belinda is up on charges for all that she was involved in, though she'll get a reduced sentence for cooperating with us. We didn't know for sure if Jim was the man we all saw on the security video at the bank's ATM where he withdrew the money that one day, so she helped to add some nails to his coffin. We'll see you and Landon in a few days then."

"See you then!"

"Congratulations again," Zelda said.

"Thanks! We're very happy."

"We knew you would be. See you soon." Odette ended the call.

Landon arrived shortly after that with the contract for her and Phillip to sign. Thankfully, the clinic's office manager was also a notary public. Gabrielle gave Landon the news about the sisters taking them to the jaguar club. Smiling, he pulled her into a hug and kissed her. "That will be fun. You know what that means, don't you?"

"Yeah." She wrapped her arms around him and gave him a hug back. "I'll have my very own dance partner all night long."

He chuckled. "It's a good thing my sisters taught me how to dance."

"Yes, it sure is. Steaks tonight to celebrate selling the house and Phillip joining the vet staff?"

"Absolutely."

"Why don't you take the car home. You can pick me up and we can have dinner then."

"I'll do that." He kissed her again. "Soon, we'll be home."

———

Time was flying with all the work they had to do with packing, but they never stopped enjoying themselves, running on the beach late at night as wolves and swimming in the pool mornings and at night. Making love too, of course. The vet with the family had started the job and begun working. Which meant Gabrielle and Landon were finally set to move the day after Christmas.

Gabrielle was excited about being moved in by the first of the year. "I can't wait to see how the pack celebrates the new year."

"We'll have a big dance and this time it will be perfect because I'll have you to dance with. It will make for the best new year ever."

"For me too. I think Phillip wants into his new home pronto. I told him as soon as the moving van pulls out, he can move right in."

Landon laughed. "Sounds good to me. Burgers should be ready."

"I'm going to miss you doing all this cooking and being a house husband when you begin working again."

He smiled. "I will cook anything you want me to cook, and cleaning?" He shrugged. "Anything you want me to do, I'm game."

She slid her hands up his shirt. "The same thing with me."

"Good, then after we have burgers, we're swimming, then going to bed."

She laughed. "That sounds like a winner to me."

Despite the fact that Gabrielle was working days, they had a blast every moment they could spare together. On Sunday, they spent the day in bed, then swimming in the pool, then to the beach, grabbing a couple of meals that Landon fixed—he insisted because barbecuing in the snowy cold wasn't happening back home for a while—then in bed, then swimming. She'd even taken him to see the Magic of Lights at the Daytona International Speedway one night. They even managed to get some packing in! They'd had the garage sale, and everything she hadn't wanted to take with her that hadn't sold, she donated to the local women's crisis center.

Then it was back to work and her last four days on the job. Christmas Eve, she would work a shorter day, then off to the jaguar club with her mate and friends, and then Christmas Day was for having some more downtime with her mate. The big moving day was on Saturday.

Rather than the wolves of Silver Town coming to move them over the holidays, Lelandi had arranged for a mover to pick up everything Gabrielle wanted to take with her on Saturday. She still couldn't believe all they had done for her to help her move. She loved the pack for it.

She couldn't wait to get settled into her new home.

CHAPTER 23

Four days later, it was time for the jaguar sisters to pick up Gabrielle and Landon and drive to Orlando to the jaguar club for Christmas Eve. This was going to be the best Christmas Eve ever. Landon was glad he could take his dream mate dancing. And doing it with her friends would make it even more special.

When they finally arrived at the club, they could hear the music spilling into the street, and cars were parked all along the block and in the parking lot.

"We made a reservation," Zelda said. "It gets packed because the place is so much fun. They used to only serve drinks, but now they serve hot or cold sandwiches so that people can eat while enjoying their beverages."

"This looks like fun," Landon said, not sure what to expect. But when they went inside and he saw dance platforms above with dancers—both male and female—dressed in jaguar-print loincloths and dancing to the riveting music, he thought it was terrific.

The place was filled with live tropical plants and vines. Colorful disco lights flashed across the high ceilings painted as a starry night. Patrons were on the dance floor having a great time as Odette told the hostess that they had a table reserved under Zelda and Odette.

"Right this way." The lady motioned to a table and handed them menus. "Welcome to the Clawed and Dangerous Kitty Cat Club." She smiled at all of them. "We don't get wolves in here very often."

"We're the best of friends," Zelda said.

When the waitress came, they all ended up ordering the southern baked ham and buns and fries.

"The snow cocktails look good," Gabrielle said, "for a place that doesn't have snow."

Landon chuckled. "Rum, white chocolate liqueur, and crushed candy canes sounds good and Christmassy."

They all ended up getting the rum drinks too.

Before their drinks came, a dark-haired guy came over and asked Odette if she would like to dance.

"Sure." She stood and went with him to dance.

"That's always the way," Zelda said.

Gabrielle laughed. "You always get asked to dance too."

"Yeah, but she always gets asked first."

A little sister rivalry.

A blond guy was eyeing Gabrielle and Zelda and then he came over to the table.

"I'll dance with you," Zelda said before he asked Gabrielle instead and caused trouble. She got up from the chair and went with the guy to dance.

Then their drinks and sandwiches arrived.

"This is fun." Gabrielle leaned over and kissed Landon.

"I agree, honey." He kissed her back and they toasted to each other.

Then they took a drink of their cocktails and began eating their sandwiches.

The ladies returned after dancing to eat and drink.

"Any hopefuls?" Gabrielle asked.

Both Odette and Zelda laughed. "No. I mean, maybe, but one dance won't decide something like that," Odette said.

Landon took Gabrielle's hand. "For us, it would have." He led her to the dance floor and pulled her nice and close and danced with her. "Ever since the sisters asked if we wanted to come with them here, I've been anticipating holding you close and dancing. Man, is this nice."

Gabrielle wrapped her arms around his neck and moved

against him. "But the problem with this is we'll get so worked up, we'll want to do something else."

He smiled down and kissed her, settling his hands on her backside. "I so love you."

"Hmm, you are making me hot for you."

"The jaguar sisters have nothing on you."

She chuckled. "That's because they weren't all that interested in the jaguars they were dancing with. Not like I'm interested in this hot wolf." She rubbed against him to stir things up even more.

"Now who is being the hot wolf?"

She kissed him and licked his chin. "That makes two of us—really hot together."

Suddenly, Odette was dancing with another jaguar and moved him next to them. She was definitely leading him. She winked at Gabrielle. "Scorching, guys." Then she led the jaguar away.

Zelda danced with another jaguar up close to them, and she smiled. "Looking good."

"They're wolves," the jaguar who was dancing with her said, sounding surprised.

"They sure are." Then Zelda and the jaguar moved off.

Landon and Gabrielle chuckled. "Your friends are cute."

"They are. They will gloat about this forever. They'll say they were the ones that made this happen."

"Hmm, you have a point, but if you hadn't been a rule breaker…"

"In a string bikini…"

He smiled and kissed her. "That's for sure."

The song ended and they returned to the table and finished their sandwiches and drinks. The sisters had already finished theirs.

"I'm going to run to the little girls' room. I'll be right back." Gabrielle went to the restroom.

Landon was sitting at the table when he saw a man who looked suspiciously like Melany's husband, Jim, seated at a table nearby.

But it couldn't be, could it? The guy was talking to another man, both hunched over the table, and the other man handed him a passport. Before Landon could tell the sisters and ask if the man was Jim, Gabrielle came out of the restroom.

Then Zelda was shouting at Odette, and both ladies were running toward the man's table.

The guy Landon thought was Jim bolted from the table and ran straight into Gabrielle on a collision course. "Hell." Landon wanted to kill him.

Gabrielle fell against a man, who steadied her, and Jim was escaping out the front door. Landon knew Gabrielle was fine, but he had to help the jaguar sisters capture their perp.

Landon hoped Gabrielle wouldn't be sore with him for tearing out of the club, but he figured if he could help the sisters in their mission and protect them, too, if they needed protection, she would be happy about it. Especially if they could take the perp down.

"Jim?" he called back to the sisters.

"Yes!" they both shouted.

The man turned and had a gun, damn it. Landon was close enough to him at that point that he lunged for Jim, forcing him down onto his back on the pavement and successfully knocking the gun from his hand. The sisters pounded the sidewalk to reach them, one grabbing Jim's gun, the other pulling a zip tie out of her pocket.

"I always have a couple handy," Odette said as Landon flipped the guy onto his front and tied his hands.

Zelda was already calling for backup. "Yeah, we got the dead guy, very much alive. Melany needs to be cleared of all charges."

Landon was glad for that, but he needed to get back to his mate—and take care of her! Just in case any humans or jaguars thought she was available.

Now that was a first, Gabrielle thought. Go on a date with her mate and her two best friends and be left at a jaguar club all by herself as they chased some guy out the door! Gabrielle had raced after them after nearly falling, if a male jaguar hadn't caught her. When she reached the door, she glanced out but didn't see anyone. Ohmigod! It had to be Jim they were trying to chase down!

Landon might be a deputy sheriff back in Silver Town, but he didn't have a weapon on him. She didn't know if the sisters did or not. Well, maybe Melany's husband didn't either, if that's who it was.

Gabrielle wasn't about to run out into the dark and search for her mate and the others. She went back to her table and ordered herself another drink. She wasn't giving up their reserved table until her mate returned for her.

The club was packed with humans and jaguars, which made her think of the last time she was here with her friends, except that she had been sitting alone because they had been dancing with a throng of jaguars and she hadn't wanted to. She tapped her fingers on the table. She sure hoped they nabbed the guy. But she hoped none of them were hurt. Still, what a great Christmas Eve gift that would be—if they could catch the guy they'd been after.

She was sipping her drink when the blond jaguar who had danced with Zelda approached the table to ask her to dance.

An out-of-breath Landon quickly interceded. "She's with me." He took her hand and she had to put her drink down quickly. She smiled at Landon and then at the jaguar.

"Wolf mates can be so…unpredictable at times." She smiled up at Landon again and kissed him.

He kissed her back, then pulled her onto the dance floor, and they danced another slow dance.

"Sorry about leaving you like that, honey."

"You have a nice way of making up to me. I totally approve. Did you catch whoever you were after?" Gabrielle hoped that they had at least done that.

"Yeah. I tackled him. It was Jim, Melany's husband. We tied his wrists, and the sisters read him his rights, and now they're waiting for other JAG special agents to pick him up and incarcerate him." Landon kissed Gabrielle as they danced close together.

"Oh wow, that's wonderful. I hadn't expected you to run off all Rambo Wolf on me, but I'm glad you helped the sisters catch the bastard."

"We were meant to be together, you know?"

"Yeah, I know. You are the best thing that ever happened to me."

After two more dances—Landon continued to move slow and close with her no matter whether it was a fast or a slow dance—Gabrielle saw the jaguar sisters return to their table and she missed a step with Landon.

He glanced in the direction of their table and smiled. The sisters had ordered new drinks and raised them to Landon and Gabrielle to cheer the capture of Melany's husband.

This would be a night to remember. Gabrielle was glad they had Jim in custody and now Melany should be safe and could return home, her name cleared.

But Landon wasn't giving Gabrielle up for anything, and they danced until closing, only stopping to get a glass of water in between dances.

"I've had the best time with you." Gabrielle kissed Landon.

"The night isn't over yet." He was full of promises.

"I can't wait." She knew he'd follow through.

At closing, the sisters drove them back home. All they did was talk about catching Jim—the wild jump that Landon had made that was worthy of a jaguar's maneuver and how he had saved the day as he took the perp to the pavement.

"That guy is going to have a sore back," Odette said.

"Yeah, he was limping good by the time the other agents picked him up. We'll get a citation for this, but Landon needs one too," Zelda said.

He smiled. "All I needed was to help you out so you could end this case and aid Melany, and I could get back to dancing with my mate before some big blond jaguar swept her away to the dance floor."

"Not the guy I danced with already," Zelda said.

"Yep," Gabrielle said, "but the wolf beat him out."

"Wow, that was really the best night at the club ever," Odette said. "Not only because we had so much fun with the two of you, and we enjoyed dancing with the jaguars. But catching our perp in the process too? Absolutely the best night ever."

Everyone totally agreed.

But the night wouldn't end quite yet for Gabrielle and Landon as they were dropped off at her home and entered the house.

Of course, she was planning to make love to her one and only wolf, but then she remembered she had to prep the sausage casserole she wanted to make for Christmas breakfast.

"Come on, mate of mine. We're going to make a Christmas casserole for breakfast tonight on a really small scale, because we don't want to transport a bunch of leftovers. We'll just bake it in the morning."

"Sounds good to me." Landon cooked the sausage while she mixed the mustard powder, salt, eggs, and milk. Then they added the sausage, bread cubes, and cheese and stirred them evenly. He poured the contents of the bowl into a baking dish, Gabrielle covered it, and then they set the pan in the fridge to chill overnight.

"That looks like something we could make for Christmas breakfast next year with the whole family," Landon said.

"Oh, just wait until you eat it. It's divine."

"You are divine." He scooped her up to carry her to the bedroom. "And I'll show you just how much I know so."

CHAPTER 24

THE NEXT MORNING IT WAS CHRISTMAS DAY AND GABRIELLE woke in Landon's arms, knowing that she had gone to heaven. She didn't want to get up for anything. This was getting to be a typical trend for her with him. Normally, she practically jumped out of bed to get her day started, no matter what she had to do, whether it was a workday or a fun day off. But Landon had changed her morning wake-ups to something altogether different—and infinitely more fun and sexier.

He kissed her mouth.

"Merry Christmas, honey," she said.

"Merry Christmas, sweetheart. You know, the sooner we get up to bake our casserole, the sooner we'll be able to return to bed," he said.

She chuckled. "Are you excited about Christmas?" She wished they could have been at Doc Mitchell's house already.

"Not as much as I'm looking forward to returning to bed with you."

She laughed. "You are such a wolf."

She threw on some blue pajamas and slippers, and he dressed in some gray pajama bottoms and slippers. She had some Christmas ones under the tree, but they needed to unwrap them.

She started baking the sausage casserole in the oven while he made them a cup of coffee and hot tea.

Gabrielle was used to working on Christmas Day—at least for emergencies, since she'd been the only vet at the clinic without a family. This time, Phillip was taking the calls for Christmas and she and Landon were excited about moving tomorrow. She hadn't had anyone special like this to actually share Christmas with since her parents had died.

She and Landon were having steaks for lunch instead of a turkey or ham, because they were moving the next day and didn't want to have leftovers. And they weren't really opening a bunch of presents here, though she'd been amused he'd brought some smaller packages with him in one of his suitcases. Of course she had bought him some things, too, once he said he was going to be with her for Christmas.

She smiled when she opened the hand-carved wolf ornaments for her tree—their tree. "I was going to wait until I returned to Silver Town to get some."

He smiled. "I figured they were small enough and packable, and I wanted you to have a Christmas memory of the time you spent with us at the lodge."

"I love them."

He opened a package and found a pair of pajama bottoms for Christmas—howling Arctic wolves on red flannel. "Yes!"

She laughed.

He kicked off his slippers and stripped out of his gray pajamas right in front of her. Smiling, she shook her head. He was just so hot. He pulled on the new pajamas and looked down at them.

She ran her hand over his buttocks. "Hmm, it fits, but it's still loose enough to be comfortable for sleeping, and it's fun, Christmassy, and looks hot on you."

"They're great. Once I'm in bed with you, they'll be joining your pajamas." He leaned down and kissed her.

She kissed him back, and then she opened her present from herself so she'd have matching pajamas with him. She hadn't worn Christmas pajamas since she was a little girl. This was going to be fun.

"Now I like that." He helped her unbutton her shirt and kissed her bare breasts.

She chuckled. Then he pulled the new shirt over her head and cupped her breasts in the soft flannel top. He leaned down to pull on her pants, touching her between her legs as if he'd gotten distracted, and then helped her on with her new pants.

She was ready to return to bed with her sexy wolf.

Next, he opened a gift card that was for a store that sold great barbecue grills.

"For our new house. I'm expecting all kinds of grilling from you once the snow melts."

He laughed. "You've got it."

She opened a package and found her very own staff T-shirt and sweater. "Awww." She ran her hand over the embroidered wolves.

"As our honorary member for helping to save a snowboarding guest of our lodge, for helping with an injured skier on the slope who ended up shifting into a wolf, for locating the kittens and momma cat in the room near yours, for helping find Rosco and bringing him home, and for being one of the family."

She wiped away tears and gave him a big hug and kiss. "I can't tell you how much it means to me to be part of your family."

He hugged her to his chest. "We feel the same way about you. None of us wanted to let you go."

Then he opened one of his presents and smiled. "Blue board shorts. These are great."

"For lake swimming and swimming in the pool."

And she opened a package that contained a string bikini—hot pink. She laughed.

"I figured you might want one for the lake instead of always wearing a Christmas one out of season."

"I thought we were swimming in the raw."

He smiled. "You can start out in the bikini." He opened a package and found she'd given him a beach towel featuring a couple of gray wolves on a blue background.

He'd bought her one too—only hers was a wolf on a bright-pink beach towel to match her bikini. He'd gotten her gift cards for skis, poles, ski boots, ice skates, an annual ski pass, and snowshoes.

She'd given him a gift card for a canoe he'd been eyeing in a store in Daytona Beach. But the company had stores in Colorado too so they would deliver it to the house before they arrived home, someone from the family accepting the delivery.

The timer went off on the oven, and she hurried to get their sausage casserole out.

"Thank you for all my gifts," she said.

"I love mine. My family wants us to have a little Christmas get-together when we arrive home." He set the table, made her a cup of tea, and poured some more coffee for himself. Then they sat down to eat.

"That would be great."

"This is delicious. We'll have to make this next Christmas for the family," Landon said.

"You all make such special dishes, I'm glad you enjoy one of mine."

"You bet."

Once they finished breakfast, they were going to clean up, but she stuck the casserole dish in the sink to soak and he put the dishes in the dishwasher. Then she pulled off her Christmas pajamas and he smiled.

"Sex later. I'm trying out my new string bikini in the pool—last chance." Since they were moving tomorrow and she didn't think she'd get another opportunity to wear it in the pool. She headed into the living room to dress in her bikini.

Joining her, he stripped out of his Christmas pajamas and grabbed his new board shorts. "I'm totally game. I'm off to catch my mermaid in a string bikini this time. The first time I tried, she did a vanishing act."

She laughed and hurried to tie up her bikini top and headed for the pool. It wasn't as big a pool as the lodge's so she knew it wouldn't take any time for Landon to reach her. This time, she was perfectly happy to have her wolf catch her as she jumped into the pool.

He dove into the pool and she glanced back over her shoulder. He was gaining on her, his perfect muscular arms and shoulders rippling with the effort. She did the unexpected: stopped and waited for him.

And he smiled. This time he would catch her, and she was so ready.

He wrapped his arms around her. "Merry Christmas, my wolf and mermaid all wrapped up in one."

She wrapped her legs around him. "Merry Christmas, my hunky wolf, ski instructor, and all-around superhero. I so love you."

They began to kiss, and he untied the straps to her bikini top and let it fall to the bottom of the pool. She chuckled and kissed him back. "You will have to dive to retrieve it later. Can you imagine what would happen if Phillip took possession of the house and found it?"

"He would know I caught a mermaid in the pool before we left. Only I kept her and left something behind."

"No way. That's half of my bikini Christmas present."

Landon began to untie her bikini bottoms and once he had untied them, they went the way of the bikini top, sinking slowly to the bottom of the pool. She looked down at her bright-pink bikini down there. Two could play at this game. She pulled off his board shorts and they sank to the bottom of the pool.

He chuckled, and then he was kissing her and she was thoroughly into this. In the pool on Christmas Day with the love of her life.

Their tongues laved each other's as she wrapped her legs around his and hugged him tight. He was keeping them afloat with his hands on her bottom, clasping her close to him.

He released her bottom and slid his hands up her waist, then to her breasts and squeezed them gently, kissing the swell of them. "This makes up for me not catching you the first time," he whispered against her forehead, then placed a reverent kiss there.

"The game would have been over too quickly if you had." She kissed his mouth, her hand cupping the back of his head while she really gave the kiss every ounce of passion she possessed.

"I was glad to catch you the next morning."

"I was glad you were the one doing the catching." She kissed him again, their tongues sliding over each other's before he reached down between them and began to stroke her.

His erection was already full blown, ready for pleasure. Something about water and sex came together for them. She was a Florida girl, what could she say?

He carried her out of the pool and into the house, and they ended up on the bed.

He was kissing her mouth, her neck, nibbling on her shoulder. She was arching away from him as he applied his erotic touch to her feminine nub. The climax was coming and she was stretching for the peak. Wanting it now, to sleep afterward, and make love to her wolf again.

She kept her feet anchored around him. She couldn't think of a better way to make love to him before she left her Florida home for good. But only because he truly was the one for her, the kind of lover she couldn't ever have envisioned having. The one who gave her everything she needed when she hadn't thought she needed anything more in her life. Boy, was she wrong.

He made her whole world complete. She tightened her legs around the back of his, and before she could come, he surged into her—exquisite ecstasy, filling her to the brim—thrusting deep inside her.

The wolf was hot. Oh so hot, and heating her blood to sizzling. Their hearts were beating as if in a swimmer's race, their bodies united in that form of intimate bliss that mated wolves could share.

She was so glad they hadn't waited to mate, that she had opened her heart up to him and he had reciprocated. She'd never expected making love to him would feel this intensely satisfying.

He was holding her hips while she kept her legs wrapped around him as he continued to thrust, and then he moved one hand to her feminine nub and began to stroke her with determination.

He was a sea god in the flesh as he sent her over the edge, winging across the galaxy, the climax consuming her all at once. "Ohmigod, yes."

Then he was filling her with his hot seed and he groaned with pleasure. He continued to thrust until he was spent, and then he pulled her into his arms and just hugged her soundly.

"I love you, Gabrielle. You are the only one meant for me."

"Hmm." She kissed him back. "I love you. I will dream about this forever. But before we clean up the dishes and take a well-deserved afternoon nap…"

"I have to go diving."

"You sure do."

"But you have to retrieve my new bathing suit."

"Last one out with their treasure…" She left the bed and headed outside, him following her out to the pool. She dove into the pool to retrieve his board shorts.

He dove for her.

Life would never be the same for her, and she was so glad it wouldn't.

Gabrielle couldn't have been more suited to his personality, Landon thought as she dove for his swim trunks and he went after her. She was infinitely more fun to dive for than their clothes. And she loved how he wasn't about to concentrate on getting them, but playing with her instead. He loved her, and when they finally finished playing with each other, chasing each other across the pool, and trying to grab their bathing suits after tackling each other numerous times, they rescued their bathing suits and ended up in the shower, then in bed. And finished their Christmas off just right as two newly mated wolves would.

———————

The next day, the movers came bright and early. Landon was glad it was finally time for Gabrielle and him to move. Now they could settle down at Doc Mitchell's house and she could start working once her license came through. Until then, his siblings had said he had all the time off from working at the lodge to be with her— skiing, riding snowmobiles, ice skating, getting the house set up the way they wanted it, and whatever else they wanted to do. Call it an extended honeymoon, they'd said. One of the things they had to do was shop for furniture. Blake had said their sisters could go with them and he would hold down the fort.

Once the moving van was on its way, Phillip arrived with his own moving van and Gabrielle wished him well at the clinic. He thanked her for the house and the job and wished her well at her new home and clinic.

Then Landon drove Gabrielle's car and they headed to Colorado. His family would take delivery of the household goods when the moving van arrived, while he and Gabrielle were driving back to Silver Town at a more leisurely pace.

"I love your family," Gabrielle said, settling against the seat as they drove through Florida.

"They're great. We'll do the same for Kayla and Roxie—when they find mates too. It's what family is all about."

"You know, we're going to have to stop driving early."

He smiled at her. "At a hotel with a swimming pool and—"

"An extra-soft bed."

EPILOGUE

GABRIELLE ENJOYED WORKING AT THE VET CLINIC IN SILVER Town. Over the six months since she'd been back, Doc Mitchell had loved to come in and work with her or give her time off, and she was thrilled that he did.

She loved the changing seasons in Silver Town, the wolf pack, her new extended family, and most of all, her mate. Landon meant everything to her—and he continued to show her just why she'd made the best decision of her life to mate him and move here.

All the trees were leafing out and soon the flowers would be here. Landon had today off from working at the lodge, and Doc Mitchell was filling in for Gabrielle today at the vet clinic, so she and Landon were planning on taking their first swim in the lake as humans, and then they would shift and swim as wolves. But she had really important news to tell him when the jaguar sisters called her.

"If we wouldn't be too much of an imposition, we would love to visit you for the Fourth of July. We have it off, and if it would work out for you all, we would love to come out and see you. No new moon either," Odette said. "Plus we hoped Melany and her boyfriend could come. She wants to thank you all again for all your help in apprehending her ex-husband."

"Oh, I hope the new guy is better for her than the last. We would love to have you come and visit! Let me run it by Landon, but I'm sure he'll be thrilled."

"Okay, we'll let you go. Just text us and we'll put in the leave form."

"Will do." They ended the call, and Gabrielle joined Landon in the kitchen where he was making them eggs, hash browns, and bacon. She loved her mate. "The sisters are coming for a visit."

"When?" He gave her a hug.

"For the Fourth of July, if that's all right with you."

He kissed her mouth and that morphed into a deeper kiss. "Your friends are my friends. We'll go swimming and boating, run in the woods, and have a big barbecue with the family. We'll have a great time."

"Oh, that sounds wonderful. Would it be all right if Melany comes too?" Gabrielle asked.

"You don't even have to ask. I'm just glad she is in the clear now over the murder charges and her mate is sitting in the jaguar confinement facility."

"Me too. Um, she has a boyfriend now."

Landon frowned. "He can come, too, and we'll check him out."

Gabrielle smiled. "You are the best. And *we* have some good news too."

Landon's phone rang and he said, "Hold that thought." He answered the phone. "Hey, Blake, what's up?"

"Nicole and I have some good news to share."

"Let me put this on speaker. Go ahead, Gabrielle's right here to hear the news."

"We're three months' pregnant!" Blake sounded like a proud daddy already.

Landon laughed. "It's about time."

Gabrielle smiled. "We are too. That was the good news I was going to tell you, Landon."

"Hot damn, honey!" He set the phone on the table and gave her a hug and a kiss. "This calls for a celebration."

Blake laughed. "Well, it looks like our kids will be coming about the same time. They will be perfect playmates. They'll probably play and quarrel with each other just like we did as kids."

"Oh, absolutely," Landon said.

"How wonderful that you're going to have yours about the same time as ours. Congratulations, you two," Nicole said.

"The same to you. I might not be delivering your babies as wolf pups if I go into labor at the same time," Gabrielle warned. "We'll have to try and time it out right. You first, then me." As if they could really time it out. Of course, this early on, they didn't know how many they might have or the sex of the babies, but she was so thrilled they were having their kids about the same time.

Nicole laughed. "Well, since Doc Mitchell is continuing to work part-time at the clinic, I'm sure he would be honored to deliver your babies when the time comes. We'll check with Roxie and Kayla about the time that would be best for everyone to have a party to celebrate all our good news. We'll invite my parents and brother too."

Of course, in the meantime, they would have the family physician monitor their progress, and if things didn't work out according to plan, he could deliver either Gabrielle's babies or Nicole's. Gabrielle couldn't be more pleased to be able to mutually share the progress of their pregnancies with each other. Her sister-in-law was like the sister Gabrielle had never had. In fact, Nicole's parents had practically adopted her, and Nate was just as protective of her as he was of his sister.

"Just let us know and we'll be there. Or here. Whenever you want to do the celebrating, we'll make time," Gabrielle said.

"Okay, we're calling them next. Congrats again," Nicole said.

"Same to you," Landon said.

Then they ended the call and Landon kissed Gabrielle again. "When did you learn we were pregnant?"

"Right before the jaguar sisters called. I was going to tell you after they called and then your brother phoned us with their good news. I figured there wasn't any sense in me keeping the news to myself so that I could tell you first, then call them back when you learned of it."

"No, I'm glad you told them too. I'm thrilled we're having our own kids."

"Good, because you would be in trouble if you weren't."

"Oh, the eggs!" Landon hurried to dish up the breakfast, but she knew just what she wanted to do before they even went swimming together in the lake today. Take her mate, her lover, her wolf to bed to celebrate the coming of their baby or two, or more, in their own personal, intimate way. She had decided that sometimes breaking the rules could be a good thing—for a she-wolf in a string bikini while a hot and sexy wolf was on guard duty.

Landon adored Gabrielle and he couldn't believe he was going to be a father, just like his brother! He couldn't be happier. Everything was working out great with Gabrielle. She was loving the pack, the family, her new job, and Silver Town. She had shopped with Roxie, Kayla, and Nicole to pick out furniture, but they'd had Landon come along to ensure he was happy with everything they selected.

The house was really nice, the furniture beautiful. But what made the house a home was Gabrielle. Everyone had helped to move her and unpack all her things at the house, and she and he had been so appreciative. The pack had celebrated her joining them and shared the word she was their new vet, though Doc Mitchell enjoyed working there part-time to relieve her and help her out. He still loved the work, but he was glad he didn't have to do it all the time.

Landon had loved skiing and ice skating with Gabrielle the rest of the winter season after she'd moved there. Though Lelandi, as their pack psychologist, had had some talks with Gabrielle about her issues with ice and lakes before she could really ice-skate comfortably.

And of course they'd gone swimming at the lodge pool after hours. Now it was time for swimming at the lake, boating, hiking, and fishing. She was game for it all. And so was he.

He served up breakfast, rescuing it before it had been a disaster.

They sat down to eat. "I know we planned to swim after breakfast but—"

"We're going to bed first," she said, smiling at him and taking a bite of her bacon. "Have I told you what a great cook you are?"

"Thanks. So are you. I'm so glad we're together."

"We're totally in sync."

When it came to deciding to forgo other activities to make love, absolutely.

"I love you, Gabrielle."

"Oh, I love you, honey. Anyone who could convince me to leave my sunny, hot Florida for snowy, cold Colorado was the one for me."

"I feel the same way about you." He finished up his breakfast and so did she. "Dishes can wait." As soon as she stood, he swept her up in his arms and carried her to their master bedroom. "Loving you can't."

"Hmm, you always say the right things." Then she wrapped her arms around his neck and kissed him while he carried her into the bedroom.

"I caught my mermaid and wolf in one."

"And I lured my mate with a sexy string bikini. See? I knew how to fish before I had ever fished."

"And you caught a big one—beginner's luck."

"Luck had nothing to do with it."

"Hell yeah, it does. I'm one lucky guy." He began removing her clothes and kissed her bare belly.

"Okay, when you put it that way, you're right."

He chuckled. "I love you."

She helped him out of his clothes. "I love you too. And I'm one lucky woman."

"I'll say."

She laughed and hugged and kissed him.

Plans to swim at the lodge before work every morning never seemed to work out, though. Spending more time in bed together before they started their workday worked out even better.

It was amazing how little things that had seemed important to her before no longer were—not when the wolves were in love.

ACKNOWLEDGMENTS

Thanks to both Donna Fournier and Darla Taylor for their great beta reads, catching stuff I've missed a million times, reminding me of the cat and kittens in the story, helping me to brainstorm, and all of this during COVID-19. Thanks, ladies! And thanks to Deb Werksman, who continues to believe in my stories, no matter the difficulties that we face during the pandemic. As always, I'm excited to see what the art department comes up with, since their covers are beyond compare!

ABOUT THE AUTHOR

USA Today bestselling author Terry Spear has written over ninety paranormal and medieval Highland romances. In 2008, *Heart of the Wolf* was named a *Publishers Weekly* Best Book of the Year. She has received a PNR Top Pick, a Best Book of the Month nomination by *Long and Short Reviews*, numerous Night Owl Romance Top Picks, and two Paranormal Excellence Awards for Romantic Literature (Finalist and Honorable Mention). In 2016, *Billionaire in Wolf's Clothing* was an *RT Book Reviews* Top Pick. A retired officer of the U.S. Army Reserves, Terry also creates award-winning teddy bears that have found homes all over the world, helps out with her granddaughter and grandson, and is raising two Havanese puppies. She lives in Spring, Texas.

UNDERCOVER WOLF

STAT: Special Threat Assessment Team, from *New York Times* and *USA Today* bestselling author Paige Tyler

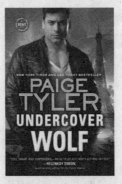

Alpha werewolf Harley Grant isn't exactly comfortable with her inner wolf, even though she's on a STAT team where she can use her abilities openly. Alpha werewolf Sawyer Bishop would give anything for his MI6 team to know about his inner wolf, but his teammates are mistrustful of anyone or anything with inhuman abilities.

When STAT and MI6 team up to stop a crew of supernatural bad guys intent on causing a nuclear meltdown, Harley and Sawyer are thrown together. And as they grow closer in their work, they can't help but bring out the inner wolf in each other.

"Unputdownable... Whiplash pacing, breathless action, and scintillating romance."
—K. J. Howe, international bestselling author, for *Wolf Under Fire*

For more info about Sourcebooks's books and authors, visit:
sourcebooks.com

FIERCE COWBOY WOLF

Ranchers by day, wolf shifters by night. Don't miss the thrilling Seven Range Shifters series from acclaimed author Kait Ballenger

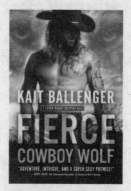

Sierra Cavanaugh has worked her whole life to become the first female elite warrior in Grey Wolf history. With her nomination finally put forward, she needs the pack council's approval, and they insist she must find herself a mate.

Packmaster Maverick Grey was reconciled to spending the rest of his life alone. But he needs the elite warrior vacancy filled—and fast. If Sierra needs a mate, this is his chance to claim her.

For these two rivals, the only thing more dangerous than fighting the enemy at their backs is battling the war of seduction building between them...

"Kait Ballenger is a treasure you don't want to miss."
—Gena Showalter, *New York Times* bestselling author

BIG BAD WOLF

First in an action-packed new paranormal romantic suspense
series from award-winning author Suleikha Snyder

Joe Peluso has blood on his hands, and he's more than willing to pay the
price for the lives he's taken. He knows that shifters like him deserve
the worst. Darkness. Pain. Solitude. But lawyer and psychologist Neha
Ahluwalia is determined to help the dangerous wolf shifter craft a solid
defense...even if she can't defend her own obsession in the process. When
Joe's trial is torn apart in a blaze of bullets, Neha only knows that she'll do
anything to defend Joe...even if that means protecting him from himself.

**"*Big Bad Wolf* is a perfect urban fantasy for the times:
clever, romantic, heroic, and filled with hope for a better
future. Suleikha Snyder has crafted an amazing world."**
—Award-winning author Alisha Rai

For more info about Sourcebooks's books and authors, visit:
sourcebooks.com

Also by Terry Spear